A
Th

T,
ren
da

Love is
a time of enchantment:
in it all days are fair and all fields
green. Youth is blest by it,
old age made benign:
the eyes of love see
roses blooming in December,
and sunshine through rain. Verily
is the time of true-love
a time of enchantment — and
Oh! how eager is woman
to be bewitched!

BRIDE OF DOOM

Fauna, the beautiful quadroon slave-girl — heroine of GOLD FOR THE GAY MASTERS — had a daughter Fleur, as beautiful, as fatally captivating as herself. This is Fleur's story. The story of an arranged marriage to the forbidding Baron of Cadlington, of her love for the young artist Peveril, of the darkly-predicted black heir who is born to her, of her fiery attempts to find escape, revenge — and fulfilment of the restless urges that burn in her fated blood.

Books by Denise Robins
Published by The House of Ulverscroft:

THE ENCHANTED ISLAND
THE FEAST IS FINISHED
I SHOULD HAVE KNOWN
A PROMISE IS FOR EVER
MORE THAN LOVE
THE SNOW MUST RETURN
SET THE STARS ALIGHT
MOMENT OF LOVE
THE OTHER SIDE OF LOVE
DARK CORRIDOR
GOLD FOR THE GAY MASTERS
THE STRONG HEART
HEART OF PARIS

DENISE ROBINS

BRIDE OF DOOM

Complete and Unabridged

ULVERSCROFT
Leicester

First published in Great Britain by
Rich & Cowan
London

First Large Print Edition
published 1998

British Library CIP Data

Robins, Denise, *1897 — 1985*
 Bride of doom.—Large print ed.—
Ulverscroft large print series: romance
1. Love stories
2. Large type books
I. Title
823.9'12 [F]

ISBN 0–7089–3897–3

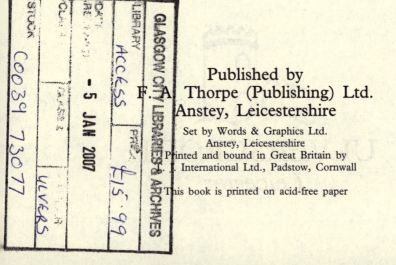

Published by
F. A. Thorpe (Publishing) Ltd.
Anstey, Leicestershire

Set by Words & Graphics Ltd.
Anstey, Leicestershire
Printed and bound in Great Britain by
T. J. International Ltd., Padstow, Cornwall

This book is printed on acid-free paper

Prologue

1

THE fierce sad baying of hounds echoed and re-echoed through the dark forests that frowned down upon the Vale of Aylesbury. Across the Chiltern Hills a mass of sombre cloud had been broken up by a wild wind and tossed across the sky. A sudden storm of rain blotted out the landscape. At three o'clock on this afternoon in October in the year 1836, the hunt organized by Denzil, Lord St. Cheviot, was at an end. Even now hounds had closed in on the limp exhausted body of the beaten stag. Its life-blood was welling from a hundred jagged wounds torn by the teeth of the savage dogs.

It had been a long disappointing day for the members of his lordship's hunt. The royal animal had given them a poor chase and only during the last hour or so had the pack found the scent and routed the wretched stag out of its hiding-place deep in the thicket.

St. Cheviot did not wait to watch the death-throes of his quarry. He was in one of his most sombre moods — in keeping with the stormy day. His friends who knew him well avoided him like the plague when he was in these evil tempers. Whispering together they looked after him as St. Cheviot wheeled round and pressing his spurs into the big black stallion whose sides were already foam-flecked and bloody, dashed like a madman along the thorny path that led out of the woods and into open country. Then he rode higher up the hill towards the summit on which stood the spectral outline of Cadlington House, the country seat of the St. Cheviots.

In all Buckinghamshire, there was no man with such a reputation as St. Cheviot's for lunatic riding — or indeed for such cruelty. He rode without mercy. It was whispered among the ladies that he had no mind whether he broke the heart of a horse or a maid so long as they satisfied him initially. His was not a pretty character. But his immense wealth and the grandeur of his ancient title made him *persona grata* in most of the Drawing Rooms in London — or Buckinghamshire.

Like a fiend, the rain lashing him, St. Cheviot with crop and spur urged his horse up the steep hill. He was in a hurry to get home to dry clothes, fires and strong wine.

Seen thus through the gathering gloom, man and mount seemed to be one hewn out of the stormy landscape.

There could be no denying the spectacular looks of the thirty-year-old nobleman. He was immensely tall and although slender of flank, had wide powerful shoulders. He had lost the green Austrian hat which he had been wearing earlier today. His raven-dark hair soaked with rain was curled, long and thick, plastered to cheek and brow. His deep-set falcon eyes had a penetrating stare. Just now they were bloodshot and angry. The anger was mainly the backwash of an incident which had taken place at Cadlington last night.

The place was full of guests whom St. Cheviot had invited to attend the chase today. There were one or two women among them — wives of the sportsmen who came to Cadlington not because of any love of the host but because they were satellites ready to fawn upon St. Cheviot and accept his lavish hospitality.

One of the ladies — Sybil Forminster — whose husband was welcomed to Cadlington mainly because he, Lord Forminster, was a crack shot and duellist, had recently attracted St. Cheviot's attention.

The Forminsters were not long married. Sybil was a beautiful girl — herself no mean horsewoman — with long golden hair and bright blue eyes. She was reputed to be as chaste as she was handsome and much in love with her bridegroom.

It was unusual for such a girl to visit Cadlington. St. Cheviot shunned matrimony and his mistresses, whom he frequently changed, were seldom either respectable or of his own class. Respectability bored St. Cheviot.

Last night, at the long rich banquet provided by the host, young Lady Forminster had been placed on the right of the host. Her husband, George, noted that St. Cheviot continually bent close to her and whispered in her ear, and that Sybil found it difficult to eat or drink. She appeared flushed and nervous. St. Cheviot had, in fact, drunk more than was usual and was in the throes of a sudden violent passion for the blonde beauty. George Forminster continued to watch gloomily — wishing, no doubt, that he had not brought his wife to Cadlinton, no matter how splendid the chase or magnificent the hospitality. He had been in two minds about it. He did not like St. Cheviot but had been attracted by the thought of the stag-hunt — there were not many these days in the district.

Later, while the musicians played softly and the guests — most of them — gathered in the library to enjoy a game of cards — St. Cheviot had come upon Sybil, alone, in the gallery, where — a lover of painting — she had been examining some of the old portraits of the St. Cheviots. The 'Black Barons' they had been called — for without exception they had the ebony hair and dark eyes which Denzil inherited.

Sybil greeted her host with innocent

courtesy. He looked splendid in his dark red coat and flowered satin waistcoat, and shewing a well-shaped leg in silken hose. But he soon let her know the evil intentions in his inflamed mind. Then she tried to elude him — it was obvious to her that he was inebriated. But he seized her in his arms and embraced her hotly. When she struggled and protested, he breathed mad proposals to her, adding:

"I am crazed by your white and gold loveliness. I will give you the world if you will leave Forminster and elope with me." This he had said and looked so wild and passionate that the young girl uttered a frightened scream.

George Forminster heard the cry and came to his wife's aid. Both men were swordsmen and weapons were drawn. In a few moments the gay mood of the festive evening changed. Cards were scattered and forgotten. A circle of men gathered around the duellists and in the portrait gallery, in flickering candle-light, the outraged husband fought St. Cheviot.

In less than a few seconds the

unfortunate George Forminster was down, bleeding from a serious wound which had only just missed his heart. St. Cheviot was the better swordsman of the two. Drunk or sober — he could use that flexible wrist of his with almost fiendish dexterity.

As for the fair-haired bride who now knelt weeping by her unconscious husband's form — she had lost any attraction she had held for St. Cheviot. He no longer glanced in her direction and was furious because he had been drawn into such a fracas. He had wanted amusement — not this. Livid, sweat pearling on his forehead, he smoothed the disordered lace and lawn at his throat and flung his sword on to the floor for scared-looking servants to pick up. Then he bowed to his open-mouthed, gaping guests.

"The party is over. Let us get to bed — we must be up early for the Meet," he said.

Nobody dissented. The people who gathered around him as a rule did what St. Cheviot bid and without argument.

An hour later the episode was over and must not be referred to. Forminster's carriage departed carrying the still insensible George and his wife away from Cadlington. St. Cheviot's own house-physician went with them.

But the memory of the episode remained with St. Cheviot and spoiled his day. He disliked weakness in himself — as well as in others. He was bitterly angry that he had drunk too much and thus insulted Sybil Forminster. The silly little fool's lips, so he reflected, had not been worth the kissing — or the consequence. It was a poor beginning to the week-end's sport. And now the party lacked one of the finest shots. Forminster would recover, but quite obviously he would never set foot in Cadlington again.

All through his life, St. Cheviot had made more enemies than friends. But though tongues wagged and women feared him — men found him interesting and the women vied with each other for his favours. It would be no mean triumph to pull off a marriage with St. Cheviot and become mistress of Cadlington, the most splendid mansion in Buckinghamshire.

The great park trees loomed out of

10

the mist of rain and frowned upon St. Cheviot as he slackened pace and drew near the top of the hill. Lights flickered from the keeper's lodge beckoning him through the October gloom. He could no longer hear the huntsman's horn or the cacophony of the snarling blood-thirsty pack behind him in the forest. All was quiet. He paused a moment to take a swill at a silver flagon of brandy. He was wet and cold. He had a mind to leave his guests to their own devices. He would like to take a carriage and drive through the dismal evening to London. A game of cards at White's — a late supper with a pretty female more amenable than Sybil Forminster — they were decided attractions.

Down came the pitiless rain, ice-cold against St. Cheviot's face. He wiped his eyes with his sleeve. Suddenly his stallion reared, whinnied, and almost shot the unsuspecting nobleman from his saddle. Nevertheless Denzil kept his seat. Savagely he swore at the sweating frightened animal. Then, peering through the rain, he saw two figures: male and female. They had their arms around each other, huddled under sacks, like peasants, trying to shelter from the storm. They must have been sheltering in the hedges, and St. Cheviot's mount had been startled by their sudden appearance out of the gathering mists.

"What the devil do you two think you are doing?" his lordship shouted furiously.

The sacks dropped from the heads of the pair who stood revealed to Denzil. One a stripling boy — no more than twenty or so at the most — supporting the figure of a hunchback girl whose head barely reached his shoulder. They were not ill dressed; the boy in shabby suit and cloak; the hunchback also covered by a long cloak, and wearing a bonnet. But they were a wet bedraggled-looking pair, and St. Cheviot, looking down contemptuously, felt his temper cool. He gave a brief laugh.

"No wonder Apollo was startled out of his wits — never did I see such apparitions," he growled. "What the deuce do you two scarecrows do here in this weather and on Cadlington Hill?"

12

The boy drawing nearer the horse and rider, spoke up:

"Sir, whoever you are, you need not insult either my sister or myself," he said.

He spoke in an educated voice with a note of pride in it that surprised St. Cheviot, who dashed the raindrops from his eyes and looked closer. He noted now that the young speaker had a delicate but handsome face with large fine eyes; his mop of light brown curling hair was wet and tossed by the wind about his temples. No peasant this — but somebody of culture. St. Cheviot was suddenly curious.

"Who are you — why are you on my land?" he asked.

"My name is Peveril Marsh. This is my sister, Elspeth."

"What *do* you here in this storm?" Denzil repeated the question and now turned his attention to the hunchback. She suddenly gave a low moan and swayed. The boy supported her, then let her fall back on the side of the road and knelt beside her. He cried out:

"Ah! For God's sake, Elspeth, beloved sister! . . . "

Denzil scowled. He recognized the fact that this was no ordinary swoon. The unhappy girl was desperately ill. He hated illness in any shape or form but even he, who was not particularly charitable, could not ride on and leave such a youthful helpless pair to the mercies of the gathering night. The storm was growing worse. He shouted at the boy:

"What is wrong with her, in heaven's name? Why are you here?"

"My sister is dying," said the boy hoarsely and raised a white stricken face washed by the rain and his own tears. "Oh, God, I did wrong ever to allow her to leave London and journey this long way."

"To see whom did you come?"

"A Mrs. Ingleby, sir, of Whiteleaf."

"Whiteleaf? That is a mile away from here across the hill."

"Yes, sir. We got lost and we had no money for a conveyance, once having spent so much on our fares in the coach which brought us from London to Monks Risborough."

"Who is Mrs. Ingleby? I have not heard of her."

"An aunt of my mother's, sir," the boy began to explain. "But she has been dead this twelve months. We did not know. We hoped to find bed and board with her. When we found her gone we set out by foot, meaning to beg a lift. We were misdirected by a woodcutter and we are here, and have been walking until, as you see, we can go no further. My sister is on the verge of collapse."

And he added that Elspeth had been very sick for a long time and that it was in the hope that the country air might revive her that he had brought her this long way. He, Peveril explained, was an artist but had had little chance to indulge in his talent, for he was the sole support of the seventeen-year-old invalid. Their parents were dead. The boy earned a bare living working for a frame-maker in Cheapside.

This information bored St. Cheviot but he said:

"I will send two of my men down with horse and cart to pick you up. You can take shelter in the servants' quarters at

15

Cadlington for tonight. But it seems to me as though the shelter of the tomb would be more in keeping with your sister's appearance," he added brutally.

The boy who called himself Peveril Marsh looked wildly up at the big dark figure of the man. His cheeks grew scarlet with anger, and with despair. Then he turned back to his sister's prostrate form. Tenderly he untied the bonnet. St. Cheviot, still peering, saw suddenly a face of astonishing beauty. It did not go well with the misshapen back, but of a certainty, he thought, she should have been a dream of loveliness. She had the same large eyes as the boy's and long golden curls. But her face was white as death itself and her lips bloodless. Feminine beauty never failed to interest Lord St. Cheviot. And being superstitious, hunchbacks invariably held for him a morbid attraction. To touch the hump meant good luck; this he had always heard. He slid from the saddle, leaned down and laid a hand on the girl's back. Immediately her large eyes opened and she looked straight up into his face. So peculiar and deep was her gaze that he felt a curious thrill run through him.

"Why, do you stare at me so, poor soul?" he muttered.

"Destiny," she said in a thin quavery tone. "I know your destiny, sir — I am a seer."

"What does she mean?" Denzil asked the boy roughly.

Peveril, with a tender look at the hunchback, said:

"My sister has prophetic powers. She has always been able to look into the future."

Now St. Cheviot was vastly interested. Rain, wind, the icy darkness of this late October afternoon, all were forgotten. He had the supreme egotist's intense desire to know what lay ahead of him. He knelt down by the girl.

"Tell me what you see?" he demanded in the voice of one who is accustomed to being obeyed.

But now the boy artist spoke up bravely:

"Sir, I fear my sister is gravely ill. I must get her to warmth and cover."

"All in good time," said St. Cheviot and, fixing his black glittering eyes on the girl, urged her afresh.

"What do you know of my destiny?" he asked.

"Elspeth, are you all right?" put in the boy with feverish concern.

She gave him a wan smile but kept her extraordinary eyes upon the handsomely-dressed gentleman who was bending over her. Then in a sepulchral voice she spoke to him once more:

"Your name — what is it?"

"Denzil St. Cheviot, Baron of Cadlington, who lives at Cadlington House," he replied.

"St. Cheviot," she echoed that name in a hollow tone. "The black barons."

Surprised, he nodded.

"So, they call us."

"Still unwed," she continued.

"By heaven, you are right," St. Cheviot gave a coarse laugh, "and likely to remain so."

"No," said the dying girl. She struggled to sit up and pointed a finger at him. "Within twelve months from now you will be wed. I, who can see into the future, do foretell this marriage. And with it comes disaster. Oh, horrible!"

18

she added and shuddered.

St. Cheviot's lips curled.

"Marriage is for a man invariably a horrible disaster," he said and laughed at his own jest.

"A horrible disaster," repeated Elspeth Marsh. And now her breath came more quickly and with difficulty. "I see red-gold hair and violets. Yes. *Watch out for red-gold hair and violets*, sir . . . and for a black St. Cheviot."

"What, another?" Denzil gave another strident laugh. "And what is all this nonsense about red hair and violets?"

Then the boy interrupted:

"You will live to see that she has spoken the truth. Elspeth is never wrong and this is maybe the last prophecy she will ever make." His voice broke. He knelt down in the mud, his tears flowing as he tried to chafe some warmth into the hunch-back's icy little hands.

Again a strange superstitious thrill passed through St. Cheviot's frame. Maybe it was true that the girl had vision. Sometimes, he knew, it was given to the dying to foretell what lay ahead. Again his hand touched the girl's hump.

"For luck," he muttered.

But the boy did not hear. He had burst into bitter tears.

"Elspeth, dearest sister," he cried.

Now St. Cheviot saw that the girl's head had fallen back. She was dead. His lordship recoiled and turned back to his horse.

"I will send my servants to assist you," he said curtly. "Wait here."

The boy did not answer but flung himself across the body of his sister and continued to sob her name.

2

ST. CHEVIOT dug his spurs into the stallion's flanks and urged the animal up the hill. He came to the great wrought-iron gates of his home. In the deepening dusk they took on a spectral aspect. Little could be seen at this hour, and in such weather, of the magnificent park surrounding the house. Two of the lodge-keepers, carrying lighted lanthorns, came running to open the gates for their master. He reined in his mount and flung a sharp order at one of the men.

"A few yards down yon hill you will find a lad — a stranger in these parts — and his sister, who has just expired. Have them brought to Cadlington and tell my footmen to see that they have attention."

"Yes, m'lord," said the man addressed.

St. Cheviot rode on between the sombre line of chestnuts that flanked the drive and were waving wildly in the gale. Soon he could see lights flickering

21

from the windows of the House. Never had he been more glad to reach home. What a disappointing chase, he thought angrily — and what infernal weather. So far the whole week-end had been a disaster. Of a certainty he would return to London and leave his guests to their own devices.

Now he was outside the front door of Cadlington — shouting in his boisterous fashion for his groomsmen who came hurrying round from the courtyard. A footman flung open the door. Spears of light cut across the soaked lawns.

Cadlington House looked huge and forbidding in the purple stormy evening light yet it had a magnificence of its own — with the hill rising steeply behind, thickly wooded to the summit. In front of the house, the pleasure gardens were laid out in terraces. From here, tall windows commanded a magnificent view of the Buckinghamshire Weald.

Godfrey, first Baron of Cadlington, had built this house for his French-born wife, Marguerite. It bore the unmistakable Jacobean stamp — half stone, richly-timbered, containing some twenty-four or

-five bedchambers, and a fine dining-hall surrounded by a musicians' gallery. At a later date, Roland St. Cheviot, Denzil's father, in atrocious taste, had added a wing. This stuck out from the rest of the building like a monstrous growth wrecking its beauty of design, for it was very lofty, rounded like a tower and turreted. It looked as grotesque as an illustration from a Teutonic fairy tale.

In the interior a winding staircase led to the highest turret which could be seen on a fine day for miles around. It had become a landmark.

Denzil, as a boy, had used it as a place of escape from parents or tutors. He had at one time kept up there wild animals that he had snared. One day a young maid-servant had been found on the staircase with her throat cut. How or why she came to such a sorry pass was never discovered. After that the tower had been shut up and the interior had fallen into a poor state of repair. It was now said to be haunted. Denzil was always intending to have the whole wing pulled down but some morbid fascination about the architectural excrescence held his hand.

Nobody ever went near the tower after dark. The local inhabitants regarded the tall frowning turrets with superstitious horror.

But the old house itself had all the graciousness and dignity of its age. And it was certain that no other in Aylesbury could boast of such fine linen-fold panelling or splendid fireplaces. The two staircases curving up to the musicians' gallery were built of rosewood, richly carved.

Throughout the last two hundred years, Cadlington had braved the elements on these wild wooded hills, buffeted by gales and storms — drenched by fierce rains. In severe winters the grounds lay buried in deep snow.

At such times the icy hills were almost impassable and then Denzil St. Cheviot would betake himself to London or go to a sumptuous villa which he rented in Monte Carlo.

But in the spring and summer, Cadlington would lose its forbidding and gloomy appearance and gain much beauty. It could, indeed, look mellow and welcoming against the green hills when the gardens were aglow with flowers and the orchards rich with fruit blossom. The time St. Cheviot loved best was the late autumn; the shooting and hunting season. Such a cold stormy October as they had experienced today was exceptional.

A few moments later, St. Cheviot was in the warmth and brilliance of the great hall standing, legs straddled, in front of a leaping log fire. He drew off his gauntlets and shouted for wine. A young footman came running with glasses and decanters. A huge wolfhound which was St. Cheviot's favourite pet, and so savage none but he dared touch her, had been lying in front of the fire. She rose and walked ponderously up to her master, wagging her tail. He looked down at her and patted the great head.

"Good bitch," he growled. "Where the deuce has everyone got to — the place is dead."

St. Cheviot had a loathing of being alone — even for a moment. Perhaps his conscience did not care for solitude — too much time for remembering — he had done evil in his life and had much to be ashamed of. At any rate, he liked

25

company and grew ill-humoured when he was alone. If his female guests were resting at this hour before dinner, let them rest, he decided — later they might find him more entertaining.

Once inside Cadlington, the wind and the rain and the lonely countryside shut out, it was like being in another world; one of luxury and wealth — the enormous wealth of the St. Cheviots. The great house was stacked with treasures — a good deal inherited from the Lady Marguerite, Denzil's French ancestress who had been an heiress in her own right. The hall in which St. Cheviot was now standing was hung with fine Gobelin tapestries. The tall-backed pointed walnut chairs with their seats of multi-coloured gros-point were French. The fine thick curtains of vermilion silk brocade, sweeping across the windows, had been brought from Paris, hung in the time of the first Baroness and never changed. Some of these gay touches in the decorations amused Denzil St. Cheviot, who had a fancy for Paris and its fashions.

But beauty, colour, art, music, all

26

things lovely crept into St. Cheviot's life only as a strange distorted foil to his inner spirit of darkness and depravity.

When he entertained here, he liked to do so with an ostentatious display of wealth and power. Tales of his astonishing banquets circulated through England. Those who had participated spoke afterwards of the lavish splendour. The long rich dinners eaten at a table laid with gold plate and rare china bearing the St. Cheviot crest — two eagles, with wings spread, their claws locked in conflict. The library in the west wing, filled with rare, handsomely bound volumes. Of a licentious nature, many were in Italian. But St. Cheviot was no great reader — the books had been appreciated by his father.

Within a few moments of the return of the master of Cadlington, the house blazed with lamp- and candle-light. He, washed and changed, sat before a fire in a small octagonal room, which he used as a private sanctum and kept particularly private documents under lock and key. When in here, it was more than any servant dared do than disturb him. Legs stretched before him, and with Alpha his wolfhound at his feet, Denzil sipped hot mulled wine. He began to feel more comfortable and agreeably-minded as the warmth crept back into his starved body. He had been soaked to the skin before he reached home.

He could not, however, forget the peculiar prophecy of the hunchbacked girl on the roadside. It haunted him.

Marriage . . . within twelve months from now . . . watch out for red-gold hair and violets, she had said, *and a black St. Cheviot.* Well, he had always been partial to blonde women and particularly to those with the white skin that accompanied reddish hair. As for the 'black St. Cheviot', that was more than possible. No blond heir had been born to this family for centuries. But it was curious that a total stranger from London like Elspeth Marsh should know so much.

Before his meeting with the brother and sister, Denzil had fully intended to take himself off to London tonight. Now he had changed his mind and decided that he would stay here in the warmth and, later, join his guests for supper and a game of cards. But first he wanted to see the boy, Peveril Marsh. There were things on St. Cheviot's mind that he wished to ask the young man. Why, for instance, one who spoke so well and looked delicately bred should have come to such a sorry pass. Even as this question entered St. Cheviot's thoughts, a knock came on the door and the boy, himself, entered.

"Ah!" said St. Cheviot, "come in, my young sir. Stand here before me."

Peveril Marsh walked slowly towards him. St. Cheviot could not but be struck now by the boy's light graceful tread and extreme good looks. He was too thin — the face almost cadaverous — but the large grey eyes were brilliant and the forehead high and intelligent, crowned by that thick mop of brown curls which were now dry and glossy. He wore borrowed clothes, white shirt and a flowing tie. His eyes were red-rimmed and it was obvious that he had been weeping. St. Cheviot said:

"Have you had food?"

"Yes, sir, I thank you. Your servants

have been very considerate. My sister . . . " his voice broke.

"Well?"

"Is no more," said the boy in a half whisper and choking. "They have laid her out in an empty room in the servants' quarters and put candles at her head and her feet. Tomorrow they say the parson will come and that a grave will be dug for her alongside Cadlington Church."

"Have you no kith and kin?" demanded St. Cheviot.

The boy seemed to struggle with his emotion. He could not answer for a moment. St. Cheviot added harshly:

"Come, you are no child — can you not conduct yourself in more manly a fashion?"

Now Peveril Marsh flung back his head and spoke with the pride that had first impressed St. Cheviot.

"I do not consider it unmanly to grieve for my sister, sir. She was all that I had."

"Pshaw," said his lordship, who was without sentimentality or, indeed, fine sentiment of any kind. He had only asked the boy to come and see him because

30

he was bitten with curiosity to know how much power the hunchback really had possessed to foretell the future. He thrust jug and tankard across the table to Peveril and bade him drink.

"The wine is spiced. It will strengthen you. Take it."

Peveril drank a few sips and some colour came back into his cheeks.

"Your sister was misshapen — better that she should lie in her grave," said St. Cheviot suddenly. "She had singular beauty of the face but with her deformity no man would ever have taken her to wife."

But Peveril winced.

"She had me, her brother, always to love and protect her," he said in a choked voice.

"Tell me your story," said St. Cheviot.

"What can it matter to you, sir? Why not let me go whence I came?"

"You will do as you are told," snapped St. Cheviot.

Peveril Marsh looked at his benefactor in some surprise. He was soon to learn that here was a man quite merciless to those who offended him and who expected instant obedience. It could not be said that Peveril found Lord St. Cheviot kindly or a man of charm, but tonight the young artist was bemused with the pain of his loss, and with a despair that arose from the hopelessness of his position. He allowed the strong-minded wealthy nobleman to dominate him. At St. Cheviot's request, he related his personal history. He was about to celebrate his twentieth birthday. Five years ago, he had been in a very different position. He and his sister lived with their parents in a small but decent house in the neighbourhood of Holloway in London, where his father had owned a smalll haberdasher's shop. His mother was a cultured lady of more gentle birth than his father and she, herself, had taught her children from infancy. At an early age Peveril had shewn signs of genius with pencil and paint-brush. At twelve years he had painted a picture which had astonished even his parents. So at the request of his mother he had been given education at St. Paul's School and private lessons in painting from an old Italian artist, a friend to Mrs. Marsh.

All had been set fair for Peveril's career. The one unhappiness in the family had been the sad deformity of the little girl, Elspeth. From an early age Peveril had learned to take care of her. Brother and sister were deeply devoted.

Then tragedy befell the family. Mrs. Marsh had suddenly been carried off by a fatal illness to which the doctors could give no name. But her demise, at the early age of forty-one, had not only caused intense grief to her young son and daughter, but altered the whole character of her bereaved husband. He had taken to drinking and neglecting his business. His son, trained only as an artist, and with little head for commerce, struggled to help keep the business afloat. But it had ended in misfortune. Poor William Marsh was taken to a debtor's prison where he languished for six months then died.

Peveril, at nineteen, found himself homeless and with a hunchbacked sister to support. Painting and selling pictures was too precarious a living, so he had taken a job in Cheapside with a firm of frame-makers. Brother and sister shared a home in miserable lodgings. From that time onwards it had become evident to Peveril that the delicate girl would never survive another winter. Thus he had taken the decision to leave London and take Elspeth to the country, to this aunt, Mrs. Ingleby, whom they had once or twice visited as children in happier days. Peveril had felt sure that she would care for Elspeth and allow her to stay in Whiteleaf where the good pure air might help to restore her failing strength.

"It was foolish of me," said the boy in a low voice, "not to have ascertained first that my aunt was still living, but as I had not heard of her death, I took it for granted that we would find her there."

After that, things had happened as formerly described to St. Cheviot. How the fare from London to Monks Risborough had taken all the money the brother and sister had saved; how Elspeth was taken ill during the journey and what had happened once they found that Mrs. Ingleby had died and her cottage was sold to another.

"I feel responsible for having hastened my beloved Elspeth to her grave," ended the unhappy young man.

"Nonsense," barked St. Cheviot, "the girl was already doomed, but I would have you tell me about her powers of prophecy. Am I to believe that she really possessed such supernatural knowledge or was she merely raving?"

"She was not raving," said Peveril. "She developed powers of fortune-telling even when she was a child. I've known her tell me even the exact number of marks I would get at school for certain subjects. Alas, she also foretold our mother's passing, only none of us believed her."

"Then you think she may be right and that I shall find myself wed to a female with red-gold hair, and within twelve months . . . " said St. Cheviot, rose to his feet and laughed harshly.

"Indeed, it will be so, sir."

St. Cheviot put his tongue in his cheek.

"We shall see."

"Have I your leave to go now, sir?"

"Go where?"

"I must no longer encroach on your hospitality."

"Would you not stay and see your sister entrusted to the tomb?"

Peveril shuddered.

"Yes — that I must certainly do, but after . . ."

"After, you will return to London and starve?"

"I will not starve if I can work with these, sir," said Peveril proudly and displayed his slender, well-shaped hands.

St. Cheviot locked his own fingers behind his back and frowned at the boy, who although tall was a head shorter than himself.

"How far are you skilled at painting, I wonder?" he drawled.

Peveril did not seem to hear. He stared into the flames with dull sad eyes. For so long now his sister Elspeth had been the one love and care of his life — he could not picture an existence without her. He dreaded the sad loneliness. Once, when they were talking together, she had prophesied that he would at a young age meet and experience a great love and passionate happiness. But that seemed

36

almost impossible — so far Peveril's heart had never beaten fast at the sight of any woman. His affections had been claimed entirely by his family.

St. Cheviot's voice startled him out of his reverie.

"Supposing I keep you here at Cadlington and give you the wherewithal to paint my portrait? It is time my likeness hung on these walls amongst my ancestors . . . " and he gave his sardonic laugh; a laugh which Peveril found sinister rather than humorous. But regarding the nobleman's spectacular appearance, the artist in Peveril stirred. Indeed — what a portrait Lord St. Cheviot would make in rich and flowing oils, on a vast canvas worthy of his height.

"Well?" thundered St. Cheviot.

"I should like to paint your portrait, sir," said Peveril, and his grey eyes regarding the older man with an expression of cool confidence that St. Cheviot found intriguing. One of those sudden whims of fancy which must always be satisfied in his lordship, seized him now. For no particular reason he decided that he would commission this unhappy youth who had so far suffered a disastrous beginning to a wished-for career as an artist.

"Then you shall stay here, and from time to time I will bore myself by reposing before you so that you can reproduce my likeness," he said. "Who knows but you are a genius in disguise? We shall see. Borrow paper and crayon and go into the hall now and draw for me a likeness of any one of my guests whom you see there, I do not care whom. Then bring it to me."

With some eagerness Peveril assented. For the past year while working as an assistant in a shop, he had had neither time nor heart to use his talents. He felt a sudden wish to prove to Lord St. Cheviot that he was, in truth, a real artist.

He was gone an hour, during which time St. Cheviot took a nap, overcome by the heat of the fire and the fumes of the wine he had drunk. Then his lordship opened his eyes to find the boy standing beside him. Respectfully Peveril handed him a sheet of white paper. On it was sketched in charcoal the head of a man; one St. Cheviot instantly recognized as that of Sir James Barnett — a bachelor of middle age who had come down from London for the shooting and was staying in the house. Unmistakable, the several characteristics of Sir James . . . the broad nostrils, the long face and the double chin, the pouches under the eyes, and the rather sheeplike expression. St. Cheviot burst out laughing.

"Gad! But this is quite remarkable. Yes — I can see that you have considerable talent, my young man. It is a dashed good likeness of that fool James, and if you get as good a one of the present Lord Cheviot — in oils on a full-length canvas — you need no longer starve. You shall become my portrait painter-in-chief. You shall also paint my house and gardens."

Peveril's cheeks flushed but the gleam of triumph in his eyes was short-lived. Too late, he thought sombrely, too late for Elspeth, whose tragic little body was even now lying on a bier. Peveril hung his head but St. Cheviot's hand clapped his shoulder.

"It is well done. I shall give orders that you be appointed a room in the tower, high up where you can have good light. You shall reside here. I will take you to London when next I go. There you shall purchase the necessary paints and canvasses, then return here to start your work."

"I thank you, sir," said Peveril in a low voice.

"First bury your sister," said St. Cheviot, in a voice of indifference, "and bury with her your melancholy. I do not like gloom around me. Now go get some supper and sleep. I've had enough of you for today."

Almost it was in Peveril's mind to reject the nobleman's offer of work even though of such a pleasant kind, for to become a great painter had always been his heart's desire. But he could not find it in him to like this man who had befriended him. There was something so brutal and callous about him. 'Perhaps,' Peveril thought bitterly, 'I am over-sensitive and take my sorrows too much to heart.'

So he decided to stay at Cadlington

and accept the unexpected opportunity that heaven had sent him; even though that help came from what Peveril vaguely suspected a devilish quarter. He bowed and left St. Cheviot. But he went not to eat and drink, but to kneel beside the candle-lit lifeless frame of his sister; there to pray for her departed soul.

Part One

1

IN the following year, 1837, on a fine cold morning in May, Hélène, Lady Roddney, sat in her boudoir reading a letter. The weekly mail arriving by post chaise had just reached Pillars. Sir Harry was out with one of his neighbours, shooting. The house was quiet except for an occasional peal of girlish laughter which made Lady Roddney lift her eyes from the closely written pages which she was scanning, and smile. It was as though she could see through the walls to the adjoining room where her young daughter, Fleur, was entertaining a friend. The merry laughter pleased her.

There was nothing she liked more than for Fleur to be happy. Ever since the child had been born on the twenty-fourth of this month, eighteen years ago, the Roddneys had lived with but a set purpose: to make beautiful the life of their daughter. The only child they would ever have, for Hélène had been told after that long and difficult birth that she would never bear another living infant. She had, in fact, never meant to have children — fearing the dark strain that might be inherited by the next generation and grievously embarrass them all. It was not that Hélène had any wish to forget the fine old African who had been her maternal grandfather. Indeed, he was unforgettable. Just as she could never totally eradicate all memory of her own terrible childhood and the sinister events that had followed. Those ghastly days of slavery, when, with her people, she had been sold into bondage.

But it was a period that above all things Harry wished her to forget. And now it all seemed barely possible that it had happened. Nearly twenty-eight years ago, it was in fact, since she had become Harry Roddney's cherished and adored wife. They had been so happy together that it had not seemed to matter that their union was fruitless for the first ten years. It was as Hélène wished. Then — Fleur had come.

Listening now to her laughter, silver-sweet and gay, knowing that Fleur was as beautiful as an angel and with a disposition as sweet and docile, yet with some of her father's fire — Hélène had no regrets.

She had been born on the very same day as a certain small girl at Kensington Palace; although just how great Victoria, daughter of the Duke and Duchess of Kent, and niece of William IV, was destined to be, nobody then could dream.

Hélène was only half way through perusing her letter — the pages of which were scrawled in violet ink. She was a little bored with the long epistle — and its writer. Dolly — Mrs. de Vere — was a cousin of Harry's. A silly, fussy little woman who cared greatly for money and position. She married Archibald de Vere, a wealthy business man much older than herself, but he deplored the manner in which she spent his money.

They had a house on Knightbridge Green, a son younger than Fleur and a pair of fat daughters, twins, now nineteen, whom everybody except their mother found excessively stupid and plain. Cousin Dolly, nevertheless, from the very start of her cousin Harry's marriage to Hélène, then the widow of the famous Marquis de Chartellet — had proved herself a staunch friend. She had welcomed the advent of the beautiful and quite famous Marquise into the Roddney family and taken considerable pains to invite the married couple, on their return from Italy, to stay with her. This had pleased Hélène, who did not wish Harry to be totally cut off from the Roddneys. In addition, Archibald was a powerful member of the East India Company wherein Harry had started his life as a man of affairs — and from which he had only retired a year ago.

Harry got on well with Archibald who in character and demeanour very often reminded him of his uncle, James Wilberson. And Hélène tolerated Dolly, but she was a gossip and that sharp unkind tongue of hers often ran away with her. In Hélène's estimation one had to be careful of the things Dolly repeated.

Through half-shut lids, Hélène's dark velvet eyes dreamed out of the windows at a white billow of cloud that drifted across the blue clear sky. It was so peaceful here, except for the light-hearted chatter and laughter of the girls next door.

And Hélène's heart was as a rule full of quiet. But today, for some strange reason, the past arose to haunt her. It was too terrible to lay for ever buried, and must at times disturb her peace. Sometimes she asked herself cynically how many of their present friends would accept her if they *knew*. Knew that she, the proud Lady Roddney, had been born in an African kraal of a white father and a half-caste mother. That as a fabulously beautiful quadroon girl of tender years she had been sold into slavery — become the chattel of a spoiled vicious society woman, by name Lady Pumphret, and that later when Lord Pumphret who had been her only friend, expired, been submitted to a terrible bondage from which she had fled to the protection of the noted young rake and charmer, Sir Harry Roddney. All these things that had happened she would not today allow herself to remember in detail. They were too terrible. And through a terrible misunderstanding Harry had gone out of her life again. So once more she had been sold — and this time to the erudite old Marquis de Chartellet. In his house, known as 'The Little Bastille', on the Essex coast, she had found refuge and lived for some years. Her whole life had altered. Lucien had educated her and lifted her out of her misery. She had ceased to be the unhappy quadroon once known as *Fauna*. She had become *Hélène* — the name de Chartellet gave her, and in due course she had become his wife.

As *Madame la Marquise de Chartellet* she had been revenged upon the society that had once tortured her. But as far as she knew, not a living soul knew of that other hellish existence or of the dark strain in her blood.

After Lucien's death, when she had married her old love, Harry, she found all the happiness that had once eluded her. London accepted Lady Roddney just as they had once toasted her as *Madame la Marquise. Fauna, the quadroon slave, was to all intents and purposes, dead.*

But today as Hélène sat in her beautiful boudoir listening to her daughter's laughter, she was disturbed not only by the phantoms of the past but by the thought of Fleur's future.

The child was only seventeen but it was the day of early marriages and both Hélène and Harry realized it was time Fleur found a husband.

But whom? Who was there worthy of her, the mother asked herself this morning. Young Thomas Quinley — son of neighbouring Sir David Quinley, doctor and scientist — a nice boy, and Fleur liked him and rode sometimes with him and his sister. But he was to her no more than a brother — a companion. The Hon. Vyvyan Lockhart — a good-looking, amiable lad — would ride a good many miles from the Hertfordshire border to see Fleur for an hour. Fleur had convinced her mother that she would never accept a proposal from young Vyvyan.

This morning Hélène also fell to wondering who would care for Fleur should she be still unwed when her parents died. Death was not probable yet — but it was possible. There was, of course, Cousin Dolly. But Fleur had no great faith in the cousin, whose way of life Fleur herself despised. No — she would not want Fleur to make a home with the de Veres.

Other than that there was only Harry's lawyer (he had been legal adviser to Sir Arthur Fayre from whom Harry inherited Pillars). In case of an early demise, Harry had made Caleb Nonseale Fleur's legal guardian. Hélène found Mr. Nonseale polite, even servile, but deep down in her heart she did not trust him.

2

FLEUR RODDNEY bent low over a handful of exquisitely coloured silks with which she was embroidering a tea cosy for her mother's wedding anniversary. She chose a strand of deep violet and held it up to the light.

"Look, Cathy — is this not a pleasant hue?" she asked.

Catherine Foster — a pleasant, freckled girl with long brown curls — looked first at the violet silks, then into her friend's eyes. Catherine was — like many others — always fascinated by the shape and colour of Fleur Roddney's eyes.

"Truly, your eyes are more violet than blue — and like your silks," she sighed. "You *are* lucky! Your lashes are dark, yet you are fair — and they are the longest I have seen. Lucky, *lucky* Fleur!"

Fleur gave her musical laugh.

"Foolish Cathy — what have you to complain of? You have the dearest face," she murmured.

53

Catherine grumbled, glancing sideways at a mirror over the fireplace in her friend's boudoir. It was a charming room — white and madonna blue — Fleur's favourite colour — and full of spring flowers. Over the mantelpiece hung a painting of Hélène by a contemporary artist. To the young girl — who had received this on her seventeenth birthday — it was her dearest possession. Always she admired her lovely and fascinating mother.

Lady Roddney, superb in a grey velvet ball gown of that period, with low corsage; sapphires sparkling on her snowy throat and bosom; rich red-gold curls falling over the matchless shoulders.

Fleur's hair was a shade paler but she had the same contours; high cheekbones, small pointed chin and ripe curving mouth.

The girls chatted intimately as they worked. They were vastly entertained by the prospect of the dance which Lady Roddney was giving at Pillars next week to celebrate Fleur's eighteenth birthday.

Suddenly Catherine remembered a certain gentleman who had figured at a dinner party which Fleur's Papa had given here, at Easter. He had not left Fleur's side all evening and had turned the pages for her while she played *Sheep May Safely Graze* on her spinet.

"Do you know whether Lord St. Cheviot is on your Mama's list of guests?" she asked, and looked slyly under her lids for Fleur's reaction. It was surprising. Fleur stiffened and her pink flush faded.

"I hope not," she said. Her voice was quite changed. She looked almost *scared*.

"But why, Fleur?" Catherine asked curiously. "He was so very handsome. You said so. You told me you were quite bowled over."

"Only at first — then almost at once I drew back," said Fleur and accidentally stuck her needle into her finger. She withdrew it, then, like a child, sucked the tiny pin-prick of blood.

"I do not think I want him to come to the Ball, nevertheless," she added.

"But why?" persisted Catherine.

"He — frightens me. And I do not find him sincere — he is too bold," said

Fleur thoughtfully.

"But handsome."

"Oh, vastly so! I admire it."

"And entertaining."

"I do not know. We did not speak much together, but I believe he is greatly travelled," said Fleur. "He was originally of French extraction. He spends much time on the French Coast. Papa says he is a fine rider and a deadly shot. It was at a shooting party they met. The Baron is also famous at fencing, and I have heard it said that in Paris he once killed two opponents when he was attacked, on either side — ran them both through like this and this . . . "

And Fleur with a turn of delicate wrist, flicked her needle in the air from left to right. Catherine screamed.

"Ooh — how horrid!"

"I have a notion that Lord St. Cheviot, for all his gallant manner — is horrid," said Fleur frankly.

"But he sounds *fascinating*," breathed Catherine. "Wickedly, deliciously attractive, dear Fleur."

The other girl did not comment for the moment. She recalled her first meeting with St. Cheviot at a dinner party given by her Papa. Certainly, St. Cheviot had dominated the dinner. He was a witty conversationalist and *raconteur*.

When he had singled Fleur out for favour, she had at first been shyly flattered. Quite overawed, she had sat clasping her long slim fingers, listening while he bent over her chair and told her how her several beauties had enslaved him on sight.

"The white swan on your father's lake has not more grace than that which is yours," he had said. "The first time I gazed into the violet of your eyes, I was dazzled, and I am still blinded. I have never seen greater loveliness, Miss Roddney." Those were the sort of things he had murmured into her ear all through the evening. He had told her, too, about Cadlington — his vast residence. How lonely it was in all its magnificence — how wasted its army of servants — and the priceless jewels that lay in the family safe. All waiting for a bride; for the girl who would become the wife of Denzil, Lord St. Cheviot.

Heady, significant words — whispered

throughout an entire evening — by the most dazzling man in the room. What wonder it had gone a little to Fleur Roddney's innocent head. Yet after he had departed, and she had discussed the evening with her mother, she had said:

"*What is it about Lord St. Cheviot that repels me, Mama?*"

Hélène had hesitated to answer. In her opinion, St. Cheviot was, despite his looks and title, too fierce, too coarse for her darling whom she and Harry had so long protected from the wickedness of the world.

"I do not personally care for him, my darling, and if you like, you need not see him again," the mother had told Fleur before they retired that night.

But Harry Roddney had other views. He was intrigued by St. Cheviot. Twice, since Christmas, Harry had stayed at Cadlington House as a member of a big shooting party. Hélène had of course been invited, but she declined. She preferred to remain at Pillars with her daughter.

When Hélène had suggested that strong rumour had it St. Cheviot was not a good man, Harry had laughed and carelessly caressed the frown from the noble forehead of her whom he loved so well.

"Dear heart — he is a *man* — and unmarried. He cannot be expected to live the life of a saint. Was Harry Roddney's past life so speckless that he can afford to pick faults in others?"

"If Harry was not faultless in his youth — he was always kind — who should know better than I?" Hélène had answered. "But it is my opinion that St. Cheviot knows no charity."

"My dear love, do not worry your beautiful head about him."

"But he is enamoured of our daughter," sighed Hélène, "and makes every effort to see her."

Again Harry, with all the simplicity and gaiety of nature that Hélène had first loved in him, laughed.

"What man does not kneel at the feet of our Fleur? Let St. Cheviot fall. She will not have him."

"Would you wish her to?"

Harry pulled the lobe of his ear.

"N-no," he said at length, "I would not. He is, as you say — too worldly — and perhaps too old for her. Let her marry a simple youth — it is best."

With that, Hélène was content, and troubled herself no more about the master of Cadlington House. But since then she had discussed him with Cousin Dolly, and Dolly, the little gossip, shed further light on the magnificent baron — none too good a light.

"It is rumoured that a well-born girl recently drowned herself because he betrayed her," she had said. "Isn't it romantic? But I would adore to entertain him. He is so handsome and so *wicked*! They say, too, his house has a haunted tower where a crime was committed." She giggled. But her information did nothing to endear Lord St. Cheviot further to Hélène.

It was the last paragraph in the long gossipy letter from Dolly that finally made Hélène open her door and call to her daughter.

"Fleur — can you come to Mama a moment?"

Catherine, hearing Lady Roddney's voice, rose to her feet and said that she must depart. The carriage was waiting.

Her Mama had sent the brougham for her, with Miss Spencer, her chaperone; and she must go.

"Come back tomorrow, dear Cathy, and we will finish our needlework," said Fleur, kissing her friend's cheek.

In her mother's boudoir, the young girl gazed fondly at the elder woman's grave, lovely face. To her it was a face that bore traces of deep suffering — but the mother never spoke of it, and Fleur never asked questions. She could only guess (dimly) that her mother had been through great pain in the past, and once her father had said to her:

"Be always angelic to Mama, my Fleur, for she has known tragedy that you are too young to understand — and come through her ordeal with flying colours. Now 'tis for you and for me to make sure she never sheds another tear on this earth."

Hélène put an arm about her daughter and began to read her what Cousin Dolly had written.

'*It might interest you, my dearest Hélène, to know that yesterday Archibald and I rode together in the Row and who should canter alongside us and greet us but the wicked St. Cheviot himself. He has grown handsomer than ever and wore a black riding coat and white breeches. He spoke of your little Fleur . . .'*

Hélène paused and glanced enquiringly at her daughter. A carmine flush had crept up under the fair skin. Hélène continued:

'Indeed he seems to find her so fetching that he is anxious to see her again and asked if I would not induce her to come and stay with my girls. Now if you would let me I could present her, providing his Majesty recovers and can hold a Court next Season . . .'

Fleur listened attentively until her mother had finished reading the letter, then moved away from the encircling arm and thoughtfully touched the glossy leaves of a small palm which stood in a corner.

"Well, my love," said Hélène, "what about it?"

"It must be as you wish, Mama. If Papa wants the Baron at my dance, he must come."

At that moment there came the sound of horses' hooves in the drive. Mother and daughter exchanged glances of pleasure.

"Your father has come back," said Hélène.

Together they went down the handsome staircase and into the hall which had been greatly enlarged since the first day Hélène (then known as Fauna and a year younger than her own daughter was today) had set foot in it. Harry Roddney came through the door.

He kissed his lovely wife and then his daughter.

"How is my Darling?" he asked, pulling one of the fair silky curls that fell upon her shoulder.

Fleur with the artlessness of youth plunged straight into the problem that was worrying her.

"Mama and I have something to ask you, Papa."

"Concerning what, my darling?"

"Mama will tell you."

"It is a question of the proposed guests

63

for her birthday dance," said Hélène.

"Ah, yes," said Harry, "the great day when our Fleur becomes a woman of the world!" and playfully he swept a bow in cavalier fashion to his daughter.

Fleur laughed merrily.

"I don't think I shall ever be *that*, Papa, and do not want to be. Indeed, I do not want ever to leave you and Mama, and our home."

"Let us then talk of the guests for your Ball," said her father.

Hélène, who knew what the girl was struggling to say, said it for her.

"It is of Lord St. Cheviot she would speak, Harry. She is not sure in her mind that she wants him here again. She did not care for him."

Harry Roddney, who was inclined to be a little vague about people, put a finger against the side of his nose and reflected.

"St. Cheviot, ah yes, has he then been asked to Fleur's party?"

"Not yet. All the other invitations have already been sent," said Hélène. "But we know, dearest, that you have been his guest at Cadlington and have said several

64

times that you wished me to return some hospitality other than the once he dined with us."

Harry poured himself out a glass of sherry and sipped it, smiling amiably at his wife.

"It is for you to say, my angel. What do you want to do in this matter?"

But Hélène knew her husband. Harry was not always tactful and had no memory. She put a hand on his shoulder and looked at him whimsically.

"Are you quite sure that when you last went with St. Cheviot to the Anglo-French cock-fight you did not mention Fleur's birthday and suggest that he attend? It would be so like you, Harry."

His handsome face flushed. He looked apologetic and coughed.

"In truth, my love, now I come to think of it, I believe I *did* mention the fact. For St. Cheviot asked if he might be permitted to send Fleur a box of the orchids that they grow at Cadlington and for which the forcing houses in his garden have long been famous."

Hélène's expression changed. Fleur bit her lip.

"I hate orchids," said the girl under her breath.

"That's all right, my dear, you can receive them, then give them away," said her father grandly.

But Hélène shook her head.

"Harry, Harry, you were never a diplomat, although you are my heart's love."

"Have I done wrong?" he asked with so woebegone an expression that Hélène immediately took one of his strong fine hands and laid it against her cheek. The gesture of a young girl.

"My heart's love," she repeated under her breath. "If you have already made the invitation, do not trouble. We can entertain St. Cheviot once more and Fleur can receive the orchids, but it must be firmly understood that we are not interested in any serious advances from him now or ever. He is not for Fleur."

"Certainly not," Harry agreed promptly. "He is too old and a devil, but by gad, what a wizard with pistol or fowling piece or sword. I've never seen his like. Well, well — I will get changed . . . "

66

He walked off. Hélène smiled at her daughter.

"Too late now to stop St. Cheviot coming — your naughty Papa has been so indiscreet. He is too lavish with his invitations."

"It is no matter, Mama," said Fleur. "I shall only give Lord St. Cheviot one dance and can send the orchids to Cathy's mother who likes them."

Hélène bent and touched her daughter's cheek with her lips

"You need never be afraid of the Baron of Cadlington — or of any man. Your father and I will always be here to protect you, my angel," she said.

Not long afterwards, in the bitter agony of the storm that even now was clouding Fleur's horizon, the young girl remembered those loving words. They were words spoken from the heart, but in blissful ignorance. For soon neither her mother's devotion — nor her father's strength — could protect Fleur from the doom that awaited her.

3

ON May 24th, when the Roddneys held a Ball to celebrate their daughter's eighteenth birthday, another birthday was being celebrated at Kensington Palace. Another young girl was entering her nineteenth year; Victoria with a royal destiny and a brilliant future before her.

All day it had seemed to Fleur that her own destiny was every bit as wonderful as that of any Royal Princess could be.

Hélène tried to make her rest but the excitement had conquered. Fleur wanted to have a hand in everything, and when all was done, had wandered arm in arm with her mother through the house. Never had the reception-room looked more magnificent. The Aubusson carpets had been rolled away. The floors were waxed and polished until they looked like golden glass. Banks of flowers, and tall palms, were placed in all corners and there was a raised dais for the orchestra that had been especially engaged for the night.

Three great chandeliers hanging from the carved ceiling glittered with light from hundreds of wax candles. All over the house, the candles burned in their gilt or silver sconces. Fires crackled in the grates, for the May night was cool. But it had been a lovely day and fortunately it was a lovely starlit night without the fog that Fleur had dreaded, and which might have kept some of the guests away.

The guest chambers at Pillars were full. Cousin Dolly had come to stay with the twins and her son Cyril, who was a little less gloomy and dumb than usual because he had just passed his entrance examination for Oxford. Nobody knew how he had managed it but it had given his mother something really to boast about at last with her dull-witted family. Now, she was telling everybody that 'darling Cyril was the cleverest boy in the world and would *astonish* the dons, when term began'.

The Roddneys had spared no expense to make this birthday party a perfect one for their idolized child. In the dining-room, the servants had already loaded side tables and buffet with every variety of food. Great dishes of stuffed veal in aspic, York hams, cold game, French and Russian salads; towering confections of jelly, fruit, and cakes with whipped cream and nuts; bowls of fruit salad; trifles in silver dishes and of course, in the centre, the birthday cake made by the Roddneys' chef who came from France and had surpassed himself. What a wonderful cake it was, thought Fleur. Three tiers of white icing like turrets, edged with pink, and studded with glazed cherries. And Fleur's name was written across it in pink icing, with 'HAPPY BIRTHDAY' and the date.

The sight of the eighteen candles which she would light later this evening, made Fleur clasp her hands together like an enchanted child.

"So many! Oh, Mama, I am growing too old, and too fast. I wish now to go back and not forward."

But her mother had kissed her and laughed.

"We must never go back in life, my

darling — always forward. For you, I pray, it will be ever upward, too — to the starry heights!"

Now Fleur was dressed waiting for the guests.

St. Cheviot arrived early. He was at the moment in residence in London. He was standing at the foot of the staircase when Fleur appeared to take her place beside her mother and father who were receiving.

She had a few moments ago run up to her room for a moment in order that her maid should put a stitch in the flounce of her ball gown which had a tiny tear in it.

Lord St. Cheviot's black eyes, which had been full of boredom and indifference, smouldered suddenly into an unholy glow of admiration. As his glance fastened greedily upon the girl who seemed to float rather than walk down the staircase, his pulses gave a wild throb — as they had throbbed and beaten upon the first night he had seen her at Lady Roddney's dinner party. Now, as *then*, he seemed to hear an echo of the prophecy made by the crippled girl who had died in her

71

brother's arms that stormy October night outside the gates of Cadlington House.

"*Within twelve months from now you will marry,*" she had said before she expired. "*I who can see into the future foretell this marriage. But with it comes disaster. Red-gold hair and violets — watch out for red-gold hair and violets . . . It shall be . . .*"

He remembered those words and tonight with more than ordinary excitement he continued to watch Fleur Roddney.

The dress chosen by her mother, and made by the French *couturier* who had come especially to Pillars to fashion it, was as snow-white as the girl's long neck and delicately rounded arms. Flounce upon flounce of the fine frilly lace — until it reached the tips of small white satin shoes. The corsage was cut low but modestly so, with rosettes of satin ribbons, drooping a little of the shoulders. A wide violet-blue sash was tied around the small waist. Her curls clustered silkily about her neck. Those large shining eyes, the hue of violets in her hair, made St. Cheviot catch his breath. In vain he looked to see if she

72

carried the orchids he had sent, but she did not.

"Devil take it," he muttered to himself, "I do not think she fancies me."

As Fleur reached the last stair, and stood there a moment, he impeded her further progress. The thought flashed through his mind:

'*I must have her*. The hunchback's prophecy shall be carried out. Fleur, and Fleur alone shall be Lady St. Cheviot — Baroness of Caddlington.'

He bowed low.

"Your servant, Miss Roddney . . . "

She looked up at him but she did not return his smile. She did not like it; it had the quality of ice — and behind the ice — the threat of fire. She did not like him. Yet he was the most handsome man in the room.

Black hair well oiled, curling across his brow, side whiskers, high collar, satin cravat; and like most of the gentlemen here, he wore knee breeches, silk hose and a cutaway coat. He was handsome and haughty and towered above the others because of his remarkable height. Fleur murmured a timid greeting; she felt at the same time as though his presence too greatly overshadowed her. She could no longer see the sparkling chatting laughing crowd — nor her parents who were near the front door. She had a wild sensation of terror, almost claustrophobic in its origin, and although St. Cheviot would have detained her, rushed past him and fled to her mother. She was pale and trembling as she reached Hélène's side, but said nothing of what she felt. Hélène was too busy welcoming late-comers to notice her daughter's distress.

Now the music was playing and young Tom Quinley thrust through the crowd to ask Fleur to open the Ball with him. She was about to write her initials on his programme when a tall figure slid smothly between them. St. Cheviot, a hand on his heart, bowed.

"If you will grant me the pleasure, Miss Roddney . . . "

She wanted to say 'No'; to cry to Tom to stay. But the boy was much too overawed by the age and magnificence of the well-known baron, and grimacing his disappointment moved off.

"Keep the next one — the schottische — for me, Fleur," he called as he went.

St. Cheviot crooked an arm. Fleur had no choice but to place a hand through it.

"I shall esteem this a very great honour," he murmured, "and might I say that tonight you look like the Spirit of all the flowers in the world?"

She made no answer. As before when she had listened to Denzil St. Cheviot, she was silent before his flattery. She was a little angry, too, because she felt this had been forced upon her. She had wanted to open the Ball with Tom, her friend. St. Cheviot was too masterful. Perhaps it was that he gave one such a feeling that he expected his wishes to be carried out instantly that she disliked. She, the least rebellious of people, wished suddenly to rebel.

The opening dance was a polka. St. Cheviot placed a kid-gloved hand at the back of the girl's slight waist. She placed her right hand on his. It might have been a snowflake, he thought, for all the impression it made. And when he considered what he had just said to

75

her about being the Spirit of all flowers, he thought sardonically:

"Twould be a pity to cut her down and watch her die.'

But immediately, as he moved with her on to the polished floor, a less merciful thought followed.

"Tis a pity, too, that I hold her here with formality and for all the world to see, and must contain myself, for I would like to crush her against me and bruise that meek young mouth with kisses; teach her that Denzil St. Cheviot is to be reckoned with.'

Unmindful of any such hateful reflections, Fleur danced with the man whom her father had invited here. Those looking on were whispering what a handsome couple they made — the tall dark man and the slight fair girl. St. Cheviot was a graceful dancer and a good match for Fleur, who moved exquisitely. For a moment the other guests watched them and then Hélène, not wishing her daughter to be thus exhibited, followed with her husband. Soon the floor was crowded with couples.

The gay polka ended, St. Cheviot

crooked his arm and escorted Fleur towards the conservatory. He manœuvred her through a doorway and she found herself seated on one of the red plush sofas.

"May I get you some refreshment, Miss Roddney?" he asked.

"Nothing, I thank you," she answered breathlessly.

His dark sombre gaze held hers. He saw how she shrank from him. It did not deter him. On the contrary it fired his longing to overcome her reluctance.

Fleur sat twisting the little painted fan which she held between her lace-mittened fingers. She attempted to discuss the crowd.

"Many people have come to my birthday," she murmured, "and I have had some wonderful presents. Look — my papa gave me this . . . "

Artlessly she held out a delicate wrist on which there glittered a little bangle of pearls, simply set in gold. St. Cheviot gave a smile that was more a sneer.

"A pretty bauble," he said, "but unworthy of that exquisite arm. At Cadlington there is a diamond bracelet that belonged to my French grandmother. It was Marie Antoinette's and is valued at thousands of pounds. I would like you to wear it."

Fleur swallowed. Her lashes fluttered. She looked to the right and left like a startled fawn.

"I — treasure my father's gift — but I — am not really interested in valuable jewels," she stammered.

But St. Cheviot was thinking:

"Her waist is so small I could almost take two of the old *Comtesse* Marguerite's bracelets and make them into a diamond belt for Fleur. One day I shall. *And I myself shall clasp it around her.*"

"Where are my orchids?" he asked suddenly with a bluntness that defeated Fluer. Once again she was distressed, not wishing to appear rude.

"The orchids were splendid, thank you. I — but I could not wear them, they — it was necessary for my attire tonight that I should wear violets," she said in the same stammering frightened little voice.

St. Cheviot folded his arms and looked

down at her with his humourless smile.

"I will have more sent to you from Cadlington tomorrow. You can make a carpet with them and tread upon them with your little bare feet. I do not mind."

Such talk merely terrified her. She half-rose.

"No, sit down again," he said in a softer voice, and told himself that he must control his rising passion. He was used to putting out a hand and taking what he wanted. Such women liked force, but this one he could see must be wooed, *tamed*.

"Sit down, I beg of you, Miss Roddney," he repeated. "I apologize if I have said anything to offend your ears."

She put a hand on her fast-beating heart.

"I hear the strains of a schottische. I promised Mr. Quinley — "

"Will you not stay and talk with me?"

"No — " she began, and now saw to her utter relief the tall boyish figure of young Tom Quinley. He was not remarkable to look at and just now appeared rather red-faced and clumsy beside the magnificent baron, but to Fleur he was a sweet sight — a rock of refuge.

"Our dance, I think, Tom," she said.

He bowed and crooked his arm. She took it and walked away with him without so much as a backward glance at St. Cheviot.

He narrowed his lids until his eyes were like black slits. Up went his brows. A sardonic grin widened his lips. The first round to *her*. The first of many, perhaps, in the tussle that lay before them. Instead of returning to the ball-room, he called to a passing footman to fetch his hat and cloak. He was driving back to London at once. He left behind him a note for Harry Roddney.

Your pardon but I have been taken ill and have called my carriage. I do not think your daughter likes me but I wish you to know that I would lay my life down for her gladly.

St. Cheviot.

When Harry received this note he passed it, in some surprise, to his wife.

Hélène shrugged her shoulders.

"I doubt if it was illness — I warrant it was pique. Fleur has just told me that she found him and his talk detestable, and shewed it."

"Dear, dear," said Harry and pulled the lobe of his ear, not pretending to understand his womenfolk in this matter. He saw only the loss of some very good shooting and entertainment if St. Cheviot should remain 'piqued'. But certainly if his darling did not care for the man, he must be allowed to go.

4

A LITTLE less than a month later, on the 20th June, the star that had hung over the head of the Duchess of Kent's daughter flashed into sudden prominence. Her uncle, William IV, died on the 20th June, and the young Victoria became Queen of England.

When Fleur heard this news she was staying in London with Cousin Dolly in their tall narrow elegant house that faced Knightsbridge Green. They all heard it — the salute of guns — the newsboys dashing through the streets — the hurry and scurry of shopkeepers to put up the shutters and fix the crêpe to doors and hats. England was plunging into mourning for a King who had left no particular mark in the world. But that young fragile-looking girl with the lion's heart who had received the kiss of homage from her ministers in the early hours of this morning, was destined to rule over the greatest Empire history had ever known.

It was exciting news for England and for every family, including the de Veres. Archibald de Vere had gone out early and come back to tell them of the vast crowds surging round the Palace and the excitement that prevailed. Cousin Dolly immediately rushed the twins upstairs to find black dresses, and sent a message to Miss Golling, her dressmaker, to come at once. There were not many black gowns in Dolly's own wardrobe. Fleur, too, must get into mourning instantly, she declared.

Fleur meant to enjoy London but had not come here very willingly she had to admit to herself, although she behaved with the utmost sweetness and docility and tried not to let the twins — or Cyril — see how bored she was by their incessant vapid chatter.

Quite unexpectedly, Papa had been called to Paris, there to investigate the unfortunate death of a man who had worked for many years both for his old friend and benefactor James Wilberson; and for Harry while he had served in the

Far East with the East India Company.

The man appeared to have died under particularly tragic circumstances and left a widow there, a helpless invalid. Harry Roddney, ever generous and conscientious, had deemed it his duty to go over and do what he could for the wretched woman; even bring her home. On a sudden impulse, Hélène had volunteered to accompany her husband. At this time of the year, the Channel crossing would not be rough and she might, she said, find it pleasant on a sunny day on one of the little paddle-steamers that took passengers from Dover to Calais.

"Papa shall drive me down the *Rue de la Paix* and I shall buy a new bonnet and choose one for you, my dearest," she had smiled at her daughter.

"Oh, yes, Mama, do," had been Fleur's eager reply, "for I hear the summer bonnets in Paris this year are very fetching."

They had had a happy dinner together the night before Harry and Hélène took their little voyage, although Fleur had found her Papa preoccupied with sad thoughts of the excellent head clerk who had come to such a sad pass on the Continent; it would appear through gambling.

But the next morning as Fleur had kissed them farewell and watched the carriage drive them away from the portico on their journey to Dover — a strange presentiment of trouble had shaken the psychic consciousness of the young girl. She had had an irresistible presentiment to fly down the path and scream after them:

"Come back — oh, my beloved parents, *come back*."

Cousin Dolly, who was with her, had been surprised when Fleur burst into hysterical weeping.

"Fie on you for being such a baby! Your parents will not be gone more than a week," she had said and led the girl back into the house, where the twins sympathetically offered their handkerchiefs!

Fleur had done her best to recover from this strange depression and to deem herself foolish and over-sensitive. Mama and Papa meant to stay in Paris only for a few days it was true — and then they would all be together again.

"I do believe you will weep at your own wedding!" Cousin Dolly scolded her.

Fleur had hastily assured Cousin Dolly that there was no wedding in sight, and that she meant to remain with her parents as long as she could.

With this, Cousin Dolly had little patience. Here she was, desperately trying to find suitors for the twins, and men from all sides milling around to get the beautiful Miss Roddney to smile at them. If *she* were Hélène, she would be positively annoyed with the obstinate young miss. As for the St. Cheviot business — that was more than annoying to Mrs. de Vere. For unknown to her Cousin Harry or his wife, she was in secret contact with St. Cheviot; in a manner which would have greatly angered both the Roddneys had they known.

St. Cheviot had not taken the slight he had received at Pillars very well. Dolly had heard reports that he returned to town in a towering rage and let everybody know it. He had even spoken of Fleur

86

as a 'spoiled pampered brat who needed a lesson'. Nevertheless, he was so far challenged that he had, since the Ball, persisted in his advances. Lady Roddney gave him no encouragement, and when he saw Harry on occasions at the Club, the kindly jovial baronet spoke with him but seemed embarrassed about his daughter and avoided the subject.

Dolly knew that every morning now for four weeks, huge boxes of orchids had arrived at Pillars from Cadlington House. Valuable exotic blooms, purple and red and yellow-green — all shapes and sizes on long sprays. With each box, he sent a card always with the same words:

Make a carpet of these if you so wish but do not ignore me.
St. Cheviot.

Dolly would have given her silly empty little soul for this mark of favour from such a splendid and handsome person, devil though he was. Yet she had been told by the girl, herself, that as soon as the orchids came, she gave them away to anybody who wanted them.

"They are poisonous and they terrify me," she said. "I do not wish to receive tokens from *him*."

"But what have you against him?" Dolly asked, looking at the girl with round astonished eyes.

"I do not know," was the reply. "I just do not care for him."

But the orchids continued to come. Now, although Fleur did not know how he discovered it, St. Cheviot found out that she was staying in London with the de Veres. Every morning that same box was delivered at Knightsbridge from Buckinghamshire; brought thither by a rider on a sweating foaming horse. The very sight of the poor mount (Fleur had seen it arrive several times) disgusted her. He must be a cruel man, she thought, to allow an animal to be ridden almost to death in order that she should receive his flowers so early.

She refused to acknowledge her receipt of them, and once when Cousin Dolly suggested that St. Cheviot should be allowed to call, she turned so white that Mrs. de Vere had to capitulate with a shrug of the shoulders.

"As you wish, my love, but you are missing a great chance."

On this the morning of the King's death and the accession of the young Victoria, Fleur permitted Cousin Dolly's maid to measure her for a mourning gown and thought longingly of her parents.

At any moment now they would surely return from Paris and take her back to Pillars. She felt stifled in this fussy, ornate, noisy little house where it seemed to her that Cousin Dolly and the twins screamed all day.

Cousin Dolly, becomingly attired in black, with black bonnet and black fringed shawl, peered in to see what Fleur was doing. Fleur showed her a book that she was about to read. It made Cousin Dolly shudder. Gibbon's *Decline and Fall of the Roman Empire*. Heavens, she thought, what an uncomfortable girl! She enjoyed *history* instead of joining with Isabel and Imogen in the search for attractive mourning apparel.

"Oh, well," murmured Dolly, "we will gather together for the midday meal. I have an appointment with Miss Ply. *Au revoir*, dearest Fleur."

Little did Fleur know that Cousin Dolly was hastening to a rendezvous with Denzil St. Cheviot, himself. Veil over her face, and tiny parasol to shield her from the sun, the plump little woman sat puffing on a bench beside the Baron. He looked immensely bored.

"Is is not exciting that we have a Queen on the throne and when the time of mourning is passed, we can embark upon a brilliant social life in London," Dolly twittered.

"I did not come here to discuss the new Queen," said St. Cheviot in his most icy voice. "What of *her*?"

"Oh, it is tragic, but I cannot induce Fleur to see you or visit Cadlington," sighed Dolly.

St. Cheviot's lips drew into a thin line. He tapped his thumb-nail against the tall beaver hat to which was affixed a rosette of black crêpe. He looked taller and leaner than ever in his mourning clothes. He said:

"She receives my flowers daily?"

"Yes, my dear St. Cheviot, and throws them away."

"As she is trying to throw me," said

St. Cheviot grimly.

Dolly floundered in her mind for a method of bringing Cousin Roddney's rebellious daughter to heel. St. Cheviot had struck a financial bargain with Dolly. He had discovered that she was heavily in debt.

At their last meeting, St. Cheviot had promised her a reward — handsome enough to make her senses swim — if she could aid and abet his courtship of her young cousin. The Roddneys need never know and it would be a solution to Mrs. de Vere's present embarrassment.

"Well," said Denzil curtly, and dug the end of an ebony stick which he carried, into the gravel, "have you no suggestion?"

"Oh, dear, it is so *difficult*," said Dolly. "Fleur is such a determined child."

"I, too, am determined," said the man coldly.

"Youth is temperamental," added Dolly. "She does not care for orchids."

"Bah!" said St. Cheviot, "then I will send — violets."

Dolly brightened.

"You might *try* them. I know she dotes

91

on them. Meanwhile I will continue to sing your praises."

He bowed, escorted her to her carriage and left her.

He went down to Cadlington only at week ends. His temper was frayed. The servants were in fear and trembling. Only Peveril Marsh dared speak to him. The young artist often received visits from the master.

Denzil would pace up and down the studio in the tower, gloomily watching the boy bring his splendid painting of Cadlington to life. He only half recognized the genius of the artist. It was in himself and his affairs that St. Cheviot was interested. Again and again he would question Peveril as to the validity of his dead sister's power of divining.

"Had she truly the gift of seeing into the future?" the Baron would demand repeatedly — tormented with desire for Fleur.

Peveril would look with his grave eyes at the bitter face of his strange patron and answer:

"I believe so, my lord. That is all I can tell you. Always when Elspeth told fortunes her prophecies came true."

Then Denzil would lose interest in the picture — and in his protégé — and return to his own quarters, to drink heavily until dawn.

5

FLEUR sat in the small writing-room at the back of Cousin Dolly's house, scanning the weekly newspaper which had just been delivered and which was widely bordered with black.

It was some forty-eight hours since King William IV had breathed his last.

This morning, Lord Melbourne had brought the first message from the Queen to the House of Lords, and Lord John Russell moved a similar address to the Commons.

Fleur, brought up by her father to be interested in her country's affairs, looked with interest at an article which described the present period as one of 'perfect tranquillity'. The young Queen had ascended the throne at a great moment in history. The country could look forward to a reduction in taxation, an improvement in the standard of living and a relaxation of the terrible severity of the present criminal laws.

It was expected, the paper said, that the young Queen would open Parliament in November; surrounded by wise elderly advisers there seemed little doubt that this new sovereign would inspire loyal devotion from her subjects.

Fleur continued to read the article, then lifted her eyes from it and thought deeply about this young Queen who was her own age. Henceforth Victoria Regina must live constantly in the fierce light that beats upon the throne. Nothing that she could do or say could be concealed. A husband would be chosen for her; she could not even fall in love and marry as Fleur Roddney hoped to do — a man of her own choosing.

"Who would be a queen?" Fleur asked herself and sighed in sympathy, wondering whether that very young girl, now immersed in state duties in her palace, every felt lonely or afraid. *As I would feel in her place*, Fleur said the words aloud. *God bless and strengthen the poor little Queen!*

Then a feeling of happiness replaced the melancholy that Fleur had been enduring at her parents' absence. Last night a gentleman who knew Papa had brought a sealed message from Paris. A letter from Papa, telling his darling that they would be back in England tomorrow. Papa suggested that Fleur should drive with her maid to Pillars and there wait for the coach which would bring Mama and Papa from Dover. The little family would be reconciled in their own home.

"Oh, heavenly thought!" Fleur exclaimed and folded the newspaper which Cousin Dolly had said must be preserved for Archibald. Fleur had seen little of Cousin Archibald except during meal times. He seemed to her to be a docile silly gloomy man. He was always vainly grumbling at the cost of things and accusing the servants (if not his wife) of reckless extravagance in the house.

That evening, Fleur attended what she hoped would be the last family dinner with the de Veres. She was wild with excitement at the thought of returning to her own home. Cousin Dolly remarked on her colour and high spirits.

"It is not flattering to us," she pouted, "I hope you will not let your Papa think we have failed to amuse you."

"Oh, dear no, I have been much amused, Cousin Dolly," said Fleur with her exquisite *politesse*.

Dolly was growing more than a little afraid of the debts that were growing about her ears and terrified that Archibald would get to hear of them. She had warded off most of her creditors by assuring them that she expected to receive a fat legacy any day now and that 'legacy' should have come from St. Cheviot — after his engagement to Fleur. Devil take the girl for being so obstinate in her dislike of him, and her stupid childish attachment to her family, thought Dolly.

This morning, the horseman from Cadlington had brought, instead of the usual orchids, a magnificent box of red roses lying upon a solid bank of violets. When Dolly had opened this box and shown the exquisite blooms to the girl (who declined the offering) she had screamed with rapture:

"How can you *resist*? *Really*, my love,

you are rejecting a *great* passion from a *great* man."

Fleur had merely touched the violets with the tips of her fingers, a faint regretful smile curving her young lips.

"The flowers are beautiful, Cousin. One cannot help but love them, but I do not wish to accept favours from the gentleman who has sent them," she said.

Archibald de Vere rose from the dinner table and his family rose respectfully with him. As they trailed through the drawing-room, the master of the house glanced at Fleur out of the corners of his eyes. He said:

"So you leave us tomorrow, my pretty dear?"

"Yes, Cousin Archibald," said Fleur.

Dolly sniffed. Archibald never alluded to his own daughters as 'pretty dears'. Drat that girl! All men seemed to fall for her; even Archibald, who had little time for females.

"Let us hope," continued Mr. de Vere, settling himself in his favourite armchair in the drawing-room, "that the weather grows more clement for your parents' crossing. I fear they say the seas are running high."

Fleur walked to one of the windows and looked anxiously out at the rain. Yes, it was a wild drenching night. She could see the trees tossing on Knightsbridge Green, and the carriage horses slipping and straining in the muddy roads. Nobody would dream that this was June. She thought of poor Mama being tossed about on a rough Channel in one of those little paddle steamers. She bit her lips, Papa loved the sea but Mama would be *very* indisposed, indeed.

Fleur played a game of backgammon with the twins, then retired early to bed.

She wakened early and untying her little cambric cap, ran quickly to the window to look upon the weather. Alas, it was still blowing hard and the park looked sad and sodden.

"Oh, poor Mama, how she will dislike the homeward journey," thought Fleur, and rang for her maid. Now to pack — delicious thought — to pack and prepare for the carriage which was to take them down to Essex at eleven o'clock. It was anticipated that her parents would arrive at Pillars before dark.

The farewells to her cousins were said. The twins blew their noses and professed to shed a tear. Cousin Dolly said that 'she regretted Fleur's short visit' and dared to murmur at the last, while a coachman tucked a plaid rug around Fleur's knees. "Do not be too harsh with poor Denzil St. Cheviot. He is eaten up with longing for you."

But all that naughty greedy Dolly got for her pains was a toss of Miss Roddney's lovely head and that mutinous twist of rosy lips that were usually so soft and smiling.

Dolly watched the carriage depart, feeling that she had failed on Denzil's behalf, and wondering miserably when the storm of debts would break over her foolish head and bring the wrath of her husband about her ears.

Meanwhile Fleur enjoyed every moment of the long drive from Knightsbridge Green to Essex; stopping only once or twice while her maid tossed pennies at the turnpikes as the young lady's carriage passed through. But she chatted merrily with her confidential maid. Molly had tended her since she was twelve years old. She was simple, direct and passionately devoted to Fleur's mother.

"There lives no finer lady in the land than my Lady Roddney, your dear mother," she would say to Fleur from time to time. "God's blessing be on her head."

Today Molly was a little more subdued and less talkative than usual. When Fleur asked what ailed her, the young woman blushed and drew a lugubrious sigh.

"I trust you are not sick, my good Molly!" exclaimed Fleur.

To which the maid then confessed that she was sick of heart, though not of body, and gradually there tumbled from her the confession that she had fallen in love for the first time, and with one of the serving-men in Mrs. de Vere's household. Noggins was his name. Vaguely Fleur called to mind the said Noggins who cleaned silver and worked mainly in the pantry. Decidedly a plain young man with a shock of red hair. But Molly seemed to think that he had all the graces. Well, well, Fleur thought, and smiled to herself; poor Molly was no beauty and Noggins appeared to be the first man who had ever paid serious court to her.

"Poor Molly, and you have been dragged away from your suitor. Alas, you must be very unhappy. What can I do for you?"

Molly fervently assured Miss Roddney that she could do nothing. Noggins had promised to remain sober and respectable and to save until such day as he could ask her to wed.

Once home, Fleur thought no more about love and Molly was too busy to remember to weep for Tom Noggins. There was much to be done. The lazy servants to marshal, special flowers to be arranged in Lady Roddney's room, a fine dinner to be prepared for the master and mistress who were returning home.

Later on Fleur attired herself in a dress of pale blue silk, which was a special favourite with her father. She fixed forget-me-nots in her bright hair. She sat in the withdrawing-room, an enchanting picture of maidenly loveliness, her ears strained for the first sound of horses' hooves in the drive. How late her dear ones were in coming. 'Twould be a pity, she thought, if the dinner were spoilt.

It was some time before Fleur began to be anxious. Then she rang the bell for Molly. She must talk to someone, for now the young girl was truly disturbed. Darkness had fallen long ago; still no sign of Sir Harry and Lady Roddney.

Fleur looked at her maid anxiously.

"Oh, Molly, there must have been an accident."

"No, no, miss," muttered the maid, although within herself she felt a rising apprehension.

Fleur clasped her long delicate fingers together.

"What else can have delayed them so? If only we were not so isolated and could communicate with Dover and find out what time the steam packet arrived. But, alas, we cannot."

"*If it ever arrived*," thought the maid grimly, although she dared not say so. But in the servants' hall they had been talking; Vyler, the butler, had recalled a terrible storm some years ago (Miss Roddney was still an infant) when one of the paddle steamers had sunk to the bottom of the sea.

It was nearing ten o'clock and at last there came the sound of carriage wheels. At once the colour returned to Fleur's face and she rushed into the hall.

"At last they are come, Molly. Oh, thank God!"

She did not wait for the servants. She herself flung open the heavy oaken front door.

A gust of wind whirled the flounces of her gay dress around her ankles. Then the chill, as of death itself, struck the girl as she saw the man who stepped out of the carriage and walked towards her. The greeting prepared for her parents died on her lips, never to be uttered. For it was her cousin-by-marriage, Archibald de Vere, himself, who walked into the hall. The man to whom she had said farewell early this morning.

He looked strained and grave, muffled in a thick grey cloak. He removed his high-crowned hat as he walked slowly towards the girl and shut out the rain-swept night behind him.

"Fleur, my dear child — " he began

but stopped as though he could go no further.

Such terror seized Fleur's soul in that instant that she could make no movement, neither could she speak. Rooted to the spot she stared at Cousin Archibald. Before he spoke again she realized one thing — that he could be no harbinger of good news. She stared at him wildly, seeking mutely for the truth, no matter how terrible. Then de Vere, who was kindly despite his inherent meanness, and was desperately sorry for Fleur, cleared his throat and spoke again:

"Alas, my dear child, what I have to say to you can bring you nothing but great pain."

Molly, the maid, drew nearer, her hands clasped, her own face pale as she strained her ears to hear what was being said. But suddenly Fleur gave a piercing cry.

"*Mama*! . . . *Papa*! . . . What has happened to them?"

Archibald told her, faltering a little. The thing must be said. Dolly had sent him down here with two of their fastest horses to draw the carriage, in order that the news — which had already reached London — should be conveyed to the unfortunate girl.

The steam packet which had left Calais this morning had not reached Dover, nor ever would. One of the worst summer storms in history had broken over the small boat within sight of the English coast. The details were as yet unknown but coastguards reported that the steamer had sunk and that there were no survivors.

The unhappy Archibald, who had never been on a more distressing mission, fingered his hat, scowling at it. He dared not look at the young girl. He heard her low anguished cry:

"God have mercy . . . *have mercy* . . . do not let this terrible thing be true!"

De Vere spoke again.

"There is no hope. Of that we are certain, such is the violence of the storm — and it is still blowing — the seas were mountainous and even the strongest swimmer could not reach the shore."

Fleur only half heard these words. Her

voice rose hysterically:

"They are drowned! My Mama and Papa are drowned . . . forever lost to me."

"Mary, Mother of God, have mercy," muttered Molly, who was a Catholic, crossed herself several times and went down on her knees in the hall.

Before Fleur's eyes she seemed to see those cold relentless waves . . . Mama, so beautiful, so delicate, sinking, sinking, choking for breath as the cruel water closed over her lovely head. Papa, so gay and handsome, trying to save Mama and failing. Death for them both. A cold watery grave — together still even to that agonizing end.

It was too much for the highly sensitive and imaginative girl — child of that great love which Harry and Hélène had borne each other. Darkness engulfed her. She fell senseless into Archibald de Vere's outstretched arms.

6

TWO months later, on a hot day at the beginning of August, Fleur sat in the writing-room opposite her Cousin Dolly in the little house in Knightsbridge which she had left so gaily that morning in June for the anticipated reunion with her parents.

For the last hour, Dolly de Vere had been saying the same thing over and over again.

"You have no choice, my dear. You must do as you are told, and you *must* remember that until you are of age, you come under Mr. Nonseale's jurisdiction, and my care."

Fleur made no answer. She had really hardly spoken during this conversation any more than she had spoken during the last eight weeks. It was as though the shock of the tragedy that had befallen her had robbed her of normal speech. She answered only in monosyllable. '*Yes, Cousin Dolly*', '*No, Cousin Dolly*'. Mrs.

de Vere found it most aggravating. She would almost rather have had an out and out quarrel with the girl.

"It's time you stopped this grieving," continued Dolly in a pettish voice, "and took a little more interest in life. A girl cannot weep for ever because her dear parents are accidentally drowned — " She broke off, for suddenly the silent black-robed figure of the girl jerked and moved as though she was a marionette, and this was the cue for her to come to life. She sprang up and turned on her father's cousin with such fury that Mrs. de Vere shrank back, flabbergasted. Fleur's face was colourless. Her eyes, dim with crying, flashed with a mixture of hatred and defiance that made even silly Dolly de Vere feel frightened. A hoarse voice said:

"Why do you not leave me alone? What have I ever done that you should plague me so? Why can I not be left in peace to mourn for my darling Mama and Papa? Oh, I hate you, *I hate you*, Cousin Dolly, and I wish I had never been born!" And now the tears came in a flood, scorching down Fleur's cheeks.

She rushed to the door. Mrs. de Vere, quick as an eel, wriggled herself there first and spread-eagled her arms to prevent the girl passing.

"Why, you ungrateful girl — to speak to me so," she panted, her own plump little face scarlet with mortification. "We took you in and gave you a home and this is your way of thanking us. I must say I feel very affronted."

"Let me pass," stammered Fleur, shaking. "Let me go to my own room."

"No, you will stay here and listen to me," said Mrs. de Vere. There were ugly thoughts twisting in and out of her foolish brain; thoughts very much connected with the future of this orphaned girl — *and* Denzil St. Cheviot. So far, despite all Dolly's efforts — her pleadings, arguments, or reproaches — she had not been able to induce Fleur to meet St. Cheviot. That gentleman, however, was now a regular visitor at the de Veres' house. And now Archibald was no longer in the way. His old business house in Calcutta had sent an urgent demand for his presence owing to a money crisis in the Company, and a couple of weeks ago, Mr. de Vere had sailed for India.

In consequence, Dolly had redoubled her efforts to pitch Fleur into St. Cheviot's arms. Her personal affairs were in such poor shape that she dare not delay any longer. She needed the golden sovereigns that St. Cheviot metaphorically rattled for her hearing, and she salved her conscience by telling herself that it was 'for the twins', not for her own sake, that she wanted money so badly.

Dolly screamed at Fleur:

When St. Cheviot came to dine this evening, Fleur was please to be present. She was to take off that mourning gown and put on something more colourful and fetching. She was to sing and play for his lordship's amusement. Later, when she was alone with him, and when he proposed, *she was to accept him*.

This marriage had been arranged by Mr. Nonseale and Cousin Dolly herself. It had their full consent.

"But not Cousin Archibald's! He will protect me!" Fleur broke in at last, her lips quivering, her huge eyes tormented.

111

"Your Cousin Archibald is now upon the ocean voyaging to Calcutta and will not be back until Christmas," announced Dolly triumphantly.

Fleur looked to the right and to the left, moving her graceful head with the frantic gesture of a hunted fawn. Mrs. de Vere added a few more sharp words.

"Understand, Fleur, that the time has passed when you can defy me."

"My parents would not have wished this. My Mama did not like Lord St. Cheviot any more than I do," said Fleur in a desperate voice.

"Regrettable though it is, I now stand in the place of your Mama," said Dolly arrogantly, and marched out of the room and shut the door behind her.

Fleur looked at the closed door. It might well have been barred and bolted like the gate of a prison. And Cousin Dolly was her jailer. The change in Dolly was incredible to Fleur. Never before had she experienced spiteful cruelty or ill-treatment. She had always lived in innocence and joy with her parents. Could it be only nine weeks ago, she asked herself, that they had so gaily celebrated her eighteenth birthday at Pillars? She was still only eighteen, but now no more young. Her girlhood had been murdered as though the dewy blossom were crushed by the heavy fist of the misfortune that had fallen on her.

Brought back to London by Mr. de Vere, Fleur had remained in bed, too ill to care what happened to her.

All England was shocked by the appalling disaster that had overtaken the little paddle steamer in that Channel storm.

Many friends visited her at first but Fleur had not been able to understand why her bosom friend, Cathy Foster, should have abandoned her in this hour of need. Later, the twins let out the fact that their mother had been very rude to Mrs. Foster. It was, of course, at the back of Dolly's mind to separate Fleur from all her closest friends. For this was, Dolly felt, a heaven-sent opportunity to get Fleur completely under her control and so bring about the engagement to St. Cheviot.

When, at length, Fleur rose from her bed, a pale ghost of herself, it was only to be hurled into a vortex of legal discussions and arrangements which were all being made over her innocent head. She was too bewildered to understand half of them. But she was at least forced to comprehend at last that life was not the simple happy affair that her parents had brought her up to believe. Now she began to suffer for the tender care that poor Hélène had taken of her beloved child. And she was the victim, too, of Harry Roddney's deepest failing. He had always been too happy-go-lucky and unwise in his choice of friends. Just as he had thought there was no real harm in the rakish St. Cheviot, so he had placed his trust in his Cousin Dolly. Fleur knew (for she had heard him say so) that he had always deemed her a butterfly, but had also believed her a fond kindly mother. He had never dreamed that she could be anything else to his unhappy daughter. Amongst the papers in the dead man's bureau, Archibald de Vere found his final Will and Testament. It declared that in case of the death of both parents, the young daughter was to be entrusted to the care of the de Veres

114

and of Caleb Nonseale, Harry's lawyer. Hélène Roddney had never cared for Mr. Nonseale but Harry took no notice of the dislike. Nonseale had been adviser to his uncle, Sir Arthur — that was enough for *him*.

Fleur had so far had only one interview with Mr. Nonseale, and then every instinct had warned her that her good-natured father's trust in the lawyer had been misguided. So also must Harry's late uncle have been taken in by the wily, smooth-tongued legal gentleman.

When Caleb Nonseale spoke, he continually rubbed his hands together as though washing them. He never stopped smiling but it was not a smile that gave Fleur confidence. He discoursed at length and with much detail about affairs of her parents' estate which had no meaning for her. The only thing she could understand was that all her father's money, as well as the de Chartellet fortune (from her mother's side), would come to her when she was of age; and be entrusted to her husband should she marry.

At the end of the hour with Mr.

Nonseale, he had said something to Fleur which had frightened her horribly.

"You are eighteen — already past the age when many young ladies are given in marriage," he observed, his beady eyes taking note of her several beauties (for beautiful Fleur must always be despite her sunken eyes and hollowed cheeks). "Mrs. de Vere and myself have discussed the matter, my dear, and decided that it will be a good thing for you to accept any — er — good offer that may now come along."

Nervously Fleur had made haste to assure Mr. Nonseale that she felt that it was far too soon after the demise of her dear Mama and Papa for her to consider a wedding.

"Besides, I have not yet met one whom I desire to wed," she finished.

Mr. Nonseale had frightened her still more.

"Now, come, come," he said, "your hand has, I understand, been asked for repeatedly by a fine nobleman. A great Baron — one who offers you title and riches beyond the expectations of most young ladies, I may say, my dear child."

Her blood froze as she judged his meaning.

"If it is of Lord St. Cheviot you speak, I will certainly never marry him," she said in a low voice.

The lawyer had continued to smile but he raised his bushy brows significantly.

"Ah well, we shall see!" he murmured.

From that time onwards, Fleur knew no peace. Dolly made merciless efforts to change her mind. Fleur thought she would go mad, listening to repeated praises of St. Cheviot.

When the poor harassed girl cried that she would sooner drown herself than become Lady St. Cheviot, Dolly called her conduct 'disgraceful'.

"What would your Mama and Papa have said to hear you make such an unchristian threat," she exclaimed.

To which Fleur, weeping, replied:

"Mama and Papa wished only for my happiness and said that I might choose my own husband."

Dolly answered that Miss Fleur Roddney was a spoiled brat.

Later on Fleur had gone quite humbly to Cousin Dolly and asked if she could draw enough money from the estate to live in retirement with her maid. If not at Pillars (dear, *dear* Pillars!) then in one of the cottages that had belonged to her father. This request was received by Cousin Dolly with a shrill laugh.

Fleur felt an increasing sense of despair and homesickness. She pined for Pillars but the place had been closed down. Donna, her mother's greyhound, picked up some poison in the grounds, sickened and died; so one by one the things that Fleur loved were being wrenched out of her life.

She did not feel well. The heat of London in August weighed her down.

Sometimes she considered running away. But to whom could she run? She was too proud to ask for succour from the Fosters since Cousin Dolly had affronted Mrs. Foster and Cathy was no longer her friend. And no gently nurtured girl born and brought up in the country could think of facing the sinister streets of London alone and penniless. One of the most outrageous of Dolly's acts had been to arrange with Caleb Nonseale that not one shilling of the fortune which was rightfully hers was to be paid to Fleur. Without money, she was powerless, and Dolly knew it.

Throughout the rest of this particular day Mrs. de Vere was more than ordinarily ill-tempered and spiteful. At last Fleur looked at her with beseeching eyes and said:

"Oh, Cousin Dolly, my unhappiness is too great to be borne. I do not feel I shall survive it!"

With a slight touch of anxiety, Mrs. de Vere regarded the young girl's sadly altered appearance. Drat it, she thought, she did not want Fleur to die. She controlled the wish to slap the girl. She tried once more to be affectionate, put an arm around Fleur and patted the poor bright head that drooped so piteously these days.

"My poor child, lean on my bosom," she said. "Oh, believe me I wish to comfort you and if I appear harsh it is only for your sake. I know what is best for you," she added with honeyed sweetness.

So starved was Fleur for a little love and understanding — so hungry for the warmth and devotion she used to receive from her parents — she flung herself into Cousin Dolly's arms in a touching manner.

"Oh, pray, Cousin Dolly, do not be harsh with me any longer, for my heart is breaking," she sobbed.

"Come then, do as I beg and consent to see his lordship at dinner this evening," cajoled the wily little woman. "You have built up in your imagination a false picture of him that has no truth in it. He is very splendid and would cherish you with his life."

A shudder went through Fleur's too-slender body. She kept her streaming eyes hidden against Mrs. de Vere's shoulder.

"Be sensible," Dolly wheedled, "and let him pay his respects to you, my love. Then you will be Cousin Dolly's own good little Fleur. And I am sure your Mama and Papa would rejoice if they knew that you were to make such a magnificent marriage."

Another shudder convulsed the girl. She whispered:

"And if I do not . . . will not . . . see him?"

Then Dolly played her trump card. Quite suddenly she went down on one knee before the girl, not caring what a ridiculous figure she cut, with her cap a little awry on her flaxen head; her big china blue eyes brimming with tears. She threw herself on Fleur's mercy. Now at last Fleur must be told how important it was that she should make an effort . . . if not for her own future's sake, for the sake of Cousin Dolly who had done everything for her since her Mama died. Dolly poured out to the astonished young girl the disgraceful story of her mad extravagance, and accumulation of debts; what disaster would befall her, and Isabel and Imogen, if those debts remained unpaid. Indeed so much did Dolly owe that she did not think Archibald would ever forgive her. He might punish her by leaving her to languish in a debtor's prison. Poor darling Cyril, he would have to give up Oxford. He would be ruined. *They would all be ruined . . . unless Fleur married St. Cheviot.*

Scarlet and confused, Fleur stared down at her father's cousin.

"But I surely have some means and

could help you . . . " she stammered.

Whining and sniffing, Dolly explained that Fleur could not touch her money until she was of age — or had a husband, who would be able to control her fortune. Unfortunately, Harry Roddney had so worded the Will that Dolly could claim Fleur's money only with Mr. de Vere's consent; he being joint guardian. And him she dared not tell. Certainly she could not ask him to co-operate in drawing large sums of money from Fleur's estate.

Fleur was scarcely able to comprehend the legal facts that Dolly poured out. But she could and did understand that she might ruin Dolly and her children by refusing St. Cheviot.

"And is it only through my betrothal to Lord St. Cheviot that this money can be obtained?" Fleur asked in a low voice.

"Yes, my love," said Dolly, and she eyed the girl slyly, feeling that at last she might win the day.

A long sigh came from Fleur.

"You ask a terrible sacrifice of me, Cousin Dolly."

"Even so, I *do* ask it," said Cousin Dolly eagerly. "Oh, remember that I am your flesh and blood! Do not let me languish in a debtor's jail."

"If only Cousin Archibald were here," said Fleur in a despairing voice.

"But he is not," said Dolly. "My fate lies in your hands. Oh, my sweet Fleur, do not abandon me. I have been foolish, but it was for my children, and you know how well *your* Mama loved *you*!"

Fleur shut her eyes. She hardly dared think of her beautiful gentle mother and that love that was so cruelly lost.

To marry well seemed to be the first duty of a woman, she thought wearily. Not only Cousin Dolly, but many society matrons would think her crazy to hold out against Lord St. Cheviot.

Suddenly she felt that she could no longer go on fighting. She would at least consent to *see* and speak with Lord St. Cheviot again. In a voice of despair she said:

"I will dine with you tonight and — consider Lord St. Cheviot's proposal."

But when Dolly with an ecstatic cry

123

sprang up to kiss her and called her 'angel', Fleur shrank from her embrace. She did not even weep. She experienced an unutterable fatigue of body and mind; the loneliness of death, itself.

7

ALL through dinner St. Cheviot sat opposite Fleur and kept his dark desirous gaze upon her. He saw nobody else at that table. Even had Fleur not been there, he would not have bothered to look at Isabel and Imogen. Plump, giggling, they ate hugely, one course after another, and ogled the gentlemen beside whom they had been placed. Dolly had invited two young officers of the Dragoons, who were acquainted with the de Veres, to make up her numbers. She had also spent — in a wild gamble — a great deal of money on this important party. It was quite a banquet. The sombre, rather stuffy dining-room, was brilliantly illuminated with candle-light. The table shone with the best de Vere silver and glass. Dolly, herself was in pink taffeta with a little lace cap on hair done in coquettish ringlets that bobbed against her rouged and powdered face.

She addressed St. Cheviot in the most servile fashion, complimenting him upon his looks, his taste in wines, etc. — or spoke in a voice of honeyed sweetness of her 'beloved Fleur' as though she had never in her life nagged or bullied Harry's daughter.

To Fleur, the festive dinner was one long-drawn-out torment. Nothing that Cousin Dolly said could persuade her to change her mourning garb for a more colourful one. Her darling Mama and Papa had only been dead nine weeks. But she had never looked more alluring. The black evening gown made her skin look like the camellias that grew upon the south wall at Cadlington, he thought. Not once did she look straight into his eyes. She wore no jewellery, no ornament. Only two white roses. *His* roses, pinned to her corsage. He told himself cynically that no doubt Dolly had forced her to wear the flowers, but it was an encouraging sign.

When the dinner ended, Dolly marshalled her girls and bade them take their escorts into the drawing-room for some music. To Fleur, she said:

126

"Lord St. Cheviot is most anxious to see that strange plant which your Cousin Archibald brought me from Covent Garden in the spring. Pray show it to him, my love."

Fleur's slight fingers twined convulsively around the little Dorothy-bag which she carried.

"Go along, my sweet child," said Dolly gushingly.

St. Cheviot crooked his arm. Fleur seemed to brace herself, as though for an ordeal, but she allowed the man to lead her into the conservatory. Useless to battle any more against this man's stubborn passion for her — or Cousin Dolly's determination. All day Fleur had thought about it — and of the reason why Dolly so much desired this match. All day she had asked herself if she could possibly bear her lot and make such a sacrifice; and if Papa would have wished it. To refuse and to send Cousin Dolly to a debtor's prison and disgrace the family — that would surely be too cruel.

Like a lamb to the slaughter she accompanied St. Cheviot and sank on to a small red plush sofa under a huge palm. St. Cheviot stood before her. Somehow the tremendous height of the man, and the breadth of his shoulders, frightened her. His ebon black hair was curled and pomaded. He held a lace-edged handkerchief in a white-gloved hand. Handsome, impeccable, and as Cousin Dolly kept reminding her, excessively rich, and always moving in that aura of wickedness which some women find mysteriously attractive. But not Fleur. After a moment she knew that he had seated himself beside her.

"It has been a long while, Miss Roddney, since we last spoke alone."

"Yes — oh — yes."

"Too long. A protracted misery for me. Why have you been so cruel?"

Her breath began to come quickly. The man's personality overawed her.

"I — did not mean to be cruel," she replied.

"You are very pale," he murmured. "Do you suffer so much? Is it an illness of the mind that weighs you down and has taken from you all the childish sparkle?"

Now she raised her eyes and gave him a long sad look.

"That sparkle, as you call it, my lord, vanished for ever beneath the waves with my adored parents."

St. Cheviot scowled. He wished to let her think that he was a man of sympathy and understanding but emotions such as these displayed by this young girl were so foreign to him as to be incomprehensible. He had had no fondness for his own mother and father and regarded them in their lifetime only as barriers to his hunger for entertainment of a kind which they did not approve. And when they died he had mourned them only for the briefest possible time. He had been thankful for the freedom, the full control of money and possessions which their decease afforded him.

Now he cleared his throat and said:

"Alas, that sinking of the Channel steamer was a terrible tragedy. I know how you must feel."

"Do you?" she asked almost wistfully, as though seeking to touch one answering chord in him which might lead her to believe that this arrogant man had some real kindliness in him.

He bowed and answered:

"Most certainly. Who would not understand your grief? I respect it, also. But you are far too young to shut yourself away and, like Niobe, drown yourself in tears."

"Two months is not long," she said in a choked voice.

"For one who has so longed to look at you and hear your voice, it has seemed Eternity," he said glibly.

She sat silent. Her thoughts were with her parents. An Eternity, St. Cheviot said. Yes, so it seemed since she had looked upon Mama's beautiful face or heard Papa laugh, or walked beside them through the sunlit corridors of their country home. Long, so *long* . . . yet she did not want to emerge from her retreat in the shadows. The very sound of laughter or music hurt her now.

To her dismay she suddenly felt iron fingers grip one of her delicate hands. St. Cheviot had gone down upon his knee and was pressing his lips to her palm. It was a kiss so scorching that it terrified her. He seemed unable to

130

control his terrible desire and continued to kiss the hand and to mutter wild protests of passion.

"I do so adore you . . . I beg . . . I implore you to thaw for me," he exclaimed. "You are all that is pure and perfect in my sight. I do most truly respect your grief and pain. I beseech you to turn to me for comfort. You are alone in the world now. Fleur, *Fleur*, take me for your husband. Give me the right to hold you evermore in these loving arms."

Well-chosen words. She listened to them dazedly. Deep within her she knew that had they come from the lips of a different man — one chosen by *her* — they might indeed have brought her the consolation she so badly needed. It would have been pleasant, indeed, to be able to lay her aching head against a heart that beat with tender love for her. But somehow every instinct in Fleur still recoiled from Denzil St. Cheviot. Now that she listened to him she knew that nothing could change her. She tried to drag her hand away from those greedy kisses.

"Lord St. Cheviot!" she protested faintly.

"Nay, do not shrink from me. Most lovely of flowers — all that I possess is yours for the asking. Marry me. Come to Cadlington House as its mistress, and my wife, and I swear that I will deny you nothing."

She sat there shivering. She knew that she wanted nothing that he could give her. A title, riches, all the furs and jewels in the world could not bring back her lost youth and happiness — or her parents. While she listened to St. Cheviot's frenzied appeals, two great tears rolled down her cheeks, sad twin diamonds glittering in the candle-light.

But the man did not note the tears nor had he it in his nature to show tenderness. He was consumed only with his longing to touch Fleur's young mouth. He spoiled the moment which might have been victorious for him, by suddenly sweeping her up into his arms.

"You shall not refuse me," he muttered. "I have your cousin's word for it that you will accept my proposal."

For the first time in her life, Fleur

was kissed with a brutal passion that not only shocked her but decided her once and for all that she could never go through with this sacrifice, even for Cousin Dolly. Gasping, she pushed St. Cheviot away. She struck blindly at his hot face with one small clenched fist.

"I *loathe* you. How dare you insult me so!" she breathed and before he could speak again, picked up her flowing skirts and ran from him as though pursued by the devil himself. She rushed up the stairs to her room and locked herself in.

St. Cheviot stood still, panting, bitterly affronted. He was in a white-hot passion of rage. He sought and found his hostess.

For her he had only a few brief words.

"I have been refused and struck across the mouth by your charming cousin. Either you see to it that she retracts what she has done, and marries me immediately, or not one golden guinea will you get from me, Madam."

With this he left the house; Dolly wailing and shrieking after him in vain. Now it was her turn to be the bully. She darted upstairs and pounded upon

Fleur's bedroom door, which was locked.

"Let me in at once, you wicked ungrateful girl!" she hissed.

No sound. Fleur was not weeping. She lay silent full length upon her four-poster bed, with the curtains half drawn. She had wiped her lips with a handkerchief again and again until they were almost raw, as though seeking to erase the vile imprint of St. Cheviot's kisses. She heard her cousin's voice reviling her, and threatening to turn her out into the streets, but she made no reply. She only knew that she would not be forced into St. Cheviot's arms, no matter what Cousin Dolly said or did to her. At length Dolly had to give up her efforts to gain entrance into Fleur's room. She was too afraid that the two young officers downstairs in the drawing-room with Cyril and the twins would hear and spread a scandal around town.

"Very well, my fine friend, we shall see who is to be ultimate winner of this battle," she flung at Fleur through the keyhole. "You have behaved like a lunatic. You shall be treated like one. I shall send you to a Madhouse. You shall finish your days among mad people like yourself."

Fleur did not reply but she heard, she trembled from head to foot. She did not know how to deal with the furious woman. As Dolly went away Fleur burst into tears and called helplessly on her dead parents. She sobbed: "*Mama, Papa! Why can I not die and come to you? Oh, look down and protect me now. Be with me in my helpless sorrow.*"

Later, both Dolly and the twins tried to gain access to her room, but Fleur refused to let them in. The last thing that Dolly screamed at her was a threat to take her by force to Cadlington House and leave her there. This froze the young girl's blood. She made no attempt to seek her bed but paced up and down the room alternately praying, and seeking in her mind for a way out of this horror.

Long after the de Veres were asleep, Fleur, a candle in her hand, quietly unlocked her door and tiptoed along the corridor down a small staircase to the servants' quarters. She roused Molly, her maid. The girl came out, hair in curl papers under a cap which was askew.

Her red shiny face looked frightened and astonished as she saw the figure of her young mistress, wrapped in a cashmere shawl.

"Why, *miss* — what has happened — ?" she began.

Fleur put a finger to her lips and beckoned the maid forward. Molly followed her. A moment later the two were whispering together in Fleur's bedroom.

"I rely on you, I must. I have nobody else in the world," Fleur ended pathetically.

Molly was five years older than her young mistress and certainly far more experienced after the many physical and moral buffetings she had received at the hands of both footmen and butlers in the servants' hall. She was quite a staunch young woman, and devoted to Fleur. With all her heart she detested Mrs. de Vere — and the de Vere household — with the exception of Noggins, who had made her romantic heart flutter.

But when Fleur told Molly that she wished to run away and that Molly must go with her the maid was at first hesitant.

136

"Oh, miss, but how would you do for money?" she gasped.

"Dear Molly, have you a little to lend me?" asked Fleur humbly, "and I could also sell the few jewels I have in my possession. I have a pearl necklace which belonged to my dear mother. Each pearl, I know, will be worth quite a few pounds."

Molly scratched an ear vigorously.

"I have my last month's wages not yet spent, miss. What would you have us do?"

"Leave this house before my cousin wakens, find a vehicle and drive to The Little Bastille," said Fleur.

Molly gasped again. She knew all about The Little Bastille. It had become a legend in the Roddney household. That fortress-like building on the edge of the cliff, facing the bleak wastes of the Colne estuary. It had been built by the Marquis de Chartellet soon after he had escaped from the French Revolution.

There, Hélène de Chartellet had spent much of her early married life. Because of its exceeding gloom, she had not used the place, after she became Lady Roddney, but kept it shut up and attended by caretakers because it was still full of Lucien de Chartellet's treasures.

Only once had Fleur been taken on a visit to The Little Bastille by her parents. She remembered, vaguely, narrow windows, thick stone walls and battlements that made the edifice look like a miniature prison fortress frowning down upon the sea.

It would be useless rushing down to Pillars; Cousin Dolly would obviously look for and find her there. But she might not trace Fleur once she locked herself within the walls of The Little Bastille. Fleur was certain that she could count on the loyal protection of Mama's caretakers. She doubted, too, whether it would enter even the head of her guardian Caleb Nonseale to seek her there.

"Once I am safely at The Bastille you can leave me, dear Molly, and return to your London life," Fleur told the maid, who looked as though she did not relish the thought of retirement to that peculiar house which had been built to satisfy a Frenchman's sardonic whim.

But Fleur begged so hard that she should accompany her now, Molly could not refuse. Alas, the poor lamb looked like to die, as she told Noggins later on, and seemed properly scared of being forced into marriage with his lordship of Cadlington.

Fleur, feeling more hopeful now, returned to her own room, packed a small bag. She took all that she had of value and which she might need. She crept down the stairs and out of the house, accompanied by Molly who carried a small wicker hamper full of food that she had rifled from the kitchen, as well as her own possessions.

Before the de Veres were awake, and when the first vegetable carts were rumbling over the cobbles from Covent Garden, and yawning shopkeepers were taking down their shutters, the two fugitives were well away from Knightsbridge Green.

Now, Molly, half amused and half scared by the adventure, took the initiative and begged lifts towards St. Paul's. This, Fleur knew, was on the route to Essex. Noggins, being a Londoner, had informed Molly that there were livery stables not far from Paternoster Row. They could doubtless hire a private vehicle and coachman to drive them to the coast.

Sure enough, they found both stables and the coachman willing to convey them — at a price. That price took most of Molly's wages and a small brooch, offered by Fleur. The summer morning was warm and bright as they finally drove through the narrow streets on to the main Essex highway.

As they passed through the first turnpike, Fleur became almost hysterically gay. She clasped the rough mittened hand of her serving-woman.

"Dear Molly, I am for ever grateful and if my Mama were alive she would bless you," exclaimed the young girl, two hectic flushes on her cheeks. "I feel sure that once we reach The Little Bastille, I, for one, can remain lost to the world."

"But, miss, you cannot stay there alone for the rest of your life!"

"No, but at least I shall have time in which to consider what to do. I might eventually disguise myself and enter some gentlewoman's service," said the girl.

Molly glanced at her and sighed. Miss Fleur looked bad, she thought. What a terrible strain she had been under since her noble parents had been drowned! Molly was glad she had come with the poor soul. She began to open the hamper.

"You must eat, miss, and keep up your strength. See! . . . I have found a bottle of wine to bring a sparkle to your eyes."

Fleur shuddered. She seemed to hear St. Cheviot using that same word . . . 'sparkle'. She said to the maid what she had said to *him*, "That sparkle has vanished for ever beneath the sea with my beloved parents."

But she tried to eat and managed a little of the loaf and cheese, and a sip of the wine that Molly handed her. Then she sat back against the padded, musty-smelling cushions of the brougham and gave a long sigh.

"I am surely safe now," she murmured, "and oh, Molly, whatever happens, I beg you to be faithful and never to reveal to Mrs. de Vere the name of my hiding-place."

"Never, miss, or may I be struck dead!" exclaimed Molly. But she turned from her young lady and rather uneasily glanced out of the window at the first village through which they were passing, having left Whitechapel behind. She wished, suddenly, that she had not been so hasty as to whisper to Noggins, just before leaving, the very information that Miss Roddney wished kept a deadly secret.

"No matter, he won't tell. He promised," the maid salved her conscience. "And he begged of me to confide in him."

The coachman whipped up his horses. They broke into a gallop along the rough deserted road.

8

THREE nights later, Fleur sat alone in a big bedroom in The Little Bastille, gazing out of an open window.

Twilight had fallen. The dark green sea moved steadily into shore and creamed over the rocks underneath the frowning cliffs. The sky faded from vermilion and purple into the dark mists of the night. The stars came out one by one. Fierce, sad and rugged though it was, this former stronghold of the Marquis de Chartellet had a beauty of its own. Fleur recognized and was comforted by it. She had small comfort else, for she was alone now — more alone than she had ever been in her life before.

But it seemed that her plan to escape from an enforced marriage with St. Cheviot had succeeded. Whatever the hue and cry in the de Vere household — no word of it had reached this solitary retreat. The helpful Molly had stayed here only forty-eight hours — long enough to get her mistress settled and to counsel Mrs. Leather, the caretaker's wife, to take good care of Miss Roddney. Then she had returned to London.

When, as she bade Fleur farewell, she had started to excuse herself for not remaining, Fleur in her gentle fashion begged her to say no more. She understood that Love (in the shape of Noggins) drew Molly like a magnet back to town. Possibly Mrs. de Vere would refuse to have her in her household, but Molly would soon find another job — and Noggins would go with her; he had said so.

Wistfully, the young girl had watched Molly drive away, feeling that with her vanished the last link with her old home.

Now the Leathers tried to serve her to the best of their ability. Jacob Leather was a goodly man; one-time butler in the service of the Marquis. Lottie, his wife, faithfully polished the furniture and silver, and kept dusted the beautiful pictures and tapestries and the thousands of books which the erudite Marquis used to read.

The Leathers had only been on the staff here since Lucien de Chartellet's marriage to Hélène, so they knew nothing of Lady Roddney's earlier life in The Bastille. But it was some comfort to poor Fleur to be with these amiable creatures who spoke of her mother as a great and beautiful lady.

"The spit of you she was, miss," Mrs. Leather told Fleur many times.

As soon as she was strong and well enough to tackle life, Fleur decided that she must earn a living. The first thing was to lose her identity as 'Fleur Roddney' in order that Cousin Dolly should never find her again. She would take another name.

She finished the supper which Mrs. Leather had served, and sat now in her bedgown which was of broderie anglaise threaded with blue ribbons. It made her look very young and fragile. Her glorious hair, unbound, flowed over her shoulders. Mrs. Leather had just brushed it.

"It would break my lady's heart to see you so forlorn," the good woman had murmured, "'tis a cruel shame they should have treated you so, but do not fear; if anyone approaches, Leather and myself shall conceal you. There are many dungeons under The Little Bastille."

Fleur had wept in the woman's arms, hungry for love and understanding. What in heaven's name was she going to do with the rest of her youth? It was a question she could not solve tonight at any rate, she decided, as she leaned her aching head on her hand. She could hear the faint sound of music coming from a crowd of fishermen. They were singing a gay tune. It must be wonderful to be free — and gay — Fleur reflected. She envied the humble fisherfolk; she, who until a few brief months ago had envied nobody on earth.

"Indeed, Mama would never have left me to join Papa in Paris, could she have guessed the fate that has since befallen me," the poor girl mused.

Alas, alas, that one could not turn back the clock!

Fleur knelt beside her bed and prayed, as was her habit before retiring. A while later, she snuffed her candles and lay on her pillow, thinking. She had in mind that tomorrow she would have a conference with the Leathers and consider whether or not she could find a job in this district, as a governess. For she was well educated in many subjects, and especially good at the spinet, and with her needle.

It must have been close on midnight when she heard the barking of the dogs that were kept chained in the courtyard on the west side of The Bastille. This was followed by the tramping of horses' hooves and the shouting of men's voices. Fleur woke up and sat up in her bed, her heart beating violently. She lit a candle, slid into her wrapper and straightened the little muslin cap on her head. Then she stood near the door, listening attentively. It was useless opening one of the narrow windows which only looked down on to the sea. But dread had already entered Fleur's soul. *Had her hiding-place been discovered*? In God's name, had Molly betrayed her and told Cousin Dolly where she was?

While she mused upon this, she heard footsteps and suddenly her door was opened and Lottie Leather rushed in. She was a big-bosomed woman with a fat kindly face which was, in this moment, grotesque and ashen. She quivered like a jelly. Her night cap was awry, showing the curl papers over her grey head. In her hand she carried a tallow candle which was shaking so that the wax poured on to the floor.

"Oh, miss, *miss!*" she stuttered.

Every vestige of colour ebbed from the young girl's cheeks.

"Who has come? What is it, Lottie?" she demanded.

"It is Lord St. Cheviot," the woman gasped.

"Dear heaven!" whispered Fleur.

With a moan, Mrs. Leather continued: "His man, who rode here with him, has put a knife through my husband's back. Oh, miss, *miss!*" and she fell at Fleur's feet, sobbing wildly.

Fleur neither moved nor spoke. Rooted to the spot, abject fear consuming her, she stared down at the woman and listened to her babbling cries.

"*St. Cheviot!*" Fleur repeated the name again slowly, her eyes large and wild.

'Dear heaven, Molly must have told Noggins and he has played me false,' she thought.

She was given no time to think further. She heard the heavy sound of footsteps. Then, and then only, she moved and tried to close and lock the door against the invader. But it was too late. A heavy fist crashed the door open and sent the girl reeling backward.

Denzil St. Cheviot stood before her. Fleur looked upon him with much the same terror as she would have gazed on a Fiend let loose from Hell. He was breathing quickly; garbed in riding attire. His usually well-pomaded hair was a little untidy; one black lock fell across a forehead that glistened with sweat. His cravat was awry. But he smiled. It was a smile so deadly that it made the young girl's spirit recoil.

Then he swept a bow; a mock flourish.

"Your servant, Miss Roddney!"

Mrs. Leather turned and began to claw frantically at his boots.

"Murderer, murderer of my innocent husband!" she shrieked. "You shall pay for it. I shall seek justice — "

But she got no further. He spurned her with the toe of his boot and called:

"Ivor!"

The man who had ridden with him appeared at once. Fleur, still frozen to the spot, unable to move or think, turned her attention upon him. Afterwards, she was to learn much more of this Welshman who had been Denzil St. Cheviot's confidential valet and close attendant for some years . . . and to fear him. A small sly little fellow with cunning eyes and a pair of hands that were freakishly big and powerful for his size. He was almost as good a shot as his master and utterly without scruple. He had but one loyalty and that was to the master he served, whether it be in the name of right or wrong.

St. Cheviot indicated the woman who was howling invectives at him.

"Bind this creature, take her down to one of her own cellars and leave her there. She will find it over-damp and cold, and rat-infested, but it will teach her to threaten me," he said.

Lottie turned and appealed to Fleur, her eyes bolting with fear.

"Do not let him murder me, too, miss!" she screamed shrilly.

Somehow Fleur found voice. This

was the worst nightmare she had so far experienced since her former life ended. But she was no coward. Her spirit rebelled against the brutality of what was about to be done to the innocent and helpless wife of the caretaker.

"My lord," she said, addressing St. Cheviot, "this female served my mother when she was married to the Marquis. In their names, I demand that she should be spared. Already there is one murder on your soul this night; would you have another?"

St. Cheviot laughed. It was more like a growl in the thickness of his throat. Once again he swept her a courtly bow.

"As Miss Roddney wishes . . . Ivor . . . let the female cool her blood in the dungeons for tonight only. Release her in the morning. But she is warned that if she mentions this night's work to any living soul she will die horribly. Do you hear?" He thrust his face nearer to that of the hysterical woman. "*Silence*, or you pay with your life!"

Lottie nodded miserably, reduced to a state of abject fright. The Welshman, with a sly look at Fleur, saluted his noble master and retired, dragging Lottie after him.

St. Cheviot closed the door and smiled at Fleur.

"Will you not ask me to sit down?" he murmured. "I have ridden a long way — so fast, indeed, that my first mount burst its heart, which matter held me up at Chelmsford whilst Ivor found me a fresh horse."

Fleur did not speak. Her large eyes stared up at him.

Slowly St. Cheviot unbuttoned his cloak and threw it on the bed.

"It must surely impress you that I take so long a ride, and in such hot haste, to reach you," he continued.

Then with a hand at her throat, and every effort to still the violent trembling of her limbs, the girl spoke.

"My lord, I ask you in the name of decency to leave my bedchamber instantly."

He looked around. His tall figure in the light of the fluttering candles threw a gigantic shadow on the ceiling. Now that silence had fallen over The Little Bastille again, there could be heard the faint hiss of the waves on the rocks below. St. Cheviot glanced out of the window and then back at Fleur. He raised his brows.

"You have chosen a charming retreat although a trifle gloomy for one so young and fair. But up here it is warm and perfumed, and I am in no hurry to depart."

"Lord St. Cheviot, why are you come? On what authority have you forced an entry into my mother's house and done an innocent man to death?"

"He got in my way," said St. Cheviot coldly, "he sought to prevent me from entering. My man, Ivor, is quick on the draw — quicker than your protector — that is all."

"You are the devil himself," said Fleur in a dry whisper.

He drew nearer her.

"And you an angel. An interesting combination . . . we shall see what evolves when heaven and hell unite."

His words froze her blood. She backed away.

"Who told you that I was here?"

"Who else but your Cousin Dolly de

Vere? But not until today could she bribe a fellow named Noggins into informing her of your whereabouts. You gave us all the slip in uncommonly neat fashion. When Mrs. de Vere first acquainted me with the news of your escape, I myself went to seek you at Pillars. But neither your servants there nor your friends knew anything. Then the good Noggins, who is anxious for the wherewithal to finance his marriage, informed your cousin of the facts. Until then, I must confess neither your cousin nor Mr. Nonseale, your guardian, had the slightest suspicion that you would fly to de Chartellet's Bastille."

Fleur put her finger tips against her quivering lips. She shook so violently that she could scarcely stand. So it *was* Molly who had betrayed her. Unwillingly, perhaps; but caught in the net of her own trust in the man she loved.

As St. Cheviot drew near to Fleur, she cried piteously:

"I beg and beseech you, Lord St. Cheviot, to have respect for me and leave my room. Tomorrow, I swear that I will be amenable and allow you to escort me back to London. I realize that I am defeated."

"Not quite," said his lordship with that deadly smile which made his handsome face assume for Fleur the features of incarnate evil.

"What do you mean?"

"That I intend to make quite positive, my sweet girl, you will never again refuse me as a husband," he said.

The black brilliant eyes which devoured her now were merciless, like the man himself.

When Dolly de Vere had informed Denzil of Fleur's escape he had consented to join with her in the search and to take measures to put an end to Miss Roddney's stubborn conduct. Measures that would never have been permitted were Archibald de Vere still in England. But Dolly, frantic for her own safety, showed herself willing to co-operate with St. Cheviot's vile plan. At first they feared Fleur had vanished for good. But once Noggins let the cat out of the bag, St. Cheviot immediately set out for the Essex coast.

"Leave all to me," Denzil had told

Dolly, who had seemed a trifle nervous and ill at ease about the whole concern. "Tomorrow, when I return her to you, Fleur will do as she is told. Having regard to her reputation and her virtue, I do not think she will raise any further objections to our immediate marriage in her own interests."

Even Dolly had wavered before those sinister words. She had started to whine:

"I am a mother. I needs must consider my cousin's orphaned child. Oh, be gentle with her and remember she must not be too far driven or she may not live to become Lady St. Cheviot."

His answer had been:

"She will live. The maiden may languish in her grief and be sorely afflicted by her fate, but she is young and strong withal and will grow accustomed to her new status. Meanwhile I will not leave her side, madam. She shall be given no chance to do away with herself."

Now as St. Cheviot looked at the slight and exquisite girl, white as her muslin draperies, and with her soul's terror reflected in her large eyes, he knew nothing but a brutal desire; the determination to vanquish her utterly and thus force her to the altar-rails.

"My sweet child," he said, "do not waste your breath by refusing me again. Tonight this solitary fortress chosen by yourself shall become a Cupid's paradise for us."

Fleur opened her lips to scream, but no sound came. It would have been useless even had she uttered it. She felt St. Cheviot's great arms crushing her, and the scorning passion of his kiss. Then he lifted her right up into his arms and laughed down at her.

"I think, my shrinking violet, that tomorrow you will be willing and eager to announce our betrothal, and to become my bride and the future mother of my sons," he said.

She was beyond answering, almost beyond caring in the extremity of her anguish. But the last sound that she heard before she temporarily lost her senses was the surge of the sea and a rising wind. The September night was passing into a stormy dawn. Seagulls wheeled uneasily over the battlements of The Little Bastille. Fleur wondered wildly if her mother's ghost would not arise from her watery grave to seek out and protect the daughter who had been so hideously betrayed.

Part Two

1

O N the fifteen of September, 1838, Fleur, daughter of Sir Harry and Lady Roddney, late of Pillars, near Epping, was married at St. Paul's Church, Knightsbridge, to Denzil St. Cheviot, Baron of Cadlington.

It was a big wedding attended by innumerable relatives and friends, gathered from near and far by Mrs. de Vere, and almost every family of high degree from the county of Buckinghamshire. And London was gossiping about it.

Despite the fact that all England knew of the dissipations and vices of the Lord St. Cheviot, he happened to be one of the richest men in the country; hence those who were invited, and were disposed to whisper in shocked terms of St. Cheviot's excesses, forgot them today, hypocritically gushed over his magnificence and came willingly to see him married to his beautiful bride.

There had been a brief engagement. It

surprised all who read the announcement. The affair was taking place a little soon, for conventional taste, after the tragic death of the Roddneys. But little Mrs. de Vere had explained to one and all that it was such a *love* match and the pair were so *anxious* to be together, and 'poor darling Fleur needed a husband and home'.

The church was packed. It was a pity, of course, that the late summer day was not mild and sunny. A wild wind tore through the streets bringing a shower of leaves down from the trees in Hyde Park. The gutters ran with muddy waters, and down came the rain just as the church bells started ringing. Handsomely clad gentlemen assisted their ladies to step from their carriages while coachmen held large umbrellas over them.

Mrs. de Vere played the 'mother' beautifully, dabbing now and then at her eyes with a little lace handkerchief, twittering to her guests about her 'broken heart' at losing her sweet little cousin. How 'tragic' it was, too, that dear Archibald could not return from India because business kept him there. Mr.

Caleb Nonseale, however, as the family friend and solicitor, gave the bride away. Even he — the sober-sides — had tried to clothe himself in a more distinguished way than usual for today's event. All Dolly de Vere's friends gossiped among themselves, '*Where is she getting all the money to give the Roddney girl such a show?*'

Which question might have been answered for them could they have heard the quick conversation which had taken place between Dolly and Mr. Nonseale just before setting out for the church.

"I must congratulate you, madam, on the way in which you have brought my young client to heel," said Caleb, and smiled significantly at Mrs. de Vere. She, resplendent in her blue velvet, with nodding ostrich plumes in her bonnet and a coquettish bow tied under her chin, looked a trifle uneasy, but managed to titter:

"Yes, indeed, but it's been a *great* responsibility."

"I have not asked how you achieved this change of front," he added.

"Pray do not," Dolly said, grimacing

significantly, and fanned herself, growing first hot and then cold. Caleb then informed her that a large sum of money had this very day been placed by his lordship to her credit at the bank. An equal amount had been paid to Mr. Nonseale, himself. Mrs. de Vere could breathe again. Her debts would be paid on the morrow. She was safe. Archibald need never know how near she had been to ruin. And when the will was proven, the vast amount of money due to Fleur from the double estate of father and mother would be handed over to his lordship of Cadlington. He could deal with it as he thought best.

Kneeling in the church, after having uttered a hypocritical prayer for the welfare of the young girl whom she had ruined, Dolly tried to tell herself that she had really done the best possible thing for Harry's daughter. Nevertheless, Dolly de Vere could not quite erase from her mind the memory of the trust that Harry had placed in her and how she had abused it. Almost she could feel the cold horror and hatred with which he and Hélène would regard her if they but knew how the marriage had come about.

Of course, Dolly tried to argue with herself, Mr. Nonseale was equally culpable. It could not have taken place without his consent. He, too, had been in need of money. He, too, had broken faith with Harry Roddney.

"I must try not to think about it too much," Dolly de Vere muttered to herself. But when she looked at the altar before which the bride and bridegroom were standing, she licked her lips nervously. She was really quite haunted by the memory of all that had taken place during this last few weeks.

Unforgettable, the hour when St. Cheviot had brought Fleur back to her cousin's home. Even Dolly had felt a deep pang of shame at the sight of the girl's altered appearance. Deathly pale, with eyes that bore the stamp of despair, Fleur trembled incessantly and refused to answer any of the questions put to her. Dolly ordered the twins out of the way and sent the young girl straight to bed.

Molly, her former maid, and the treacherous Noggins, had been dismissed. A new woman, older and more reliable, had been engaged by Dolly to look after Fleur. She was told that the young girl was 'sadly wanting' and must be closely guarded, and that no notice was to be taken of anything 'odd' that she said.

From the moment of Fleur's return, the key was turned in the lock. She became Cousin Dolly's prisoner.

St. Cheviot, himself, seemed rather more angry than jubilant over the affair. The evil was done, but his lordship confessed himself dissatisfied. He was in a devilish mood. When Dolly in a quivering voice began to ask him what had happened, he shut her up.

"The girl has no fire in her," he said harshly. "She is made of ice. I think, too, unless she is carefully handled, last night's shock will unhinge her. Pray look after her with tact, madam. I wish her to be in better health and spirit when we come to marry. I will wait for her one month more and no longer."

With that he had departed. Dolly returned to the girl's side feeling more than apprehensive, wondering if they had not gone a little too far in their efforts to break Fleur's resistance.

The resistance, however, seemed to be broken. Fleur neither argued nor protested, nor complained of what had been done to her. It was as though all her spirit had fled forever and she wanted no more of this world. She turned her face to the wall and lay silent without so much as a tear or a sob. Mrs. de Vere had found it an exceedingly uncomfortable job ministering to her. Her patience was sorely taxed on many occasions during the weeks that followed, but she did at least extract from Fleur her promise to announce her betrothal to St. Cheviot.

"Yes," she kept saying every time Dolly asked the question. "Yes, I will marry him."

"You *must* now," was Cousin Dolly's assertion. "No decent young girl could do otherwise."

"No — no decent girl could do otherwise," Fleur agreed in a monotone. Her great eyes stared blindly ahead of her.

"It is all very unfortunate," stuttered Dolly. "I regret that it happened. Of course I had no *idea* St. Cheviot would dare to do — as he did."

Then and then only Fleur had turned and regarded Cousin Dolly with an expression of such scorn and bitterness that the older woman writhed.

"*You* knew, Cousin Dolly, *you* sent him. He murdered my father's servant. Then he murdered *me*," she added in a low voice. "If my father could return from the dead he would avenge me. You would not dare to look him or my mother in the face."

So Dolly had crept from the room, snivelling.

But for a long time Fleur was ill — with a sickness of the mind more than of the body. Archibald, ignorant of the black crime that had been committed against the unfortunate child who had been left in his wife's care, received only a much-delayed letter to say that 'dear Fleur had consented to marry St. Cheviot'. *Little doubt*, Dolly wrote, *you will rejoice*.

Physically, because Fleur was young and strong, she revived.

Once or twice when St. Cheviot came to see her, she received him and gave him her hand to kiss but refused to look at him. Dolly, watching, saw that she trembled and that the waxen pallor of her face was suffused by painful colour. However, she was extremely polite. The betrothal ring, which he had placed on her finger (three emeralds which Dolly imagined must have cost a fortune), was too big and heavy for her thin finger. But she thanked him for it and for a fabulous necklet of diamonds which he chose for her from the St. Cheviot collection. She had grown almost emaciated. This made St. Cheviot impatient.

"You must gain weight, my dear child," he told her. "I think you will benefit once you are living at Cadlington where the air is brisk and there is excellent fresh produce from my many farms."

"Oh, dear Fleur is a tremendously lucky girl," Dolly had chirped in.

And then Fleur's heavily languid eyes turned in the older woman's direction. Dolly found her cheeks growing hot. Really, it was awful, the scorn with which the young miss regarded her.

After St. Cheviot left, Dolly had been a little cross with Fleur.

"For the love of heaven can you not smile or simulate happiness — even if you do not feel it? Do you wish to be a bore? Take it from me, even St. Cheviot's patience with you will snap."

"I do not care," Fleur had replied, closing her eyes.

Exasperated, Dolly cried:

"Can we do nothing to please you? What do you *want*, you dreadful child?"

"To be alone," she had whispered, "alone with my shame and my sorrow. Were I a Catholic, I would wish to beg permission to enter a Convent and be removed for ever from this world."

"Upon my soul, you are a little fool!" was Dolly's rejoinder.

One day St. Cheviot sent Fleur a box of camellias in the centre of which sparkled a magnificent star sapphire. On a card were written the words:

Let my care and my gifts make those sorrowful eyes of yours shine again with the blueness of this jewel. I will be good to you if you will let me.

St. Cheviot.

She had — in obedience to Cousin Dolly's request — thanked him for the priceless sapphire — but a bitter smile had twisted her sad mouth when she saw how the sharp edge of the brooch had bruised the tender creamy petals of the flowers. Already they were brown and broken.

"Like my heart," she had whispered to herself. "Like my youth."

Today — on her wedding day — the bride was attired in an exquisite dress of palest violet satin, misted over with frills of exquisite lace. There were tiny lace-frills on the rim of the bonnet. A gauzy veil floated from the crown. A small violet velvet cape, lined with ermine, covered her thin shoulders.

In one lace-mittened hand, the bride carried a posy of violets and silver leaves. Diamonds sparkled around her throat. She looked so beautiful, so pure, so pathetically young and sad — the men felt curiously disturbed — as though suddenly they felt the grossness of man's appetite to be a shameful thing. But the women — knowing nothing of the truth — envied Fleur her marvellous jewels.

St. Cheviot was magnificent in dove-grey with floral satin waistcoat and a collar so high that his chin was almost lost in it. He towered above the young girl at his side. She *felt* that strong animal presence and loathed it.

She made the responses in the veriest whisper. Then it was all over. She walked down the aisle on St. Cheviot's arm. 'His, *his* forever,' she thought in anguish. From now onward, her life would be one long martyrdom. A *respectable* martyrdom, she thought with a cynicism that would have broken Hélène Roddney's heart could she have known what lay in her daughter's mind this day.

Passively, the new Lady St. Cheviot accepted the kisses and congratulations of relatives and friends. There was but one person she would have liked here today — dear little Cathy, her childhood friend, but this had been denied her, Cousin Dolly would allow her no communication with the former intimate friends of the Roddneys.

One of the things which Fleur had most bitterly resented was being escorted to her marriage by such a man as Mr.

172

Nonseale. Loyal though she was to the memory of her beloved father, she had to admit that poor Papa had made a mistake in his solicitor. She was quite sure that Mr. Nonseale and Dolly were in league. She had had to talk with him and listen to a lot of dry legal matters which she did not understand. Wearily she had signed documents at his request. He had been suave, and servile, and made her shiver as he spoke of her 'wonderful good fortune' in contracting so fine a marriage. Lord St. Cheviot, he said, would now decide what was to be done with the properties she had inherited. He hinted that his lordship had already made up his mind to sell Pillars and the de Chartellet estates. Henceforth all would be in St. Cheviot's hands to do with as he wished. All that she possessed. From this day onward he was her guardian, her trustee, her *owner*.

If her heart ached at the thought that she would never see dear Pillars again, she could at least be glad that never would she re-enter the freakish Bastille — that house of treasure which had once been Lucien de Chartellet's pride.

173

It held for Fleur only the most appalling memories. When she ventured to ask what had become of poor Mrs. Leather, she had been told that the woman had been 'pensioned off' by his lordship. The poor creature had been threatened to such an extent that she would never let it be known what had transpired at The Bastille that night. So she kept silent when it was announced that poor Jacob Leather had met his death 'by accident'.

Fleur tried not to think about these matters as she stood at St. Cheviot's side in the reception-room at Cousin Dolly's house. Footmen handed around Marsala and Madeira and the Bride-cake. The head chef at Cadlington had sent this towering confection of white frosted sugar — on it the initial 'D' and 'F', twined together with lovers' knots, and the Cadlington coat-of-arms in rose-pink ice picked out with sugared violets. Always violets, Fleur thought, weary of them. Yet once they had been her favourite flowers.

She was glad that the sun did not shine today. It would have been a mockery. She was glad, also, that St. Cheviot did not force her to travel at once. He had wanted to take her to Monte Carlo where the sun would be warm, but Cousin Dolly's physician had warned him that Miss Roddney's health was in such fragile state (he presumed due to the shock of her parents' death), he would not advise the long journey. Especially as she might have a natural horror of the Channel crossing. So Denzil had consented to take her straight to Cadlington. They were to leave Knightsbridge at midday in his lordship's famous 'flying coach', pulled by four horses. This would mean a stop, midway, to Whiteleaf. It so chanced that St. Cheviot was friendly with a certain baronet, Sir Piers Kilmanning, who owned a fine shooting estate near the village of Fulmer. Kilmanning and his wife had offered the bride and bridegroom a suite in their house where they might rest the night. The next morning, they could proceed at their leisure to Cadlington.

The very name of 'Kilmanning' had made Fleur feel worse instead of better. She had actually heard Mama speak of

Lady Kilmanning; a woman she had known in the past when Mama was *Madame da Marquise*. One of the set that Hélène had despised; a middle-aged coquette who lived only for pleasure and whose husband was a famous buck during the period of the Regency.

As far as Fleur could see, any friends that she would have in future would be of the type that amused St. Cheviot, but against whom Mama and Papa would have shut their doors.

During the drive from the church, St. Cheviot with attempted gallantry raised her hand to his lips.

"May I not have one word, one smile from you, Lady St. Cheviot?" he asked.

She did not raise her lashes, nor answer. Then she felt his fingers grip her wrist like a vice.

"Answer me. I will not tolerate this contempt."

Now obediently she raised her magnificent eyes.

She said:

"What would you have me say, Lord St. Cheviot?"

"First, that you drop that odious

method of addressing me. I am your husband and I have a name."

She bit her lip. *Her husband.* She found it hard to believe. On the rare occasions when she had talked to Cathy of a 'possible husband', it had been in terms of exquisite romance.

St. Cheviot saw the working in her long slender throat. He was furious because whenever he spoke to her she looked ready to flinch as though before a threatened blow. For what he had done he had drowned his conscience fathoms deep. It had been the girl's fault for being so stubborn; anyhow, what had she to grumble at? Had he not given her his title and was she not in a position that his own mother before her had found flattering? He began to pity himself because of the difficulty of drawing one spark of response from this strange girl. Ignorant she could no longer be called but her innocence was still curiously unsullied. It was like an impenetrable wall between them.

"My name is Denzil," he said harshly.

"Denzil." She repeated the name as a child repeats what it is taught but without interest.

"Deuce take it," he said scowling. "This is not a good beginning to our married life. A bridal should surely be a happy affair."

"*Happy*?" That word was repeated most bitterly by the girl, and she laughed. It was not the first time that Denzil St. Cheviot had heard her laugh. Once at Pillars — months ago — he had stood watching her silently, listening to the light happy laughter of a radiant being. It was then that he had begun to desire her. Now she was his, but she had lost that radiance and her laughter was dreadful and humourless. The sound of it irritated him, when it should have filled him with remorse. He did not pause to consider that it was *he* who had murdered the soul in her, as surely as his man had plunged the knife in Jacob Leather's back.

"I will not have people think that I take an unwilling bride," he muttered.

Now Fleur spoke with a cold dignity that half annoyed and half amused St. Cheviot.

"I fear, Lord St. — I mean Denzil," she stumbled over the christian name, "I cannot be responsible for what others think. I have not supernatural powers."

He shrugged his shoulders.

"And you do not intend to be a willing partner?"

She looked at him with that loathing which he found so boring.

"I was *not* a willing partner," she said between her teeth.

St. Cheviot flung himself into his corner of the coach and folded his arms, scowling at her.

"Have it your own way. You are as obstinate as a mule."

She shut her eyes. As the coach rumbled along taking her towards her new home, she thought:

'Not only am I unwilling, but everything that is in me shrinks from carrying out my duties as Lady St. Cheviot. I wish I could die.'

But she was denied the merciful oblivion of death — of joining those dear ones who were lost to her.

She carried with her a tiny sable and velvet muff. She locked her hands in it and leaned her head back against the cushions. Exhaustion claimed her. Utterly worn out in spirit and in body, she sank into a doze. Her bridegroom glowered at her from his corner but kept silent. There were times when to taunt Fleur afforded him sadistic pleasure, but for the moment he left her alone. He looked forward to what he knew would be an excellent meal with the Kilmannings. Sir Piers was a genial host and Arabella his wife had ever shown a willingness to receive St. Cheviot's attentions. She was a good-looking woman despite her age, with a pretty ankle.

St. Cheviot yawned, then he, too, slept.

2

CADLINGTON HOUSE was bathed in sunshine. All morning there had been a scurry and a bustle among the servants both indoors and out. The master was bringing home his bride. They were expected home before midday.

Floors had been given an extra polish; stonework and plaster washed. In the immense kitchens, the head cook — he was a French chef — pompous and perspiring, chivvied his under-cooks, kitchen-maids, and scullions, and set to work on the superb menu which he knew, from practice, would please a difficult master.

Head of all the staff was Mrs. Dinglefoot, the housekeeper; a woman of character who ruled her big staff of females with a rod of iron. A steel purpose lay hidden behind a terrible smile. She was marshalling them all this morning like a general who knows that the enemy is about to attack. The enemy in this case was the new Lady St. Cheviot. Matilda Dinglefoot had held her position as housekeeper at Cadlington when Denzil's mother was alive. *She* had been a meek silly lady who suffered from wretched ill-health and was only too glad for Mrs. Dinglefoot to take entire control.

For years, Mrs. Dinglefoot (alluded to by all members of the staff in hushed and awed voice as Mrs. D.) had swept through Cadlington House imperiously, the keys of still-room, linen-cupboards and silver chests dangling from her waistbelt. Her strident voice issued commands which were instantly obeyed or immediate notice was given to the recalcitrant. Rarely did she come face to face with his lordship. His orders were, as a rule, passed to her through the medium of his confidential valet, Ivor. And Ivor, it could truly be said, was the only human being of whom Matilda Dinglefoot was afraid. She knew how high he was held in his master's esteem. His power was great and any woman servant to whom Ivor took a dislike would rapidly find herself outside the door. Mrs. D. hated and feared Ivor, and appeared outwardly as his friend. For him, in the servants' hall, was reserved the finest titbits from the kitchens; the choicest wine. Linked in a curious and ferocious fidelity to the Baron, these two were, in truth, St. Cheviot's loyal servitors. But they would willingly have slit each other's throats.

This morning, Ivor had been busy giving orders at the stables and bidding the grooms make sure that St. Cheviot's hunters were in trim for a week's hunting. Then he had to attack the gardeners and see that the orchid house — the only part of the garden in which St. Cheviot took personal interest — was ready for inspection.

Ivor had just now come indoors to remind Mrs. D. that at any moment the bridal pair would arrive, and to warn her to make sure that the rooms for the new Baroness were ready.

"Don't fret yourself — all is prepared," Mrs. D. assured him and suggested that he might sip a glass of Madeira with her in her sitting-room. Over this drink, the crafty Welshman eyed the housekeeper with a touch of wicked humour.

"A little depressed are you not, Mrs. D.? It is many a day since there was a lady in the house to tell *you* what you may or may not do."

Mrs. D. smiled.

"I doubt if my new mistress will be greatly interfering — from what I hear of her. I tackled his lordship's mother — I do not doubt I can manage his wife."

Laughter gurgled in Ivor's throat.

To be sure, he thought, Mrs. D. could manage anybody except *him*. He knew too much about her and the way she feathered her nest in her master's absence. Never could she treat *him* as she treated the rest of them here. What a smile she had, to be sure! She had very big teeth like a horse. The smile was less an expression of mirth or pleasure than a drawing back of two lips which exhibited those fearful teeth. She was an immensely tall woman — a good head taller than the little Welshman. She had a poor complexion and used a kind of paste to cover her blemishes which gave her an ugly whiteness. Her hair, of a light shade of rusty brown, was dyed and done in a vast array of sausage curls always so neat that Ivor believed that she wore a wig.

To preserve an impression of youth, however, had become a passion with the grotesque old spinster, and when she had had a drop too much, she simpered and acted the coquette which was nauseating in the extreme. Ivor had suffered on occasions. To his master, he told tales of her gigglings and posturings. A coarse jest went down well when the Baron was in the mood for it.

"From what you say, her ladyship is not of too forceful a disposition," observed Mrs. D. as she finished her wine, and looked meditatively round her well-furnished parlour.

"You are right, ma'am, she is not forceful but she is of a stunning appearance."

Mrs. D., who had moved towards a mirror, patted one of her false curls and observed with dismay that more hairs than usual sprouted from her chin. The beauty of other females had power only to rouse the utmost hatred in the bosom of Matilda Dinglefoot.

"Well, well, Master Ivor," she said, "you have seen my lady — so you should know."

A mask fell across the saturnine face of the Welshman. *He* alone knew what wickedness had transpired in de Chartellet's Bastille, that turbulent night. In a curious way he had been disappointed in his master for he regarded it as a sign of weakness that a man should be driven to such lengths for love of any woman.

Mrs. D. took her leave of Ivor and went on her rounds. Underlings scurried away at her approach. There was none who wished to come under the lash of Mrs. D.'s tongue.

She marched up the stairs and into the rooms that had once belonged to her late mistress, Denzil's mother.

There were flowers everywhere. Big fires burned, in case the September evening should grow chill. All was spick and span.

But Mrs. D.'s face expressed a sour disapproval as she stood looking around her. Previously, these two communicating chambers were dark, gloomy and so filled with ornament that it took three servants at least a week to spring-clean the suite. The old Baroness had favoured rococo extravagance. Today the place was unrecognizable. A miraculous change had been wrought — not by his lordship who had only paid the bills — but by Peveril Marsh, the young painter.

St. Cheviot had, in his moody fashion, grown to like the gentle young artist, and to admire his able work. Not only had Peveril executed a very creditable likeness of his lordship, but several large and wonderful paintings of his friends. It amused the Baron to boast that he had inaugurated a new member of the household as his 'Painter Extraordinary'.

The boy had taken a fancy to the old disused tower, from the top turrets of which one could command such magnificent views of the Weald; the Baron allowed him to occupy it. Here a studio had been furnished for him. The boy lived his solitary life there. When he was not painting, he was poring over his books. If he felt lonely, he did not complain. Once when St. Cheviot had told him that it was not good for so young a man to become a hermit and suggested that he should find a mistress to amuse him, the boy had blushed crimson and shrunk from the suggestion.

"I want no mistress, my lord. I crave only the opportunity to paint and to improve my mind," he had answered. Whereupon St. Cheviot, shrugging, left the boy alone.

Peveril had become a familiar figure at Cadlington — emerging from his turret studio only to take fresh air and exercise, and eat his meals in the servants' hall. The young girls of the staff tried to coquette with him. He had a kindly word for them but no mind to make love to any of them. They found him an enigma, but everybody liked him well. If there was any help needed among them, Peveril was the first to offer it.

He had extraordinary powers with animals. He could do anything with a wounded bird or injured dog. Even the ferocious Alpha, who never allowed any person but St. Cheviot to touch her, went willingly to Peveril. In fact, she often voluntarily climbed the steep circular staircase, and sat at the young artist's feet while he painted, through the long sunny hours.

But in Mrs. D., Peveril had a bitter antagonist. She was jealous of him and of Denzil's interest in him. As a rule if the Baron saw anything to admire in any one of the staff Mrs. D. speedily found reason to send them packing. But this she could not do with Peveril Marsh. She was exceedingly indignant when his lordship instructed the young artist to rearrange the bridal suite.

"He is an artist — let him design for my lady the most beautiful bedchamber and boudoir that can be created and spare no money in the project," Denzil had commanded. So Mrs. D. was forced to stand aside.

Peveril had enjoyed the job. It appealed to the poet and the dreamer; this inauguration of beauty for a bride who was said to be the loveliest ever seen. He knew nothing of Miss Fleur Roddney's origin or sad story, just as he knew little of evil, itself. He knew little, really, about his master, the Baron. He could not altogether shut his ears to the wild stories that were whispered of

St. Cheviot's misdeeds, neither could he altogether forget the callous indifference which his lordship had first exhibited towards poor Elspeth as she lay dying. But during his twelve months at the House, Peveril had had little cause to complain of personal cruelty from St. Cheviot. He was not a good man; he was not an amicable one; Peveril, the idealist, could never love such a master. But he was grateful for the protection and home St. Cheviot had given him after Elspeth died.

His one ambition now was to profit by his experience in painting, save what money St. Cheviot or friends in the district paid him for portraits commissioned, and finally leave Cadlington and start an independent life. He had no wish to accept permanent charity.

He had flung his whole heart and inspiration into the decorating and refurnishing of the bridal chamber. Mrs. D., who was as blind to beauty as a bat, stood now staring around her thinking only that it was all wasteful and foolish. It was a fairy-tale room and there was no part in Matilda Dinglefoot which could attune itself to gossamer fantasy.

All in white — glittering and delicate — the very reverse of the dark wine colours the old Baroness had favoured. The walls were panelled in ivory satin, frosted with silver thread. There were great white bearskin rugs stretched across the floor. Sweeping ivory-velvet curtains were looped back with silver cords on either side of the tall windows. From the windows one could look right across the green forest, or downwards to the blue mists of the valley.

The great four-poster bed had been stripped, repainted and hung with transparent, gossamer curtains. Overhead, painted cupids hung by silver chains, each one carrying in his chubby hands a silver lamp which would be lighted tonight for the bride. The bed was covered by a white satin spread smothered in an exquisite foam of lace. On the huge square pillows the bride and bridegroom's names had been embroidered. *Denzil and Fleur.* That name '*Fleur*' fell pleasantly on Peveril's music-loving ear. It was lovely; and he pictured her as a flower of beauty whom he would immediately wish to paint. Certainly his lordship would command it. A likeness of the new Baroness must eventually hang among her predecessors in the long gallery.

There was only one painting — it hung over the fireplace — a gilt-framed *Madonna and Child*, after Raphael; one of the many treasures in this fabulous house. Peveril had picked it out from the gallery and bade the servants hang it so that it could be seen from the bed.

Mrs. D. sneered, her arms akimbo.

"What does he think — that her ladyship will be inspired immediately to give birth to an heir, and so turn this mansion into a vast nursery for snivelling brats?"

She feared that his lordship had forsaken liberty and married in order to get an heir; there could be no other reason.

And she also presumed that there would be no more wild parties held here; no crowds of gentlemen for hunting and gaming. Mrs. D. would now be asked to run a milk sop, pious household, like most of them round here. Alas, it meant that the good old times at Cadlington were over!

The communicating chamber was her ladyship's boudoir (his lordship occupied the suite on the opposite side of the corridor). Here again, Peveril had allowed his artistic fancy full flight. The room was panelled in some light fruit wood. The predominant colour was olive green — carried out in the velvet curtains, and draperies on sofa and chairs. There was a little Queen Anne bureau by the window at which her ladyship could write if she had a mind; and a bookcase for which Peveril had chosen the books — the poets in particular. Portraits of the bride's parents brought from Pillars hung on either side of the carved wood mantelpiece. The ornaments were few — one or two delicate porcelain figurines and a pair of silver candlesticks. Much to Mrs. D.'s disgust Peveril had cleared away the many old framed photographs and pictures; the wax flowers under glass cases — the busts of previous St. Cheviots — all the sentimental trophies of the old Baroness who had taken a long time in dying and left an odour of decay in her rooms. But all that had gone now and the windows were open to the sunshine. In Mrs. D.'s memory so much fresh air had never before been let into this suite. A week ago Mrs. D. still hoped that his lordship would dislike it when he saw the new rooms. But St. Cheviot had approved — with certain reservations. A few days ago he drove down to make his final inspection and remarked to Peveril:

"Do you then think that a young lady will like such scarcity of ornament, and such simple design? By gad, it is too cold and chaste for *my* liking."

The boy had flushed and answered:

"It was my belief, sir, that the chasteness would please the bride."

That had brought a roar of laughter from St. Cheviot, but he had shrugged and said:

"This one — perhaps. We shall see. I must admit, at any rate, that you have achieved quite a stunning effect. Never before has Cadlington boasted such odd decoration."

This morning Peveril came up the stairs with an armful of lilies. He placed them in a silver gilt vase on a table beside the *chaise-longue*, over which he had thrown a white Spanish shawl. Masses of violets had been forced by St. Cheviot's gardeners, and were cut and ready for Peveril to bring in here as soon as the bridal pair were within sight. It was Peveril's idea to scatter them over the bed and the floor. His lordship had hinted that violets were the bride's favourite flowers.

"Stuff and nonsense," was Mrs. D.'s opinion, but she turned her back on the poetic bridal room and made her way down to the great hall. Thank goodness the interfering brat of a boy had not been allowed to touch *this* part of Cadlington and all was as before.

3

U P in his studio Peveril Marsh thought much of the young bride who was being brought to her new home. All that was romantic in him favoured the day and the hour. He had been depressed lately, wondering when he would ever have enough money to go forth on his own and face the world. With all the benefits that Cadlington offered, he did not really like it here. But today his depression gave place to a pleasurable anticipation.

This turret was his only home. The circular room still had a slightly mouldy odour. The walls were shabby — half concealed by many paintings and sketches. A trestle bed, a table, two high-backed chairs and the artist's easel, served for furnishing. There were eight narrow windows in the circular turret. Peveril kept them uncurtained. He liked to look out on the landscape, in sunlight or shadow, in rain or snow. It was enthralling to him to watch the clouds race across the sky, to see at times the heavens open and let down a torrent of rain. He liked, at early morning, to glimpse the first bar of gold that cut across the darkness of the night and heralded the dawn. And in the summer he enjoyed gazing up at the stars, and marvelling at the infinity and splendour of the constellations. He was happy — yet unhappy — not knowing what lay behind his strange restlessness.

Gazing down on the sunlit vale this morning, he suddenly saw a dark shape winding up the hill towards Whiteleaf. The silence was broken by the unmistakable sound of horses' hooves, and the crack of whips. A look of excitement came into Peveril's eyes. *At last* — this must be the Baron's coach.

Peveril turned and ran down the stairs. Entering the great hall from the passage which led from the tower into the main house, he collided with Mrs. Dinglefoot. She tottered back.

"Careless young devil!"

"Your pardon, ma'am," he said, "but

I have seen his lordship's coach coming up the hill."

Mrs. D. dived into a voluminous pocket for a handkerchief. She blew her nose loudly. Her small eyes — cunning, like an elephant's — blinked at the boy.

"Contain yourself, my good fellow. There is no need to knock over a defenceless lady in your transports."

A young footman, wearing the smart green livery of the household and who was drawing white gloves on to his sweating hands, sidled up to the young artist. He made an uncomplimentary gesture towards the back of the retreating housekeeper.

"Defenceless lady, indeed! It is the likes of us poor folks who need be defended from *her*!" he muttered.

Peveril spoke to the man with his usual kindness but with just that touch of dignity which proved his breeding.

"If I were you, Jukes, I would hurry to your post. I am going to fetch the violets for her ladyship."

And with his light quick tread, Peveril ran to the greenhouses where a gardener handed him a huge basket of the dewy flowers.

Upstairs in my lady's chamber, Peveril sprinkled the starry purple blossoms over the white rugs, and upon the foam of lace across the bed, until the whole room looked and smelled exquisite. Pleased with the effect, he ran downstairs again and presented himself with the rest of the staff who were lining up on either side of the hall. They were marshalled into position by Mrs. D. and the head footman, Mr. Wilkins; all present, down to the lowest scullery boy. Being a mild warm morning, the front doors had been flung wide open. In the sunshine, grouped around the portico stood the outdoor servants; the gardeners, the groomsmen, the stable-boys.

St. Cheviot's Welsh valet was well in evidence — smartly dressed in his best dark grey coat, pantaloons and Hessian boots. He occupied a foremost place of honour, and would be the first to receive the master and his bride. He beckoned genially enough to the young artist who had also attired himself in what was his finest apparel — a sober suiting of a dark cinnamon shade with which he wore a white frilled shirt; and, for once, a high collar and cravat. His frank handsome face was not as full as it should have been. He looked pale and haggard. There were shadows under his eyes. Peveril worked far too long and too late — sometimes in a fading light — and his whole expression was that of one who gave much time to philosophizing. He was for ever preoccupied with morbid reflections on the sorrowful loss of his beloved sister, his shattered family life. His, too, was the temperament of the artist whose work never satisfied him. He suffered (quite mistakenly) from the fear that he would never achieve a real work of art.

Now the coach with the four high-stepping greys appeared round the bend in the drive and was brought with a fine flourish to the front door of Cadlington House. A cheer went up from the staff.

A postillion climbed down and opened the door. From the coach emerged the tall haughty figure of St. Cheviot. His face bore no expression of pleasure or gratitude for the cheers that came from his retinue. He looked sour and rather yellow in the golden September light.

At Fulmer, he had sent his bride early to bed and stayed up, himself, until the small hours, dicing with his host and a few bloods who had been invited to gamble with him. He had drunk too much. His tongue was thick. He had no stomach for festive entertainment at home. But he had a new reputation as a husband to consider, and must make some hypocritical show of settling down to matrimony, or all doors in the district would be shut to him and his lady.

But last night when the amorous Arabella had whispered in his ear: "'*Tis but a child you have wed, my lord St. Cheviot. Truly, you will soon be bored*," he had agreed with her. Now that he had got Fleur — he was already bored; more especially because of her lack of response. A prize obtained by St. Cheviot never possessed the same stinging attraction of things still out of reach. But he had a quick answer for Arabella. In the absence of her husband he had taken toll of her lips.

"I have married only for the purpose

of getting me an heir, madam," he had whispered with meaning.

Which indeed he felt would soon become the sole *raison d'être* for his excursion into domesticity. His passion for Fleur was likely to be washed away by her continuous weeping. However, with punctilious courtesy, he lifted her out of the coach and, holding her up in his arms, carried his bride across the threshold. He set her down on the tiny feet in their white kid, pearl-buttoned boots.

A roar of applause went up from the indoor staff. There were cries of:

"Welcome to his lordship and her ladyship."

"God bless the bride and bridegroom!"

"God bless you, my lord . . . and you, my lady."

Mrs. D., her eyes like gimlets, searching for what she could deduce from the bride's face, curtseyed to the ground, breathing heavily as she did so. The lesser servants peered over the shoulders of those in front.

And so Fleur, once Miss Roddney, beloved child of Sir Harry Roddney and of Hélène, one-time *Madame la Marquise de Chartellet* — came to Cadlington.

She came here as the Baroness, Lady St. Cheviot. She found herself in a great house of ornate magnificence. She looked at the rows of bowing, fawning servants; at the double staircases, and fine gallery, at the grand display of hothouse flowers. Even the banisters were entwined with exotic orchids. How she hated the orchids; she regarded them with horror. They reminded her of *him*.

Now at last Peveril Marsh set eyes on Lady St. Cheviot. His rapt gaze embraced her, marvelling at her pure extraordinary beauty. But what struck him most forcibly was the look of crushing sorrow stamped on that youthful face. How pale she was! How transparent! Was she very delicate? What was wrong? Never in his life had he seen hair of such a colour. It made him catch his breath; filled him with a mounting desire to reproduce immediately on canvas the rose-gilt hue of her curls. The slender perfection of her body was intensified by the fine cut of the lavender-coloured velvet skirt and short tight coat she was wearing. There was a drift of expensive lace at her throat. On her bonnet was a waving ostrich plume which made her look tall, but Peveril noted that she barely reached her husband's shoulder.

All that was true artist in Peveril rejoiced in this vision. He was not yet twenty. At his age many a young man had clasped many a woman in his arms, for lechery if not for love. But Peveril Marsh had had neither time nor money for the cultivation of female company. He had known, of course, that he could never become a true painter until he had fallen in love; for great talents and great passions are more often than not linked by a single creative force. The sight of St. Cheviot's bride struck at his being — like lightning — almost paralysing his senses.

St. Cheviot turned a jaundiced eye in his direction, and nodded.

"Good day to you, Peveril! How goes the latest master-piece?"

"No masterpiece I fear, my lord — but the new painting continues — I thank you," he answered. But he continued to look with awe and wonder at the young Lady St. Cheviot. Suddenly she raised lashes that seemed too heavy for the languorous lids. Her eyes met his. The deep violet of them astounded him. Once again that lightning flash struck at the trembling young man. Immediately he lowered his own eyes. Fleur did likewise.

During the journey from London, and last night at Fulmer, she had felt only half alive. The same deathly lassitude seemed to have settled on her limbs, and in her mind, this morning while they drove through the sunny Buckinghamshire countryside to Cadlington.

She could not raise one spark of enthusiasm when St. Cheviot had first pointed out the tower that rose above the forest of trees, and finally the park which surrounded the great mansion. He boasted of the many beauties of his ancestral home.

"Cadlington is all yours now, madam," he had said in a cold boastful voice, "and much more, if you would only appear a little less frozen in manner towards me."

She had answered:

"I care nothing for worldly possessions. I have already told you that, sir, and I cannot alter what I am."

"Sometimes I wonder *why* my choice ever rested on you," he snarled at her.

"Let it be remembered, then," she said with all her mother's dignity, "that the girl upon whom you first fastened your regard bears no resemblance to the one who was destroyed that night at The Bastille."

St. Cheviot had grown red, then pale. He said through his teeth:

"Do not mention that night — do not dare speak of it again."

Then Fleur, with her new unhappy laugh, said:

"If the memory shames you, my lord, that is one point in your favour."

He had sunk back in his corner of the coach muttering that the sooner my lady had a parcel of brats in the nursery to keep her busy, the better. Ensure that the race of St. Cheviot will be carried on; that was all now that he wanted. He took the trouble to tell her so. She said nothing but looked at him with a fresh disgust. Everything that she said or did proved to him that she had gone though with this marriage only in bitter revulsion.

Now she was being asked to admire the magnificence of her new home — the luxury of the life that she would lead here. But it did nothing to comfort her. She wished bitterly that she could be like Cousin Dolly or the twins, who would gladly have accepted the pollution of this husband for the sake of worldly possessions.

Who, she wondered, was the grey-eyed boy who had looked at her just now with such deep respect and admiration? She seemed to notice none of the other faces; only Peveril's alone. Then she passed on. She came to the foot of the staircase. Here, a gigantic woman wearing a frilled bonnet came and bobbed and spoke to her, mittened hands meekly folded over her breast.

"Your servant, my lady. I am Mrs. Dinglefoot, the housekeeper; here when the sainted Baroness, his lordship's mother, was still alive."

"I give you good morning, Mrs. Dinglefoot," said Fleur with the exquisite politeness which she never failed to show to the lower classes.

Mrs. D.'s malevolent gaze travelled critically up and down the girlish figure. The beauty that had struck Peveril Marsh's soul and ravished it, filled her with new sensations of malice and spite. Truly, my lady was a great beauty. But she looked tired — almost *crushed* — the housekeeper thought with some pleasure. Maybe already she had been brought to heel by the Baron. He was not one to suffer any nonsense, nor bow to a woman's whim. Perhaps Mrs. D. need not anticipate that she would receive opposition from this quarter. Fawning, her lips drawn back to show the horse's teeth, Mrs. D. murmured something to the effect that she hoped her ladyship would be pleased with her rooms; and would she like to inspect the kitchens and the rest of the house now or later?

"Later, please," said Fleur.

She was tired — always so tired. She craved to be alone; to be left to sleep. Only in such oblivion could she find relief from the misery and degradation of what was now to be her life. Through the laces at her throat was thrust an arrow of large white diamonds. Diamonds sparkled around her wrists and on her fingers. Not one of these maidservants but envied her, she knew — and she would rather have been the very least of them than Lady St. Cheviot.

Denzil came forward and put a careless hand on her shoulder. Immediately she flinched away from it. That gesture did not escape Mrs. Dinglefoot.

'Ah ha!' she thought, 'there is not much love lost between *them*. I fancy my lady has not come here as a willing bride. So much the better. She will not want to rule me or my domain, for she will not be particularly concerned.'

And hugging this observation to herself, Mrs. Dinglefoot bobbed, withdrew and whispered fiercely to the rest of the female staff to get on with their business. Lunch was not to be served in the big dining-room but on a small oval table *à deux* in a morning-room; a more intimate meal for the 'bridal pair'. Tonight there would be a banquet to which many guests from the district had been invited. Fleur knew about this and her fainting spirit shrank from having to be presented to St. Cheviot's friends and acquaintances so soon; and from playing the part of the blushing bride. She hated hypocrisy; but she knew that she must go through with it. She thought, *This is only the beginning*.

When St. Cheviot had carried her into the hall just now she had felt as though his strong brutal arms were pitchforking her into a prison. Henceforth there was to be no escape for her, no privacy, nothing left of *Fleur Roddney*. Within these walls, as Lady St. Cheviot, she must 'love, honour and obey' this terrible man — until she died.

Suddenly there came the deep-throated bark of a big dog. Fleur saw a white wolfhound bound through the open doorway. She liked animals, but she thought this one had a ferocious aspect. It sidled up to St. Cheviot and licked his hand. He caressed the dog's head and said:

"So! Always a welcome from my favourite! This is Alpha — Alpha, go to your new mistress and show that you are pleased to greet her, too."

Fleur held out a hand. Alpha moved forward, gingerly, sniffed at the extended fingers and then backed, snarling. She preferred men. She had never made friends with any female at Cadlington. But she saw Peveril Marsh and went up to him for a caress. St. Cheviot laughed.

"A true woman," he said. "You must have a care, Fleur. Cross her and she will show her fangs."

"She has already shown them, my lord, and I shall not seek to cross her," said my lady coldly.

The bitter and sometimes misplaced humour that lay in St. Cheviot moved him now to exhibit his power over the animal — and over Fleur, herself.

"Alpha will guard you at my bidding. And if I say so, she will allow no one else to approach you. Watch!"

He spoke and gestured to the wolfhound, who immediately turned and caught a fold of Fleur's skirt between her yellow fangs. Fleur stood stock still, a frozen expression on her face. There was no fear in her eyes. Of this ferocious dog she was less afraid than of her amorous master.

211

"Now," said St. Cheviot, and beckoned to Ivor, "try to take her ladyship by the arm," he commanded.

The Welshman obeyed sourly. He knew the bitch's temper, but he was no coward. When he was almost within a few inches of taking Fleur's arm, however, the wolfdog sprang at him, snarling horribly. Ivor retired, muttering that one day he would cut the beast's throat. St. Cheviot rocked with laughter. The rest of the staff joined in. Everybody seemed to think it a fine joke. Fleur had not moved but her face had grown a shade whiter. Then Peveril Marsh dared to speak to her.

"Do not fear, my lady. Alpha's bark is worse than her bite."

"I am not afraid," said my lady in that same cold little voice, but her eyes held kindness for the young man who tried to put her at her ease.

St. Cheviot whistled off his hound. He was tired of the sport.

"Now, my sweet child, I have a surprise for you," he addressed Fleur in a dulcet voice intended for his staff to hear, although his dark eyes were still full of the resentment which he felt towards his young wife. "Let me present to you, Peveril Marsh — the young man of whom I have already spoken. A genius in our midst. My Painter Extraordinary. You shall sit to him for your portrait — all in good time."

He beckoned to Peveril, who came forward a trifle shyly and bowed low to my lady. At once she felt drawn to him. He looked so youthful and gentle beside the dark massive figure of St. Cheviot. Art in any form appealed to Fleur. Both her parents had cared greatly for beautiful paintings and she, herself, in her early teens had been commended for her brushwork. (Ah, heavens, she thought, with a sudden anguished pang, how far away those dear dead days at Pillars. Oh, gone for ever, those happy blissful days!)

"I am honoured to meet you, my lady," said the young artist. His voice was low-pitched and as gentle as his expression. Instinctively Fleur held out a small gloved hand. He looked at it as though not knowing what to do. St. Cheviot gave a sarcastic laugh.

"You may kiss her hand. She will

not bite you," he said with a return to humour.

The boy's thin face burned. He took the little kid-gloved hand. It looked very small and white lying against his brown palm. He noted with some dismay that his own long fingers bore smears of paint that no amount of scrubbing with soap and water had been able to remove. He barely touched his lady's little hands with his lips — then dropped it as though it was a hot coal. St. Cleviot roared.

"Our young artist has not the cavalier touch. But you will mark, my lady, that he can use a brush with great perfection. Damme, if his portrait in oils of myself is not the finest in the collection of St. Cheviots. Come, show it to her, boy."

Fleur said:

"If you will excuse me, my lo — " she stumbled and added, "Denzil. I would go to my room. I am a little faint."

"Women are always faint at the wrong moment," grumbled St. Cheviot, and turned and shouted: "Which one of you is the temporary maid to her ladyship?"

In a day or two there would come from Paris a French woman whom St. Cheviot had engaged as his wife's personal maid, but for the moment Mrs. Dinglefoot had found a nicely-spoken girl from the village who understood the care of clothes and would not be too clumsy.

This maid — younger than Fleur — stepped forward and bobbed.

"I am Phoebe Withers, my lady — daughter of Reuben Withers who is head gardener at Cadlington, so please you."

"Good day to you, Phoebe," said Fleur kindly. "I shall be glad of your services."

St. Cheviot glanced at the little maid and told himself coarsely that he, too, might one evening be glad of them. She was a pretty wench who had not so far come within his notice. Reuben Withers had charge of the orchid house and was second to none at his job. Little Phoebe had a trim figure and a pair of sparkling eyes. Behind Fleur's back, Denzil chucked the girl under the chin. She blushed and giggled. These actions did not pass unnoticed by Peveril, who frowned and felt some astonishment if not disgust. It seemed an extraordinary way for the Baron to behave. Did a gentleman, then, bring home a bride and within twenty-four hours of his wedding, pay attention to a female servant?

Peveril looked a trifle anxiously at Fleur. She turned and said, "I would be glad if Phoebe would come and show me to my rooms."

"Not so. I shall show you the rooms myself," said St. Cheviot, "and with us shall come the one who has so cleverly designed them. To this young artist, I entrusted my decorations. All has been newly done in the attempt to please you, Fleur." He added the last words in a low voice meant only for her ears. She did not answer. She walked up one of the fine thickly carpeted staircases, a small hand on the rosewood banisters; her head held high.

Peveril followed, his heart beating fast. Now that he had looked upon Fleur St. Cheviot's face, he hoped passionately that his decorations would please her. And he was glad that he had spent so much time and effort in making the rooms beautiful for her. For now he knew that he had chosen well. The virginal, sugar-white

216

loveliness of the bridal chamber was the right background for Lady St. Cheviot's cool flawless beauty.

He had the satisfaction of hearing a cry of approval fall from her lips. Indeed, Fleur wakened suddenly now from the nightmare of her thoughts, and came to life if only for a few moments as she looked upon the enchantment conceived and carried out by the young painter. Despite her misery, her profound despair, all that was feminine in her was gratified by what she saw. The glittering lace-covered bed, the cupids overhead with their gleaming silver lamps, the painted ceiling, and most of all the sweet-smelling scattered violets — violets for her to tread upon. What a charming idea!

"It is indeed bewitching," she murmured and some colour crept up under her skin.

Peveril bowed low. He was ready to kiss her feet for joy.

"I am rewarded — and more — by the mere knowledge that it pleases you, my lady," he said.

Now she looked him straight in the eyes. She even smiled.

"Thank you," she said. And she was glad that *he* had done this thing and not St. Cheviot.

But almost at once the towering form of St. Cheviot came between them, blotting out of sight the boy's happy face. Denzil encircled her tiny waist with the long fingers of his two hands.

"So you are really pleased? You are blushing. At last, perhaps, you begin to realize what I feel for you and all that I would do for you if you would be a little kinder," he said under his breath.

At once her pink colour faded. She shrank away. The glorious shining bedroom was veiled from her as though by a mist of loathing and despair. If this had been prepared for her by a bridegroom whom she had loved, if in this heavenly room she could have been bride to any other man than St. Cheviot — how different it might have been! Little did Peveril Marsh dream that this pretty chamber could be only another setting for her abasement — her martyrdom — and that when St. Cheviot's hands touched her, it was as though they grasped those lilies yonder, staining the matchless whiteness to a bitter brown.

Indeed, Peveril Marsh, knowing nothing of such reflections, walked happily with the bride into the communicating room. This, too, satisfied her. Once again in her gentle way she smiled and thanked him.

"I have never seen lovelier rooms," she said. "This one in which we now stand reminds me a little of my parents' home; of the boudoir that belonged to my dear mother. She, too, favoured pale wood panelling, and this same shade of green."

Peveril looked at Fleur, speechless with gratitude. His searching gaze noted that the girl's full underlip trembled and that a tear glittered on the longest lashes he had ever seen. Once again he was sorely troubled. Why, why did Lady St. Cheviot look so sorrowful; so *defenceless*? What was her history? What had led her to marry the Baron? Did a woman not give herself for love? What in heaven's name lay behind this curious atmosphere of disaster which the sensitive young artist was quick to sense?

He felt that it was time he absented

himself. Bowing first to Denzil, then to the bride, he murmured a few words and departed.

Phoebe tripped into the room.

"Mrs. Dinglefoot wishes to know if my lady would like a cup of camomile tea or a cordial before her luncheon — " she began.

But St. Cheviot interrupted.

"Leave us."

"Yes, my lord," said Phoebe and hurriedly shut the door again.

Fleur began to untie the ribbons of her bonnet. She walked back into the exquisite bedroom, moved to one of the windows and stared down at the wonderful gardens; at clipped yew hedges; the flower borders, pink and scarlet with late summer roses, or magnificent chrysanthemums; the upper terrace with its Italian marble balustrade; an artificial lake embroidered with water-lilies. Then she stared into the distance across the blue-green mist of the forest down into the valley.

She was an exile, utterly alone, as though in a foreign land — far removed from everybody, everything she had ever known. Her spirits were so low that she even felt she would like to be back in Cousin Dolly's house; at least with her own kith and kin. Yet no! Cousin Dolly was her enemy, and poor Cousin Archibald knew nothing of her betrayal. There was no one to protect her from any further infamy to which she might be subjected. She had been made a respectable wife — yes — now she bore a fine old title — and she was mistress of this palatial home. And she wanted none of it.

The slow tears began to trickle down her cheeks. With a heart-broken sigh she brushed them away. She knew that it angered her husband to see her cry.

Now he was at her side. His eager fingers began to unbutton her little jacket. His face was flushed with the passion she had grown to dread.

"You are a lovely thing," he muttered. "It is a pity you are also an icicle."

She stood dumb. She had little spirit with which to fight. What was the use, anyway? She was his wife, she had her duty. Always Fleur had been conscious of her duties in this life. Thus, she had

221

been brought up by her mother.

"Can you not say one word of thanks for everything I have done for you?" St. Cheviot demanded savagely, his black eyes glowering at her.

"I thank you," she said in a low voice.

Enraged, he pushed her away — so roughly that she stumbled and fell. She lay still on one of the white bearskin rugs — crushing the violets — her face hidden on one curved arm. But she did not cry.

222

4

TWO months later, one cool wet morning in November, Fleur climbed the circular staircase that led up to Peveril's studio. She climbed slowly for one so young. She could not overcome that lassitude that had fallen on limbs and spirit since her marriage to St. Cheviot.

At the moment she was feeling better than usual, because St. Cheviot was away. He had had a fiery row with his head gamekeeper over some shooting incident. Cadlington had been full of gentlemen enjoying the shooting last week-end. All day, the forest had resounded with the crack of guns. But following this row, St. Cheviot, in one of his black moods, had taken himself off to London. There, Fleur knew he would spend his time at the clubs, playing cards or supping with his mistresses. She knew that he had mistresses. He had told her so, to add to her shame and horror.

"Man cannot live with a block of ice," he had told her one night, "and I can easily find attractive females who think me a fascinating lover."

To this Fleur had made no response. Always when he insulted her, she remained dumb. It was this very patience and resignation in the face of her misery that angered him most.

Once, and once only, he had muttered an apology when, after a peculiarly unhappy scene between them, she had faced him, driven beyond endurance, and cried:

"Oh, God! The day will come when the ghosts of my beloved parents will rise from their watery grave to haunt you. Your monstrous behaviour cannot go unpunished — you will see."

She had noted the way he backed from her. She knew that he was superstitious.

After a week or two of trying to accustom herself to her new life at Cadlington, Fleur consented to sit for her portrait to the young artist, Peveril. She saw him quite often — either in the house or wandering in the grounds. She never failed to stop and speak to him.

His great gentleness — coupled with a certain boyish dignity — appealed to her. He seemed the one member of the household she could like and respect. On the whole she disliked the Baron's staff. It had not taken her long to discover that the housekeeper was her enemy, and a most unpleasant one.

Phoebe had long since been replaced by a French woman of over thirty years, by name Odette; sharp-featured, sharp-tongued and not at all the pleasant or motherly type that Fleur's mother used to employ at Pillars. But Odette was a clever needlewoman and took excellent care of my lady's wardrobe. This satisfied St. Cheviot — so Odette remained. One of the many burdens of Fleur's existence was the number of times the Baron liked her to change her clothes. She was dressed up like a doll to amuse him, she thought bitterly.

She disliked not only her husband, but his friends. Many people had called — one or two matrons with young daughters who might have been pleasant company and were highly respectable. But the mothers seemed to fear the

Baron (rightfully, Fleur told herself with irony). In such a way did he look at their virginal daughters! So the nicest of the neighbours came rarely to Cadlington, some not at all. It was left to the unfortunate young bride to find but one modest friend; Peveril, the painter.

She grew to look forward to her hour of sitting while he painted. They talked fluently together nowadays. They found much in common — these two young things who were much of an age. She learned of his early life, his struggles, his misfortunes. His knowledge amazed her. He was a scholar and a poet as well as a painter.

There were moments during these last two months as autumn drifted into the beginning of the winter and the weather kept her much indoors, when Fleur had wondered how she could have borne her life without Peveril's company.

This morning she was a little more breathless than usual when she reached the top of the tower.

She, like Peveril, found in this turret studio a refuge, a retreat from the rest of the world. In her own rooms she was suffocated by the very magnificence with which he surrounded her.

Peveril heard her light slow step. He went quickly to the door and opened it. As he watched Fleur climbing up the last few stairs, his eyes bore the expression of one who looks at a sacred image.

In all his nineteen years, the young artist had never experienced a rapture more intense than that which he felt at the sight of the beautiful young Baroness; nor a respect more profound. But whereas hers was burdened with an intolerable sorrow, his was disturbed only by the anguish of love.

As she reached him, he bowed low, touching with his lips the slender hand she extended. *This* was how he liked her best; in the simple gown in which he was painting her. It was of madonna-blue velvet, the violet-blue hue of her eyes; she wore no jewellery. She seemed to him to look no more than fifteen or sixteen years old. The pearly quality of her skin like the rose of her lips was nature's masterpiece.

A thrill of pure joy would frequently

shoot through the young man while he painted her.

The Baron, one morning, had said to Peveril:

"Mind you execute the portrait of my lady in gay mood. I want no hint of tears. Women cry too much and too often!"

Peveril had repeated this to Fleur and been horrified by the bitter little laugh which had escaped her. She said:

"Paint me as you see me, Peveril — a true artist can only reproduce what he sees with his own unfailing vision."

But he feared that St. Cheviot might not be satisfied. He begged him not to look at the painting until it was finished.

Peveril led Fleur into the studio. She seated herself in the high-backed chair in which she always posed for her picture.

"Will you feel a draught, my lady?" he asked anxiously.

"No," she said, "I like it here."

And she laid her hands on the arms of the chair, crossed her small ankles, and shut her eyes, while Peveril knelt before her and arranged the folds of her blue velvet gown. He looked up.

That perfect head was drooping like a lily overweighted on its slender stem. As ever, he marvelled at the length of her silken lashes. This morning the shadows beneath those huge eyes were deep. Seen thus with sealed eyelids she made his heart ache. Oh, that tragic curve of lips! Now, and every day of his life, he brooded over the mystery of her. Knife-points of doubt and anxiety entering his tender heart until he felt that he was bleeding from a thousand wounds. What was wrong with her? *Oh, what?* He loved her so deeply that he would gladly have died to bring one smile of true happiness to her dolorous mouth. But he hardly ever saw her smile.

Her lashes lifted. Peveril trembled. He could not look too closely into the purple depths of Fleur St. Cheviot's eyes. Sometimes he felt that he did not *want* to learn what lay in them.

"The morning is grey," he said hastily, "I will start to paint while the light is good," and he turned to the canvas. It was nearly five foot high. He felt it would be his masterpiece if ever he was to paint one. Today he was concentrating on that sweet mouth with the divine cleft in the lower lip. He dipped his finest brush into rose-madder and began to paint.

She watched him and talked a little.

"It is dreary at Cadlington when the rains come."

"Yes, my lady. Last winter it was worse after Christmas. Fearful gales come sweeping across the valley. The whole house seems to rock with the thunder of the storm."

"I shall not mind the storms. But the vapours — the autumnal mists add to my gloom," she said.

"There should be no gloom for you, my lady, only the joy of spring," said Peveril.

One of her brows lifted. She said:

"It is a long time since I have tasted the joy of spring."

This was the sort of reply which he hated to hear.

"The Baron is away for long?" he asked.

"Until the end of this week, I believe."

Now it was Peveril's turn to raise a brow. How could any man leave such a bride for a whole week? he asked himself.

Said Fleur:

"Tell me, Peveril, have you any supernatural powers such as your poor sister possessed?"

"None, my lady. Elspeth, alone, was born with that psychic spirit."

"I laid a flower upon the poor child's grave when I was in the churchyard, yesterday, with my maid."

"I thank you, for my sister's sake. She suffered much and I often reproach myself that I brought her all this way from London and hastened her death."

"You did it for the best," said Fleur who had heard his story so often that she knew it well, "and at least the strange fate that led you here did you also a kindly turn. For it gave you work and a domicile at Cadlington."

To herself, she said:

"And it gave me my one, my only friend in the world."

The young artist murmured:

"I owe much to his lordship."

Fleur shut her eyes for a second. It was well, she told herself bitterly, that anyone had anything to thank *him* for. Oh, she knew that St. Cheviot could be free

231

with his money — even tolerant when the mood took him; but as a rule his whims and fancies turned in the wrong direction. He was more prodigal to those people who amused him, than to the ones who deserved his generosity. Least of all was he generous to *her* in the only way she wanted. He did not wish to give her peace, or let her lead the kind of life that she wanted.

"How long do you think you will stay at Cadlington, Peveril?" she asked him.

"I do not know, my lady," he answered. "There are moments when I feel I must get away. I do not wish to be beholden for ever even to such a good master. But when I have spoken to his lordship he has refused to allow me to leave."

Fleur nodded. She knew from what Denzil had said to her that he liked to keep Peveril here because others envied him his young 'Painter Extraordinary'. For St. Cheviot, he was just another treasure in the great house, but if and when Denzil tired of the boy — he would ruthlessly abandon him. That was St. Cheviot's way.

Peveril continued to paint. He was not

working well and he knew it. He was strangely restless. Fleur had become the inspiration of his life yet, today, he felt uninspired. He would like to stop work, throw himself at her feet and ask her a hundred questions about herself.

He was not altogether ignorant of what was going on. There was much gossip in the servants' hall, to which he could not entirely stop his ears.

There was always intimate gossip, too, from Odette, the French maid. Odette was a Parisienne, not averse to some coquetry and, although twice Peveril's age, had an eye for the handsome boy with his singular talents. Once or twice she had waylaid him in the gardens and whispered that she could teach him much if he was interested. He rejected her advances. Subsequently she grew spiteful and never missed a chance to tease him. And although she dared not speak her mind, she was quite sure that the young artist was genuinely enamoured of my Lady St. Cheviot. So she took special pleasure in letting Peveril hear the kind of talk that would make his spirit recoil.

She carried tales of his lordship's

overwhelming passion for my lady. Of his terrible rages. She, Odette had seen him rush out of my lady's room, cursing her. And later found my lady in tears which she tried to hide but could not. Once, Odette whispered to Peveril, she saw livid bruises on my lady's slender arms; imprints of his lordship's fingers. There must be dark terrible scenes in that enchanted bedchamber that Peveril had designed for the 'happy bride'. Scenes of unbridled passion on the Baron's part — of reluctance from my lady.

Such tales drove Peveril into a state of deep distress. Each fresh story only confirmed his dread suspicion that my lady had come here as an unwilling bride. More than that, it began to destroy what had been his boyish respect and homage for the man who had befriended him.

This morning, Peveril talked to Fleur of the Queen.

On the 20th November, he told her, the young Victoria would be going in state to open the Houses of Parliament.

"I wonder," said Fleur, "whom she will marry."

"No doubt it will be whosoever her

statesmen choose for her," said the artist, leaning forward to smear with his thumb a tiny coil of thick oil paint.

"Alas, that most women must marry the men chosen for them rather than make their own choice," sighed Fleur. "I shall pray every night that our young Queen's fate will be happier than — " She broke off, crimsoning from brow to chin. How nearly she had let that disloyalty fall from her lips. *Happier than mine*, she had been about to say.

Peveril dropped his brush. He grew suddenly pale. His brows contracted. He walked to the fire and kicked a log into position, making the sparks shoot up the chimney. He knew exactly what the unspoken word should have been. And today he knew beyond all doubt that Lady St. Cheviot did not love her husband.

"If my lady will forgive me, I am not in the mood to paint well today. I would sooner leave it till tomorrow," he muttered.

Fleur stood up and stretched her cramped young body, moving towards the warmth of the fire. Now the wind had changed. Spear-points of rain tapped against the several windows of the turret. In here it was warm, but outside it was cold and bleak. As bleak as the future that stretched before her, Fleur reflected. She could hardly tolerate the thought of the Baron's return.

"Would it disturb your work, Peveril, if I stayed here with you a little longer?" she asked with the meekness of a very young girl, not conscious of her dignified status in this vast establishment.

Peveril sprang to his feet. Nervously he fingered the Byronic tie which he favoured.

"But, my lady — it is for *you* to give *me* orders," he stammered. "If my humble studio pleases you, it is an honour and delight for me to entertain you here."

She looked at him with sweetness, and a faintest uplifting of her sad lips.

"I like to be here," she said gravely and spread her chilled fingers to the flame.

"My lady," he said, "to paint you is my privilege. To converse with you also is like a strange unfettering of all my thoughts."

236

"And mine," she whispered.

It was the first time the two young things had ever dared openly to express such pleasure in one another's company.

Peveril continued:

"I would like to do more — so much more! My dear lady, tell me, how best I can contribute to your happiness?"

She turned the small head with a movement both graceful and proud. But there was all the sadness in the world in her voice as she answered him.

"I have not known what happiness is since my Mama and Papa were taken from me by a monstrous cruelty of fate."

Then suddenly they heard above the sighing of the wind and the rain the sound of heavy footsteps. Someone was coming up the circular staircase. Fleur was first to recognize that step. All the colour that both the fire, and the sweetness of Peveril's words, had raised in her face, drained from it now.

"It is my husband. The Baron has come back earlier than intended," she said.

The full frightfulness of his suspicions

broke over the young painter's head, for he could not help but read the stark misery and dread that had so suddenly aged and blanched that young fair face before his very eyes.

'*Oh, God,*' he thought, '*she hates him.*'

And immediately there followed another thought: '*Then I must hate him, too.*'

5

THE studio door burst open unceremoniously. In sober but fashionable clothes, St. Cheviot stood there. He wore a cape and carried gauntlets in his hand. He looked as always after he had been away in London for a few days; dissolute, moody, his face ravaged by the excesses in which he had indulged. His great height made it seem as though he filled the doorway. There was a sinking sensation in Fleur's heart at the sight of those broad shoulders and that florid handsome face. He looked her up and down and then a lightning glance round the studio — a glance that barely included Peveril. Then he turned to his young wife again.

"Well, well, *well*, so this is where my loving wife has hidden herself. I looked for her in vain in her own apartments."

She moved forward.

"I did not expect you home so soon."

"Obviously," he said with a sneer, loosed his cape and flung it on a chair. He ran his fingers through his thick ebon-black curls, still smiling in that cold cruel way.

"I came early because Mrs. Dinglefoot sent for me," he said.

Fleur started.

"*Sent* for you? On what grounds?"

St. Cheviot did not answer at once but moved across the studio to the easel. He examined Fleur's portrait. Legs straddled, hands in his pockets, he rocked to and fro, on toe and heel. His eyes narrowed. He said:

"Mrs. Dinglefoot, the excellent creature, always has my good at heart. I asked her to communicate with me should she see anything amiss down here."

"And pray what does she see amiss?" asked Fleur, putting her hand to her breast. Her heart was beating violently.

Peveril stood rigid and silent.

Said St. Cheviot:

"The good Mrs. D. sent me a carefully worded letter to the effect that she did not think you look well and that you spend too much time in weeping."

Fleur, with a nervous glance at Peveril, said:

"I do not consider that my health — or my tears — should concern Mrs. Dinglefoot."

St. Cheviot took no notice of this. Staring harder at the painting, he said:

"She deemed it her duty as an old and confidential servant of this household, to express the opinion that you expend far too much time and energy upon climbing these steep stairs, and remaining in this studio. You might be better employed out of doors in the new phaeton, driving through the countryside or calling upon the neighbours. That conduct would, of course, also be more fitting to your ladyship's dignity. More in observance with the conventions, shall we say."

The inference behind St. Cheviot's words brought the hot blood to the young painter's sensitive face. But Fleur remained deathly white. Then she said:

"I consider it none of Mrs. Dinglefoot's affair if I come up here. I resent such interference."

St. Cheviot turned to her. His dark eyes glowered.

241

"My dear Lady St. Cheviot, Mrs. D. acts under my orders."

"As a spy — ?" began Fleur with passionate resentment, but cut the sentence short. "Nay — we must not embarrass Peveril by discussing our private affairs before him."

Suddenly a new suspicion smote St. Cheviot. *Could it be . . . was it possible* . . . he threw a slantwise look at the girlish figure in the madonna-blue gown. It was early days . . . of course . . . but that *might* just be the good reason for her ladyship's sickness in the mornings.

He rose, yawned, and turned a sour gaze on young Peveril.

"You have been making too many demands upon her ladyship's time. There have been sittings enough," he said. "Finish the portrait without her ladyship."

"As your lordship pleases," said Peveril, but his breathing quickened.

To cut short these moments of joy . . . to see Lady St. Cheviot only at a distance . . . to talk with her no more . . . what cruel deprivation! He looked at Fleur anxiously. She stared at the

242

ground, as though not wishful to meet his gaze. Heavens, how pale she was, how she trembled, he thought.

"Incidentally I have some criticism to make of the portrait now that I have at last seen it," added Denzil. "The flesh tints and the hue of the hair have that remarkable quality which even old Clarissa Rustingthorpe (and she is a connoisseur) declares is reminiscent of the Venetian masters. But why no adornment? I will have the St. Cheviot jewels sent up to you. Paint them into her ladyship's picture, if it is ever to hang in the gallery beside the other ladies of quality."

The harshness of the command did not disturb Peveril. Indeed, both he and Fleur had suspected that this was what his lordship would say. But he could not bear to see the look, as of a drowning woman, that came into Fleur's eyes as his lordship put an arm around her.

St. Cheviot said:

"You do not appear well, madam. Come — let us go. Mrs. D. is right. It is high time I came home and personally organized your life. Come!"

She opened her lips as though to protest but closed them again. Her whole body seemed to shiver from the contact with him. She was stricken dumb by the thought that he had returned. That after today these little moments of innocent happiness spent in this studio must end.

Peveril said:

"If your lordship would permit *one* more sitting . . . "

"No," said St. Cheviot in a rough voice, "and remember to paint in the jewels. I give you good morning." He added: "The Marchioness of Rustingthorpe is sending her carriage for you the day after tomorrow. She has a grand-daughter in residence at the moment. I have given my word you will accept a commission to paint her. She is an ugly brat, but you can do your best."

Now Peveril spoke up:

"It is my earnest wish, my lord, that I start to make my own way. If I can add this fee for painting the Marquis's granddaughter to my small savings, I shall have enough to enable me to set up a small studio in London."

St. Cheviot, who had been walking to

the door with Fleur in the circle of his arm, looked at Peveril over his shoulder and frowned.

"It is for me to say when it is time for you to leave Cadlington," he snapped.

Fleur thought:

'St. Cheviot is only happy when he is curtailing liberty — imprisoning a human being for some vile or egotistical reason of his own. Alas — poor Peveril! He has outgrown the pleasure of accepting charity *here*.'

The boy saw that this was no time for argument with his lordship. But anger was bubbling in him — a proud resentment against tyranny.

Suddenly Fleur felt faint and put a hand to her temples and murmured:

"Oh, pray support me, sir — I fear I am about to swoon."

St. Cheviot's arms lifted her from the ground.

"The devil take it, she is, indeed, indisposed," he muttered.

Peveril, sick with pity and anxiety, looked to the right and to the left.

"Alas, I have no vinegar — no feathers to burn . . . "

"No matter. I will carry her downstairs."

And without even saying farewell, he turned and began to walk slowly down the stairs bearing the unconscious form of his wife.

Slowly Peveril shut the studio door. The rain was coming down in torrents now, lashing against the windows, blotting out the Vale of Aylesbury. He walked to the easel and looked at the portrait in despair. Then he turned to the chair in which Fleur had but recently sat. He clasped it as though he were clasping the shade of her living presence.

In Fleur's exquisite bedroom, Fleur was laid upon her bed. Imperiously, St. Cheviot called for servants, cordial, burnt feathers, and vinegar. He also sent a footman hurrying down the hill to fetch the parish doctor. This physician, an old man by name Dr. Boss, was adequate at his job, if not up to date.

Fleur struggled back to consciousness reluctantly. She found her room full of people. She was at once conscious of the presence of her husband on one side of the bed, of Odette bathing her temples and applying burnt feathers to her nostrils and of the menacing figure of Mrs. Dinglefoot in starched apron and bonnet, giving orders to the lesser maids to bring in hot water, warming pans for my lady's cold feet, and to remove the lilies which were filling the bedchamber with their overpowering scent.

St. Cheviot bent over his young wife.

"So, my love, you are reviving," he said in the smooth voice which he sometimes used to her when in the presence of his staff. Let it be said in the neighbourhood at least that he was a devoted husband.

Fleur felt faint and sick. There was a frightened sensation in her heart and the moment she was conscious, she *remembered*. Never again was she to be allowed to go up to the studio in the tower and sit with Peveril Marsh. Her last and only happiness had been taken from her. A tear rolled down her cheek.

"Courage, my love," said St. Cheviot in his most dulcet voice. "Dr. Boss is on his way."

"Lawks, ma'am, my lady, but you gave us a fright," began Mrs. Dinglefoot who was in some triumph because she had managed to get her master back to Cadlington and upset what she called 'the apple cart'. The wily woman had become well aware of her young mistress's desire to spend a great deal of her time conversing with the young painter.

She had sent for the Baron not from a spirit of loyalty nor any genuine anxiety for her ladyship's health, but out of the spiteful wish to rob my lady of any joy that she had found in life. Gentle, long-suffering though she was, Fleur inspired nothing but hatred and malice in the heart of the ugly old woman. Only last night, Mrs. D. had remarked scornfully to the French maid, who was her friend and ally, that her ladyship was a poor sickly thing who would no doubt die bearing her first child.

Mrs. Dinglefoot had served the late Baroness when she was first *enceinte* with the present Baron. She knew the signs of pregnancy in a female. She was sure that accounted for my lady's nausea in the early mornings.

Fleur's eyes looked with distaste at Mrs. D.'s hairy chin. The sight disgusted her. She whispered:

"Denzil, please to clear my room. I wish to be alone."

"With me, of course, my darling," said St. Cheviot in a breezy voice, clapped his hands and dismissed the maids who were running to and fro like a lot of silly useless hens.

Outside the door, Mrs. D. eyed Odette.

"You will see. Dr. Boss will confirm my suspicions."

Odette tittered. She was thin with a foxy face, a woman of inordinate vanity. She wore a frilled cap with long streamers, perched on the top of her mountain of coarse black curls.

"*Oo la! la!* It will tie down *Madame la Baronesse*. She will not be able to carry on with her intrigue with ze young *Monsieur* the artist."

"I would dearly like to find out if it *is* an intrigue," muttered Mrs. D. "Come, my girl, I hear Dr. Boss's carriage."

The physician from Monks Risborough examined Fleur carefully.

She did not dislike him. He had white hair and beard and a noble forehead. Anything of nobility — that quality which used to surround her in her childhood but seemed now so rare a thing — appealed to Fleur. She lay against her huge lace-edged pillows looking wan and pathetically young, her beautiful hair tumbled about her throat. The old doctor was much moved by the sight. When he told her the reason for her swoon and for her *malaise* of the last week, he was perturbed to see how badly she took the news. She went scarlet then pale . . . then turned her face away. The physician held one thin little wrist between his fingers, feeling the flutter of a weak pulse. He heard a low sob from her. Bending over her, he said:

"Nay — my dear child (your pardon, my lady Baroness, you seem such a child to me, for I am a very old man), but you must not grieve over what is an entirely natural state of affairs. The Baron will be delighted and surely you — "

"I am not delighted," she broke in. "But I do realize that it is my duty to bear my husband an heir."

"When it is born you will love the infant," Boss encouraged her.

She shuddered. She could not imagine

herself loving any child of St. Cheviot's. What a monstrous thing nature was, arranging to unite her shrinking flesh with that of a loathed husband and thus conceive a new life. Monstrous that from her reluctant body there would emerge flesh of his flesh . . . A son or daughter? Who could tell? But it would be a St. Cheviot *through her.*

Dr. Boss continued to offer comfort and counsel in his kindly way. She must rest a great deal, take a little exercise — not much — and plenty of fresh air. She must conserve her strength for the approaching birth which Dr. Boss reckoned would be early in June.

Of course the good doctor knew a great deal about St. Cheviot. He had, in fact, brought the Baron into the world. And he had attended the old Baron and Baroness and closed their eyes after they had died. He could not say that he cared overmuch for the family; and, like others in the neighbourhood, he had heard ugly rumours of the excesses to which the present young Baron was prone. But like everyone else, Dr. Boss waited upon St. Cheviot with deference

251

and civility because of his wealth and title. It was expected of a physician who had his living to earn. St. Cheviot paid well — better than the villagers who called Dr. Boss to their stinking hovels — only for death — seldom to attend a birth. Many a medical service he had to render around here for no payment at all. The farmers and most of the local inhabitants were ground down by heavy taxation. The cost of living was high and wages disgracefully low. The country, in Dr. Boss's opinion, was in a sorry state. Pauperism was spreading through England like an ulcer. In recent months, cholera had almost wiped out several of the adjoining hamlets. Maybe now with Queen Victoria on the throne and Lord Melbourne in power things would grow better. Meanwhile such autocratic and wealthy landowners as the St. Cheviots or the Rustingthorpes continued to wield a despotic tyranny over the lower classes. Dr. Boss deplored such facts but could not escape from them.

Suddenly Fleur turned to him, her eyes unnaturally bright and wild.

"Some births are difficult and even

dangerous. Maybe I will die when my child is born."

He looked up from the bag in which he was packing his instruments and clicked his teeth in a shocked way.

"I beg you, my Lady St. Cheviot, not to consider any such calamity. You are not well. You need a tonic which I shall prescribe or you, but you are excellently fashioned by the Almighty, and should bear a fine child. With care, my lady, *with* care."

He made his exit. He would come again in a few days' time, he said, to ensure that her ladyship was making good progress.

A moment later, St. Cheviot burst into the room. There were many times when Fleur asked herself why the crystal loveliness of the bedchamber that Peveril had designed for her did not shatter to fragments whenever that dark powerful figure thundered into it.

She felt Denzil pick up one of her hands and cover it with kisses — an act of homage rare from the Baron.

"My love . . . my dearest! So it is true! Mrs. D. has not brought me home for nothing, You have conceived. That is the reason for your present delicacy and lack of appetite. Ah, my love, this is a happy day for your devoted husband. What could be finer than to know that in seven months' time an heir will be born to Cadlington!"

She lay motionless. St. Cheviot's kisses left her unmoved. But she permitted herself to give a humourless smile.

"Do not be too sure of a son, Denzil; it may be a daughter," she said.

"No, it must be a son," he said, rubbed his hands together and stuck his thumbs in his waistcoat. "It would be a new and amusing thing, my dear, if we should have a red-head like your own in the family. It would be the first red St. Cheviot. Well, well, I would not mind."

"Maybe," she said in a barely audible voice, "the babe will not live."

St. Cheviot frowned and seating himself on the edge of the big white bed, imprisoned both her hands in his strong hard fingers.

"I forbid you to speak in such vein," he said loudly. "You know my burning ambition to have an heir. It was for this that I married you. Besides," he added with a slight laugh, "the rest of the hunchback's prophecy has still to be fulfilled. And now I recall that she promised that it will be another black St. Cheviot. Yes . . . it cannot be red-haired but black like myself."

"Pray leave me to myself for a while," said Fleur.

"Not, madam, until you have reassured me that you will do all in your power to conserve your health and strength and give me a fine son. It shall not die, do you hear, Fleur? *It must not!*"

"That will be as God wills," she whispered.

"Bah!" said his lordship, and taking a tiny gilt box from his waistcoat applied snuff to each nostril. He sneezed violently several times.

Fleur thought:

"If only he would go away and leave me alone."

But St. Cheviot raved and ranted about the fine race — the former Barons — and what he would do with his son. How he would teach him to shoot, and

255

to ride, and to be a man.

"None of your namby-pamby artists," he ended, "and thinking of artists — if that young genius Peveril likes to flaunt his independence in my face now that he makes money through my benevolence — I may well bid him go before the child is born. I fancy, too, that I shall pull down the tower, and wipe out its sinister ugliness once and for all."

Fleur made no answer. She only knew that the tower had never seemed sinister to her. As for sending Peveril away, the very idea chilled her and made her frighteningly conscious of how dear he had grown to her. She was human enough to allow herself, for a moment, to remember Peveril and the unspoken sympathy that ran like a golden electric current between them. If the studio and the little winding staircase were demolished her dearest joy would be buried under a heap of stones.

St. Cheviot took her hand again.

"Come, Fleur, I am pleased that you are *enceinte*. Ask for whatever you want. Some new pearls? Another emerald for your finger? Speak! I will send to Paris for whatever you desire."

"I desire nothing," she whispered.

"Do not be so foolish," he said impatiently. "There are many women who would envy you the magnificence of this house, my gifts, and even of my embraces," he ended with a significant look.

She looked up at him. He was uneasy before the expression in those huge sorrowful eyes. Dammit, he thought, must she always make him conscious of his villainy towards her? He shouted:

"I give you everything. What more do you want?"

"Nothing, I tell you, save to be left alone."

He glowered around the virginal bedchamber.

"You have become as frozen as this sickly white room. After your child is born these decorations shall be altered. A new setting shall be created — more fitting for my wife. There shall be scarlet satin, a gilded bed, erotic pictures. No more of such religious stuffs as *that* . . . " He pointed at the Raphael Madonna over the fireplace. "You need to be encouraged if you are to participate in passion's pleasures, my dear; that is obvious."

She set her teeth. To destroy this beautiful room would be only one more act of violence and unkindness on Denzil's part.

"Do you think, my lord, that a changed environment could alter my feelings towards you?" she suddenly asked him. Through their long lashes her eyes glittered, rejecting him. "Oh, go away, go away," she added, and flung herself face downwards on her pillows.

"You are a fool!" he shouted at her, "and unwise to show so much contempt. You belong to me. Take care that I do not exert my rights and keep you chained to one room as I would chain a slave, and allow you no further contact with the world."

No answer from Fleur. St. Cheviot's blood cooled. He reminded himself that if she were to give him a healthy babe he must curb his passionate temper and leave her alone. Yes — he would take himself off to London again where flesh-and-blood women were waiting to receive him with open arms. He could be bothered with her ladyship no longer. As he walked to the door, he said:

"Perhaps you wish that I should send for your Cousin Dolly since you have no mother of your own to advise you."

Now Fleur sat up, her feverish face bathed in tears.

"No — no — on no account do I want to see her. I could not endure her presence. *You* know why, my Lord St. Cheviot."

His sombre gaze fell. He shrugged his shoulders, striving as best he could to be tolerant because of her condition.

"Then is there anyone you would like to see during these coming months? I daresay I shall be much in London," he growled.

She hesitated. Into her mind had flashed the awe-inspiring thought that she wished only for the sweet comfort and friendship given her by Peveril Marsh. Her cheeks flushed a deep crimson at the very idea. She hung her head.

"I know of no one," she whispered.

"Then good day to you and I bid you take care of yourself, my lady," he said gruffly and walked from the room.

6

CHRISTMAS came.

Cadlington was cut off from the rest of the countryside, once the long winding hills were covered with snow and the puddles were blue with ice. It was a severe winter. Nobody in the district called on the poor young Baroness although all the ladies knew from gossip that she was bearing a child. One or two of the more kindly ones might have bothered to take a glass of cordial with her, but the weather conditions made a good excuse for not doing so.

Fleur, therefore, was left very much alone. This she did not mind. And in particular she was relieved because St. Cheviot spent much of his time with his cronies in London. Also, when he came down she was not so much as before subjected to his violence, his possessive passions. For now she was advancing in her pregnancy he was so anxious that she should bear a living child, he controlled himself and acceded to a few of her wishes.

He even went so far as to put the brake on Mrs. Dinglefoot. The very sight of the woman's ugly countenance upset Fleur. She told her husband so. He laughed and tried to make a jest of it and called her fanciful, but she insisted that she would not have anything to do with the housekeeper. Fleur did not like Odette overmuch but she preferred the French woman who sewed so well and had begun, with Fleur, to stitch exquisite tiny garments for the coming infant.

When Mrs. Dinglefoot received orders from her master not to force herself on her ladyship's presence but to send word on matters concerning the household through others — her hatred became overwhelming. If she could do anything to spite Fleur for daring to snub her in this fashion (for it became a matter of jest and snigger in the servants' hall) Mrs. D. intended to do so.

Fleur received Christmas greetings from Cousin Dolly and the twins. She knew that Dolly wanted to come to

262

Cadlington. But such was Fleur's loathing of the woman who had betrayed her to St. Cheviot that she tore Dolly's Christmas letter in two and left it unanswered. She wanted no more to do with her. Dolly was a widow these days. Cousin Archibald was dead. He had succumbed to the cholera in India a few months ago. One of the twins — Imogen — wrote to Fleur and said that Mama might possibly give them a step-Papa in the spring — a gentleman of some means and wasn't it 'a pity that Cousin Fleur would be *hors de combat* and unable to attend the wedding'.

Fleur did not send congratulations to Cousin Dolly. Even were she able to go — nothing would have induced her to attend such a wedding. Cousin Dolly was a wicked woman. Perhaps it was as well that poor Archibald de Vere had died before he could return and discover why, in truth, Harry Roddney's hapless daughter had been forced into marriage with St. Cheviot.

One letter only at Christmas time brought some warmth to Fleur's starved heart. An unexpected communication from her girlhood's close friend, Catherine Foster. Catherine informed Fleur that a month ago she had married their mutual friend in Essex, Tom Quinley.

Catherine wrote:

I have often thought of you, Dearest Fleur, and the happy days we knew together at Pillars when your dear Parents were alive. Mama and I were exceedingly Distressed to hear of your Misfortunes and I would have communicated with you before now but you did not answer the letter which I wrote to you just before your Marriage. I thought perhaps that you had no more time for our Friendship. But now I am Mrs. Thomas Quinley and dear Tom makes me an excellent Husband. We reside in a very elegant house not far from Bishop's Stortford.

I feel an overwhelming desire to look upon you again and to know your news. To think that you became the Baroness of Cadlington after all. Do you not remember how uncertain you were about your Affections when first St. Cheviot came to pay his attentions to you? One hears things but I trust they are not all True. I would prefer to believe that you are happy and not too fine a lady now to remember Mr. and Mrs. Thomas Quinley . . .

When Fleur read this letter — the day after Christmas — she was sitting by the fire in her boudoir. She had been reading, trying to pass the time. It grew dark early on these winter afternoons; the nights seemed long and dreary. Already one of the footmen had lighted the candles and set a lamp upon her table.

Fleur seated herself at the bureau in order to answer Catherine's letter. Alas, she thought, if Catherine but knew the truth! It was because of that ugly truth that she had not written to her before now. She did not wish the Fosters to know her dreadful fate and subsequent unhappiness. And she was afraid that if she saw Cathy she could not conceal from one who had known her as a child, the dreadful havoc that had been wrought in her.

She was writing to Cathy when she heard a knock upon her door. Without

265

turning her head she said, "Come in" thinking it one of the servants; Odette perhaps, to help her change into a lose velvet gown which she wore before the evening meal. She was always cold in spite of the fires. Cadlington was so huge and draughty that during this severe weather it struck chill at her very bones. She felt perpetually ill. Dr. Boss promised that she would begin to have better health once the child had quickened but as yet she had not felt the stirring in her womb.

"My lady . . . do I disturb you?" said a boy's low voice.

She dropped her quill and swung round. Her heart leaped for pleasure as she saw the unaccustomed sight of Peveril Marsh. He stood before her, smiling — a parcel under one arm. He was dressed plainly in a velveteen suit with wide cravat. He looked changed, she thought, fatigued and curiously older; a new maturity sat upon him though she knew not the reason. She had not seen him face to face for six weeks now.

Peveril advanced and bowed respectfully.

"It is to give my lady my Christmas

greetings and to give her this humble offering," he said fingering the parcel. He added: "I did not come yesterday. When Mrs. Dinglefoot saw me approaching your apartments she informed me that it was no use making any attempt to see you because you were too ill to receive me."

Fleur stood up. Her cheeks coloured angrily.

"Mrs. Dinglefoot was not acting on my instructions," she exclaimed.

"Today I dare to steal, unnoticed through the house and up to this door," Peveril confessed. "I have been so concerned, my lady, to hear many tales of your indisposition."

"My illness is — natural. I am in no danger, I thank you, nevertheless," she said in a low voice.

"I am much relieved," he said.

They stood silent now, surveying one another. The blood was flowing fast through the veins of both these young creatures who had been denied the consolation of each other's presence for so long. The boy with his keen artist's perception noted little indication of her approaching maternity. Somehow he was fiercely glad. It had brought him the most strange repugnance to hear that she was to give the Baron an heir.

He had missed her friendship sorely and hungered for a glimpse of her. He lapped up every item of news of her that he could gain from the servants' hall, even though it was news he did not wish to hear. With the greatest reluctance he had altered her portrait and painted in the jewels the Baron had sent him, upon Fleur's throat and wrists. But for the artist, the whole significance of the painting had lost its meaning. It was just another to take its place in the gallery amongst the former ladies of Cadlington. The sad Madonna had become a bejewelled, tragic figure. Peveril could no longer bear to look upon it.

Reading his thoughts, Fleur said:

"My portrait is now being framed, I hear."

"Yes," he said and lowered his lashes. "I did not care for your picture once I had painted in the jewels," he confessed.

"One day, perhaps, I shall sit for you

again, Peveril," she said.

"I wish I could think so, my lady," he exclaimed before he could restrain the impassioned impulse. To cover his embarrassment he handed her the parcel he had brought. "A humble offering for Christmastide," he said.

It was wrapped in white paper and sealed with wax. Opening it, she found a small painting in a carved wood frame which, afterwards, he told her he, himself, had fashioned. The painting was of such perfection that it drew a cry of pleasure from her lips. A pair of delicate, slender hands clasped as though in prayer, resting upon a tiny cushion of ruby velvet with tassels on each corner. Against the rich red material the hands looked very white and fragile. The long fingers, with nails almond-shaped, were entwined, upraised, suggesting intense supplication. *They were her hands*. Fleur's face grew rosy with a sudden radiance that Peveril had never seen before. It made him catch his breath. She looked so young and so startlingly happy.

"Oh!" she exclaimed, "what matchless work!"

"You know whose hands they are?" he said in a low voice.

She laid down the gift and spread her two hands to the fire by which she was sitting. They looked transparent in the light. She answered:

"Yes."

"I remembered every line, and wished to reproduce their beauty. I trust that you are not annoyed."

"Annoyed," she repeated, "but how could I be? It is a charming compliment and the little painting is a gem — like a Dutch masterpiece. With all my heart I thank you for it."

Now Peveril said awkwardly:

"I trust his lordship, also, will like it."

Fleur knew that those formal words were forced but that he had painted her hands for her alone.

"It shall hang in this room," she said.

"Thank you," he said.

Now they held each other's gaze with a look of almost frightening concentration. Each was stirred by the sudden glorious warmth of feeling which ran so positively between them. Neither spoke.

At this juncture Odette knocked on the door and walked in. She tossed her head, her long muslin streamers fluttering as she saw Peveril. She eyed him wickedly out of the corners of her slanting eyes. He did not return the look but hastily took his departure knowing how vile Odette's tongue could be. Knowing too, that Mrs. Dinglefoot from some secret spying place must have seen him steal up here and sent Odette further to spy.

Fleur said nothing. But long after she was alone again with her thoughts and dreams, she studied the exquisite little painting of her folded hands. Then she folded her own flesh and blood fingers in the same anguished entrancing manner that he had reproduced, laid her forehead upon them and wept bitterly for all the joy of life and love that was forbidden her.

She did not see Peveril again for a long time.

A bitter February came — cold, savage weather, holding the Buckinghamshire countryside in its icy grip.

Wrapped from head to foot in rich furs, the lady of Cadlington was taken for a short drive in the sledge which St. Cheviot had imported from Russia and given to her as a present. It was a gay affair, painted in red and white, and drawn by two sturdy ponies with bells on their tossing heads. It amused Cheviot to present his wife to the world as some fabulously rich Russian Princess who might have appeared thus driving from her palace in St. Petersburg. When he had first shewn this equipage, with two groomsmen from his stables, in the new livery, he had said to Fleur:

"This will enable you to go out more often. Horses slip much on these roads. It is a unique gift. I trust you are grateful."

She thanked him in the cold proud but courteous way in which she always acknowledged his extravagant presents.

"It is an amusing idea," she said.

St. Cheviot looked at her gloomily.

"One would not think to look at you that you are amused."

She turned her face away. She could never look upon him as a friend, a kindly husband, but only as the man who had slain her youth.

In this, the fifth month of her pregnancy, much of the original nausea had passed. She would have felt quite well but for her deep depression, the perpetual hunger of her heart. The worst thing of all was her dread of the future, when she knew she must share St. Cheviot's bed and board again.

However, he did not nag at her nowadays, but tried in his selfish fashion to be conciliatory. On this February morning he himself took her for a drive in the gay sledge and was pleased when the villagers turned out to wave and cheer as they passed by. They called: "*God bless you, my lord.*" "*God bless you, my lady.*"

Fleur looked sadly at some of these people who were her husband's tenants. Their threadbare garments and cadaverous faces — their sickly infants — saddened her. How gladly she would have thrown them all the jewels that weighed down her throat and her hands. She wanted to visit their dwellings, to act the lady-bountiful. But St. Cheviot had forbidden her to go near any of the cottages on his vast estate in case she caught a fever. He had a dread of contagion.

During that drive in the sledge they met Peveril walking alone with Alpha, the wolfhound, padding behind. St. Cheviot bade the sledge driver (whom he had fitted up in character, in bearskins) to pull up the sledge for a moment. He called to the boy:

"Is it not time you put the final stroke to the portrait of that Rustingthorpe child — you have been far too long over it. Do you grow lazy, my young friend?"

The young painter doffed his cap. He allowed his gaze to linger for a single pulsating moment on the beautiful girl who sat with lashes downcast — silent, motionless in her sable wraps. He said:

"The portrait was finished this morning, my lord. I am on my way now across the fields to Rustingthorpe. The Marchioness has sent for me."

St. Cheviot puffed at a cigar which he had just lighted. He pulled the fur rug closer over his knees. A few snow flakes were drifting down from the grey sky and it was very cold and raw. He said.

"The old woman seems satisfied with what you have done. She is a lewd old

harridan and likes a handsome lad . . . "
He laughed coarsely. "She wishes you to
make other studies of her family to which
I have given my consent."

Avoiding Fleur's gaze, Peveril said:

"If your lordship would grant me the
time, I wish greatly to converse with
him about taking a final leave from
Cadlington."

Fleur felt a knife go through her heart.
She opened her great sad eyes. But her
face remained expressionless. Yet she
could not restrain the relief that seized
her when St. Cheviot, himself, thwarted
Peveril's desire for independence.

"Rubbish," he snapped, "why show
such longing to leave Cadlington, ungrateful
fool? Stay where you are until my friends,
who are also your patrons, want no more
of you."

Then without waiting for the young
artist to answer, he ordered the driver to
whip up the ponies and go ahead. Peveril
stood still, watching the sledge slip over
the narrow glassy road till it was out of
sight. The bells on the ponies jingled
faintly through the frosty air. The bleak
wind cut the boy's sensitive face. He put

his cap back on his head, shivered under his cape, and went his way uneasily. The desire to be near *her* was growing too strong. He had seen her sometimes from afar — watched the slenderness of her waist thicken. He knew, indeed, that she was heavy with St. Cheviot's child. But he adored her. Night and day he craved to lift some of the burden of sorrow from her young shoulders. Night and day, his hatred of the tyrannical Baron intensified. But he decided that he would accept St. Cheviot's despotic orders to remain at Cadlington until he knew that the birth of the heir was safely over. Far too often he had heard whispered gossip among the staff that her ladyship was delicate and might not survive. The idea appalled him.

February passed. The snows melted and ran in muddy streams down Cadlington hill, and Fleur was still to be seen moving about her garden, or out driving in the phaeton. Her spectacular Russian sledge could no longer now be used.

Peveril lingered at Rustingthorpe — working on a new portrait. But sometimes in the evening, after the Marchioness's carriage (graciously lent for the occasion) brought him back to Cadlington House — he saw Fleur. They would wave to each other. If they passed in the gardens, then they would pause to converse — but only for a moment. My lady was sensitive to her increasing size and too much the victim of conscience. For she knew now, that she loved Peveril with all the tenderness of her woman's heart and her sad despoiled youth. Just now passion could have no part in her life, and because she was a deeply moral being nothing would have induced her to forsake the dignity of her present position as St. Cheviot's wife.

Then later when the savage winds of March shook the great house and kept the young mother-to-be huddled before her fires, her mental and physical sufferings increased. Sometimes St. Cheviot stayed with her, but he seemed always ill-at-ease now in her company. He was, however, exceedingly careful of her health, continually giving orders and countermanding them. She must not do this, she should do that. He had heard that a prospective mother should drink special milk, and eat rare food. He sent for new cows from Jersey. He ordered delicacies from the London stores — even from Paris. Fleur was surrounded with his gifts — suffocated by them — wearied by his incessant hectoring. He even badgered her to smile.

"You must be gay or the babe will be born as melancholy and as sickly a being as yourself," he flung at her one evening when he was spending a few days at Cadlington. He quite enjoyed the spring weather now. A fair April had drifted into a warm sweet May. The forest was green and the sun shone often over hills and valleys. "Do you not find some humour in these new books I brought you?" he added irritably. "I am told they are amusing."

She looked at him with her grave eyes and fingered the novels he had chosen.

But she was obedience itself. She said: "I will try to smile, Denzil. It is not easy if you do not feel in good humour. But I beg you to cease troubling yourself over my health. It is very good at the moment and Dr. Boss tells me that we have nothing to fear."

"He will get a bullet through his throat if he isn't right," muttered Denzil.

She looked at him with scorn in her clear eyes. How violent he was in his loves and his hates!

It was on this particular evening that he mentioned Peveril's painting of her hands.

"Our young genius grows impudent. He did not ask my permission to present you with this. How came he to portray your hands so faithfully? Have you been posing for him — have you dared — "

"He remembered them from the big portrait. He thought that in giving me the little painting it would be a gesture of gratitude — towards us both," she added.

"I do not care for it," said St. Cheviot, "a pair of hands — what a dull subject!"

"Perhaps they suggest the act of prayer in which you are distinterested," she said with unusual sarcasm.

He frowned at her. She lay on a couch by the fire in one of the smaller drawing-rooms which they used when they were alone. A Cashmere shawl was thrown over her. She looked, he thought, less sickly than usual. She was damned handsome. It was a never-ending irritation to him that he could not entirely break this young girl's spirit.

"Ah, well, if you like religion proceed with it, Lady St. Cheviot. You are too saintly for me. But no doubt your saintliness will make you a fond mother."

She did not answer. 'Fond mother,' alas she thought bitterly. Far advanced in pregnancy though she was, she could not yet feel one grain of longing for St. Cheviot's child. Poor little unwanted thing! Of a certainty she would be good to it, and no doubt grow in time to love it. She had but one more month to wait, then it would be all over. She had ceased to yearn for death because she believed it to be wicked, for if the infant lived and she died, who then would mother it?

St. Cheviot began to walk restlessly up and down the room.

"This is the 28th May," he said. "Boss said that the child should be born ere another month is over. It is as well, for

I hope to be in London for the Queen's Coronation."

Fleur showed a modicum of interest in what he said. She was always entertained by stories of the young Queen Victoria. She listened while St. Cheviot began to discuss the Coronation. It would, he said, be one of the most colourful and brilliant affairs in the history of the nation. Already the Duke of Dalmatia, Ambassador Extraordinary from France, was at the Embassy. All the crowned heads in Europe would follow. There were to be fêtes and banquets more splendid than the metropolis had ever known.

"They say," added St. Cheviot, "that the expense of this affair will be in the nature of £70,000. I myself am having a new fine suit made for the occasion."

And he described at length the French brocade chosen for his waistcoat; as he smoked, and sipped his after-dinner brandy. Just for a moment it was as though they were a happily married couple, Fleur thought sadly. St. Cheviot was quite genial. But only for a moment. Then he tired of her and took his leave.

He had invited Sir Edmund Follyatt, one of his few friends in the district, to sup with him and play cards.

He picked up one of Fleur's hands and pressed his lips against it. Immediately he felt the shrinking of her flesh, so he flung the hand down again and laughed.

"Very well, my dear, if you prefer it — twine your fingers in prayer. I do not care. Good night. Do not forget your hot milk. I will send Odette to you."

She nodded.

St. Cheviot added:

"By the way, I have had a talk with Mrs. D. She greatly resents the fact that you will not receive her, and it is my wish that once our child is born, you alter you behaviour towards my good Mrs. D."

"Oh, Denzil," said Fleur suddenly, "could you not find me another house-keeper? I cannot tell you what disgust Mrs. Dinglefoot inspires in me."

"We have already had this argument," he said coldly.

She looked up at him with her soft lovely eyes.

"You give me so much that I do not

want, would you not do this little thing for me?"

He hesitated. It was the first time his young wife had ever made so direct or intimate an appeal to him. The old violent passion stirred in him. Turning he flung himself by the couch, put his hot face against her neck and feverishly kissed one of her long silken curls.

"I will do anything — *anything* once you are well again. I will even turn poor Mrs. Dinglefoot from Cadlington — only swear to love me," he breathed.

But she shuddered away from that embrace. The very infant seemed to move in protest. She felt sick with her old fear and disgust. Always she must see him as he had been that night at The Little Bastille, satanic in his merciless passion.

"Leave me alone," she panted, "go away. Go back to your mistresses."

He stood up, brushed his sleeve and gave an ugly laugh.

"As is customary, your virtue freezes me. But I apologize, my dear. This is not the time for advances. If our young genius in the tower were a sculptor, I would suggest he fashioned you out of marble."

"So that you could take a hammer and smash the statue?" she asked him, and flung back her long throat and looked up at him. He avoided the scorn in those huge eyes and marched to the door.

"Good night," he said.

After he had gone the proud head drooped. Fleur could be brave in his brutal presence but not once she was alone. Her thoughts moved irresistibly towards the magnet of that high tower — so near yet so far from her. It was long now since she had spoken a bare word of greeting to the 'young genius' whom St. Cheviot mocked, yet in whom he took such a possessive pride.

"Ah, Peveril, dear, dear Peveril," she whispered.

The child leaped again. Fleur sighed, placed her incomparable hands upon her stomach and began to weep bitterly.

7

IN the last two weeks before St. Cheviot's child was born, such a summer settled over Cadlington as no one living in the district could remember. The keen winds that blew so incessantly across the Chiltern Hills died down. There was a lushness in the meadows; a stillness over the dreaming woods; a warmth in the high-walled gardens around Cadlington House almost tropical in its languor. So long and hot were the days that even the birds seemed to grow dumb and to cease their singing as they dozed on the leafy branches. The herbaceous flowers in the great borders shot up too rapidly in the sun. The rose petals were scattered by the heat before twilight, despite the efforts of a small army of gardeners to keep the place watered. Many plants perished. Only the orchids that Fleur hated, flourished and grew more fat and wicked-looking. The great lawns changed their velvet green for the hue of burnt-gold. The servants grumbled at the heat. The windows of the big house were opened wide; doors, too, so that a draught could blow through the corridors.

St. Cheviot no longer drove to London because Dr. Boss had warned him that any day now the child might be born. So, for the time being, he abandoned his haunts in Piccadilly and his new mistress. Bored, yawning, he stayed at Cadlington and slept or drank away most of the golden summer hours. He saw little of his wife but had installed two midwives recommended by the doctor. Fleur was never left alone for a single moment now. Always she was under the watchful eye of the trained women. The Baron did not intend that anything should go wrong with his lady's confinement.

A few months ago when Fleur had asked if her old friend, Catherine Quinley, could stay here, Denzil had acceded to her request, thinking that the visit might be good for her spirits. But fate did not allow her even that small pleasure for Catherine was laid low with the smallpox a few days before she was due to take the journey.

Now with the birth of her infant imminent Fleur was very much alone in spirit. The constant presence of midwives and servants tormented her. She was irked by the mere knowledge that St. Cheviot, too, was hanging around the house . . . waiting . . . ready to spring upon her like a tiger in case she should do something to annoy him . . . something that he did not deem good for the child. It was always of the child he thought. Never of her.

She no longer went downstairs but stayed up in her bedchamber or boudoir. Just a little longer she could enjoy her romantic fairy-tale bedchamber — knowing that once the birth was over, St. Cheviot meant to destroy Peveril's creation.

"Queer in the head, I'd call her," Mrs. Dinglefoot snorted one evening while the servants were eating supper — they were all gasping in the heat which drifted from the kitchen. "Maybe the infant will be half-witted. My late mistress would turn in her grave."

As usual Peveril was forced to listen to this kind of talk, though he finished his meal as quickly as possible and went back to his solitary tower to continue painting until the light faded.

Upon this occasion, he made one of his rare protests. Fixing the malicious housekeeper with his clear candid gaze, he said:

"No one who has spoken with her ladyship would call her 'queer'. She is reserved but has many talents."

Mrs. D. fanned herself, and with the back of one red hand, wiped the sweat from her forehead. She looked particularly repulsive in this heat. She said:

"Ah ha! Listen to our young artist. Always a champion for my lady."

Odette, who still cherished a secret passion for the handsome painter, leaned near him and nudged his arm.

"You are wasting your time, Mr. Peveril. *La la*! If *Monsieur le Baron* thought that you held my lady in such high regard he would shoot you through the throat like this — " She pointed a fork at Peveril and clicked her teeth.

Mrs. Dinglefoot snorted. Ivor had loosened his cravat and was fanning himself but his sharp eyes cast a side glance at Peveril. He was bitterly jealous of Peveril and had been since the first day that Peveril had come here to live. He was equally jealous of the beautiful young bride who took up so much of his lordship's time and attention. Like Mrs. Dinglefoot, he greatly preferred the old days at Cadlington and the excitement of the wild parties that the young bachelor used to hold. He said in his sing-song Welsh voice:

"And it is swollen-headed our Master Painter is getting — painting all the Quality in this district."

"I am not swollen-headed," said Peveril quietly.

"But you have ideas above your station, Master Peveril," put in Mrs. Dinglefoot folding her arms over her enormous bosom and eyeing him sourly. "Creeping up to her ladyship's bedchamber when his lordship was away. Don't forget that we know about it."

Peveril sprang to his feet.

"You are vile and unspeakable," he said.

Odette caught at the boy's fingers and

tried to pull him back beside her.

"*Tiens, tiens,* sit down and eat your pudding, *chéri.* They only tease you," she said.

He wrenched the hand away. He was quivering with an indignation which was for Fleur — not for himself. The valet cocked an eyebrow.

"Better take care. Let it be known to his lordship that you have such a fancy for my lady and he will not take kindly to it."

"Do not interfere in matters about which you are totally ignorant," said Peveril passionately.

The Welshman's eyes slitted.

"Beware also of my ill-humour. I am not a good enemy but I can shoot as straight as his lordship. In fencing, also, I am an expert. Might one ask, *Sir Peveril,* if *you* could fight a duel?"

"I am no swordsman and I have no wish for fighting. I am a painter," said the boy.

"Or a coward?" suggested the Welshman softly.

Silence. The other servants ceased their noisy chatter and set down tankards, knives and forks with a clatter. A meagre-sized pantry boy wiped his greasy hands on his apron and came forward to listen. Everybody was agog to see what line the young painter would take after Mr. Ivor's open insult.

There was only one line that Peveril wished to take. Delicately made, totally unfit for physical violence, nevertheless Peveril Marsh was not going to be called coward by any man. He sprang at the Welshman. The next moment Peveril found himself down on the floor and Ivor's thin steely fingers were at his throat, his thumbs pressing cruelly into the flesh. None of the other men dare interfere. The Welshman was too much in his lordship's favour. If ever a chef, or footman had dared to cross the Welshman, he regretted it. But Odette screamed and pulled at Ivor's arm.

"Leave him alone — *mon Dieu!* — you will kill him. He is no match for you."

"Let them fight," said Mrs. Dinglefoot, her eyes blinking with pleasure as she saw the young painter's frantic efforts to extricate himself from those merciless thumbs.

Then suddenly the doors of the servants' hall were flung open. One of the midwives, a stout rosy-cheeked little body, her cap awry, ran in waving bare dimpled arms at the housekeeper.

"Mrs. D.! Mrs. D.! Hot water and plenty of it, pray. *Her ladyship is in labour.*"

At once an excited clangour of voices broke the silence. All the servants, including the housekeeper, stood up. So the Great Moment for which the whole household had been waiting had come. It saved Peveril. The unfortunate boy had almost lost consciousness. Ivor released his grip. This was no time for delivering punishment to the young painter. He prodded Peveril gently with the toe of his shoe.

"See, my fine gentleman — I am your victor. Next time I shall squeeze the life out of you."

Peveril stood up, swaying on his feet, one hand at his bruised throat. He was scarlet with mortification. This night, the gentle painter had become a man who wished to God he had learned to fight and could give Ivor as good a punishment as he meted out.

The infatuated Odette put an arm around the boy, steadied him, and held a glass of wine to his lips.

"Foolish one to have roused the Welshman's temper," she whispered. "*Zut alors*! You show too openly that you are her ladyship's admirer."

Peveril drank the wine. Ivor had disappeared. The staff were scampering in all directions.

"What has happened?" Peveril muttered.

Odette informed him.

"Her ladyship is in labour. I, too, must go, I shall be wanted. Come — Peveril, do not waste your time on a fine lady who will soon be closeted with her nurses and physicians and later with a new-born babe. A fine boy like you needs a fine girl for kissing . . ." She giggled and sidled close to him. "I'll steal over to the tower and visit you tonight. Folks will be too busy to see which way I go."

"Thanks, but I do not want you in my tower," said Peveril shortly, and he walked through the hall conscious of

293

nothing but a tearing blinding anxiety.

She was in labour. Oh, God, what an atrocious thought! From that sweet body which he worshipped with the same homage that he adored her mind and her soul, tonight or tomorrow there must come forth St. Cheviot's child. She would suffer. The young man was ignorant about these matters, but imaginative. He could not bear to dwell on the details. Burning as one in a fever, he escaped from Odette and ran up the circular staircase to his studio. Kneeling down by the open turret windows, he began to send wild prayers up towards the stars that glittered over Cadlington.

"God in heaven, do not let her die this night."

From every window of the great house lights were glowing. Since the midwives had informed him that her ladyship was about to be confined, St. Cheviot had been in the throes of mingled delight and apprehension. Delight because he could thank God (or the devil) that the long waiting was over. But his apprehensions were sinister. Fleur might die in labour and the child with her. Or it might be deformed.

He marched up and down, through the long galleries, the corridors and the big drawing-rooms, pausing only to shout for more wine and drink it. He told himself that if Fleur did not bear him a fine son he would make her suffer for it. He would drown the two midwives in the pond at the bottom of the garden. He was filled with crazy murderous thoughts, his brain inflamed by much wine. Then he would start thinking of the handsome boy who might be born tonight; how he, Denzil, would repent his evil ways and become a good father and better husband. He would even give money to the Church and attend to religion. He would turn into a leader of respectable society — have done with his Hungarian mistress, his dicing, his secret sins. He would make Peveril paint the new-born child.

Dr. Boss told him that the thing was taking its normal course but that her ladyship was very narrow and it would be a difficult birth; to which both the midwives agreed.

The doctor then looked a trifle awkwardly at his lordship and added:

"It is customary, Lord St. Cheviot, to ask the husband if things go badly and a choice must be made between the life of the mother or the child, which am I to save?"

Without hesitation, St. Cheviot answered:

"The child. I can always find another wife."

The old doctor recoiled, deeming this a savage reply. But he bowed and went back to his patient. Coatless, sleeves rolled up, he waited in the boudoir for the midwives to inform him that the birth was advancing and that his help was needed.

When he had last seen Lady St. Cheviot, the old man was filled with unspeakable pity. She was as white as the cambric nightgown in which the old women had dressed her. The shining hair was bundled up into a white cap. Already she was enduring those sharp rhythmic pains which succeeded one upon another with remorseless regularity. One midwife exhorted her to pull at a rope which she had tied on the bed post; the other bathed her temples with perfume and vinegar. Fleur made no sound. That was what distressed old Boss who had delivered many a shrieking lady in the district. Fleur, her face contorted, bit on her lips and stayed silent save for that low moaning in her throat.

"Why do you not call out, my dear?" Dr. Boss had asked her gently. "It would greatly relieve your feelings."

She opened her large eyes, purple, wild now with pain. The sweat poured down her cheeks. She answered:

"I do not care for his lordship to hear me cry. The pain is severe but less terrible than all the agony I have lately suffered in my mind."

Those low words, for him alone, made the old doctor draw back in shocked silence. St. Cheviot was a devil, he knew. The old man could do nothing to comfort Lady St. Cheviot.

"His lordship will be delighted once you give him his son," he said hopefully.

Fleur made no answer. She battled dumbly with her travail.

That was the beginning. But the night

merged into the dawn and the labour continued.

Every now and again St. Cheviot stalked up and knocked upon my lady's door and asked for news. When Fleur heard his voice, she shuddered and bade the women in attendance upon her keep him out at all costs.

By three o'clock Cadlington was hushed, though few slept. Still the babe had not been born. Dr. Boss was anxious. Her ladyship was more exhausted than any of them and her pulse was feeble. It seemed that the child would never come, for all her brave efforts to bring it forth.

Now such hideous suffering engulfed the young mother-to-be that she prayed to die.

She implored the old doctor to give her chloroform.

"I cannot endure much more," she gasped.

He shook his head, muttered to himself and kept a finger on her fluttering pulse. He was sorely tempted to give my lady a drug to ease her pain but dared not in case it harmed the infant. The Baron was in such a state of nerves and ill-temper that the old doctor was afraid of his own life. He would not put it past his lordship to do some violence this night, if things went badly.

Downstairs in the great hall, Denzil marched up and down, his clothes disordered, his shirt stained with wine and his eyes wild and inflamed.

Alpha, the wolfhound, padded after him. Once in a fury, he lashed out at her with his foot and she cowered away, bitch-like, submissive.

Into St. Cheviot's drink-inflamed mind came one of his crazy notions. He sent a footman to the tower.

"Bring Master Marsh to me. Bid him come immediately."

8

PEVERIL presented himself to his lordship, feeling taut and nervous. St. Cheviot tried to force wine on him.

"Drink with me, you white-livered young fool," St. Cheviot snapped, fixing the boy with his falcon eyes. "Painter or not, you are still a man, are you not?"

"Must one then drink in order to be a man?" the boy asked quietly.

"Yes, and get drunk, too," said Denzil, and added coarsely: "and tumble a pretty female in your bed."

Peveril said nothing. He stood silent, feeling a profound repugnance against this animal-like person. How could he act thus with that sweet saint upstairs struggling for her life? The boy's grey eyes lifted to the musicians' gallery, beyond which lay her ladyship's apartments. Denzil followed the boy's gaze and gave another harsh laugh.

"You, too, wait for news, eh? Well,

none is forthcoming, so you can settle down to drinking and I will teach you to play a game of cards. According to Boss, it may be hours yet before the child is born."

"I grieve to hear that the waiting is so prolonged," said Peveril in a low and scarcely steady voice. How much more could Fleur St. Cheviot endure, he wondered.

"Sit down, sit down and do not annoy me," muttered St. Cheviot, and flung a pack of cards on to the table beside which they were standing. "Here, cut — let us see if I have any luck?"

Peveril sweated. With all his heart he wished to escape from this *tête-à-tête* with the Baron.

St. Cheviot goaded the boy into drawing a card. He would not be satisfied, either, until Peveril had drunk a measure of wine. For the first few moments the boy was the winner. When finally he drew the Ace of hearts against St. Cheviot's King, the Baron tossed the whole pack on to the floor and laughed scornfully.

"So! Beginner's luck! You should take

to gambling, my young friend. You seem fortunate."

"I would not consider it good fortune to win money in this fashion," said Peveril quietly.

"Bah! You painters — with your mamby-pamby fancies — what then would you consider good fortune?"

"To paint a great masterpiece."

"So you have said before. But you have painted many masterpieces, have you not, my little genius?"

"There can be but one in an artist's lifetime."

"Then it shall be the portrait that you paint of my son. Yes, I have decided that as soon as he draws breath, you shall paint a great portrait of the new St. Cheviot," said his lordship. He spilled more wine on the frilled front of his fine lawn shirt. He had divested himself of his jacket. The heat did not seem to mitigate with the dawn.

Peveril kept silence. He felt sick and bewildered. He only knew that the last thing he wanted in the world was to look upon the newly-born baby even though it was partially hers; neither did he wish to add a single portrait more to the gallery of St. Cheviots. He knew now that they were a bad race and that this one was the worst of them all.

St. Cheviot walked unsteadily to the windows and flung back the curtains.

"Ah!" he muttered. "As I thought — this appalling sultriness heralds a storm — look yonder!"

Peveril went to his side. Together these two men who made such an incongruous pair — the great broad-shouldered Baron and the slender boy — gazed upon an awe-inspiring sight. It was five o'clock. The stars had faded. The paling moon was obscured by clouds. Dark monstrous clouds rolling up from the valley. A great storm was approaching Whiteleaf. Even while they watched, there came a low growl of thunder and the first streak of lightning tore a livid jagged fork across the sky.

Peveril stood in silent appreciation of the magnificence, but when the first rain drops spattered down, St. Cheviot gave a drunken laugh and wheeled around.

"So — my son and heir comes in on a clarion note; born in a storm like his father! Yes — old Dinglefoot remembers if none else — that I made my entry into Cadlington while a thunder storm was in progress. She told me that my mother screeched because she feared lightning — and as her lungs gave out that note — I, her son, joined with her, uttering my first cry."

Peveril shuddered, A nausea seized him. Perhaps it was the wine, or perhaps the abominable thought of St. Cheviot's birth. Once more Peveril was filled with wild and feverish imaginings of what went on upstairs. No cry would come from *her*; he knew that . . . not though she died.

"God be merciful to her ladyship," the words were torn from Peveril's lips.

St. Cheviot laughed, staggered to the foot of the staircase, and called out:

"Are you there, Boss, my good old fellow? Have you no news?"

Thunder crackled over Cadlington. The hall was illuminated by sudden blinding lightning. Down came the rain; in torrents now. At least it would cool the air, thought Peveril. Already the temperature was dropping. With the back of his hand, he wiped his damp forehead and sighed.

Suddenly there appeared at the head of the staircase the figure of the white-bearded doctor. He looked ghastly pale. But St. Cheviot leapt up the stairs, two at a time, and seized him by the shoulders.

"The birth is over? I have a son?"

Dr. Boss trembled. The old man was not a coward and he had been through many terrible moments in his career. He had seen birth and death in its ugliest aspects, but this night would be one that would live in his memory, for ever.

He stuttered:

"Your lordship . . . St. Cheviot . . . the news is bad . . . "

Peveril caught those words and his muscles tautened. The colour forsook his tired face. He heard the Baron shouting.

"You mean the child is dead?"

"Alas, *yes*, my lord."

"Dead!" repeated St. Cheviot furiously. "Ten thousand devils! I knew that my lady would never bear a living child. The poor imbecile!"

Peveril Marsh hearing those brutal

words was roused to such shocked resentment that he gave tongue to his feelings.

"Great God, my lord, but what of *her*?" he exclaimed.

St. Cheviot did not answer. The old doctor intervened.

"Lady St. Cheviot lives, but only just. She is very weak, your lordship. The child was ill placed and has almost cost her her life."

"What was the sex?" demanded St. Cheviot.

"It was a son," said the doctor in a low voice.

"That makes it worse. You old fool, could you not have saved it?" St. Cheviot said savagely, and raised a fist as though to strike the physician in the face.

Boss looked fearfully into the enraged face of the Baron.

"The infant never breathed," he stuttered. "There was naught I could do, *and it is as well*," he added to himself.

St. Cheviot did not hear the last words. He said:

"So I am the father of a dead son. This is fine news. A fine end to my hopes."

306

"Have you no thought for your lady?" asked the old man timidly.

"It was a mistake that I ever married such a weakling," said Denzil.

Peveril put his hands to his ears as though to blot out the sounds of the Baron's voice.

"My lord!" Boss uttered the protest.

"Well — how is she? How is she?" asked St. Cheviot impatiently. "I suggest Dr. Boss, sir, that you apply all your medical skill to ensure that my lady will bear other, healthier children to me."

"She will never bear another child," said Boss sombrely.

"Never another? What do you mean?"

"What must be said, though I deplore it. This is the first and last child that Lady St. Cheviot will bring into the world."

"She is dying, then?"

"No. You mistake me. She will live, but motherhood is not for her in the future. All hopes of that are over." And once more the old man muttered the words, "*It is as well.*"

St. Cheviot let out a roar of rage.

"Then she is utterly useless to me,

and the hunchback was wrong, for she promised there would be another black Baron of Cadlington."

Peveril heard this allusion to his sister's prophecy. His whole body had flamed with a secret and forbidden joy when he heard the doctor announce that Fleur would never bear another child. Thanks be unto God, thought Peveril, that there would never be born of her flesh, another vile St. Cheviot.

St. Cheviot was beginning to sober up. His first violent rage was cooling. But he was sick with disappointment. He tried to pass by the doctor.

"I wish to look on the dead body of my son."

Then the older man, visibly shaking, stayed him.

"Do not do so, Lord St. Cheviot, I pray you."

"Why not?"

"It would — only distress you," muttered the doctor.

St. Cheviot hesitated, then shrugged his shoulders.

"Very well. Tell Lady St. Cheviot that I am thankful that she is spared to me and that I will see her after I have rested," and he lurched past the doctor, down the corridor and into his own apartment.

The old doctor walked slowly, descended the stairs pulling down his cuffs. He looked with red-rimmed eyes at the young man in the hall.

"This is a sorry night," he said wearily.

"Indeed, yes," agreed Peveril with a deep sigh. "How is she, sir?"

"Weak but not critically ill. She bore her travail with amazing fortitude. Truly, in these moments the most frail woman seems to possess the courage of a lion."

"She, in particular, is courageous," said the young painter in a moved voice.

The doctor peered at him.

"You are the artist who has executed some exceedingly fine portraits in recent months."

"I am Peveril Marsh — yes, sir."

"Then if you live here you must see and hear much of what goes on at Cadlington?"

"Too much," said Peveril in a low voice.

"God grant that worse is not to come,"

muttered the doctor.

"What do you mean?" asked Peveril, startled.

"I must hold my tongue," said the old man, "and I can but pray that those two good women who assisted me will hold theirs."

"You speak mysteriously," said Peveril.

"What I know, I wish that I did not know," said Dr. Boss.

Before Peveril could speak again, Cadlington House resounded with a crash that was not of thunder but of a slamming door. There came the sound of St. Cheviot's voice echoing through the lofty corridors. The doctor turned pale. He avoided Peveril's startled gaze and muttered:

"Great heavens, I believe he knows — *one of those women has talked.*"

"What is it — ?" began Peveril.

Now the figure of the Baron appeared. He wore a striped silken bed-robe, and a night cap on his head. His eyes were black slits. Uncomprehending, the young painter watched this malignant figure come slowly down the stairs. When the Baron reached the bottom of the

310

staircase, he fixed the old doctor with a menacing gaze.

"So," he said softly, "*do not go and see the child because it would distress you*! Yes, yes, my good Boss, now I can well understand your concern for my feelings."

The old man licked his lips.

"I tried only to spare you, my lord St. Cheviot."

"You tried to deceive me, you old liar," snarled St. Cheviot. "You would have let me think that my lady had given birth to a normal still-born son."

"Who has said that he was not normal?" asked the old doctor, playing for time.

"My good friend and counsellor — my one and only loyal servant — Mrs. Dinglefoot. One of the midwives whom you tried to bribe, told her the truth, and my good Mrs. D. deemed it in my interest to enlighten me."

"The child was no monster. It was beautifully formed, and with the violet eyes of her ladyship."

"And it was *black*!" Now St. Cheviot's voice rose and he thundered the words "*black as ebony from top to toe.* Mrs. Dinglefoot saw it. *Black as the child of a full-blooded negro, even though he had the features of my lady.* I know all now, so do not try to dissemble. *Beware of a black St. Cheviot,* eh?" He swung round to Peveril, drawing his lips back from his teeth. "Now I see that your sister's prophecy held a deeper significance than I understood. We are known as the Black Barons, but this misbegotten infant to which my lady gave birth has *coloured blood in it*. I have been inveigled into marriage with a female who has black blood in her veins. Ten thousand devils!" he added, his face contorted and fearful to see, "if that child had lived, I would have stained my soul with a double crime for I would have murdered both the child *and* its mother."

Peveril and the doctor recoiled. St. Cheviot continued:

"Is it not true that this is a throw-back? That if the history of the Roddneys were unfolded, I should find that somewhere a Roddney has sprung from Africa?"

"It could be so, your lordship," said Boss, trembling.

"Very well. Do you dare suggest that the *faux pas* can be laid at the door of a St. Cheviot?" thundered Denzil. "No — *you* know that that cannot be so, for my line is pure and unbroken. It is the breeding of her ladyship which is at question, and it shall be examined." He added more to himself than the other: "Mrs. de Vere shall pay for this. I shall see her tomorrow. I shall leave no stone unturned in order to discover the full facts."

The doctor dared to lay a hand on the arm of the enraged Baron.

"Pray, Lord St. Cheviot, listen to an old man who has known you and your parents from birth. I deplore this terrible thing. It is not your fault, nor that of the hapless young mother. She lies in her room, semi-conscious and unknowing of the tragedy. Treat her gently, and with mercy, I implore you."

"If I find that her family was aware of the strain that she brought to her marriage, she shall receive no mercy from me," said St. Cheviot in a blood-curdling voice.

Then Peveril Marsh, who had been

an unwilling yet fascinated listener, was stung to speech:

"Good God, it cannot be my lady's fault. She is as innocent and pure as the driven snow."

St. Cheviot did not so much as look at the boy.

Peveril turned and walked across the hall and out of the house. The horror of the whole night had laid a mark on him from which he would never recover. At last, the poet, the dreamer, and the painter had come face to face with knowledge of the terrible things that could happen in the life which he had deemed so beautiful.

He knew nothing of heredity, or of the possibility of a 'throw-back'. But at least he was positive that if such a thing had happened, it could not be any fault of *hers*. She must once more be an innocent victim; and this time victimized in so terrible a fashion, thought Peveril, that the very angels must be weeping for her.

9

AFTER that night of the storm the weather changed. It grew cold for the time of year. Rain swept across the vale and washed hills and forests. The trees dripped around the great house. The sodden flowers were beaten into the muddy earth. The lawns were bogged. Carriage wheels stuck in the ruts on flooded roads; there was little of summer left; the whole place was sunk in incipient gloom.

For Fleur St. Cheviot, too, everything changed. Following that night of fearful pain when she had so nearly died in childbirth, she was flung into a new nightmare of fear — without any understanding of what was going on around her.

She recovered consciousness, asked to see her child, and was told that it had died. St. Cheviot did not come near her. She found that bewildering. She had expected him at least to pay her a

315

courtesy visit. One of the midwives bent over the bed and told her that the Baron had left the house early, before breakfast, taking with him his travelling coach and four servants, including the Welshman.

For a while Fleur was relieved. As for the infant, she thought of it, the tears trickling down her cheeks. She had never wanted it because of its monstrous father. So she gazed up at the midwife — an Irishwoman — and whispered, "*It is better so.*" Even then she was conscious of a peculiar look cross the woman's face, when she repeated those words.

"Yes, my lady, it is better — indeed to goodness it is!"

But they would not let her see the tiny corpse.

For a few days she lay dozing, gaining strength, nursed by the Irish midwife. The other one had gone. Nobody came near Fleur, not even Odette, which surprised her. But on the fifth morning, when she asked for her maid to come and dress her hair, the midwife told her that Odette had returned to France.

This was the first of many astonishing

episodes which Fleur could not fathom. Sometimes she heard carriage wheels; lay listening and imagining that there were callers, come to leave flowers and express their sympathies. Long afterwards she found out that this was so.

She supposed that St. Cheviot must be in a towering rage, because the heir he wanted had not lived. But it seemed abominable that he should be so unkind to her. It was not her fault that the child had died.

Dr. Boss came to assure himself that my lady was being properly looked after. Fleur tried to talk to him, but the old man seemed ill-at-ease and would not meet her eye. Neither did he make more than a vague reply when she asked him for details about the poor little babe.

Timidly she asked about St. Cheviot.

"Perhaps he went to London expressly to attend the Coronation."

But she knew, and Dr. Boss knew, that the Coronation of Queen Victoria had taken place a fortnight ago — on the 28th June. Now it was mid-July.

While her ladyship was recovering from her confinement, the village of

Whiteleaf had taken part in the Coronation celebrations. All over the Buckinghamshire countryside there had been dancing and singing. But the gates of Cadlington remained closed.

Boss had had his orders from the Baron. He was to ensure that her ladyship regained her health, then not to enter Cadlington again.

After the last visit, as he rode home, Dr. Boss met the young painter, Peveril Marsh. He reined in, and spoke to the boy, who looked strained and unhappy, but asked about my lady. The doctor told him that she was recovering.

"I thank God!" said Peveril in a voice of relief. "I have been unable to get news of her from any of the staff."

The old doctor leaned down from his mount and added in a low tone:

"Have you seen his lordship?"

"No — not since he went away. But I fear for Lady St. Cheviot. When he left Cadlington, he looked like the Fiend himself."

The doctor sighed.

"Alas we can do nothing but trust in Almighty God that her ladyship will be spared further misery," he said.

"I have tried to visit her," said Peveril. "They will not allow it. One by one the old servants are leaving. A new and rougher lot have come, and Mrs. Dinglefoot grows more and more difficult — and more powerful," he added sombrely.

"Take my advice, young man, and get out of the place. It has a curse on it," muttered the doctor.

"I shall not leave Cadlington whilst I may be of service to her ladyship," was the reply.

"Take care!" warned the old man.

He did not visit his patient again.

All these things remained unknown to Fleur. Revelation came for her only on the first day that she was allowed to leave her bed.

It was a cool misty morning in July. She had walked into the boudoir which she had not seen since her confinement. She had grown so thin that the velvet negligée which she put on hung on her loosely.

The first thing that struck her startled gaze was the sight of her bureau. It looked as though it had been ransacked. Personal papers and letters scattered on the carpet. Quills broken, ink spilled, seals broken, sealing wax smashed to powder. And what horrified her even more was the sight of the gilt-framed portraits of her mother and father which she had brought from Pillars. These had been ripped across with a knife. The faces were unrecognizable. It looked for all the world as though a lunatic had entered the room and wantonly destroyed everything in it. In particular Fleur was agonized by the desecration of that superb painting of Hélène Roddney in her grey velvet gown.

Fleur felt shocked and bewildered. She managed to pull the bell and summon the midwife who was still in attendance on her. She pointed to the chaos.

"What do you know about this?"

The Irishwoman looked uncomfortable. She knew all — but dared not tell her ladyship. There were in fact many things that the old woman knew and about which she dared not speak. For like Mrs. D., who shared with her the terrible secret of Fleur's child, she had had her lips sealed by dire threats from the Baron. She was, in fact, looking forward to the day when she could get away from this house of horrid tragedy.

She did not answer Fleur.

Fleur put her clasped hands to her fast-beating heart.

"Was it his lordship?" she persisted.

"Do not ask me," said the woman.

"I do not understand. I must go downstairs," said Fleur. "Help me dress."

Then the midwife, nervous, curtseying, stammered:

"Impossible, my lady. Oh, pray, my lady, do not blame me but your doors are locked from the outside."

Fleur stared. Her face had grown very white.

"You mean I am a prisoner in my room, and by his lordship's orders?"

The midwife gulped again.

"Yes, my lady."

"Who holds the key?"

"Mrs. Dinglefoot, my lady."

Fleur drew a breath. She sank wearily on to the edge of her bed. Her knees were shaking. Now she imagined she understood exactly what was going on.

Denzil was mad with fury because she had not borne him a living son. This was his revenge. But why ransack her bureau? *What had he been trying to find?* And why by slashing those poor portraits desecrate the memory of her beloved parents?

"This is too much," Fleur said aloud. "I shall not stay at Cadlington and submit myself to such abomination. Under no circumstances will I remain the prisoner of Mrs. Dinglefoot."

She put out a hand and gripped the midwife by her plump arm.

"Will you take a message for me?" she asked breathlessly. "If I write a note will you keep your counsel and see that Mr. Peveril Marsh receives it?"

"The young painter in the tower, my lady."

"Yes," said Fleur, and two hectic spots burned on her hollow cheeks. "He, I know, will help me. I must secure a carriage. I have been degraded and ill-treated long enough. I must leave this terrible place and seek the protection of my friend, Mrs. Catherine Quinley."

The midwife fell on her knees before

Fleur and burnt into tears.

"My lady, do not ask me to take a letter to the painter or to anybody outside this house. It is more than my life is worth."

"I implore you," Fleur wrung the woman's hand. "Look — I am young and helpless and you can see how I have been treated. Only confined three weeks ago, and my husband has not yet come to utter one word of regret for the loss of our child, nor to enquire after my health! Will you not assist me to escape from such a man?"

After a few moments, the midwife consented. She was not unkind and she was touched by the helplessness of the poor young lady. She, herself, did not understand why his lordship should treat his wife in such a manner, although, of course, there was that dark-skinned infant which must be explained away. (God help the little Baroness, for who else would, the Irishwoman thought, and crossed herself, being a good Catholic.)

Fleur found a piece of broken quill, and enough ink with which to scratch a note to Peveril.

Something is going on which I do not understand and which fills me with fear. You are my only friend here. After dark, I pray you come beneath my window and I will speak with you.

She signed this F. St. C.
But that note was not destined to reach Peveril. The midwife, terrified that she was being watched, carried out her promise to the hapless girl she had nursed. She took the letter up to the studio. Finding no one there, she pinned it to Peveril's pillow and went down again, intending to tell my lady she had done this. But she never saw Fleur again. On her return to the house Mrs. Dinglefoot paid her off and bade her leave. Dr. Boss had said that my lady required no more nursing.

Nobody went near the tower, so for the moment, nobody found the note. Peveril, himself, was in fact at Rustingthorpe. The Marchioness had received an unexpected visit from one of her married daughters, and insisted upon Peveril staying to paint her likeness before she left again. She offered double fees if Peveril would remain. The young painter had grown weary of hanging around Cadlington, knowing that the implacable Mrs. Dinglefoot would not allow him to pay my lady a visit, so he saw no reason why he should not spend a couple of days at the home of his patroness. Each painting upon which he worked meant more pay. And a new desire had come over Peveril. Idealism and artistic fancy had given way to the human need for storing up money. It was almost as though he sensed that he might one day need every golden guinea that he could earn — for *her*.

The tragedy of Fleur's marriage to Lord St. Cheviot was drawing to a swift and terrifying end — of that he was positive.

Meanwhile Mrs. Dinglefoot, supremely triumphant, entered Fleur's apartments and took control of her.

"Pray, ma'am, do not continue ringing your bell for the other servants for they will not come," the housekeeper told Fleur. Her small eyes blinked at the girl malevolently. "I have his lordship's orders to serve you myself."

"I do not wish to be served by you," began Fleur. "Kindly leave my bedchamber, Mrs. Dinglefoot."

But Mrs. D. stood her ground.

"It is foolish of you to order me out, and it would be worse for you if I obeyed, my lady. You would starve — and quickly. For I, alone, shall be bringing you your food in future."

Fleur looked at the woman with a proud attempt at defiance.

"I am Lady St. Cheviot. Do you forget that?"

"No, but first and foremost I remember that I am the humble servant of his dear lordship."

"And do you tell me that it is his wish that I remain locked in these rooms, and that no one comes to clean them and that I am to have my food thrust in here as though in a common jail?"

Mrs. Dinglefoot shrugged her shoulders.

"It is not for me to give you any information, my lady, nor to find reasons for the Baron's orders."

Gathering her strength Fleur spoke again.

"What have I done to deserve this? What crime have I committed that I should be submitted to this outrageous indignity?"

Then Mrs. Dinglefoot gave her an ugly scornful look.

"Better ask his lordship when he returns," she said. "You'll hear — *you'll hear*!"

Cackling with that horrid laughter, she walked out of the room. Fleur heard the key turn in the lock again.

She ran to the window and looked down. The gardens were deserted. The countryside presented a melancholy aspect. So high up was she, that she could not jump from these windows except to dash her brains out on the marble balustrade underneath. A frightful despair engulfed her. Her life seemed to go from bad to worse. At least before her baby was born she had been allowed some dignity here as the Baroness. She had given her orders. She had been free to walk the grounds, to drive into Whiteleaf, to talk to Peveril.

Oh, God, now that she remembered *him*, her one and only friend, her heart was torn with misgivings. Had the midwife delivered that note? Would he come? *Was he still here?* She dared not ask that question of Mrs. Dinglefoot.

For the rest of that day Fleur stayed alone in a state of suspense and puzzled misery. She even began to wish that Denzil would return. She could not endure being left at the housekeeper's mercy.

The food brought up to her now became unappetizing and obviously not cooked as usual by the chef. The wine was watered. A tray was put on her table by Mrs. D. who flung her an ugly look and departed, without a word. No hot water was brought nor any attempt made to clean or tidy my lady's apartments.

Fleur began to wish that she had died with her child. She walked around the room, clutching in her hands the torn faces of her father and mother which she had tried in vain to piece together, like a jigsaw. She wept over them, as a child over a smashed treasure. There was nothing left for her to look at with pleasure but the Raphael, and Peveril's painting of her hands. She feasted her hungry gaze upon these, and waited for darkness to fall. Then she walked to her windows and watched for Peveril. She felt if she did not see him and know that she still had one friend left in the world, she would go mad.

But Peveril did not come. And she did not know the reason why he stayed away. So she thought that even he had deserted her. She no longer wept. She was too bitterly unhappy. Nobody came to light her candles. She sat in the darkness until her body ached for weariness, her mind grew numb with misery and she fell upon her bed. Then at last she slept, wretched and uncomforted.

She awoke at midnight to hear the sound of horses galloping through the grounds, then closer, the scrunch of wheels on the drive. She sat up, listening, her heart pounding. A few moments later her door was unlocked, and St. Cheviot, in sombre travelling attire, carrying a lamp in one hand, walked into her room.

Fleur's heart beat fast. She sat up, reached for a little shawl and folded it modestly over her breast. She looked like a sleepy lovely child but as the man approached her bed and set the oil lamp down upon the table, not one spark of tenderness lit the satanic darkness of his mind and purpose.

"Ah! I find you awake, my love," he said in a pleasant tone. "I bid you good evening."

For a few seconds she was deceived by this tone and the smile which made him look devilishly handsome. She had been so lonely, so unhappy, her starved heart went out even to *him*, the cause of her downfall and oppression.

"Oh, I am glad that you are back, Denzil," she began. But she got no further, for although the smile lingered on his lips, now that she had become accustomed to the dim lamp-light, she could see the expression in his eyes. It froze her very marrow. He turned from her, walked to the wall facing her bed, and unhooked Peveril's painting of her hands. He came back to her, and held up the picture.

"Your hands, madam, your beautiful little hands which, when I saw them first, seemed to be those of a high-born lady sprung from excellent stock. I kissed the rosy tips and, on the correct finger, I placed my marriage ring. In the hollow of those hands I placed my hopes. The hopes that my charming wife would bear me a fine new St. Cheviot — ” He paused and drew in his breath with a sucking sound.

Clutching her shawl to her bosom, the young girl looked up into the face of this sinister man whom she called husband, and knew that she need expect neither kindness nor tolerance from him. She was thrust back into the bottomless pit of her despair. But she spoke quietly:

“From my heart I beg your forgiveness, Denzil, that our child died — ”

He interrupted her, using a low but venomous voice.

“If it had not died naturally, my lady, I would have provided the means for its demise.”

She shrank back further against her pillows.

“How can you say such a terrible thing?”

“Firstly,” he said softly and his smile broadened, “I intend to destroy this painting of the charming lily-white hands that Master Marsh would have handed down to posterity. Already his portrait of you lies in ribbons. Mrs. Dinglefoot took much pleasure in burning the pieces. No likeness of the present Lady St. Cheviot shall ever hang in the picture gallery at Cadlington among ladies who were more worthy of their titles. Your portrait must be forgotten — wiped out of memory, *like yourself.*"

These words froze Fleur's blood, but she neither moved nor screamed. She was too paralysed with fear. Her dilated eyes watched while he smashed the little, exquisite painting of her hands; first the frame, then the canvas which he tore from end to end. The rasping sound of the ripped material grated on her every nerve. She shuddered and whitened. Despite herself, a low cry broke from her.

"You are mad — you have destroyed a masterpiece."

"To the devil with that," he said through his teeth. "Now for your bridal chamber, my fine wife. Peveril spent his genius and my money on preparing this nest for you. He made a grave error."

"But what have I done?" Fleur cried. "Is it so desperate a crime to bear a dead child?"

St. Cheviot seized her by both wrists and jerked her out of the bed. He stood her up before him. From his towering height he glared down into her eyes.

"*It is as well it died*," he said savagely.

"You — its father, say so!" she panted.

"Its father, yes — and one who sought to raise fine sons through you. You, the virginal Miss Roddney — the innocent maid, so modest and so fine that she could scarce endure a lover's caresses. It makes me laugh. Do you hear? It makes me *laugh*."

She thought, truly, that he had gone out of his mind. She would have fallen, only his steely fingers held her up, shaking her now and then like a doll until her teeth chattered.

"The infant's skin was black," he said in that low and sinister voice. "*Black*, my dear, do you hear? *It was a negro. My* child — yes, no doubt I fathered your vile spawn. I cannot accuse you of adultery. The child was conceived at The Bastille. It was yours — and mine."

Fleur gasped: "What are you saying? Oh? Monstrous, abominable thing. It is not true?"

He shook her again.

"You married me knowing what blood ran in your veins. Knowing that the taint was there and might well be passed on to your offspring."

She stared up at him with eyes so terrified, that St. Cheviot, crazy with rage though he was, could not pursue this line further. He realized that she did not understand one word of what he said. But her ignorance made him no less violent in his anger against her. He released her, throwing her on to the bed. He added:

"Then if you did not know — I curse the memory of your mother. *Your quadroon mother*, my dear. Do you hear that? Proud beauteous Marquise de Chartellet — later Lady Roddney — was a *quadroon*. Through her, you committed this enormity, and I was nicely fooled into giving you my name."

Fleur could not begin to take in the significance of what he was saying to her. She still thought that he was out

334

of his mind. He began to prowl around her room like a malicious animal seeking what he might kill. He ripped the delicate laces from her bed and her dressing-table; the satins and the bows, all the feminine fripperies that had made it such a charming nest. He trampled on the gleaming, snowy draperies, defiling them with his heavy riding boots.

"Tomorrow they shall burn," he said.

He smashed the ivory brushes and perquisites of her toilette. Unlocking her jewel-cases, he took out the gleaming jewels and thrust them into his pocket. "These," he said, "my family heirlooms, shall never be worn by you again."

Then he took the Raphael painting down from the wall, and studied it a moment, sneering.

"This shall be spared for it is valuable. But it shall no longer hang in here. There is no link between you and any Madonna; nor, they tell me, will you ever bear another child. It is as well, lest it be another throw-back from Africa — abominable evidence of your maternal history. *Now* I understand the hunchback's warning, '*Beware of a black*

St. Cheviot.' Great God — how inspired she was — infernally so. We are the Black Barons — but your son's blackness came from hell itself and scorched my soul!"

The unfortunate girl lay where he had thrown her, her eyes glittering up at him through the tangle of her hair. Her face, her form were damp with sweat. She shuddered convulsively. She kept moaning:

"I do not understand. *I do not understand.*"

When he had completed the thorough destruction of her room, it presented a spectacle of terrifying disorder, and bore no resemblance to that gracious lovely chamber which she had first entered as a bride. Even her clothes were pulled from the cedar-wood closets, and flung into a heap. Henceforward, he added, she would need no fashionable garments. She would need very little, in fact, *for she would never leave this room again.*

For the moment that dire threat passed over Fleur's head. Neither did it trouble her to see her valuables wrecked before her eyes for she had never wanted them. But suddenly the implication of what he was saying about her dead child became too terrible to bear. She sat up and with sudden spirit blazed at him.

"You say that my child was *black*. You call my mother a *quadroon*. These can only be the ravings of a maniac."

Denzil came to the foot of the bed. He flung at her several sheets of paper closely written upon in a small hand.

"Read this. Now, every word of it," he said.

"Denzil, I am ill — " she began.

He thundered, "*Read*, I say, and *then* tell me that I am mad!"

Fleur, who felt her reason tottering, took the papers. Her fingers shook so that she could hardly hold them. She dragged herself nearer the lamp. St. Cheviot stood motionless, a dark vengeful figure, watching her out of his cruel eyes.

She began to read . . .

10

THE document which Fleur devoured that midnight, set the final seal of sorrow on her unhappy young life. A revelation of her dark inheritance — contained in a letter written to the Baron by a firm of London solicitors. They had been approached by his lordship, on the day after the Coronation, when their offices had re-opened. His lordship had demanded that they should trace the history of the Roddneys, late of Pillars in Essex, near Epping Forest.

Dolly de Vere, cousin to Sir Harry, had sworn on her oath that she knew nothing of Hélène's past and neither threats nor bribes could make her revoke that statement. Denzil had to seek elsewhere for his information. It was known that Sir Harry Roddney had married the widow of the French aristocrat, Lucien, Marquis de Chartellet. But the firm of lawyers had their sleuths. By various means, old newspapers and diaries were unearthed. Once, much had been written in fashionable journals about the fabulous Marquise whose wit and beauty had taken London by storm.

Note had been taken of the fact that two of the well-known ladies who attended the first reception given by the de Chartellets were the Lady Henrietta Hamton and the Marchioness of Rustingthorpe. Discreet enquiries were made — first of the Hamtons. It chanced that Lady Hamton's daughter (by her first marriage a Miss Pumphret) had married a young gentleman who was also a client of the very firm dealing with St. Cheviot's affairs.

Mr. Groves, the junior partner, noted for the remarkable fashion in which he unearthed secrets of the past — betook himself to visit this Miss Pumphret who was now a Mrs. Cuthbertson, residing at Kew. She was the elder of two daughters and could remember that her father Lord Pumphret had brought home from Bristol a female quadroon slave whom they called *Fauna*, and who remained for some years in the service of Lady

Henrietta Pumphret.

Mrs. Cuthbertson could, indeed, remember quite a lot that went on in her mother's lifetime — the Balls, the Drawing Rooms, and the quarrels between her parents. In particular, a certain incident which had been described to her gleefully by a maid-servant (recounted in turn by a footman who witnessed it). The cutting of a monster cake by Sir Harry Roddney. Out of this cake had stepped a small girl of incredible beauty with long red-gold hair. She was called Fauna, and was a quadroon slave. She became the talk of society. For although she had black blood in her on her mother's side, her own skin was as white as driven snow. Mrs. Cuthbertson could recall even though it must be over thirty years ago, seeing this little slave girl and hearing people chatter about the splendid blackness of her eyes and the gold-red glory of her hair.

When Fleur reached this part of the document she paused a moment to wonder what this had to do with Hélène Roddney. True, her beautiful mother had been noted for that strange combination of red-gold hair and dark eyes, *but what could be the link between a quadroon slave and Lady Roddney?*

Fleur read on. As she did so, her blood turned to ice in her veins.

Mr. Groves discovered many more things from the one-time Miss Pumphret. He could tell his lordship how Fauna, the slave, had run away from the Pumphrets' house in London never to be seen again *until* the night of the great reception given by the Marquis de Chartellet in order to introduce his new young wife to society.

Miss Pumphret related a further story of how her mother, after being received by *Madame la Marquise,* was brought home in a dying condition. She had had a stroke. But before she closed her eyes she swore to all in her household that *Madame la Marquise and Fauna were one and the same.*

Mr. Groves — a little sceptical about this matter — passed on from Mrs. Cuthbertson to the Marchioness of Rustingthorpe who resided in the same district as his lordship.

From the fat, pock-marked little

Marchioness he heard a similar story. *She* had whispered to him that she was *positive* that *Madame la Marquise* was once the slave. She imagined that Fauna must have found some Gentleman to raise her from her lowly state and later had the singular good fortune to marry de Chartellet. She, Clarissa Rustingthorpe, old though she was, could recall her own vast astonishment at the sight of Hélène de Chartellet. There could be no two such women alive, she said — with those eyes, that hair and those features.

She had not dared to impart this information to St. Cheviot, however, since she had no proof. But Mr. Groves, was not long in finding that proof. He turned supposition into certainty.

He paid a visit to The Little Bastille, which in these days had become derelict. But in one of the dungeons there remained a strong-box bearing the Marquis de Chartellet's name. This Mr. Groves had forced open. Therein he had found papers which he sent on to St. Cheviot. An account written by a man who signed himself Aubrey Birkett — one-time secretary to the Marquis. This separate document (read with such horror by Fleur thirty-four years later) struck the final nail in her coffin. After all, St. Cheviot was no maniac — his accusations had hideous foundation. For Mr. Birkett described in detail a purchase made by his master, the Marquis, at a secret auction in the East End of London — the sale of a young quadroon slave named *Fauna*. Then how she had been taken back to the Marquis's residence, and her name changed to Hélène, and her original identity changed. How during the next few years she was secretly educated by the erudite Marquis who finally married her and helped her to revenge herself upon society. Particularly to revenge herself upon a certain nobleman named Sir Harry Roddney whom she thought to have betrayed her, although this was not a fact. Later, of course, Harry had married her.

All this was set down by the secretary, including a faithful account of the loveliness, the sparkling mentality of the one-time slave who had been so cruelly ill-treated by her purchasers. Now at last, Fleur learned of her ancestry. Of how her mother — then the child, Fauna — had been taken on to a slave ship from the African coast to Bristol. And how her grandfather, a gentle negro of Christian upbringing, had died before reaching his destination.

"He was my *great-grandfather*," Fleur looked up from the papers and whispered the words inaudibly. "So I have an eighth of black blood in me. The dark strain escaped my mother and myself but was handed down to my unfortunate babe."

She knew little about matters of heredity but she knew her Bible; that terrible warning. '*The sins of the father*' it began, and something about 'being handed down to the third and fourth generation'. Her poor darling mother! Even now Fleur could think of her only with tenderness. She was not to blame for her ancestry. But if only she had warned *her* that she should not marry, and why — what a lot of misery she might have been spared! Fleur could only presume that her parents had hoped that as they had been lucky, she, too, might escape the curse.

Oh, shameful, shameful doom! Fleur

reflected. God be praised that the old doctor had promised that she would never bear another babe.

Utterly exhausted by the enormity of the truth which had been unfolded to her this night, Fleur dropped the paper and fell back on her pillows unconscious.

When she opened her eyes again, St. Cheviot had gone. She stared at a scene of utter devastation. July sun poured into the outraged bedchamber and struck cruelly against the eyes of the young girl who must have lain unconscious through the small still hours of the morning. Then beside her bed she saw the overpowering figure of Mrs. Dinglefoot. Her face bore a formidable expression. She set down a tray on which there was bread and milk.

"Come on, my girl, sit up and eat," she said tartly. "No playing the fine lady with me. I'll not bring burnt feathers or vinegar for any of your swoons."

Fleur could hardly struggle into a sitting position. Her whole body ached and she fancied she had some fever.

"Where is his lordship?" she whispered.

"Gone back to London — the poor

gentleman — he could not bear to remain here and breathe the same air with you, who should not call herself by the proud name of St. Cheviot."

"I will not argue with you as to that," said Fleur, "but I wish to know when his lordship intends to return."

"Never," said the housekeeper, and gave her high-pitched laugh as she looked around the ruined room.

"A nice nest — and suitable for the daughter of a slave," she added, and the hairs on her monstrous chins quivered with secret and malicious mirth. "I wish our fine young painter could see his work now. I was aware at the time it was wasting my Lord St. Cheviot's money and that his marriage to you was a calamity."

For a moment Fleur was silent. From the woman's words it was obvious that she knew everything. What respect could she demand now, the poor girl asked herself hopelessly.

'*Oh, my mother, my poor mother, what have you done to me!*' she inwardly cried.

Out of her apron pocket, Mrs. Dinglefoot

produced a letter written in his lordship's flourishing handwriting.

"I was told to give this to you. When you've read it, please to make some order out of this bedlam in here. You will be cleaning it yourself in future. There will be no more maids to wait on you." She walked toward the door.

Fleur called after the housekeeper: "Am I to be kept a prisoner then?"

"Yes, and it's what you deserve."

"Shall I be allowed to see nobody?" asked Fleur faintly.

"Nobody," was the answer.

Fleur struggled with the anguished desire to ask what had happened to Peveril. *She dared not mention his name* in case he should be implicated — and the terrible man who was her husband would also visit his wrath upon the innocent youth who had been her friend.

She had not seen or heard of Peveril for so long now that she could only suppose he had left Cadlington. So, she thought, she was deserted by all, at the mercy of Mrs. Dinglefoot.

Once the key turned in the lock she read what St. Cheviot had written. It was a cruel letter and did not add to her comfort.

Madame,
    Any kindly feeling that I ever had for you died when I discovered what you are and of the wrong you and your family have done me. At a later date I may seek annulment for I consider that your relatives deceived me by marrying me to one of black blood without warning me of the menace to my issue. At the moment I am unwilling for this horrible scandal to become public. I have, therefore, told all and sundry that the birth of your child has unhinged you and that you must in future be kept away from the world, and nursed like a mad-woman. Nobody will be allowed to visit you. My faithful Mrs. D. will be your sole attendant. Had you extended a greater generosity to me in the past I might now feel more tolerant towards you. However, the thought of your beauty fills me with disgust, aware as I am of your tainted blood. I shall spend most of my time henceforth in London or

*upon the Continent. As your husband
I remain in control of your fortune and
have acquainted Mr. Caleb Nonseale
of the sad fact of your insanity.*

This monstrous letter was signed '*St.
Cheviot.*'

The young girl looked up, stared
around her with dull apathetic gaze.

She could expect no better treatment
from the Baron of Cadlington, she
thought bitterly. After nearly a year's
intimacy with him she could believe him
capable of any abomination.

*Had you extended a greater generosity
to me in the past I might now feel
more tolerant towards you.*

Those words stood out in St. Cheviot's
letter. Yes, he might have still desired
her had she fawned upon him. But now
— no longer desiring her, he could
sadistically gloat over the thought of
her unhappiness. She had no weapons
left with which to fight.

There stretched before her an endless
vista of loneliness. If Cousin Dolly or

her family or Mr. Nonseale, her trustee, asked for her, they would be told that she was out of her mind. In truth, if she stayed here long enough, she might lose her senses.

Dropping Denzil's note, Fleur flung herself upon her disordered bed, and with tearless eyes pressed against the rumpled pillows, lay without moving for a long time. Later that day Mrs. Dinglefoot came into the room. The woman looked at the girl on the bed and snapped at her:

"Still too lazy, my fine lady, to start tidying your bed-chamber, eh? Well — you will learn. Here, take this and get into the next room and begin to clean up there . . . " She flung Fleur a mop and duster. "I have two good souls here who are to measure your windows for bars."

Fleur slipped into her muslin wrapper, threaded with blue ribbons, one of the few garments which St. Cheviot had not destroyed.

"Meanwhile," continued Mrs. Dinglefoot, "you shall have somebody to watch you and ensure that you do not attempt suicide."

And suddenly she opened the door. Alpha, the wolfhound, bounded in. Fleur stood still, her gaze riveted on the animal's ferocious mask. Lover of animals though she was she had never been able to make friends with Denzil's pet. That was not the poor dog's fault, she knew, but that of Alpha's master who had maliciously trained her to snap and snarl at his bidding.

Mrs. Dinglefoot had red raw meat in her hand. With this she tempted the hungry dog. He went to her, greedy, slavering. But now the woman pointed at Fleur.

"Hi! Alpha, let her see what you can do," she said.

Alpha sprang at Lady St. Cheviot. The animal's teeth closed into a fold of the muslin negligée. She growled in her throat, pulling at the frills, keeping her eyes on Fleur. The girl trembled but refused to cry out. Mrs. Dinglefoot laughed.

"Come, Alpha, sit down and wait for it," she said. "Later you shall be on guard, my good creature."

Fleur put a hand to her throat.

"Am I to be left to the mercy of this animal?" she asked faintly.

"Alpha will not touch you unless you make an attempt to reach those windows," said Mrs. Dinglefoot.

Fleur shut her eyes and shuddered.

Came the sound of men's voices. Mrs. D. bundled her into the boudoir. After a moment, huddled against the communicating door, Fleur heard the voices of two of the workmen from the estate. In their strong Buckinghamshire dialect, they chatted about the size of the windows and the type of bars that must be cut at Whiteleaf Forge.

Fleur closed her eyes. She tried to pray. Oh, fearful fate — locked behind closed doors and barred windows and treated like a poor deranged creature! *Peveril!* her lips formed his name. *Peveril, if you but knew you would not let them do this to me*. What had happened to *him*?

Peveril had, in fact, been told little by anyone at Cadlington. For since the fearful night when Fleur's baby had been born, the boy had spent much of his time at Rustingthorpe. It was from the old Marchioness herself that he finally heard

352

the whole sordid story.

Clarissa Rustingthorpe, approaching her sixtieth year — bore little traces of the beauty which had once won for her a wealthy husband with a great title. Her hair was always dressed nowadays in dyed auburn curls, and she wore bright coloured dresses and too many bows. She was very fat and waddled on high heels. But she was quite amiable and had taken an enormous fancy to young Peveril Marsh.

The Marquis was an invalid and remained in his own rooms attended by his gentlemen. Clarissa coquetted with the handsome young artist. He found her repulsive but pathetic. She was always trying to induce him to leave St. Cheviot and establish himself here in one of the rooms of her vast mansion. She chatted to him endlessly while he painted, feeding him with bon-bons that he did not want, or trying to force wine on him. This, Peveril found very trying, but she paid well for his work and without saving money he could never hope for the independence he craved.

Clarissa also plied him with endless

questions about Lady St. Cheviot. She was never tired of hearing Peveril describe the Baron's wife. He spoke with eloquence of Lady St. Cheviot's beauty but more guardedly of her personal life. Clarissa stubbornly persisted in trying to find out the true state of affairs at Cadlington. She even tried to whisper malign stories about Hélène Roddney and her mysterious life before she became *Madame la Marquise de Chartellet*. But Peveril politely but firmly shut his ears to them.

After the birth of the child, however, a certain Mr. Groves visited Rustingthorpe. He had a long session alone with the Marchioness. Afterwards she waddled back into the room in which Peveril was putting the finishing touches to the portrait of the little Victoria Rustingthorpe.

"My goodness, now the fat is in the fire," the Marchioness giggled.

"With whom, my lady?" Peveril asked only vaguely interested.

"The St. Cheviots."

Then Peveril's expression changed.

"What has happened, my lady?"

Clarissa seated herself beside him. She

allowed herself an ecstasy of gossip. She made no effort now to guard any secret she might hold but poured out the whole story into the boy's ears. That same story that she had told Mr. Groves.

So Peveril heard in detail the scandal of the Marquise de Chartellet. And now at last he understood the nature of the tragedy that had taken place at Cadlington a few weeks ago.

"They say Lady St. Cheviot has been deranged ever since her confinement," chattered Clarissa.

"*Deranged!*" repeated Peveril.

"So they tell me," nodded the Marchioness fanning herself. "Poor creature! From what you say, so like her mother, and she was uncommonly handsome."

Peveril stood up. His eyes held a stricken look.

"God be merciful to my sweet Lady St. Cheviot," he said in a low voice that held much of horror.

Clarissa waved a lace-edged handkerchief at him. From it floated a cloud of scent.

"Oh fie!" she said, "do not tell me that

you have a naughty fancy for Lady St. Cheviot. It would do you no good. The poor soul is out of her mind and they tell me St. Cheviot has left Cadlington and gone upon the Continent. Everyone knows he keeps a mistress in Monte Carlo."

Peveril remained speechless. He could think of nothing but Fleur. He was shaken to the depths of his sensitive being by the thought of her terrible sufferings. *Out of her mind*? Maybe so. But maybe it was only one of the Marchioness's fancies. Her imagination often ran away with her.

He could scarcely bear the flirtatious perfumed old woman. But for once in his life he felt the need to dissemble. He must go to Fleur St. Cheviot's aid, and without money he was lost. He had some savings but he would need more. He threw down his paint brushes and bowed low to the Marchioness.

"Your servant, my lady," he said hoarsely. "I beg you to excuse me. I have urgent business to which I must attend. What you have told me leads me to suppose that it were better for me to leave Cadlington. I will go and pack my things."

"And come back here to Rustingthorpe?" asked the silly old woman, peering at him from short-sighted eyes.

"I will consider it, my lady."

"You want money? I will give it to you."

He flushed.

"I want only payment for my work."

"Yes, yes, little Victoria's portrait. You shall have twenty guineas for that. Wait — I will give it to you now — but only if you promise to return here."

Peveril bit his lip. Twenty guineas was a small fortune and could do much for him. He must be in a position to place himself and his services into Lady St. Cheviot's hands *should she need them*.

He permitted himself the lie and hinted to the infatuated old Marchioness that he would return. Later with the money in his pocket he set out to walk to Cadlington. He refused the phaeton offered by Clarissa. He felt that it might be better for him to make an unobtrusive return after his two days' absence from the tower.

11

THE day was warm and the hedgerows sweet with wild flowers. Fleecy clouds hung like cotton wool in the blue sky. The countryside was green and pleasant after the recent rain. While he walked the long road toward Cadlington hill, Peveril was bathed in sunshine but his heart was filled with misgivings.

What would he find at Cadlington?

He unbuttoned his coat and loosened his cravat as he began to climb the steep hill to Whiteleaf.

For the rest of his life, he was to thank God that he refused the Marchioness's offer of her phaeton. For half-way up the hill, he was waylaid by a young girl who darted out from the woods and caught at his arm.

"Oh, Mr. Peveril, zur!" she exclaimed. She was well-spoken and had only a slight Buckinghamshire accent.

"Why, Rabbina, good morning to you!"

he returned her greeting.

She was a young servant — one of the between-maids on St. Cheviot's staff. She had only come here a month ago, just before my lady was confined. She was a timid little thing, small for her age and easily bullied; the daughter of a low-born cowman on St. Cheviot's farm. Mrs. Dinglefoot, recognizing that Rabbina was poor and ignorant and also very nervous, had immediately picked upon her. Peveril had witnessed some of the bullying and tried to help her. From that time onward, the humble Rabbina became Peveril's slave. In her adoring way she performed many small services for him. She answered his greeting today, her small freckled face puckered with anxiety.

"I thank God that I have seen you in time and can speak to you, Mr. Peveril, zur!" she panted.

He looked with surprise at her hot perspiring face.

"What is it, Rabbina?" he asked in his kind way.

She clasped her hands together and plucked at the strings of her sunbonnet.

Last night, she said, she had been given orders to serve cooled cider in the housekeeper's private sitting-room. The child knew that Mrs. D. was entertaining Mr. Ivor. Ivor had gone to London with his lordship, but returned yesterday to fetch some important documents which his lordship had forgotten and which he would not trust with any but his personal servant. Rabbina had spilled some of the cider just outside the housekeeper's door. While stooping to mop it up, fearing that the irascible housekeeper would see the puddle and cuff her, she had overheard an conversation that was going on between Mrs. D. and the Welshman.

"Well?" asked Peveril tensely. "What has this to do with me?"

"It is of you they spoke, zur," she peered up at Peveril with adoring gaze. "You wuz always good to me, sir, and this is my chance to give you a warning."

Aware suddenly of danger, Peveril took Rabbina by the elbow and drew her into the shade of the glade. There hidden from the road, he listened intently while Rab repeated what she had heard.

360

Mrs. D. had been describing how the bars were now being made, down at the blacksmith's, for her ladyship's windows.

"How fearful . . . " muttered Peveril. "It is worse than I anticipated."

Rabbina continued:

The pair in the housekeeper's room mentioned Peveril Marsh by name so Rabbina remained outside to eavesdrop. *Fleur had written to him*. Ivor had informed Mrs. D. that his lordship had discovered a note which Lady St. Cheviot had sent, appealing for Peveril's help — for Denzil had ransacked the studio before leaving Cadlington.

At first St. Cheviot instructed Ivor to seek Peveril out at Rustingthorpes and horsewhip him. Then his temper cooled. Peveril was for the moment under the patronage of the Rustingthorpes. Even St. Cheviot did not fancy creating a scandal under the Marquis's roof. The wealthy Marquis was too close and too powerful a neighbour. And as Denzil had destroyed Fleur's indiscreet letter, Peveril would never now receive it. When Peveril returned to Cadlington, Ivor had his lordship's permission to thrash the painter within an inch of his life, then despatch him from Cadlington. Lady St. Cheviot would never look upon her poetic painter again.

"So you will see, zur," ended Rabbina, "you must not return to the House. Mr. Ivor may kill you."

Peveril stood silent a moment, racking his brains. He was a man of peace but no coward. He had learned neither to wrestle, to spar, to shoot nor to defend himself from physical attack. It would be madness to pit his strength against the trained Welshman. *That* was not the way to help Fleur. No — he must be more wily. With cunning, he might rescue Fleur St. Cheviot from terrible doom that had hung over her since she came here as a bride.

Rabbina remembered something else to tell Peveril.

"Zur, there is a great fierce dog guarding her ladyship day and night until the bars have been made for the windows."

"Ah?" exclaimed Peveril. "A white wolfhound?"

362

"Yes, zur, Alpha, and I heard Mrs. D. say that it sits by the window and if my lady moves towards it and so much as tries to open it, the bitch will fasten her teeth in my lady."

Peveril shuddered. He knew well how fierce the wolfhound could be. Even the Welshman was afraid of her. His poor sweet lady! Oh, what a monstrous man was Denzil St. Cheviot! To think that there had ever been a time when Peveril Marsh had thought him fine and noble. Then a sudden thought struck the boy. The colour returned to his cheeks. With *him*, Alpha had always been astonishingly docile and submissive. Many of the old servants had remarked that they had never seen the bitch more friendly towards any one. *That might prove vastly useful.*

Rabbina was speaking again, her roughened fingers plucking firmly at a bunch of nettles that grew close to them.

Peveril followed the action and muttered to himself:

"Grasp firmly at the nettles and they will not sting. Yes, I must emulate this little maid's example. I have spent too much time painting fine portraits — gathering the lilies, dreaming my foolish dreams. Now I must take action even if it is violent. For violence is being done to *her* who is the idol of my soul. God give me strength and wisdom for I am in sore need of both!"

He had not heard what Rabbina said to him but he gripped her arm.

"Have you ever seen the Baroness? Would you do her a kindness even though it endangered you?" he said hoarsely.

Rabbina nodded.

"Aye, I saw her once and thought her most beautiful and pitiful. I would willingly do her a kindness and you, too, Mr. Peveril, who have been so kind to me."

"Then you shall," said Peveril.

12

IN her great bed lying under the tattered linen and lace Fleur lay motionless. She had not dared to stir since darkness fell. Earlier she had drunk some soup that Mrs. D. brought her, only because the woman forced her to do so.

"We'll not have you starve to death and let folks say his lordship has done you a cruelty," the woman had snarled at her. "Drink every drop of it!"

Afterwards, when Mrs. D. had left, locking the door behind her, Fleur became horribly conscious of the white wolfhound lying by one of the windows. Mrs. D. had opened that window in order to give the animal air, for the night was particularly warm. Until now Fleur had scarcely been able to support the atmosphere.

Another storm was gathering; heralded by those black clouds that could be seen rolling up from the valley. Mrs. D. had brought her no light. Fleur could only dimly discern the shape of the wolfhound but could hear her panting.

Fleur felt the sweat pour down her limbs. She did not particularly wish to have the animal spring at her again and, perhaps, sink her fangs into her flesh and draw blood. She lay in a stupor. She was singularly uncomfortable. She had been allowed neither to wash herself nor comb her hair. She felt begrimed. Her lips were dry and sore. She had not yet fully recovered from the effects of her confinement. Brought up like a delicate lady she had never before experienced such rough usage or deprivation of things like warm water and soap, a brush and comb for her hair, or clean linen. She wondered indeed, if any gentlewoman alive had ever experienced such a fate as this in the hands of her husband.

She wondered if it was St. Cheviot's intention that she should be driven insane so that he could ease his conscience and feel justified in locking her away from the world. Yet even during the worst of her torments she kept telling herself that she preferred to lie here like this, forsaken and neglected sooner than submit — as she had done in the past — perfumed and bejewelled, and in loathing, to his demands.

The night was silent save for the hooting of the owls down in the forest.

The night seemed uncommonly long. She could not sleep. She could not bear this tension — this feeling that she dared not move because of the animal guarding her.

Then suddenly she heard a low growl rumble in Alpha's throat. Fleur sat up, her heart beating faster. What did the animal hear? *Something — somebody* — but what — who — at this hour, for it must be well into midnight.

Rubbing her eyes, Fleur saw the shaggy creature pad to the window, still growling. But all of a sudden she saw an astonishing sight. Alpha, having ceased to growl, began to wag her tail furiously. Dully, Fleur told herself that it must be that the animal heard familiar footsteps.

Now there rose above the window-sill the dim outline of a man's head. She heard a whisper:

"Alpha ... good soul ... good

girl . . . lie down, Alpha . . . take this . . . "

Fleur put the tips of her fingers to her lips. Huddled on her bed she stared, not daring to believe that she had recognized the voice.

Alpha padded into a corner and began scrunching some titbit that obviously pleased her. The next moment a slimly built man vaulted into the room and moved soundlessly towards Fleur. Once beside the bed he paused. He looked down at Fleur. She stared up at him. Then a low sound issued from her throat. She uttered his name.

"*Peveril!*"

"My lady," he breathed.

"Oh, God!" she whispered, and held out both hands to him, frantic with excitement and joy. "You have come to take me away."

He knelt by the bed, took those outstretched hands and raised them each in turn to his lips, covering them with kisses.

"My sweet lady, what have they done to you?"

Her head sank. Her forehead touched

368

his shoulder. Both his arms supported and held her. She wore still the crumpled muslin negligée which she had not been allowed to change. He could barely see her but he could feel how hot, how feverish she was, and the dampness of her silken tangled hair. He held her not in passion but in love — a love that was profound; full of pity. For the moment he knew that it was what she needed and what he must give. He pressed his cheek to hers. With his own heart beating wildly, he dared to kiss her hair.

"My dearest — my beloved lady — oh, *Fleur*," he whispered.

"Peveril," she spoke his name again, and by the frenzy with which she clung to him, he measured the extent of her pleasure at this reunion. She trembled in his arms. Her tears drenched his face. He heard her hoarse whispering.

"How did you come? How did you know where to find me? Is it safe? Have you not endangered your very life by coming here, like this, to me?"

He answered only the last question.

"If I have, it is worth while — I am

privileged to risk such an unworthy life for you."

She said:

"You cannot be aware of the truth about me?"

"I know everything," he said. "I loved you before I knew. I love you still more now. Your husband has forfeited the right to protect you. I beg to be allowed to do so."

"You are the only true friend I have in the world." She wept and Peveril felt her lips against his cheek. He said:

"We must be quick. At any moment Ivor or Mrs. D. may wake and hear us."

"How did you get here? Where have you been?"

He told her everything that had led up to his meeting on the hill with Rabbina, the between-maid. Fleur learned how the little maid had also risked terrible punishment and met Peveril underneath Lady St. Cheviot's window. Rab kept watch below there now while Peveril climbed the strong creeper that grew as high as her ladyship's bedchamber.

"Praise God," said Peveril, "I am agile

and have a good head for climbing."

During the afternoon he had bought stout rope. This he would tie to the bed post. He would let Fleur down first, then follow. None of this could have been achieved had he not made friends with Alpha.

"How thankful I am that the hound was my constant companion before you came here," whispered Peveril. "I have only to tell her to lie still and she will not move."

Wild excitement gathered in Fleur's heart.

"What clothes have you?" Peveril asked her.

"Alas, only a shawl for my shoulders. The Baron . . . in his rage . . . destroyed everything that I have."

"He is indeed a madman," muttered Peveril.

"Worse than that."

Peveril stuck a match. The tiny light illuminated Fleur's face and figure. Almost he uttered an exclamation of horror. She was so emaciated. Her hair was tangled and matted, her lips cracked. It broke Peveril's heart to see her. But

371

she pulled the shawl over her breast and smiled at him. A smile of unearthly sweetness. He extinguished the match, took her hands in his, and covered them with kisses.

"If heaven has given me the right to call myself your protector, I am the happiest of mortals. Henceforth my life is dedicated to you," he said.

Then quickly he tied the rope to the post of her bed, gave an order to Alpha who wagged her tail and continued to gnaw the delectable bone he had brought to her. He moved to the window, looked down and whispered:

"*Hist!*"

Rabbina's voice floated up to him.

"Yes, zur, all is quiet."

Then Fleur St. Cheviot became once more the vivacious spirited fleet-footed girl who had once graced her parents' household and for whom nothing ever held terrors. He tied the rope round her waist. He lowered her safely to the ground. She felt a pair of strong young arms receive her.

"Oh, my lady, my lady," whispered Rabbina, the little maid, and then let her

372

ladyship go and curtseyed and bobbed, much embarrassed. It appalled her to see a lady of quality in such a state. Why, the poor young thing, thought the raw country girl, she is not much older than myself — all eyes and a bag of bones.

Fleur caught the little servant's hand in hers.

"With all my heart I thank you for the risk you have taken for me tonight," she breathed.

Peveril had swung himself down beside them.

"Ssh, still a moment," he whispered.

All three of them stood tense, listening. Fleur felt that the beating of her own heart must make a noise in the quietness which had fallen upon Cadlington. Even the owls had stopped hooting. Now they heard the church clock from Monks Risborough strike the hour of one. But the great House remained wrapped in an almost uncanny silence as though it would aid and abet Peveril's rescue of the Baron's ill-fated wife.

Peveril breathed again.

"Come — all is well — let us go," he said.

Fleur took the arm he held out to her.

"What are your plans?" she asked.

He told her. His paints and a few clothes were in a carpet bag which had been collected from the tower by Rabbina and left in the bushes.

They must not pass through the main gates, for the lodge-keeper might waken and see them. They would turn off the main drive and make their way through the hedgerows leading out on to the road towards Great Missenden. If Lady St. Cheviot could walk so far as half a mile, Peveril had organized a horse and gig to wait for them at the cross-roads.

"Once we are in the thicket we shall be safe," added Peveril. "Our only danger is lest somebody should awake and see us running across the lawn into the trees."

"Oh, let us hurry!" exclaimed Fleur frantic with longing to be gone.

Peveril took one of her arms, Rabbina the other. The next moment the three shadowy figures flitted across the lawn. They they were gone, and safe behind the shelter of the tall trees.

An immense thankfulness filled Fleur's

heart and warmed yet more of life and vitality back into her. She moved as swiftly as the little servant girl in her home-spun cloak and stout boots. Once the fleecy shawl fell from her thin shoulders. Peveril picked it up and wrapped it tenderly about her. She felt his gentle touch and smiled up at him. He had never seen her thus before. It was as though the sorrowful statue of his madonna had come to life, with the blood surging through those alabaster limbs. Her new feverish beauty enthralled the painter.

But they were not yet out of danger. Once on the high road bearing the wooden sign-post 'To Great Missenden' Peveril picked up the carpet bag which Rabbina had packed for him and hidden beside her own modest bundle. Rab, too, was leaving Whiteleaf for ever. It did not particularly grieve her to know that she must remain away from her family from now onward.

Her apprenticeship at the great House under Mrs. Dinglefoot had offered little so far but ill-usage and hard work. She had begged Peveril to allow her to go with him when he left Whiteleaf and become maid to her ladyship.

Now it was Rabbina to whom Peveril and Fleur must turn for immediate help. She had an aunt in Great Missenden; by name Mrs. Tabitha Gomme, who was sister to Rabbina's dead mother. She had always been a favourite with Rabbina, but the child had the chance to visit her only rarely. Mrs. Gomme, a widow, was a respectable body, a lace-maker, who occupied a tiny tumbledown cottage on the outskirts of Great Missenden. She would, Rabbina knew, give a haven tonight to the runaways.

Peveril then bribed a man named Amos from Monks Risborough, who owned horse and gig, to convey them all to Missenden. He would not recognize the Lady of Cadlington. Nor did he know the young artist by sight. He was a dull-witted fellow who minded his own business and would not ask questions or give information even if it were demanded. What he wanted was gold. Peveril had offered plenty for the journey and received his promise of complete discretion. He fancied that

Amos would not bother to tittle-tattle about his nocturnal passengers, and in any case, even if Amos was suspected, Peveril and Fleur would be well away before he could be accused.

Peveril outlined his further plans for Fleur as they walked swiftly along the long dark road to the cross-roads at the top of the hill.

Rabbina was to introduce them to Aunt Tabitha as an 'eloping couple'. Peveril apologized to Fleur with humility, for this impertinence. At once she replied:

"As if I could take offence since you plan all for my well-being," she said with her loveliest smile.

"Thank you," he said in a low voice and pressed her arm against his.

It was when they reached the cross-roads and the end of that half-mile that they first encountered a setback.

As arranged, Amos, from Monks Risborough, sat with his gig and piebald mare, chewing a piece of straw, waiting for them. He eyed the two females with small interest.

He was anxious to get on and earn

the full purse the young gentleman had promised him.

"'Tis sta-army, zur," he said with his broad accent. "I'll be fair aggled if does ra-ain afore we git to Missenden."

Rabbina giggled suddenly and whispered to Peveril.

"He means he'll be angered, zur. *Aggled* is what we calls it in Buckinghamshire."

"I shall be 'aggled' too, if the rain starts and my lady is soaked," muttered Peveril drily. "We will get poor shelter in this tumbledown gig."

"I am very happy — do not bother about me," Fleur begged him.

But when she was settled inside the gig and seated snugly between her two rescuers, a man suddenly sprang out of the hedge at them. He shouted that he wished a lift if it was to Whiteleaf they were going.

Fleur smothered a scream. She clutched Peveril's hand. He covered it with both of his, reassuringly.

"Ssh — do not move or speak," he whispered.

The sudden apparition was a thin, sandy-haired man wearing gaiters, and

378

with half a dozen rabbits slung over his shoulder and a fowling-piece under one arm. He started a controversy with Amos. Amos having explained that they were bound for the opposite direction, the stranger began to argue that Amos should first turn back and take him home. He was obviously inflamed from a plethora of raw gin, for now he offered a swig from a large flask to Amos, who rejected it.

Peveril cut in sharply:

"Come, my good fellow — we are in a hurry — do not delay us, if you please."

The man began to mumble that he had caught his foot in a hole, wrenched an ankle and wanted a lift.

He was causing Peveril some real concern, revealing himself now as Jack Hommock, nephew of old Hommock one of the lodge-keepers from Cadlington. Jack began to climb into the gig and peer at the three occupants. He recognized at least two of them. (Fleur had hidden her face against Peveril's shoulder. He could feel her trembling violently.) Hommock said:

"Well, if it isn't little Rab — the cowman's girl — and with the young gentleman-painter. Where are you two a-going might I a-ask?" He drawled the question.

"Get down and mind your own business," said Peveril sharply.

Hommock swayed, and peered closer to him.

"Taking a night trip wi' the cowman's daughter, eh, my master painter?" he sneered.

Peveril felt in the darkness, the feverish clasp of Fleur's fingers.

"Do not start trouble, for dear God's sake," she whispered.

But it was too late. The poacher lurched towards her and rudely snatched her scarf. The silken tangle of curls fell across her bosom. Hommock instantly recognized her and gave a shout which was half in fear.

"Lawks-a-mussy! It is the Lady of Cadlington, herself. I be scrummerous to have laid a finger on you, my lady."

Fleur gave a cry of despair.

"We are lost, Peveril."

But not so, for Peveril Marsh — who

all his clean pacific life had been a gentle lad and averse to acts of violence — sprang at the poacher, who with a hoarse cry, fell back on to the road. He lay there groaning. His fowling-piece had clattered to the ground. The rabbits followed. Peveril sprang after him. He dragged the poacher to the side of the road. The man looked up at him with inflamed, malevolent little eyes.

"Helping the Baron's mad lady to get away — is that it, my master?" he gasped. "I'll raise a hue and a cry once I'm back at Cadlington and you won't get far, I warrant."

"As I expected," said Peveril darkly. "Well, my man, you are unlucky this night for if it is a case of you or my lady — her life — or yours — you must be the one to suffer."

The clouds parted — for a moment the moon shed a ray of light and Peveril saw a flash of steel in Hommock's upraised hand.

The next moment the two men were rolling in the dust. Peveril's fear for Fleur lent him an unnatural power; a frenzied purpose to shut the fellow's mouth.

Amos sat watching sullenly. He had no part in this quarrel neither did he comprehend it.

Fleur and Rabbina clasped each other. Fleur said in an anguished voice:

"Oh, God . . . if he is injured now . . . "

"Take heart, my lady," the little maid tried to comfort her. "Jack Hommock is in drink and will not be as slippery with his knife as usual."

Such was the case. Hommock pitted his brawn against the painter only for a few moments. Peveril, his fingers about the poacher's wrist, forced him back. They wrestled and panted in the darkness. Fleur could only see dim shapes and hear the heavy breathing.

Then suddenly came a sharp cry from the poacher. The knife clattered on to the roadway. Peveril reached for the fowling-piece and brought the butt down on the other man's skull. It was the first savage blow he had ever struck in his life. Hommock rolled over and lay still, Peveril pulled him into the hedge and left him there.

"Oh, thank heaven — you are safe,"

Fleur exclaimed as Peveril sprang back into the gig. "Alas, you have had to commit a crime for my sake."

"I do not think the fellow is dead. I heard him groan. But it will be some time before he is found and can betray us," he said.

His face was pale. He caught Amos by the arm.

"Remember — once you return to Monks Risborough you will say nothing of this to a soul or I shall seek you out and make sure you never open your lips again," he said fiercely.

Amos hunched a shoulder and whipped up his mare.

"I wao-on't talk, master. I'd be a-feared. All I want is the gowld," he said.

"You shall have it," said Peveril.

The gig rattled on down the other side of the hill in the direction of Great Missenden. Now a few drops spattered from the sky.

"The storm's a-coming," said little Rabbina.

But Fleur and Peveril did not hear her. They were clasping hands again. Once more Peveril felt her breath against his cheek. She whispered:

"My dear, dear Peveril — if indeed you have stained your soul this night for my sake, it will be forgiven you. The fellow would have set all the inmates of Cadlington upon us."

"And still will — if he lives?" said Peveril in a low voice. "We must seek a refuge where the Baron can never discover you."

She sighed. Her head leaned against his shoulder as they jogged along through the ever-increasing rain. She felt weary beyond caring, yet at peace.

"Oh, how happy I am to be with you . . . " she breathed.

Then he forgot the violence he had committed. All his manhood was vibrant for Fleur. He kept her fingers locked in his as they journeyed on to their destination and she did not seek to withdraw them.

13

THE storm which growled over the Chiltern Hills all night broke with some ferocity at four o'clock in the morning. By that time the runaways had reached the cottage belonging to Rabbina's aunt.

Now Fleur sat in Tabitha Gomme's rocking chair, her small feet on a stool, drinking herb-tea from a blue and white china mug. Mrs. Gomme had found a more manly drink of ale for the young gentleman. While he drank, and ate the bread and cheese Mrs. Gomme had served, he kept his enraptured gaze upon Fleur.

Mrs. Gomme and her niece had taken Fleur upstairs as soon as she arrived, removed the crumpled negligée and helped to dress her in a grey homespun gown which belonged to Mrs. Gomme. Once more her fair fell in gleaming ringlets about her neck and bosom. Difficult, thought Peveril, to believe she had ever been wife to St. Cheviot, or borne a child — she looked so young like this.

He seated himself on a stool at her feet and began to talk to her.

"My lady — " but she interrupted, gently pressing his fingers.

"I wish never to hear that odious title again. The very sound freezes my blood. To you, henceforward, I am just — Fleur. And for me, you are my friend, Peveril."

"*Fleur*," he repeated the name as though it were something sacred. His reward was great when he saw the faint uplifting of her sad mouth.

He discussed the future.

They must press onward to London. It would be wiser, because of the poacher and what might follow the discovery of his body. As soon as Fleur had rested, they would breakfast and catch the first mail coach of the day from Great Missenden, to London. Only there — among millions — could they lose themselves and stay hidden from their pursuers.

Peveril now spoke of a great friend

who lived close to the river, near the Royal Vauxhall Gardens. By name Luke Taylor, he was, like Peveril, an artist in his spare time. He was a year or two older than Peveril whom he had met first at the Grammar School. He worked in a firm of merchant bankers in the City. The last that Peveril had heard of him was that he was doing quite well.

"Luke and I have always been much attached. He has my way of thinking and Alice, his wife, is one in whom you could put your trust," Peveril told Fleur. "She is in fact some ten years older than my friend. She has the most amiable nature. With the help of a little servant of Rabbina's age, Alice keeps the house uncommonly well for my friend. I propose to take you there. I shall tell them everything — that is if you permit it — for I know that they will offer us shelter and that Luke will help me to find work. Does the idea please you?"

"I am sure I should like your friends," said Fleur, "but I do not know why they should be bothered with me."

"They have but to see you, to love you," said Peveril, with a look that brought the warm pink to Fleur's hollowed cheeks.

"Alas," she said, "I cannot — dare not — approach my own dear friend, Catherine Quinley, or any who has known me in the past."

"Agreed," said Peveril, "and although it is best for us to be frank with Luke and Alice, it is essential that you at least change your name immediately, for it is certain the Baron will make a desperate bid to find you and take his revenge."

A shiver went through the girl.

"Yes, I can imagine his rage." She nodded.

"Let us then take asylum with the Taylors. When the excitement has died down, no doubt his lordship will seek to have the marriage annulled."

Fleur looked blindly at the boy.

"Once," she said, "I believed in the sanctity of the marriage vow. But now I no longer feel pledged to him. *Let* our marriage be put asunder. I do most heartily desire complete severance from a monster such as St. Cheviot."

"Amen to that," said Peveril.

Then he stood up and drew her on to her feet.

"You must have some rest," he said and smiled down at her.

All her heart went out in gratitude to him.

"Oh, what can I ever do for you who have done so much for me!" she exclaimed.

He was silent a moment, then said in a low voice:

"It is too soon to speak of such things for I feel you must shrink from any man's protest of affection. But I stand here and protest unashamed, my love for you, most beloved Fleur. If you would do something in return for me, I ask that you permit me to stay for ever by your side."

Now her tears fell thickly but with touching gesture she laid her cheek against his hand.

"I do not wish you to leave me," she whispered. "Through all my anguish I have remembered you. When I first went as a bride to Cadlington, the only happiness I knew was in your presence, listening to your voice."

He covered her hair with kisses. For a moment they stayed close. Then he drew away, walked with her to the casement window, and pulled aside the curtains. The little kitchen was at once filled with pearly light. Peveril snuffed the tallow candle. They looked out at the dawn. Meadow and road were white in the mist. From the distance came the crowing of a cock, and the sound of a dog barking.

The young artist turned to Fleur. She looked pallid and frail in her grey gown. He gazed at the sheen of her wonderful hair, and received from her the smile that he, and he alone, seemed able to bring to her lips. Then he dropped down on one knee and leaned his forehead against her folded hands.

"You are my saint and I worship you," he said.

She could not answer. Her heart was too full but she read in Peveril's eyes an end to her despair; a promise of a happiness greater than she had ever known.

That hope still kept her spirits high when — a few hours later — she sat between Peveril and Rabbina in the mail coach which was being drawn by four fast horses *en route* for London.

In borrowed cape and bonnet, heavily veiled, she had little fear of recognition. With every mile that they covered, she began to feel less strained. There seemed no likelihood now that they would be overtaken.

Peveril, too, was in high spirits, but the financial angle troubled Fleur.

"I am totally dependent upon you. It seems all wrong," she told Peveril. He laughed at her. He had saved for this very purpose, he kept reassuring her, and he brought a few more smiles from her by describing for her his painting of Victoria Rustingthorpe and the coquettish antics of the elderly Marchioness.

"I fear," ended Peveril, "her ladyship will be sadly disappointed when I do not return to her, but I gave her good measure of work for the money she paid me, so I need not feel guilty."

Fleur looked at Peveril with a new and personal pride in him.

"You are a great artist, and should easily be able to make both name and fortune in London," she murmured.

"I dare not offer a painting under the name of Peveril Marsh," he reminded her, "for my work is individual and might get into the hands of a dealer where it would in turn be noticed by the Baron. Thus he would trace me — and you. No, I must begin life again. I shall find other means whereby to earn our livelihood."

Fleur reflected upon this and sighed.

"I have spoiled your career — " she began.

"Hush," he interrupted tenderly. "You have spoiled nothing. You have given me the sun, the moon and the stars, by placing yourself under my protection."

She was too moved to answer.

The coach rolled grandly along the highway. It was a sunny day and there were many passengers. Some well-attired gentlemen and their ladies, chattering about the state of the country under the new Queen, and recently assembled Parliament. There was a brisk genial atmosphere in the coach which did much to hearten Fleur who had never before travelled in a public conveyance. It seemed to remove her far from the old life she had led as Lady St.

Cheviot. This new freedom and the happiness of being loved and cared for by Peveril brought her a deep pure joy.

Only once, Fleur allowed herself to dwell on the grim horror of that night when St. Cheviot had destroyed her room.

"Your painting of my hands — that little gem — oh, how it grieved me to see it smashed!"

He looked down at the perfect hands in the lace mittens which the kindly Mrs. Gomme had given her.

"Do not grieve," he said. "I shall paint you again."

They paused outside the first toll house, while the guard paid his dues to the turnpike.

Afterwards on the high-road again they sat with their fingers tightly locked, while the coach wheels rumbled through Uxbridge. Fleur stared out at the outskirts of London — the crowded dwellings, the dirty streets, the milling crowds of people. This scene flung Rabbina into transports. It was the most thrilling day of the little country girl's life.

"Lawks-a-mussy — I am in London!"
she kept saying.

So at length they came to St. Martin's
le Grand where everybody got out of the
coach. They took the final journey in a
hansom cab which was the latest thing
in private conveyance. It carried them to
the Royal Vauxhall Gardens. Fleur was
unutterably relieved when at last Peveril
conducted her into the presence of his
good friends, the Taylors.

This couple occupied a small shabby
house in a genteel but modest terrace
constructed in the reign of George III.
Sydney Terrace led off a broader and
more elegant row of houses, about two
minutes' walk from the river.

When Peveril rang the front-door bell,
the Taylors were up in the room which
Luke had made into a studio and where
he painted in his spare time. This being
Saturday, he was home earlier than usual.

Luke's pleasure was genuine and
unbounded when he saw who stood upon
the doorstep. He loved Peveril Marsh and
had held his family and hunchback sister,
Elspeth, in respect and affection. Luke
had deeply deplored it when Peveril took

394

the decision to abandon London and seek a home in the country for his invalid sister's sake.

Alice joined her husband. They looked with some surprise at the young woman in grey, and her servant who accompanied them. Peveril clapped an arm over his friend's shoulder and said:

"I have much to tell you. I would be uncommonly indebted to you if I might beg your hospitality, not only for myself, but for this lady and her servant."

"Most certainly," the Taylors chorused, being both of warm and hospitable nature.

Luke was not an inspired artist like his old school friend but sufficient of one to recognize the extraordinary talent shewn by young Peveril Marsh.

Delighted to see him again, Luke led the way through a narrow hall into parlour. Mrs. Taylor followed, keeping an inquisitive eye on the young lady. She wondered if she could possibly be wife to Peveril.

Rabbina was sent down into the basement, there to give a hand with the evening meal which was being prepared by Emma, the Taylors' own maid-of-all-work.

Now in Alice's little drawing-room, which Fleur could see at once was furnished as tastefully as a poor pocket would allow, Peveril spoke, running nervous fingers through his bright brown curls.

"It is a long story, my friends," he said, "But first I ask you for your complete discretion. It is imperative that no one should know that I am here, nor must you divulge the name of the lady."

"Pray untie your bonnet and be at home, my dear," said Alice Taylor, turning to Fleur. Fleur did so and at the sight of the singular beauty of the delicate face in the frame of rose-gilt curls, both the Taylors forgot their manners and stared. Peveril smiled. He read their minds. He nodded at Luke, who was a short, stoutly built, merry-eyed fellow, with long hair brushed into a curl over his forehead — and the side whiskers much affected by gentlemen in London these days.

"Yes," said Peveril, "she *is* beautiful, is she not?"

"Quite out of the ordinary!" exclaimed Luke, the appreciative artist in him stirring as he looked into Fleur's violet-blue eyes.

"Have the goodness, you two, not to raise the poor girl's blushes in such a manner!" Alice chided them. Fleur looked gratefully at the older woman who had a pair of sparkling eyes under a fringe of dark brown hair, and seemed both motherly and kind.

"Go ahead — tell us all, boy," said Luke. "I do assure you we can find room for you both, can we not, Alice, my love? You can sleep in my studio and our one guest chamber is at the service of this lady whom you wish to protect. But we are tremendously inquisitive to know what this means, and what you have been doing since you left London."

Peveril took one of Fleur's hands in his . . .

"All in good time," he said. "To start with I must make this lady's true identity known to you."

"Whatever secret you have to tell will be safe with us," said Luke.

"Listen then," said Peveril. "This is

Fleur, Lady St. Cheviot — wife of the Baron of Cadlington in Buckinghamshire, whence we have just come."

The Taylors preserved a respectful silence whilst Peveril outlined for them the story of his first meeting with the notorious Lord St. Cheviot and later with his bride.

When it was finished, Luke Taylor rose, and putting his hands behind his back, scowled quite ferociously out of the window.

"By heavens, Peveril, your story has made my gorge rise!" he exclaimed. "The Baron of Cadlington must surely be insane."

"Sometimes I thought as much," whispered Fleur.

Alice — a warm-hearted, friendly young woman — forgot Fleur's title and high estate and flung both her arms around her.

"Poor blessèd lamb!" she said and tears sparkled in eyes that rarely found occasion for them. "What you have endured moves me to grief for you and loathing for him whom you call husband."

"I knew you would both feel this way,"

said Peveril, his handsome face flushed and grateful. "But you see the mess we are in. For all I know, I may have committed a murder last night. In any case all the devils in hell will be let loose if Hommock lives and St. Cheviot hears that his wife has gone away with me."

"I rejoice that you rescued her!" cried Alice. "And the poor lamb shall stay here in my care for just as long as she likes. You, too, Peveril, who are Luke's dearest friend."

Luke, also turned and put a hand on the younger man's shoulder.

"Yes — stay with us and share our humble home," he said. "Great discretion is needed. You must lie low for some time to come. You, Peveril, can grow a beard and set to work a-painting under an assumed name."

Peveril fingered his chin and laughed ruefully.

"Yes — a beard would be a useful disguise. As for painting — I must make that a sideline, as you do, Luke, and earn my bread in the world of commerce."

"You have a good education and a quick mind — I am confident I can find you something," said Luke.

"But what of Lady St. Cheviot?" began Alice. Fleur put a finger against her lips.

"Not *that* — I beg of you — ever again. To you I am Fleur."

"Bless you," said the emotional Alice embracing her. "And I must set to work to fatten you up — you are most abominably thin, poor dear. Some weeks of rest in my little home and my strengthening jellies and home-made cordials and you will soon recover health and strength."

"I am deeply grateful," said Fleur.

"But how shall she be called?" asked Peveril. "She dare not even return to the name of her youth — which was Roddney."

"Alas, no," said Fleur.

Peveril gave her a long yearning look.

"Would that I could give her *my* name," he said in a low voice.

Her cheeks coloured. Her gaze met his then she turned away for she was afraid of her own heart's throbbing. He added:

"One day — *one day it shall be*, please God."

"I have an idea," said Alice brightly. "She can for the moment pass as a young widow and call herself by my maiden name, which was Trelawny — I am Cornish by birth. There — Fleur Trelawny — does it not sound nice?"

"Very nice," said Fleur. "And I cannot tell you how much more I like it than *Lady St. Cheviot*," and she shuddered violently.

"It is an excellent plan, Alice. Mrs. Trelawny she shall be," seconded Luke.

"As for her own kinswoman — Mrs. de Vere, who betrayed her into that dreadful man's hands — *she* deserves to be roasted," added Alice, tossing her handsome head.

At the memory of her weak and wicked Cousin Dolly, Fleur shuddered again. She would not dare to be seen in the vicinity of Knightsbridge Green where her cousin and the family still lived.

"I, too, must find work of a kind. I cannot be entirely be holden to you, Alice, or to *you*," she added, looking at Peveril.

But he caught her hand in his and kissed it.

"Fleur, dearest, do not take from me my greatest privilege — or my hope for the future," he said in a low ardent tone.

She sighed but her eyes filled with tears — of happiness this time. To be here with these good cheerful people who were ready to cherish her was sweetest balm to her deeply injured heart.

That night, supping with the Taylors and with Peveril, she felt a contentment that she had not known since her parents' death.

14

ALL through this same day — the day which marked a new and better existence for Fleur — chaos reigned at Cadlington House. It smashed the peace of the golden summer's morning from the moment that Mrs. Dinglefoot's piercing scream brought most of the staff scurrying up from the kitchens and pantries to her ladyship's bedchamber. They all thought at first that the housekeeper had entered the poor 'mad lady's' room to find her lying dead on her bed.

Nothing would have pleased Mrs. D. more. But instead when she unlocked the door, she found the apartment deserted, the bird flown, and the wolfhound whining and scratching to be let out.

Ivor had been just about to saddle his horse and ride to London to deliver the papers to his master who was awaiting them. They were intending to cross the Channel on the next packet to Boulogne.

He stood watching Mrs. D. ransack the room — screaming and spluttering like an outraged hen. The woman could not get over the fact that Alpha had allowed my lady to go.

"Out of the window — and someone down below to aid her. But the bitch was trained to savage her if she went near that window. I cannot comprehend it!" wailed the woman, her hairy face red and perspiring.

"Alpha was friendly with the young artist," Ivor reminded her and added: "His lordship will cut your throat for this."

Mrs. Dinglefoot put a hand to her flabby throat and groaned.

"I did all I could — what more could I have done, except sleep in the same chamber as that wretch. Oh, if I ever lay hands on her again, I shall make her suffer for this."

"You never will," prophesied the valet darkly. "I warrant my lady has friends whom you know naught about."

"Who? — tell me," spluttered Mrs. D.

"The painter is certainly one," muttered Ivor. "Who else could it be? He has eluded *me* — the cunning young reptile."

"*Your* throat will be slit, as well as mine, you cockerel," screamed Mrs. D. in a passion of rage, as she flung the bed-clothes from Fleur's abandoned bed on to the floor.

"You were in charge of her ladyship — not I!" Ivor snarled back. And the two stood there, bickering, snapping at each other — shrinking with fear of the master to whom they were responsible.

Then one of the younger servants came running into the room and bobbed to the housekeeper.

"Please ma'am — Rabbina, the new between-maid, is missing and has not slept in her bed last night."

"What can that have to do with her ladyship — ?" began the housekeeper. Ivor interrupted harshly:

"Imbecile — *there* you have the help from within — the painter and this girl, Rabbina, have spirited Lady St. Cheviot away."

"Then go after them!" screamed Mrs. D. "Do not stand there wasting time, you fool."

The rest of the staff who overheard,

fled along the great corridors of the house, whispering together excitedly. It was plain that there was going to be trouble. But more than one of them spoke with compassion of the Baron's martyred bride.

"I for one am glad the poor thing has escaped," said a young footman who had received kindness in his time from the Lady of Cadlington.

"I, for another," whispered a scullery wench. "I saw her in the gardens before the baby was born and she looked like an angel."

Throughout the rest of the July morning the staff, headed by Mrs. D., searched the house, the tower, the gardens and the surrounding park, in case they should discover the body of her ladyship. She might have taken her life.

Later they learned the truth. At noon Seth Hommock's nephew was discovered lying in a ditch half a mile from the great gates. He had a nasty wound on his skull and was semi-conscious when picked up and brought home by a carrier.

Not until sundown did he open his eyes and speak — then it was to tell his uncle what he knew. The older Hommock conveyed the information to Ivor and Mrs. D. Lady St. Cheviot had been driven away in a gig, drawn by a piebald mare, and in the company of Peveril Marsh and Rabbina.

Mrs. D. ground her teeth and called down hell's vengeance on Peveril — and on young Rab. The next thing was to discover who had driven the gig. Jack Hommock could not remember. He was addled in his mind and said he had never before set eyes on the fellow. It was no one from Whiteleaf — that was all he knew.

The cowman had no notion where his truant daughter could have gone, so he was no help. It seemed that the truth could no longer be kept from his lordship. Someone must tell him of his wife's escape.

That 'someone' had to be Ivor.

When the moment came, Ivor, the bully, became a craven coward. He stammered excuses as he stood before his master in the coffee-room of the inn in Folkestone where St. Cheviot impatiently awaited him.

"Idiot — fool of fools!" St. Cheviot shouted. "You and that old imbecile Dinglefoot — letting my wife escape while you lay in bed snoring like the sloths you are. I could slit your gullets — the pair of you."

His face was livid with rage. His mind crawled with bitter, venomous thoughts that writhed around the memory of his young wife.

It was not that he wanted her back in his embrace. He harboured too strong a hatred of her appalling heritage. His former lechery had turned to a sadistic desire to break her proud spirit and humble her to the dust.

In Denzil's evil mind — incapable of a pure or high motive — he was positive now that the young painter had been Fleur's paramour. As such, he must be routed out and the insolent flame of his life extinguished. As for Fleur, she should end the rest of her days disgraced and destitute. And St. Cheviot would find a more suitable wife to bear him an heir.

Meanwhile, Denzil's fury was further inflamed by the mental pictures he drew of those two together. All Fleur's pale slender beauty was for Peveril Marsh now — a humble youth hardly yet grown to full manhood. All given to him willingly, with the heat, the rapture, the desire she had denied St. Cheviot himself.

"I shall kill them both," St. Cheviot said through his clenched teeth.

He swung round to the valet and blazed at him.

"Get out. I shall cancel my passage to France. We return immediately to Cadlington."

Part Three

1

TWO years later. In London, on the 8th February, a cold gusty day, a tall prematurely white-haired gentleman wearing side whiskers and sombrely dressed in a dark overcoat and cape, with flat oval-shaped hat, stepped out of the coach which had just brought him from Plymouth to London.

When he took off his hat one could see many scars — of jagged and livid hue — spoiling what had once been a fine and noble countenance. A face darkly bronzed as though the owner had been exposed for a long time to tropical suns.

For a few moments, he stood shivering in the biting wind which blew down Newgate Street. One or two feathery flakes of snow settled upon his cape and hat for an instant then vanished. But sombre though the weather, the streets were full of people and much decorated. In some places workmen sat

413

astride the lamps, busily polishing the glass. It seemed to the new arrival that there were preparations in progress for some big event. He, having just arrived from Australia, and out of touch with his own country, knew nothing. He felt that he must make some enquiries. He walked into a nearby tavern and joined some of the gentlemen who sat drinking and smoking in the Commercial Room.

What he heard surprised and interested the returned traveller.

The day after tomorrow the young Queen Victoria was to be married to Prince Albert, son of the Duke of Saxe-Coburg-Gotha.

The returned traveller raised his tankard of foaming ale. "Long live the Queen," he said respectfully.

Later, as he emerged into the bitter streets again, he found it odd to remember that he had not set foot on his native soil since the young Victoria succeeded to the throne.

"All is changed in England. And heavens knows what further changes I shall find," he thought.

Buttoning up his collar, he then

made his way to a firm of solicitors whose offices were situated not far from St. Paul's Churchyard. The name was engraved upon door and dusty windows. *Nonseale, Nonseale & Duckett.*

Once inside he asked a clerk if Mr. Caleb Nonseale were in. He received the disappointing reply that Mr. Caleb was out of town attending the funeral of a country client. He would not be back until tomorrow.

"So be it, I will return tomorrow," said the traveller.

"What name shall I say, sir?" asked the clerk.

"You do not recognize me?"

The clerk, a gangling lad, peered shortsightedly at the tall gentleman's scarred face and shook his head.

"No, sir."

"Then I have changed a great deal more than *you*, young Benjamin Drew, who are much grown in height since last we met."

"Lawks, sir — then you know me?"

"Yes. You have received me here many times — my uncle before me. But no matter — I will not divulge my identity for the moment. It shall be kept as a surprise for Mr. Nonseale."

And smiling, the gentleman turned and walked from the office leaving the clerk to gape after him.

The traveller did not stand long in the cold greyness of the winter's morning. He stopped a passing cab, stepped into it and gave the address of a house on Knightsbridge Green.

"I fear this will be a shock for Dolly, too," he thought, "and for Archibald and the others."

It was snowing fast by the time the scarred gentleman pounded the brass knocker on the door of the narrow house facing the Green.

He was astounded when he was told by the butler who answered his enquiry that Mrs. de Vere no longer resided there.

The butler went on to inform the visitor that Mrs. de Vere had married again, some eighteen months ago, and was now called Lady Sidpath.

"Lady Sidpath!" The returned traveller repeated the name with astonishment. "Then Mr. de Vere died?"

"Oh yes, sir, in India — it would be two years ago."

"Alas, poor Archibald! This is the first loss of which I am to hear," thought the stranger.

Once or twice at White's, the traveller in the past had played a game of cards with Sidpath and lost to him.

The traveller now heard that Dolly — Lady Sidpath — lived in Berkeley Square. The butler added that the two young ladies, Miss Imogen and Miss Isabel, were still unwed, and lived under their step-papa's roof.

The scarred gentleman wasted no further time but made his way to Berkeley Square.

He was lucky enough to find Lady Sidpath at home. The powdered footman who received him, ushered him into a handsome, if ornate drawing-room. The caller said:

"Be so good as to inform her ladyship that I am a relative — from abroad."

The next moment, he heard Dolly's familiar high-pitched voice out in the hall. The door opened and she walked in.

She was dressed as though about to go out. He could see at once that she had put on much weight and was no longer at all attractive, despite the richness of her velvet dress and jacket, her handsome sable muff and tippet, and smart plumed bonnet.

On high-heeled boots she tapped across the parquet floor towards him. She began:

"You must pardon me, sir, but I cannot understand what Jenkins means when he says you are a relative from abroad. I have no relatives — "

Then she stopped. For she had come close to the tall gentleman and was peering up into his face. All her colour had vanished, leaving only the redness of the rouge upon it. She put a hand to her lips and gave a scream.

"Mercy on us! It cannot be — it *cannot*."

"Yes, Dolly, it is. Harry Roddney back from his watery grave," said the man in a sombre voice. "Back, alas, without my beloved wife who lies for evermore beneath those cruel waves. My poor beautiful Hélène!"

But he was speaking to himself now for the fat little woman with her furs and jewels and feathers had screamed again and crumpled up in a dead faint at his feet.

He picked her up, placed her on the sofa and rang for a servant. The footman fetched her ladyship's maid who came rushing down with burnt feathers to apply to her ladyship's nostrils. Dolly moaned, spluttered and opened her eyes. Those greedy furtive eyes from under their blackened lashes stared wildly at the man who had just revealed himself as Harry Roddney. She shivered like one with ague, and stuttered his name.

"Harry! Merciful Heavens, *Harry*!"

"I must ask your pardon for subjecting you to such a shock, Cousin," he said.

Now she sat bolt upright, her face suffused with colour and her eyes bolting. She looked like one in the throes of a ghastly fright. She waved the maid aside and bade her leave the room. Then she looked up with that same wild gaze.

"Yes, it is he — scarred and grey, but all the same it is he. The closer I look, the more certain I become."

"You can indeed be certain," said Harry Roddney with a brief laugh. "I assure you, I am no ghost."

With trembling fingers, Dolly pressed a handkerchief to her lips.

"But you were drowned!" she wailed. "You perished in the storm that swamped the Packet on that Channel crossing, three years ago!"

He seated himself by the sofa and crossed his arms over his chest. "No, Dolly, I did not perish. The others did — all — including my adored wife. I was the sole survivor."

"Then why did we not know? Where have you been? Explain to me or I shall go out of my mind and still believe that you are some dreadful apparition."

Dear Heaven, she thought, if he but knew the ugly terrors that swamped her guilt-stained soul. For now another apparition stood beside Harry Roddney — although this one was indeed in her fancy — the slender form of the young girl whom Dolly had so abominably betrayed. Fleur, whom she had sold into the hands of the vilest of men, in order to get her miserable debts paid by the bridegroom.

420

Ever since Fleur's wedding-day when Dolly had knelt with hypocritical piety in the church her conscience had pricked her. She had never heard a word of Fleur, until after the birth of the child. What had happened *then* — the scene with St. Cheviot, who had in fury and indignation snarled at her — Dolly hardly dared think about in this moment. Neither dared she dwell on the horrible possibility that since then, for all she knew, Fleur might have been hounded to her death.

She sat trembling and sweating, listening to her cousin's story.

It appeared that once in the water, after the Packet sank, he had tried to hold up his drowning wife, but in vain. Hélène's lovely head sank beneath the waves and for all his endeavours, was finally sucked under, lost to him. After, he clung to a floating spar, and although tossed and drenched by the terrible waves in the teeth of a cruel storm, managed to keep alive for several hours. He shuddered as he recalled the awful scene; the capsized Packet sinking, settling to her doom. The screams of the injured and dying; the last gurgling moans of those who fought the waves but went under, when all strength was gone.

Harry drifted awhile and when he was at the pitch of exhaustion, found himself within short distance of a sailing vessel which — although reeling — seemed able to ride the storm. Afterwards, he learned that it was a Greek merchant ship bound from the Port of London to Athens. Of his actual rescue he remembered nothing. For it was then that he had received the terrible injury to face and head which had so altered his appearance, and impaired his memory.

One of the ship's officers who spoke a little English described the rescue to him. How the officer of the watch had seen his head bobbing there on the water and they had thrown a rope to him. Harry had managed to tie it round his waist successfully, but as they hauled him up the ship's side a sudden gust of wind, which was blowing at gale force, hurled him against the ship's side. He had known a searing pain. The blood gushed down his face and blinded him. Then for him — total darkness while the Greek sailors pulled him up on to the deck. He did not recover consciousness for nearly a week. By that time the ship had sailed away from the English coast, well on its way to Greece. Because of his fine health his body recovered rapidly, but his face remained badly scarred and his mind confused and wandering. He could remember nothing whatsoever of his past — neither his name nor his history.

Strange bitter blow to descend twice upon a man who once had a fine intelligent brain. Once before in his youth, set upon by assailants, he had been reduced to the same sorry state. As before, he wandered in a mist. Since he had neither money nor papers upon him — for he had removed his coat in the effort to save his wife — no one could discover who or what he was or whence he came. Only when he began to speak, they judged he was of English extraction.

He was invited to remain on board and give a hand if he so chose, because there had been an outbreak of smallpox and they were short of crew. So for a month or two Harry Roddney turned sailor and worked with a Greek crew on a dingy ship, and under conditions that should have killed him but did not. Fate willed that he should survive.

He suffered severely, much given to fevers and fantasies. However, he recovered and even grew attached to the sea and the life on board. So he continued to serve under the Greek captain. Because he was a gentleman of breeding and intelligence, they found him useful as an interpreter at the English-speaking ports which they visited.

A year went by. Those at home had presumed him dead and at the bottom of the Channel. But Harry remained on board the Greek ship. They called at Botany Bay, Port Jackson and finally sailed into Sydney Harbour. Ashore here, Harry encountered an Australian doctor who took an enormous interest in the bronzed scarred Englishman with the lost memory. He prevailed upon him to remain in Sydney. The doctor felt that he could help him recover his memory. And so Harry stayed behind and became much attached to the Australian physician and his wife.

It was just before Christmas that another and lesser accident changed his whole life again. He was driving in the doctor's gig through the streets of Sydney. The horse took fright and bolted. The gig overturned. The unfortunate doctor was killed instantly but his passenger escaped with a broken collar bone and slight concussion. Upon regaining consciousness, Harry found that he had also recovered the memories of his past. It was a tremendous and awe-inspiring moment for him. Once again he knew himself to be Sir Harry Roddney.

He soon recovered from the shock of his return to normal. But he was at first anguished when he remembered how he had lost Hélène, his idolized wife. However, he soon experienced deep happiness recalling that he had somebody to live for now — his own dear daughter, Fleur. He pined to get back to her, and to Pillars — their home. He could only imagine what grief it must have been for her to presume that she had lost both parents. Poor beloved orphan! And it would be months before he could complete the voyage around the world and reach England again.

The doctor's widow provided him with the means, and he boarded a new clipper ship belonging to some American builders and which was on its first voyage round the world. This vessel was modern and fast and if uncomfortable, had at least the virtue of speed, which was what Harry Roddney needed.

The clipper had put him ashore at Plymouth twenty-four hours ago, and here he was.

Walking up and down the drawing-room, Harry addressed himself as much to the air as to his Cousin Dolly who had listened to this astounding story in profoundest astonishment.

"It seemed that I would never reach you in whose care I left Fleur," said Harry, "and with whom I hoped to find her again. Just now I called upon Mr. Nonseale in order to get my own money. But Nonseale was away so I came straight here."

He paused and stood looking down at Dolly, hands locked behind his back.

"Fleur is with you still?" he asked. "My own darling! Barely eighteen when

I left her, she must now be nearly twenty-one years. Ah, Cousin, speak to me and tell me how my little dear has fared all this time without her loving parents."

Dolly did not answer. She seemed struck dumb. Indeed, the wicked heartless little woman looked as though she were about to swoon again. Then for the first time Harry felt a thrill of fear.

"What is it? Why do you look at me like that? *What has happened to Fleur? Speak!*" And now it was as though an icy hand clutched his heart. "In God's name, *is Fleur no longer living?*"

Dolly groaned. She could see there was nothing for it but to tell the truth, or half the truth, and whitewash herself as best she could.

"So far as I know, Fleur lives," she stuttered.

Harry's eyes, still the blue handsome eyes of the man whom Hélène had loved so madly, regained their sparkle.

"Thank God," he said. "Then is she here?"

"No. She . . . she was married soon after your . . . your . . . you were drowned, I mean, thought to be drowned."

"*Married* — to whom?"

Dolly gulped.

"To . . . to the Baron of Cadlington, Lord St. Cheviot."

Harry Roddney uttered an exclamation.

"Good heavens, my little Fleur become Lady St. Cheviot? Impossible!"

Dolly shut her eyes tightly as though to shut out the sight of Harry's altered face. She could only sit there gibbering, wishing that she had never arranged that shameful marriage.

She stuttered:

"Indeed, Harry . . . yes . . . Fleur was married a few months after you left her — an orphan as she believed."

"Where is she living?"

"At Cadlington. Her husband's country house."

"Then I shall not see her today. She is in Buckinghamshire," exclaimed Harry in a disappointed voice.

Dolly nodded. She must be the unluckiest woman in London, she groaned to herself. How could she possibly have guessed that Harry would return to this life? And everything else was going wrong. The twins were 'on the shelf'. The one or two gentlemen who had proposed to them, they had rejected, either because they were too old or too ugly. No young and good-looking suitors had approached them. Cyril, her son, had done badly since he left Oxford and eloped with a common actress — which had greatly upset Dolly and discouraged her, for she had so longed to shine in society with her new title. And her second husband, Bertie, since his fit, had become a horrid slavering old man, who was so jealous that he kept her chained to his side and allowed her little chance to enjoy herself as the rich Lady Sidpath.

"I must know more!" exclaimed Harry. "Is my darling happy? Does St. Cheviot make her a good husband?"

Dolly panted and waved a burnt feather in front of her nose again. She stuttered and stammered: She didn't really know how Fleur was, she had been anxious because she had not heard from the child for so long. St. Cheviot was a strange, inhospitable man. Neither he nor Fleur had answered her letters. Nobody in town had seen St. Cheviot lately. And so on.

Harry grew anxious. He wondered why

Fleur had retracted all she had said when last he had seen her. To him and to her mother she had repeatedly stressed her reluctance to receive St. Cheviot's intentions.

"I must go at once to Cadlington," began Harry in a low voice.

But Dolly had fainted again. Now, feeling it a certainty that all was not well with Fleur, Harry handed Dolly over to her maid and left the house.

When Dolly recovered, she had screaming hysterics which brought her invalid husband out of his bed, demanding to know what it was all about. While Dolly concocted a dozen feeble answers and set to wheedling the old nobleman to take her to a watering-place on the Continent immediately, Harry betook himself to the house of an old friend. He could get no more out of the hysterical Dolly but he *must* endeavour to secure the latest news of Fleur. He could not wait until Caleb Nonseale returned to London. Tomorrow of course the family lawyer, who was Fleur's guardian, would be able to enlighten him.

Harry was singularly unlucky, for the

friend he called upon with eager hope, a man with whom he used to play cards and who also knew the Baron — had died a few months ago. His widow had sold up the place.

Deeply depressed, Harry turned into Piccadilly, shivering a little in the cold air. It was no longer snowing but the wind blew gustily and he was used to the heat of the Australian sun. What should he do now? It was too late to get a coach to Cadlington. He must wait for tomorrow, by which time he would also be able to see Nonseale which was essential, for Harry needed his papers — and money. God alone knew what had happened to Pillars and the affairs of his estate, he thought gloomily. Alas, could it be that Fleur — the innocent darling — had mourned her dead parents so bitterly that in her desolation she had turned to St. Cheviot?

"God grant that he has been good to her. If he has not — *God help him!*" Harry Roddney muttered the words grimly as he walked down Piccadilly.

Now luck favoured him — at the same time bringing him face to face with the truth. He was just about to pass a young couple who were standing by a hansom cab (the gentleman was paying the driver) when the young lady turned her face towards him. At once Harry recognized her. He gave an exclamation as he saw that homely but pleasant countenance, faintly pitted after her attack of smallpox.

"Why, Catherine Foster!" he cried, and doffed his hat.

The young lady, who wore a fur-trimmed bonnet and pelisse and was holding her dark brown velvet skirts above the snow-wet pavement stared at him, then gave a gasping cry:

"*Sir Harry Roddney*! But no, it cannot be. It is his double. It is a ghost! Sir Harry is dead!"

The hansom moved off with a jingle of bells. Now the young gentleman turned to Harry and was recognized by him.

"Tom Quinley!" Harry greeted him.

Tom put an arm around his wife and in his turn exclaimed:

"*Sir Harry Roddney*! It is scarcely possible . . . "

"Oh, Tom, have I seen an apparition?"

stuttered poor bewildered Cathy who was beginning to doubt her own eyesight.

"You are right, Cathy dear, it is indeed I," said Harry. "I fear that this is a shock to you and will be to all who knew me. I must explain to you what has happened. Where are you bound? Where can we talk?"

The young couple exchanged glances. Tom Quinley said:

"Cathy is now my wife, sir. We were about to call upon my aunt, Lady Quinley, who occupies this house. We are on a visit to London. My uncle, Lord Quinley, has a seat inside the Abbey in order to be a witness of the Queen's marriage, the day after tomorrow."

He paused, for Harry Roddney, clapping a hand on the boy's shoulder, interrupted:

"Yes, yes. And I most heartily congratulate you on your marriage, Tom. But I am mad with anxiety about my daughter. After three years' absence — with no news of my dear one — you can picture my mental anguish. I have just now been told by my cousin, Dolly, that Fleur is married. But for some peculiar reason she could give me no news of Fleur.

Cathy — you were my child's dearest friend. *You* must be able to tell me something of her?"

Once again the Quinleys exchanged glances. Harry's quick eye noted that Cathy looked distressed. He was prey to the deepest anxiety. But young Tom intervened.

"We cannot stay out here in this bitter wind. Dear Sir Harry, all of us who knew you will rejoice at your return from the grave. But I fear that any news we can give you of Fleur is far from good."

"Reassure me that she is alive!" Harry turned to Catherine. Her eyes filled with tears.

"Alive, yes, but — "

"When did you last see her?" the father cut in again, profoundly agitated.

"Six months ago," said Catherine, "when Tom and I were in London. We reside most of the year in our country home."

"Then Fleur is in London? Can I see her tonight? Is she not at Cadlington?" Harry asked one question after another.

"Come inside, sir," said Tom Quinley, "we will go into my aunt's house and talk." A footman opened the front door. The three of them walked into the well-lighted hall.

Lady Quinley was informed of what had happened. She at once offered hospitality to Sir Harry, whom she had not actually met but about whom she had heard much from Tom's mother.

A few moments later, Harry was seated in the drawing-room, sipping a glass of wine, spreading his hands to the blaze of a fire and hearing the awful truth — as far as Catherine Quinley and her husband knew it.

2

ON this same day that Harry Roddney sat listening to what the young Quinleys had to tell him, Fleur, one-time Lady St. Cheviot, picked her way daintily through the snow which lay thickly on Sydney Terrace and knocked on the front door of the home which she and Peveril shared with the Taylors.

Rabbina let her in. The little maid from Whiteleaf looked much the same except for her new uniform striped cotton dress, starched apron and little frilled cap.

Fleur was flushed and breathless. A hat box dangled from a ribbon on one wrist, and she carried a parcel under the other arm. She greeted Rabbina with:

"Mercy on us, what a day! It has started to snow again and the wind is bitter cold! Are the master and mistress in?"

"No, ma'am, they're both out," said

Rabbina and took the boxes from the young lady who walked into the little house, appreciating its warmth. So dark had the February day become, that Rabbina hastened to light candles and place them on the table in the dining-room where Fleur untied her bonnet.

"I have everything I need now. Where is Mr. Marsh?"

"He was painting an hour ago but just after you went a-shopping he called to me and said that there was not enough light and he could not finish the portrait."

"And then?" enquired Fleur smoothing the folds of her grey cashmere dress.

"Then, ma'am, Mr. Warren — that gentleman who so often comes here — called to see Mr. Marsh. They went off together in a hurry. If you please, ma'am, I thought Mr. Marsh seemed put out."

"*Put out*, Rab? What do you mean?"

"I heard him say: 'Good heavens, Warren, you have me much puzzled and not a little disturbed.' And then Mr. Warren said something about some gentleman of title whose agents had refused to accept Mr. Warren's word that this picture was not for sale. But I heard no more, ma'am, and I hope I did not do wrong to listen."

"That is right, Rabbina. Now you may go," said Fleur.

She stood a moment, puzzling out what she had just heard. She leaned a hand on the mantelpiece and looked thoughtfully into the fire. It was cosy in here. The gloom of the February day was dispelled by the firelight and the gentle gleam from the three-branch candelabra on the dining-table. Fleur's reflection in the mirror over the mantelpiece showed little alteration in the great beauty that Peveril had adored and painted in the tower at Cadlington. Now, at nearly twenty-one years of age, Fleur retained the exquisite transparency of skin — the lustre of fair hair with the curls pinned to one side. But she was no longer the terror-stricken girl whom Peveril had first seen and adored. She had found peace here in this modest happy-go-lucky home with Peveril and his artist friends.

She began once more to try and understand what Rabbina had just told her. Why should Peveril have gone off in a state that Rab described as 'put out'? What had Warren come to tell him?

Arthur Warren was the owner of a small but prosperous art gallery in Ludgate Hill, and Luke Taylor's godfather. After seeing Peveril's work it had not taken Mr. Warren long to recognize the touch of genius in the young man's work. In particular he had praised the portraits Peveril had painted over the period of the last two years, both of Fleur and Luke's wife, Alice. Whenever Warren came here he tried to induce Peveril to let him exhibit his work, and could never understand why the young man refused. His painting was only his hobby, Peveril maintained. He would neither display nor sell. But the more he painted, the more Arthur Warren argued with him and endeavoured to make him change his mind. Added to which Peveril refused the job which Mr. Warren offered him in his business. But gratefully he accepted as much work as Mr. Warren cared to commission, which could be done at home.

Later on, Luke had explained to his godfather that through no fault of his own, Peveril Marsh was forced to lie low for a time. Also that it was imperative that his name should not be mentioned in any art circles lest he might be traced to this address. Mr. Warren, who was very fond of his godson, accepted this explanation and gave his assurance that he would never divulge Peveril's identity. But he sent all the masterpieces which were in need of restoration to the young painter to work upon. Also orders received from clients for great paintings and portraits to be copied. Peveril faithfully carried out these commissions. It was work he did not care for, but he was glad of the money.

Looking back over the last two years, Fleur thought with deep tenderness of the young man whom she had grown to love more than life itself. It was for her sake that he had to remain *incognito* and abandon all hopes of becoming a great portrait painter. For her sake that he rarely went out in public, save to walk with her and their friends; or take a coffee or tankard of ale with Luke in one of the city taverns.

How wonderful he was! thought Fleur.

Uncomplaining about his existence as an *inconnu*, seemingly contented so long as he could be with *her*. She owed him not only her freedom from a living death at Cadlington, but now her livelihood, for it was he who by his efforts for Mr. Warren, paid for her keep as well as his own in this household.

After her arrival here, Fleur had collapsed. It had taken all Peveril's devotion and Alice's tender care to bring her back to normal. After some months of recuperation, Fleur then insisted upon doing her share of work. She, once the spoiled daughter of the Roddneys, brought up as a great lady who would never need soil her hands, became 'Mrs. Trelawny', a teacher of pianoforte. For this was where Fleur's own talents were of vast use. Her dear mother's insistence that she should be taught to play and to practise, bore rich fruit in these days of necessity. She advertised for pupils, and found them. After her initial success in preparing one small candidate for examination, she was much sought after in the neighbourhood. While Alice went about her duties in the house and the men plied their particular trade, Fleur sat daily at her piano, coaxing and teaching her small pupils. Within a short space of time she grew to be much loved for her patience and charm. But few ever saw her out of doors during that first year, save in black and heavily veiled.

That Fleur and Peveril had dangerous enemies, they were well aware. St. Cheviot, Caleb Nonseale, Cousin Dolly, who, they feared, might not hesitate to betray Fleur a second time. These were the dark spectres of the past which Fleur wished to eliminate.

Eighteen months ago, quite by accident, Fleur ran into her old and much loved friend, Catherine Quinley. It had been on a sunny day — a Sunday morning, when strolling in Kensington Gardens. Fleur, Peveril and the Taylors were approaching the Round Pond when they came face to face with the Quinleys. Catherine had at once rushed to Fleur and greeted her, delightedly. Fleur was equally pleased to see her friend, but immediately warned Cathy how essential it was that St. Cheviot should never discover her or Peveril's whereabouts.

When Cathy had heard the long sorry tale of all that had taken place since Fleur's marriage she had been shocked to the bone. At once she gave her solemn promise — seconded by Tom — that she would keep 'Mrs. Trelawny's' secret. But the Quinleys were horror-stricken by Fleur's story.

"You had every right to escape and seek a new life," Cathy assured her friend. "I always feared that you were not happy, my dearest, but could never dream that St. Cheviot was such a sink of iniquity."

And then to have given birth to a baby of dark skin — *what an appalling disaster*. Stupefying, indeed, the knowledge that there had been this black strain in the family through Fleur's mother whom Cathy remembered as the proud, dazzling Lady Roddney. Cathy wept with Fleur, convulsively pressing her fingers.

"My poor sweet friend, how you have suffered! It rends my heart. What can I do to help?"

Fleur had answered:

"Nothing — only keep my secret for I could not bear Denzil to find me. Still less could I support it if Denzil found Peveril and did an injury to him."

Cathy had questioned her about the young painter and gleaned from Fleur's rosy blush that it was in this young man now that all Fleur's hopes were centred, all her joy in life renewed. Because she was another man's wife, he had so far stemmed the tide of his passion. He was her friend and counsellor, but never once had he tried to take his reward from her lips.

"How you must admire and love him!" Cathy had exclaimed.

And Fleur had replied:

"Yes. Till I die, I shall love him and only death, itself, could separate us now. But alas, even though I am chained to a monster, I am still his wife and cannot break my marriage vows."

"That," Cathy had said with a sigh, "must be hard for young lovers passionately in love with each other."

However, a year after the meeting with the Quinleys who came often to see Fleur, Cathy herself had been able to convey the best of news to her old friend. For young Tom had heard news of St. Cheviot from Lord Quinley who frequented the same Clubs. St. Cheviot now openly stated that his wife had dark blood in her and had tricked him into marriage. He had approached the Ecclesiastical Courts in order to secure an annulment of his marriage.

This news had flung both Fleur and Peveril into a transport of joy. Safe in their hiding-place with the Quinleys to watch and listen and inform them, they waited to hear that the Court had granted the Baron of Cadlington his release.

Her whole body trembled with emotion in this moment as she remembered how, that evening for the first time, in this very room where she told him the news, Peveril had taken her in his arms as a lover and kissed her.

"Will you marry me when the day arrives that you can become my wife?" he had asked her. "I have waited so long, and I love you so well."

Whereupon she had looked up into those grey, deeply intelligent eyes, wound her arms about his neck, and answered:

"Yes, yes *and yes*. Oh, my dearest, this

promises a joy almost too great!"

So for the first time their lips had met with a fervour — a hunger, that could at last find appeasement. She had thought never to know the thrill of passionate love — never to be capable of it; she, who had learned to shrink from the base and ruthless sensuality imposed upon her by Denzil St. Cheviot. She, whose wifehood had from the very start been degraded and outraged. But this was a new heroic love — the reward of Peveril's loyalty and patience. This was passing from a long nightmare into a golden dream. Peveril held her close. His firm lips insatiable for hers, restored her womanhood. There awakened in her that glorious desire to give, to *him*, her heart's love, her dearest friend.

Luke and Alice were quick to utter congratulations. They opened a bottle of wine and toasted the young couple's future.

Peveril and Fleur planned also to find a home of their own; perhaps a cottage at Richmond. Peveril was in a position to earn enough money to support his own wife. There would be no further need for her to continue with her teaching.

"I cannot give you the sort of home you deserve, alas — " Peveril began sadly. But Fleur, radiant and glowing in his arms, laid a finger across his lips forbidding him to sigh again.

"To share the smallest cottage with you, my dearest, will be more to me than a splendid mansion with any other man," she had assured him.

So for the past six months they had lived in blissful anticipation of their future. Gradually, through Tom, more rumours had reached them — fresh news of St. Cheviot. The annulment was signed and sealed. St. Cheviot was taking to himself a new wife. No doubt he meant to get his heir, Fleur observed to Peveril, and shuddered and blanched at the memory of things which Peveril preferred she should forget.

So she had tried to put them out of her mind and thinking of St. Cheviot's second wife — although not knowing who she was — could pity her.

After that, Fleur and Peveril began to move about more freely — once they even attended a Mozart concert in company with the Taylors — for they were all musical.

The day came when Arthur Warren at last persuaded Peveril to lend him a small painting which Peveril had done of Dorothy Dickins — a small pupil of Fleur's. A girl of eight years old, with long golden hair and a peculiarly sweet intelligent face. Peveril had made a lovely portrait of the little girl in her blue merino frock and white frilled pinafore, her hair tied with a blue ribbon, and Mr. Warren praised it highly. He begged to be allowed to exhibit it in his gallery. So it hung there, but unsigned. Mr. Warren, this very week, had received a dozen or more handsome offers for it from Collectors, and Connoisseurs.

Fleur pondered over the possibility that Peveril had gone off in a pother about the portrait because he feared the gentleman of title had persuaded Mr. Warren into selling it. Peveril was meticulous about keeping his word. No matter how handsome the price offered he would not wish to disappoint Dorothy's mother to whom it was promised.

Then suddenly a new fear smote

Fleur — like a blast. *A gentleman of title* had made the offer . . . Good heavens, it was surely not . . . *not* . . . but Fleur's thoughts carried her no further. She began to tremble. She could not endure the possibility that Peveril's painting might have been seen — and the masterly style recognized — by St. Cheviot, himself. But surely Mr. Warren would know the name of his client and would have told Peveril, she thought.

She and Peveril had been so happy. They had decided to solemnize their marriage a long way out of London. They had been singularly fortunate because Arthur Warren, himself, owned a small house on the outskirts of Bath. He had suggested that Fleur and Peveril go down there and be married in Bath, then borrow his home for the honeymoon. Like this, they could avoid publicity in London. So Peveril had arranged to take the coach down to the West Country tomorrow — see the parson, and make the necessary arrangements.

This morning Fleur had gone out to buy a new bonnet and fashionable shawl for her wedding. It was all deliciously exciting — so different from that nightmare time at Cousin Dolly's three years ago when she had lived in the grandeur of Archibald de Vere's house and been fitted by fashionable dressmakers and hated it all. For then it had been for *him*, the object of her loathing and contempt.

But now a feeling of oppression replaced her gaiety of spirit.

Luke and Alice — returning for dinner — found Fleur pacing up and down the studio. She at once rushed to her good friends and told them all that she knew.

Luke offered to go to Ludgate Hill and see Mr. Warren. He might find Peveril still there.

"You must eat first — " began Fleur.

"No — let him go — the food will wait but you cannot — I know your loving heart," broke in Alice. "Do not unduly distress yourself, my dear. I am sure your fears are groundless. No doubt Peveril, in view of his coming marriage, has decided to see the would-be purchaser who so greatly admires his work and is arranging to paint a portrait for him."

Fleur bit her lip. Alice added:

"Naturally your first fear is that some danger threatens him whom you love so dearly, but I do not for one moment think the titled gentleman is aught but a stray client of Arthur's. Do you, Luke?" she turned to her husband.

"I do not," he said.

But to comfort Fleur he departed forthwith. The two young ladies toyed with the light meal prepared by Alice's cook, and served by Rabbina, after which there was to be another period of anxious waiting for Fleur.

The afternoon seemed in itself to be forbidding. For soon after two o'clock the sky grew black with storm clouds. Spires and rooftops were blotted out. Indoors, the Taylors' little house was gay enough with the fire, and the lamp-light, but Fleur could not settle down to her sewing. She kept looking at the clock — or out of the window, peering down the length of Sydney Terrace which was shrouded in the winter gloom. Oh, where was Peveril? How come he had not even returned for his meal? What had *Luke* discovered when he reached the Warren Art Gallery?

"It is to be hoped," said Alice, "that there will be brighter weather for the marriage of our beloved Queen."

Suddenly Luke came home. A Luke less cheerful than he who had left home. As soon as the two young women saw him they felt a premonition of disaster. Fleur uttered a cry:

"Merciful heavens — *you come alone. Where is my Peveril?*"

"Courage, dearest," said Alice, although her own heart sank when she saw the change on her husband's countenance.

Luke quickly told them all he knew.

When he had reached the Warren Gallery he found his godfather alone, ill as though with shock.

Yesterday, he told Luke, two gentlemen arrived by private carriage and examined the pictures which Mr. Warren had for sale. One announced that he was the agent of a famous collector. The other, of less noble mien, gave no account of himself but was of Welsh extraction. They seemed particularly intrigued with the painting of Dorothy. The agent — he, too, gave no name but remained *incognito* — had heard about this portrait

452

from a friend. Mr. Warren at once explained that it was not for sale. The gentleman then asked the name of the artist. That information was refused by Mr. Warren.

At this juncture of Luke's story, Fleur went as white as the snow outside and clung to Alice's strong arm.

"Dear God!" she gasped. "*A Welshman.* It may be *Ivor* . . . Denzil's valet. And the would-be buyer must be an agent from Denzil himself. He has remained our implacable enemy and even though our marriage is annulled and he is to remarry, his malice has not been assuaged. I believe that he has ferreted us out at last. I see it all! Until now, no work of Peveril's has appeared in public. But the gentleman who was with Ivor, and who has been paid to use his skill of detection, may have recognized the painting of Dorothy as Peveril's work. It bears the singular stamp of his genius. The lustre of the hair — the rich blue of the dress — the classic background, after the Italian school which Peveril favoured. They are outstanding qualities. I mentioned to you, Luke, and to you,

Alice, that the whole thing was executed with just that same brilliance Peveril showed when he painted *my* portrait at Cadlington."

She finished this speech breathlessly, her very ears assailed by the horrid sound of the name *Cadlington*. It conjured up a hundred sinister memories.

Luke went on to tell her that the agent had grown angry — even offensive when Mr. Warren persisted in his refusal to sell, or even give the address of the painter. Finally the Welshman drew a pistol and threatened Mr. Warren, warning him not to attempt to seek police protection. Luke said, with a heavy sigh, his godfather was not a brave man but easily intimidated and this threat of violence to his person had terrified him. On his own admission he had been a coward. He agreed to fetch Peveril to the Gallery.

Here Fleur interrupted — clutching at the gold cross and chain which she wore about her throat.

"Did he then not realize that the Welshman might be Ivor — and that the Baron was surely behind all this?"

"Yes," said Luke. "And my godfather is now greatly remorseful for having dragged Peveril into danger. But his own life was in peril and when Peveril heard it he was determined that Mr. Warren who had been his friend and patron for two long years, should not suffer in his place. So Peveril went to the Gallery to face the music."

"Oh, Peveril, my love!" muttered Fleur, and her great eyes held a look of anguish.

Arthur Warren had been obstinate only on one point — that no ill should befall 'Mrs. Trelawny' or the Taylors. He insisted that he went to find Peveril alone. The would-be purchasers must not follow, but wait in the Gallery until he and Peveril returned. The Welshman had said:

"We agree. But you are warned — any attempt to betray us or spirit the painter to a new hiding-place, and you, yourself, shall forfeit your life."

So the trembling art-dealer gave this promise and rushed to fetch Peveril. The moment he entered the Galleries Peveril saw Ivor, turned to Mr. Warren and said:

"You have brought me to my enemy. But whatever befalls me now, I pray you never while you live and breathe divulge to these men *her* whereabouts."

"Meaning me," breathed Fleur. She was ashen and Alice had to support her, she trembled so violently.

"Yes," said Luke. "And Mr. Warren said: 'As God is my judge I never will betray her address. My poor boy, I shall not forgive myself, but I feared to die.'"

Luke continued his story.

"The Welshman looked long and hard at Peveril then gave an ugly laugh.

"'So — we were right. At last, Master Painter! Vile seducer of Lady St. Cheviot. At last we have found you.'

"Peveril answered:

"'I am no seducer. It is your master who has earned that name. Do not dare to lay the crime at my door.'

"Ivor took little notice of this denial but added:

"'For two years this good gentleman who has knowledge of the arts, and I, myself have searched the country seeking for a trace of you — we have searched

456

all galleries and shops that might have held work that could be attributed to you. Lucky my lord kept the portrait you painted of *him* so that the expert was able to acquaint himself with your style.'"

Fleur, hearing this, uttered a cry:

"So I was right. Oh, God in heaven, St. Cheviot's hatred and fury have pursued us to the bitter end. Why did we ever think ourselves safe!"

Luke nodded miserably. He repeated all that Arthur Warren had told him. The good dealer would have come to see her, Luke said, but was prostrate from the shock of the outrage.

Ivor, it appeared, had said to Peveril:

"His lordship has ordered that you be taken to him at Cadlington, there to fight a duel, for he intends to wipe out the wrong you did him. You will accompany us, Master Painter, by coach to Whiteleaf."

"*A duel*!" Fleur repeated those words, her blood curdling. "Good heavens — St. Cheviot is the finest swordsman in England, and my poor Peveril a man of peace who has never learned to use either foils or pistols."

Luke, his honest face pale and agitated, nodded.

"I know. But Arthur said he put up no resistance against these gentlemen."

"'I am willing to accept St. Cheviot's challenge. I will fight for my lady's honour,' said Peveril, and then turned to Luke, and added: 'Give my dear love to *her*. Tell her I could not, as a gentleman of honour, avoid this fight — deeply though I deplore it.'"

"When is it be?" Fleur asked faintly.

"I do not know," said Luke. "As you know, my poor godfather swooned and when he recovered, his assistant told him that Peveril had been taken away by the two strangers. We presume — to Cadlington."

Luke added that Ivor had also told Peveril that the Baron intended to marry again in a month's time but he wished to vindicate his honour before installing a new wife at Cadlington.

"Who is the unfortunate lady?" It was Alice who asked this, her feminine curiosity coming to the fore. Fleur was too tongue-tied with horror to speak.

Luke answered that it was a young girl of noble blood, by name, Lady Georgina Pollendyne.

Then Fleur lifted her head. For the first time in her life she spoke with bitterness:

"I know her by repute. She is but sixteen. Once again, St. Cheviot covets the innocent. God forgive the parents who are handing poor little Lady Georgina over to such a villain."

Turning to Luke, she added:

"If Peveril dies at St. Cheviot's hands — for my sake, I shall hope also to die. I had thought we escaped — but the world is not wide enough in which to hide from St. Cheviot's monstrous cruelty. From the beginning I have been doomed. *I* do not matter, but he — my darling — my love — oh *God*, hear me!" She clasped her hands. "Be merciful and spare *him* who has done no wrong."

And she staggered out of Alice's arms to a sofa and lay upon it with her head on her outstretched arms, weeping as though her heart were broken.

Luke and Alice exchanged unhappy glances. This evil had struck — at last.

The black shadow of Cadlington hung over the once tranquil little house. A house that had been gay with preparations for the joyous wedding of Fleur and Peveril. They knew not what to say — what to do — how to comfort or counsel the weeping girl.

Suddenly there came a knock on the door.

"Tell Rabbina I will go," said Luke who was a very worried man. "This may bring us news of Peveril."

Fleur's head shot up. Through the tears, her eyes glittered with a wild hope.

"Yes, yes — perhaps he has come home after all."

But Luke met with disappointment. It was not Peveril but a tall, well-built gentleman with a scarred face browned by tropic suns who stood on the threshold. As he courteously removed his hat and bowed, Luke could see that his hair was white, but not an account of age for he was obviously still in his prime.

He asked if a Mrs. Trelawny lived here.

"Yes, sir . . . but she cannot see you.

She is indisposed . . . " began Luke. Then he stopped. For Fleur had heard the voice and, deeply puzzled by its familiar cadence, moved into the little hall. The February day was drawing to a close. But by the shadowy light of a flickering lamp, Fleur could discern the visitor's face and form. The tears dried on her lashes. She stared wildly as though at an apparition; drew nearer and stared again, peering more closely up at the stranger. Her heart pounded in her breast. Her body shook. She whispered:

"No — I am out of my mind with my grief and anxiety. *It cannot be.*"

Then the tall man moved forward and held out his arms.

"Fleur, my little darling, it is I, Papa," he said huskily. He, like the young girl, trembled with extreme emotion.

For an instant Fleur stayed motionless, as one might hover between the gates of paradise and the jaws of hell. She continued to search that scarred countenance — examining one familiar feature after another.

Harry Roddney, on his part, looked through his tears at his daughter and found her no longer the laughing child he had left but a mature young woman with the mark of tragedy on her brow. Her still slender beauty, those rich curls, that divine grace, recalled for him, with painful vividness, the comeliness of her mother. It gave him a deep pang. Then while the Taylors looked on confused, they saw Fleur fling herself into the stranger's arms. They heard her voice, almost hysterical with delight.

"It *is* you! You did not die. You have come back to me. Papa, *papa*, my dearest, my most beloved father!"

The Taylors, not waiting for further explanations, linked hands and stole away. Alone, Harry Roddney and his daughter clung to each other, the tears raining down their cheeks.

3

WHILE Fleur, seated at her father's knee, recounted all that had happened since he last saw her — Harry Roddney sat motionless. He listened with an ever increasing sense of horror coupled with an intense indignation as she blurted out the dreadful story. Her voice faltered, her cheeks burned, when she reached the point of her betrayal at The Little Bastille.

Coming home from Australia, Harry had built up a memory of Fleur as the fair, joyous child whose laughter used to echo through their quiet country home. His dearest Fleur, the treasure of his and Hélène's lives; with the dew of her budding womanhood fresh upon her.

How could either of them have guessed that a terrible doom sat upon that pure unclouded brow? Harry smote his forehead with a clenched fist, remembering that it was *he* who had insisted upon returning St. Cheviot's hospitality. He who, in an idle moment, had invited St. Cheviot to Fleur's birthday party. He could picture the man, haughty, handsome, suave. But now that picture was blotted out by the other that Fleur had conjured up for him while she told her harrowing tale. He saw the Baron as a cruel ravisher of his young and innocent darling. Having made her Lady St. Cheviot, Denzil had subjected her to appalling sufferings — in particular during her imprisonment after the birth of her child.

It was almost more than Harry could stand. His whole body was shuddering. For now he had to realize that the stigma which had escaped Fleur had spread to Hélène's grandson. The poor infant heir to Cadlington had not survived his birth. But the strain, the shame, must remain. Oh, monstrous brutality of an inexorable fate that it should have been a young and innocent girl who suffered because her mother was born a *quadroon*.

At length he interrupted Fleur.

"Stop, do not go on — I have heard enough!" And he buried his face in his hands and sobbed without restraint.

Now Fleur forgot her own sorrows and made haste to comfort her father. She kissed the tears from his cheek, smoothed his hair with loving hands and begged him not to grieve.

"It is all over now, Papa. We are together again. Even though we have lost dearest Mama, God has restored *us* to each other."

Harry raised his head.

"My child, if your mother knew but a portion of this terrible thing, her heart would break."

"If she had lived, dearest Papa, it would never have happened."

"That is true," Harry nodded. "One cannot foresee the future, and when your mother begged to be allowed to accompany me to France, I could not guess that in agreeing, I signed her death warrant — and your worse fate!"

"It was not your fault, you must not blame yourself."

Harry Roddney wiped his eyes.

"Yes, dearest child, but of one thing we were guilty — we should have told you the family history as soon as you came of marriageable age."

"But, Papa, who was to know the strain would go down to the third and fourth generation," said Fleur in a low voice. "Mama's skin was white as the dazzling snow and her hair more red than mine. But why, *why* should the native strain have passed through *me* to my unfortunate babe?"

"Only doctors or men of science could explain, my darling. But it was an appalling heritage and I know now that your dear mother was right when she said, before we ever married, that we ought not to have children. Yet we so longed for a child of our great love — and when you were born, all seemed well. The possibility of this happening to *you* did not enter our heads."

Fleur seized her father's hand and put it against her cheek.

"I beg you not to blame yourself. Never through all my miseries did I reproach you or my beloved mother."

"You are an angel," said her father and once more found it hard to check the difficult and unmanly tears.

466

"Did many people know that my great-grandfather was an African?" asked Fleur in a low voice.

"None for certain. One or two who were acquainted with your Mama when she was the Marquise de Chartellet, may have guessed: because of the singular likeness between her and the young quadroon Fauna, who was Lady Pumphret's slave."

Fleur stared blindly at her father.

"Mama — a slave — oh, how difficult for me to believe!"

"Yet it was true. And you must always revere her memory. Even as a young girl — and held in shameful bondage — she remained pure and unsullied. She gave her love to me alone. Her marriage to Lucien de Chartellet was marriage in name only. Till her death she was mine, my dear and most faithful wife."

He bowed his head. Fleur's tears fell thickly but she wiped them away and began to talk of Peveril. Harry listened, nodding once or twice.

"There can be no doubt that this young gentleman is of the finest mettle, and worthy of your love. He shall receive nothing but affection and assistance from me."

"Then you do not object to my remarrying?"

"I want nothing but your happiness, my poor little darling," he said.

He rose and began to walk up and down the room, hands clenched at his sides. His scarred face bore a look of repressed anger. He broke out harshly:

"Dolly — my own kith and kin, sold you to St. Cheviot! Well — she shall pay; before God I swear it! She, who is herself a mother, must surely be the lowest creature on earth to have committed such a base crime against a motherless girl."

Fleur did not answer. Harry added:

"And Nonseale — my own uncle's friend and my lawyer in whom I also put my trust. He, too, is guilty. My home sold — my money and estates handed into St. Cheviot's keeping — oh, the infamy! Caleb Nonseale shall be called to account."

But Fleur's mind turned to Peveril and his immediate danger.

"Papa, I beg of you to help me save Peveril," she said. "He must not be allowed to fight this senseless duel with Denzil. *You* know how expert Denzil is with the foils. Peveril is gentle and peace-loving. He has offered to fight St. Cheviot for my honour and his own, but I tell you he has no earthly chance against Denzil. And if Peveril is killed you will lose your daughter, for I could not survive his death."

Harry Roddney strode across the room and took his daughter's hand in his.

"You shall not lose him. Thank God I am come in time. It is I, your father, who have the right to avenge your wrongs. *And it is I who shall meet St. Cheviot in the dawn tomorrow.*"

Fleur put a hand to her throat. Her eyes gleamed with mingled hope and terror.

"*You!*"

"Yes. What I have to say to Dolly and to Mr. Nonseale can wait. But this matter is vital. I know St. Cheviot's worth as an opponent! The very last time I was at Cadlington I struck the foil from his hand twice in succession. I can remember how discomfited he was. He said, then, that Harry Roddney alone could do such a thing to him. Oh, merciful God!" Harry raised a clenched fist above his head, "Be Thou on my side and let it come to pass as it is written in the Scriptures: '*an eye for an eye — a tooth for a tooth*.' For every moment of horror that you, my child, have endured at St. Cheviot's hands, let mine draw the blood from him, even though he fall bleeding from a thousand wounds!"

Fleur breathed quickly.

"You were once called the finest swordsman in England. Do you think, Papa, that your wrist will have lost its magic?"

"No," he said grimly. "*I shall kill St. Cheviot* — and before he has time to take a new bride to Cadlington."

Fleur glanced wildly at the clock on the mantelpiece. She rushed to the window and peered out. She saw to her relief that it was no longer snowing. The sky had cleared during the last hour. It was cold but crystalline stars winked high above London. She turned back to her father.

"The weather is grown clement. Can we get to Whiteleaf in time? Oh, Papa, Denzil's creatures have already gone and taken Peveril with them."

"The duel will not be fought until daybreak," her father reminded her. "Whatever St. Cheviot does, he will respect the formalities. For his reputation's sake he will not attempt to kill the young painter in cold blood tonight."

Fleur shivered.

"Let us go quickly!" she said.

Harry Roddney passed a hand over his brow.

"Wait, my dearest. I am financially embarrassed. I have landed with little money and — "

"You need not lack money. I have my savings and Luke will assist us," broke in Fleur.

"He shall be rewarded. In time the law will restore to us all our lands and my fortune," said Harry Roddney.

"Do not let that trouble you now, dearest Papa. Oh, I implore you, let us go."

"Are you sure you wish to come with me?" he asked, looking doubtfully at the girl who appeared so fragile, so deeply in need of care.

"Yes. I must be there."

"Then you shall be, my darling."

At that moment, Luke knocked on the door and entered, offering wine and refreshment to Fleur's father. Harry Roddney said:

"I thank you, my boy. A little wine and food will not come amiss while we wait for a conveyance."

He then told Luke Taylor what he proposed to do. Peveril's friend was, as usual, most helpful. He, himself, would go at once to the nearest livery stables and secure the fast coach that Sir Harry needed.

"No expense is to be spared," said Harry, in the old voice of authority that Fleur remembered in her father. "Hire four of the fastest horses available. In five to six hours, with a change of horses half way, we shall be at Cadlington soon after the Baron's men get there."

Luke ran to carry out this order, while Alice helped Rabbina serve a quick supper to Sir Harry and his daughter. Alice looked with some anxiety at Fleur.

"It is a bitter night. You must wrap up well. Would you like me to go with you?" she asked.

"No, I shall be all right. I have my father now to look after me," said Fleur, and flung a tender grateful look at the white-haired man, who lovingly returned it.

Harry then spoke to Alice:

"Some other time, ma'am, I will thank you in more detail for the inestimable service you have rendered my poor child."

"Peveril was our friend," said Alice, "and Fleur holds an equal place in our hearts."

"Oh, and you, too, will love Peveril, Papa," put in Fleur.

"If he is your choice I know he will also be mine," said Harry Roddney.

Fleur kissed him then hurried upstairs with Alice to change into a thicker dress, and put on her travelling cloak and bonnet.

Left alone, Harry Roddney picked up the stick he had carried when he arrived. His eyes narrowed. With a turn of his wrist he swished the cane through the air — pointing it this way and that as though at an invisible opponent. Finally he lunged forward, lower lip caught between his teeth, breath coming more quickly.

"Die," he muttered, "die, dog, *die!*"

Then he drew back, flung the cane into a corner and laughed a little, grimly, in his throat.

4

IT was three o'clock in the morning. The coach bearing Peveril and his captors neared Whiteleaf.

Peveril was stiff and half-frozen with the cold. The drive had been a long, arduous one over bad roads. The snow had held off and the heavens glittered with frosty stars. But the cold was intense and the pace slow; the horses continually slipped on the icy surface. One animal broke its forelegs. Another was brought to replace it but the delay was considerable. Ivor cursed and swore — he, himself, found this wintry journey unattractive. But they stopped at the *Saracen's Head* at Beaconsfield, where drivers and passengers were heartened by strong hot rum before they continued towards Wycombe.

Ivor and the art-connoisseur who was in St. Cheviot's pay, kept up a running flow of conversation when they were not attempting to doze under their rugs. Peveril sat apart from them in a dignified silence. Neither spoke to him and he did not wish for conversation. With folded arms he leaned back in a corner of the coach, brooding over what had transpired. It must be confessed that when he faced the thought of what was likely to happen, he could not be anything but apprehensive. Cowardice was not in Peveril Marsh, but he had always been something of a fatalist as well as a philosopher in his quiet artist's way. It seemed probable to him that he had signed his own death warrant when he agreed to accompany these men to Cadlington. But how, he asked himself, could he have faced his conscience — or a future with Fleur — if he had tried to evade the duel? He even felt a queer exultation at the thought of facing Fleur's one-time husband. It would be an honour to fight — and, if necessary, to die — for her sake. But he could not altogether overcome his grief at the thought that he might never see her again.

Tomorrow he should have been on his way to Bath to arrange for their marriage. Now all was over and *she* might be alone in the world save for their kind friends.

A thousand poignant memories assailed him as the coach climbed the hill and he saw the dark tower of Cadlington House pointing towards the luminous sky. Whiteleaf again; the familiar little village asleep at this bitter hour of early morning. Ah! . . . *his* tower! He had never thought to set eyes upon it again. Up there in that studio, his love for Fleur had been born. There, the boy had become a man — capable of deep and passionate love.

Peveril felt his heart sink as the coach rolled through the wrought-iron gates and the lanthorns, raised aloft by the lodgekeeper, shed a rosy glow across the snow. It lay a foot deep. The carriage wheels stuck to the surface and the horses strained and pulled but did not slip. As Peveril stepped out of the coach, he thought of former days when he had roamed through those magnificent gardens — and painted in freedom and tranquillity, days before St. Cheviot had brought Fleur here as a bride.

Was she never to know peace?

The front doors were flung open. A sleepy footman, buttoning his coat and yawning, admitted the visitors. Peveril glanced at him. He did not know the fellow. No doubt most of the staff here had been changed. The Baron's wrath had descended upon those who had allowed my lady to get away.

But now suddenly Peveril saw an all-too-well remembered figure approaching him. Mrs. Dinglefoot moved into the hall. She carried a lamp. It threw her vast shadow behind her. She was wrapped in shawls and wore a nightcap on her head. When she saw Peveril, her eyes blinked first with astonishment and then with an evil delight.

"Lawks-a-mussy! Peveril Marsh! So you've got him at last," she exclaimed to Ivor.

"Yes, and we're all frozen and need refreshment, Mrs. D.," said Ivor, rubbing his fingers.

Mrs. Dinglefoot, keeping her gaze on Peveril, said:

"Well, well, my fine little painter — and how does it feel to be back in the house that once gave you shelter, in return for which you did his lordship such abominable wrong?"

Peveril, weary and cold, tried to unfasten his cloak with numbed fingers. He answered the woman briefly:

"I have nothing to say to you or to anybody in this place."

She came closer to him, peering into his face.

"And what of my lady? The pasty-faced little hypocrite with her native blood — did she find your bed more to her taste than her lawful husband's?"

But here she stopped for Peveril raised a clenched fist.

"Say one more word like that, you female monster, and whether you are woman or not I will strike you!" he said.

The housekeeper shrank back. So, she reflected, the gentle artist had become a man. The glare in his eyes frightened her. She gave a teetering laugh and turned to Ivor.

"He will change his tune once his lordship sets upon him. Better take him to the tower. Let him sleep in his old bed. It is running with damp and the rats are up there. Maybe that will cool my young gentleman's hot blood."

Ivor spoke in the housekeeper's ear.

"I presume his lordship has not heard us arrive."

"No, he was dicing and drinking until late last night with his friends and I imagine he is snoring," Mrs. Dinglefoot whispered back. "He wouldn't be down here at all, but that Lady Georgina's mother and father wished to come and see the place yesterday. We had them here preening around like peacocks. They drove back to Aylesbury just before dark." She added confidentially: "I do not fancy the new Baroness will interfere with me for she's a silly simpering creature who giggles a great deal and is madly in love with his lordship. She will do anything to please him. She calls me 'her dear good creature' and will leave the running of the house to me, little doubt. None of my former lady's airs and graces or icy innocence."

She flung a wicked sidelong glance at Peveril.

"But the icicle thawed towards *him*, hey?"

Peveril glared at Mrs. D. so fiercely that she moved away, muttering.

480

The Welshman eyed Peveril and yawned.

"Come — better lock you in the tower," he said.

"There is no need to lock me in. I am here of my own free will and willing to meet your master on his own terms," said Peveril coldly.

"All the same I'm not risking losing you after the long search and trouble you put us to," said Ivor, drawing his upper lip back from his teeth.

At that moment there was the crash of a door and the sound of footsteps. Those in the hall looked upwards to the musicians' gallery. There appeared the flickering light of candles. Then came the tall figure of the Baron, himself. Wrapped in a thick velvet gown and holding a three-branch candelabra aloft, from which the grease dropped as the draught played with the spears of flame — Denzil St. Cheviot came slowly down the staircase.

Peveril's heart started to beat more quickly. Some colour flowed into his pale serious young face. For the first time for two years he looked at the man who had been Fleur's husband. St. Cheviot, he

481

noted in some surprise, had aged during the last twenty months. There was a touch of grey in the raven locks tossed untidily about his brow. Roused suddenly from his sleep and with the stubble on his chin, he looked blear-eyed and vicious.

Slowly he set the candelabra on the long oaken table in front of the fireplace. Then, tightening the girdle about his dressing-gown, he turned and surveyed Peveril from head to foot in a slow critical manner that could not be other than offensive.

"Well, well, *well*," he drawled, "so it is indeed you. My good Ivor was justified when he sent me word that he fancied he had traced the work of the master painter. Welcome back to Cadlington, my young cockerel. You have been left in peace long enough to crow on your dung heap."

Peveril made no reply. Steadily his grey eyes looked up into the glittering black ones of St. Cheviot. He caught a whiff of sour alcoholic breath. With all his soul, he loathed this man.

St. Cheviot continued:

"So, after all, the stroke of genius in

your brush gave you away — or shall I say your vanity? For at last you were compelled to display your work to the public gaze. Or was it that you were in need of funds?"

"I needed nothing, thank you," Peveril rapped out the words.

"Are you not ashamed of yourself?" continued the Baron. "Just now as you came up that hill on which your sister breathed her last, did you not remember how willingly I gave you succour, and afforded you, my young painter, the opportunity to practise your talents and save your gold? Does your conscience not smite you knowing how you turned upon the one who showed you this generosity and came like a thief in the night to steal his wife?"

Peveril clenched his hands. His forehead was a trifle damp under the crisp brown curls of hair but his voice was steady and clear as he answered.

"If we must talk of conscience, my Lord St. Cheviot, would it not be more fitting for you to examine yours and ask yourself why I grew to despise you. If I aided the escape of her — the lady who was once your wife — you even more than I — must know the true reason why it was done, and that I acted with full justification."

St. Cheviot gave a short laugh.

"Young fool. Do you think to hold yourself up as a crusader, imagining that you had the Almighty on your side when you assisted the lawful Lady St. Cheviot to climb down from the room into your lecherous embrace?"

The scarlet blood rushed to Peveril's cheeks.

"There was no lechery between us, nor has ever been and well you know it!" he said.

"I know nothing of the kind."

"Then you are informed of it now. It is the absolute truth and may the Almighty, whose Name you have so little right to use, my Lord St. Cheviot, strike me dead if I have spoken a falsehood."

"Bah!" said his lordship, but his malicious gaze fell before the young man's clear shining eyes.

"What is more," continued Peveril, "you are aware that you subjected Fleur to insupportable anguish, and that she had neither kith nor kin to champion her. I was her only friend. As such, I befriended her."

St. Cheviot raised his voice a trifle higher, working himself up into a passion against Peveril which he knew to be unjust.

"Sir — you abducted my wfe and for that I am going to take your life."

"Sir," said Peveril, "you have locked up that defenceless wife, treating her as a lunatic and leaving her to the mercies of a fiendish woman who does not know the meaning of the word 'mercy'. It was from that fate that I saved my lady. I am glad of it and ever shall be — come what may."

"Come what may!" repeated St. Cheviot with a loud laugh. "Well, it is your last hour which is coming fast towards you, my little painter! I shall fight you as a gentleman — pistols or swords, I do not care — you shall have the choice. But I shall feel the better when I have rid the world of you."

"His lordship gives words to sentiments I would like to express towards himself," said Peveril.

St. Cheviot laughed again and turned to his servant.

"You hear that, my good Ivor? Does our young genius hope to match me in a duel? Shall he plant a bullet in my head, or the point of a sword in my bosom?"

Ivor echoed the laugh.

"Your adversary is as good as dead already, my lord."

If Peveril's blood froze a little in that moment, it could not be held against him, but he showed no sign of fear. His only terror was for Fleur; lest the long arm of St. Cheviot's spite should reach out and destroy *her*.

St. Cheviot's next words considerably alarmed him.

"And I warn you, I shall not rest until I find that flower of purity for whose sake you are about to die. And to trace her, now that we have found you, should not be impossible."

Peveril's heart sank.

"But why — why, my Lord St. Cheviot, do you wish to extend your vengeance to *her*?" he broke out in a low poignant voice. "The religious Courts have severed you from your matrimonial ties. You are about to take a new bride. Can you not leave poor Fleur alone? Have you not done her harm enough already?"

"What I do or do not do about the former Lady St. Cheviot, is my affair," said St. Cheviot harshly. "You will not be alive to attempt interference."

For one wild moment, Peveril sought in his mind for a means to escape — to reach the side of her whom he adored and protect her as had always been his dearest wish. Just for a moment he regretted that he had ever allowed himself to be drawn into this trap. He could not, must not die and leave Fleur alone. Then he pulled himself together. If it was the last thing he did, he would prevent St. Cheviot from thinking that Fleur had given herself into the keeping of a man less courageous than himself.

He said:

"Let us proceed with the duel."

"It is not yet the dawn," said St. Cheviot shortly. "I shall return to my bed. You, too, can sleep if you have a mind to do so. Ivor will call you. We shall meet in the meadow — beyond the south wall. It shall be a fair fight, correct in every detail. Dr. Boss is dead, the old fool. The new one, Mr. Barnstaple, shall attend us and since you have no seconds, I will provide you with them. This gentleman for one . . . " he turned to the art-collector who had assisted in the discovery of Peveril . . . "shall act for you."

"I thank you," said Peveril stonily.

St. Cheviot put a hand up to his mouth to conceal a yawn. He was feeling cold. His liver was out of order and he was aware that it was going to bring him little satisfaction to put an end to this young man's life. He had even admired the nerve and skill with which Peveril had spirited Fleur away from this house. The full measure of his vengeful feelings were directed not so much against the young painter as against Fleur, herself. Through these long months before he had secured the annulment he had thought of her with a mixture of loathing and desire. Loathing for the black strain that had tarnished even for a few seconds of life, the pure blood of his son and heir. Resentment against the barrier of pride and coldness that she had erected between them from

488

the very moment he had first snatched her into his embrace. Yet his desire for her remained. For a while it had died but it had re-awakened; in his dreams, even in his waking hours, he remembered that incomparable beauty; the ice that he had never been able to thaw. It had driven him mad at times to remember his frustration and her spiritual triumph even in the hours of her deepest degradation at his hands.

Now, as he was so soon to take another bride, there seemed little reason left for his malice. He had cast Fleur off absolutely. He had a new fancy, Georgina Pollendyne was a pretty child with a handsome dowry behind her. But her somewhat infantile adoration for himself had brought him little satisfaction. She would be a pliable wife — no doubt she would bear him healthy children. But she did not appeal to him as that *other* had done. There was nothing in him for Georgina of the wild, hot passion that had stirred his blood when first he looked upon Fleur; Fleur with the violets twined in her rose-gilt hair, and in the dazzling loveliness of her maidenhood.

Even now on this cold grey February morn he felt the old gnawing anger because she had never really been his. He could and would kill Peveril.

He snarled at the young man.

"Well — which is it to be? Swords or pistols?"

The painter, who had no knowledge of either weapon, made a valiant effort to answer with nonchalance:

"It would give me much pleasure to run the point of a sword through your throat, my Lord St. Cheviot."

"Idiot!" exclaimed St. Cheviot, shaking now with a fury roused by the black demons of his own vile memories. "You have only a few more hours in which to live. You . . . " he swung round to the valet, "lock him in the tower and let him stay there until six o'clock."

Peveril started to argue but St. Cheviot, seizing the candelabra, turned his back and walked up the stairs.

"Come along," said Ivor roughly, addressing Peveril.

The young painter turned and followed.

Once again he climbed that well-remembered circular staircase while the

Welshman followed with a lighted lanthorn. Nobody had entered the haunted tower since Fleur and Peveril left Cadlington. The place lay hidden under a thick coating of dust. The studio, itself, presented a grim and forlorn aspect when the young painter entered. Cobwebs, opaque with filth, hung across the dirty panes of the turret windows. Peveril's own easel still stood in the centre of the room. One or two old canvases lay on the ground full of holes — gnawed by the rats. Even as Ivor opened the door — squeaking on its rusty hinges — a dark object scuttled across the floorboards. Peveril followed its progress with a thrill of horror. He had no liking for rats. Ivor said:

"Not nice, eh — but good enough for you, my little painter. You have a few hours left in which to think about the life which you are so soon to leave. Good night — or shall I say good morning!" And with a mock bow, he departed, closed the door and turned the key in the lock.

He took the lanthorn with him.

Peveril stood a moment in darkness

until his eyes got used to the lack of light. It was not pleasant in this bitterly cold room with the sound of rats squeaking and scuttling in the corners. Such surroundings would have struck gloom into the stoutest heart. Peveril's spirits dropped now to zero point. Dear God, he thought, what a way in which to spend the last hours of life — if they were to be his last. He knew every inch of this room. He groped his way to the windows and threw one open. The air was piercing but fresh and he drew it gratefully into his lungs. The studio had been long shut up and stank. Peveril could not bring himself to lie down on the rat-gnawed couch. So he stood at the window staring out at a view which once he used to find so glorious but which filled him now with the utmost gloom. Slowly but surely the night was passing; dawn had already laid a glimmering finger across the eastern sky. It would not be long before he must go down there to the meadow to meet his opponent in what would be the first, and surely, the last duel of his life.

How white and still it was over the countryside with the mists curling through the forest, half obscuring the Vale of Aylesbury from sight. Accustomed to the sombre light, he turned now to look for the high-backed chair in which Fleur used to sit. Yes, it was still here. He could almost see her there in all her delicate loveliness; feel the rich velvet of her blue gown; catch the fragrance of her hair as he arranged a silky curl before starting to paint her. He remembered her grief, recalled the terrible punishment that her vindictive husband had inflicted upon her when she most needed love and care.

Peveril had hoped once he was Fleur's husband to give her the devotion and happiness which she had never known. Now probably it would never be. Down there in that white meadow beyond the south wall he would do his best, but, as St. Cheviot well knew — it would not be a fair fight.

Peveril sank down on his knees and laid his feverish forehead against a curved arm.

"Oh, Fleur, my best beloved, how hard it is to leave you now," he whispered.

The cold was intense. He reached up a shaking hand to shut the window.

Crouching thus he stayed for a while until his eyes closed and an urgent need of sleep overpowered him. Being young and strong — even with that degree of discomfort and so much on his mind — he could still fall into a brief uneasy slumber.

He was wakened from it by the grating sound of a key being turned in the lock.

Ivor and the art-collector, who had been detailed by St. Cheviot to act for Peveril, had come for him.

Dawn was breaking over Cadlington.

5

OUT of the curling mists of the morning, Cadlington rose like a dark spectral shape, the grisly tower pointing as though in vengeance to the sky.

A little wind suddenly sprang to life and chased the clouds across the heavens. The sickle moon was paling fast before the rising sun. The forest still lay sleeping, but down in the valley, smoke wreathed upwards from the chimneys of the cottagers. They wakened early. The cattle from their byres began to low mournfully; the sound was like a protest against the cruelty of man — of birth and of death.

In the meadow which was approached through the orchard, a small group of men were gathered.

The Baron of Cadlington stood with his seconds behind him, and the new young medical man, Dr. Barnstaple, who carried his little black bag and looked nervous. He was gloomy about the whole proceedings for he was a peaceful country physician, but newly qualified, and unused to violence. This was his first attendance upon a duel.

St. Cheviot appeared to be in excellent spirits. He continually showed his fine white teeth in a smile while he divested himself of his upper garments and stood at length dressed only in his small clothes and silken hose. He began to roll back the full white sleeves of his fine lawn shirt carefully over each elbow. As he saw the slenderly-built figure of the young painter walk towards him, he continued to smile but his eyes narrowed. Peveril came nearer and bowed. The younger man looked pale and heavy-eyed but showed no sign of fear or embarrassment. Denzil St. Cheviot returned the bow punctiliously. A slight feeling of admiration once more entered his heart for this young man who was so nobly offering up his life on the altar of honour and human love. No such sacrifice, to St. Cheviot's meaner mind, could be worth while. It might be that he would fight for his so-called honour, but always with the confidence of victory.

Now, swords were brought forward by Ivor. The art-dealer and a young gentleman who had been staying at Cadlington and had been roused from his bed for the occasion, presented themselves to Peveril as his seconds. He, too, divested himself of his outer garments and rolled up his sleeves. He shivered as the wind stirred his hair. Raising his face to the sky he saw a rift of blue. A sudden shaft of sunlight pierced the green glade fringing the meadow. Almost it might have been the dawning of spring. The first promise of an end to the long bitter winter. How strange, mused Peveril, that this was the eve of Her Majesty's wedding. London today would be chaotically engrossed in preparations for the ceremonials. It was entirely irrelevant to his own tragic situation that he should pause to utter a silent prayer that her dear young Majesty would be happy with her chosen prince. Then he forgot everything but Fleur. He drew a long sigh and, with fatalistic courage, made pretence of testing the quality of the sword which he had been handed.

One of the seconds whispered to Dr. Barnstaple:

"Do you know what this is about? I have no notion."

"Nor I," the doctor whispered back, "save that there is some question of the Baron's honour being involved, in respect of the former Lady St. Cheviot. Their marriage was recently annulled." And he added: "But I have heard that this young gentleman, Mr. Marsh, is an artist by profession and has little knowledge of duelling. Lord St. Cheviot will kill him."

"May the Almighty have mercy on him," muttered the other.

This young gentleman who was St. Cheviot's guest of honour at the moment was a Frenchman by the name of the Marquis de la Poeur. He now took control of the situation. He was experienced in duelling. He warned the two antagonists of the rules and placed them face to face with their swords pointing to the ground. In every respect now, Peveril struggled to follow the motions and actions of the Baron. But he wondered grimly if he would be allowed to strike a single blow, or even once hear his sword echo against the other's blade before he was disarmed. But when the Marquis asked if the antagonists were ready, Peveril was the first to utter the word 'Yes'. The Marquis said sharply:

"*En garde, messieurs.*"

The two lunged towards each other. With a swift blow the Baron struck the sword from Peveril's hand. He laughed and said through his teeth:

"Pick it up."

Peveril, face and ears dyed scarlet with impotent shame, picked up the weapon. Once more he lunged desperately in the direction of his adversary.

"For *her*," he said, desperately.

"Imbecile," said St. Cheviot, and made a swift parry. Once again the weapon spun from Peveril's hand. The blood began to drip from his sword arm.

The Baron arched his body.

"What now?" he snarled.

Peveril's heart hammered almost to bursting but he took no notice of the blood that was fast dyeing his shirt and again stooped to retrieve the weapon.

His next movement was lightning

quick — not so much a thing of skill as of despairing desire to make at least one creditable stand against Fleur's husband. The two blades clashed. Even Denzil St. Cheviot was surprised by this sudden slight display of swordsmanship. But it could not last. It could only be a question of St. Cheviot playing cat and mouse with the unhappy young painter. Dr. Barnstaple watching anxiously, uttered a low cry of protest.

"My lord — it is not a fair fight — it will be murder!" he said with spirit.

"I shall kill him all the same," said St. Cheviot.

The sweat ran down Peveril's face. There was a second wound in his shoulder now but he shouted at the Baron:

"Continue! On guard, my lord!"

Now with grudging respect (for he could not but admire great courage when he saw it) Denzil lunged again. The fine point of his sword pierced Peveril's right hand. For the third and last time the sword fell from his bloody fingers. He staggered and would have fallen had his seconds not sprung forward and supported him. The young man's face was ghastly. His eyes bore a look of chagrin and despair.

"Let me go," he muttered, "I will fight with my left hand if need be."

"Fight then and die — " began St. Cheviot who was growing sick of such poor sport.

But at that moment the silence of the countryside was broken by the cry of a man:

"*Stop!*"

The duellists and the rest of the little party gathered there in the meadow, turned and saw three people coming through the arched doorway that led from the gardens of Cadlington. Two were men — one tall and wrapped in a cloak, one shorter and sturdier, and the third a female whose face was heavily veiled.

St. Cheviot stared in amazement at the intruders. It was highly improper that a duel should be thus interrupted. Besides — who were these strangers who dared enter his grounds? St. Cheviot handed his sword to one of his seconds and walked forward as the two men advanced towards him, leaving the female standing alone by the gate. Dr. Barnstaple was busy trying to staunch the two or three wounds which Peveril had received. They were superficial but he was bleeding profusely. He, with startled gaze, stared at the short curly-headed younger man of the two. It was Luke Taylor. What could Luke have come here for, Peveril wondered dizzily. Then suddenly he turned and saw the girl who stood by the gate. The young woman had raised her veil. Peveril was some way away from her but he would have recognized her from any distance. His whole heart seemed to turn over. He cried:

"*Fleur!*"

Now the taller of the men was face to face with Denzil St. Cheviot, and he removed his hat and stood a moment with his sombre gaze fixed on the Baron.

With every moment that passed it was growing lighter. The pale February sunlight was fulfilling its promise of an hour ago, drinking the snow from the long wet grass. St. Cheviot, nonplussed by the unexpected digression, starred at the scarred face and white hair of this

502

gentleman whom he did not recognize.

"May I ask the meaning of this, sir . . . who are you?" he began.

"Look closer at me, St. Cheviot," interrupted the other, "look close *and remember.*"

St. Cheviot stared. Anger was replaced by a vast astonishment. At first he told himself that it *could not be.* Then his very tongue seemed to dry against his teeth. He said in a gasp:

"*Harry Roddney*! No, not he but his ghost, come to haunt me."

"I am no ghost," said Harry, and unfastened the clasp of his cloak which he let fall to the ground. "I have been away for three long years — at the other side of the world where for reasons which I have no time to explain to you now, I was unable to communicate with my daughter. I have come to avenge her, sir. We have had trouble with the horses or I would have been here before. Thank God I am in time," he added with a swift look at Peveril.

Peveril, pale and shaken, leaned on Dr. Barnstaple's arm and stared at the tall gentleman.

"*Fleur's father*!" he exclaimed incredulously.

"Yes, my boy," Harry said in a more gentle tone. "I know all that has happened. You can rest assured that I am your friend as well as *her* father."

Denzil St. Cheviot continued to stare at Sir Harry Roddney in dumb amazement. Harry again addressed him.

"I know all, Denzil St. Cheviot. For what you did to my defenceless daughter in the absence of her parents you shall answer to *me*. Not to this lad who would have avenged her if he could, but is without knowledge of duelling."

St. Cheviot put a hand to his throat. He was momentarily robbed of his usual arrogance.

He began to bluster:

"I protest. The Ecclesiastical Courts granted me my Annulment admitting I had grievance, being tricked into marriage with the daughter of a common quadroon slave."

Harry changed colour. He took his glove and slashed St. Cheviot across the face and mouth with it.

"You shall not say such things and

504

live," he said in a voice of rage.

St. Cheviot stepped back, eyes glittering.

"Not so fast. It may well be *you* who shall die. That young lecher abducted your daughter from her lawful husband's side. Where is her innocence? As soon as my back was turned she took the low-class painter for her paramour. What of that?"

Speechless with fury, Harry snatched the sword that one of Peveril's seconds was holding.

"You were not tricked!" he said through his teeth. "For a sum of money you purchased my daughter's innocence when she had none to defend her."

"And what of her black blood? Have I no cause for indignation? Was I told of this abomination?" demanded St. Cheviot.

"There was none to warn you of Lady Roddney's ancestry. But once you knew — had you acted as a gentleman of honour — you would not have punished a wife who bore her child in helpless ignorance."

St. Cheviot opened his lips to say more, but now suddenly, the veiled female by

505

the gate came running towards them. The raised voices of the men had reached Fleur across the quiet meadow. She approached St. Cheviot. After two long years she looked once more upon his hated face. Her eyes flashed.

"You know well, Lord St. Cheviot, that I was faithful to you, even though you would, if you could, have broken my spirit," she said.

For a moment the Baron was unnerved. Least of all had he expected to look upon *her* again. He tried to brazen it out and gave a mock bow.

"My compliments, madam. You look well, even at this early morning hour. Welcome home to Cadlington," he sneered.

Harry Rodney put a hand on his daughter's shoulder.

"Go to the coach with Peveril, my darling — he needs your care. He is hurt."

Fleur uttered a cry and ran to her lover who put his uninjured arm about her.

"It is nothing," Peveril said, "but I protest against the interruption of this fight that was solely between Lord St.

506

Cheviot and myself."

Sir Harry took him up on those words.

"A one-sided fight is not good sport, my boy. I am better equipped to deal with St. Cheviot. You have but lately entered my daughter's life — I am her father, and it is I who have first right to challenge the Baron to combat. Stand back . . . "

The seconds whispered among themselves. The doctor shrugged his shoulders helplessly. He understood nothing and wondered if he were in a bad dream. Ivor, St. Cheviot's servant, who had been watching from afar, had heard enough; more than he wished, for his own good. The miraculous and mysterious reappearance of my lady's father upon the scene boded ill for *him*, should Sir Harry win this fight. For Mrs. Dinglefoot, too.

Harry Roddney, now prepared, stood still — with his sword pointing to the ground. He had tested the quality of the steel, his face a mask of hatred and resentment, as he bethought himself of the evil that St. Cheviot had practised upon his young daughter. As for those words 'common quadroon slave' that had fallen so scathingly from the other man's lips . . . they, apart from anything else, thought Harry, had sealed St. Cheviot's doom.

The Marquis, who enjoyed a duel between well-matched opponents, and had known Harry Roddney in the past — and his prowess as a swordsman — looked eagerly from one man to the other. This would be something to talk about in the London clubs — and in Paris. He would not have missed it for worlds.

"*En garde, messieurs,*" he said gaily.

Fleur led Peveril away.

"You have lost a lot of blood — you must come back to the coach and rest," she said.

He bent his head and kissed her hand. His face was flushed and his eyes bright with fever. "I have failed you," he said, "I shall never recover from the shame of it. I was beaten before I started. But I meant to kill him for your sake."

Fleur seized the hand that St. Cheviot had injured and pressed it to her lips.

"My dearest, you must not regret

508

Papa's decision to take your place. He deems you chivalrous and gallant for ever having entered upon this contest.

"But I wanted to kill the Baron," groaned Peveril.

"With God's help my father shall kill him for you. And think what it would have meant to me, my dearest love, if *you* had paid the price this morning with *your* life!" exclaimed Fleur.

For a moment Peveril stood looking down into her tender eyes, his mind whirling.

"Last night I believed it to be the end, and that I would never see you again," he whispered.

"Now we shall never have to leave each other," she whispered back. "We have my father to champion our cause."

"Dearest, do not ask me to return to the coach just yet," Peveril begged her, "I must stay and witness what takes place."

She nodded.

So they stood there with their arms around each other, watching. The pallid sunlight flashed upon the swords of the two men as they lunged towards each other. There was a sudden sharp clashing of blade upon blade.

All of them who witnessed that fight, and the Marquis de la Poeur in particular, were to remember it as a remarkable affair, both men being superb swordsmen.

Every time Harry Roddney lunged with parry or *riposte* the name *Fleur* was upon his lips.

For ten full moments, they fought and thrust — neither man drawing blood. On and on — magnificently matched — lunging and parrying, breathing heavily until both panted and the Baron's face grew livid and his upper lip drew back in an animal-like snarl. He, better than anybody, anticipated what he might expect. He had fought with Sir Harry for the love of the sport in the days that were past. But this was no idle sport. This was a fight to the death and he knew it.

It was St. Cheviot who drew first blood — and pierced Harry Roddney's arm. Harry's sword clattered on to the ground but with remarkable celerity he picked it up again and fixed St. Cheviot with a murderous gaze.

"For *Fleur*," he said again in a gasping breath.

The spectators looked on, holding their breaths. The Marquis muttered:

"*Dieu*, but this is a most excellent sight."

Fleur and Peveril, their fingers convulsively entwined, regarded the duel with less pleasure and with anguished intensity.

"Oh God — do not let Papa be beaten!" Fleur sent up a voiceless prayer.

Now the two men fenced again with deadly and ferocious intent.

"*This*," said Harry Roddney, "for what happened at The Little Bastille . . . "

And with a lightning turn of the wrist he drove the point of his sword into his opponent's right shoulder.

This time it was the Baron's sword that fell to earth. He muttered an oath. Harry stood panting while his adversary picked the weapon up again.

Once again the two gentlemen engaged. Now only their heavy breathing and the clash of steel upon steel could be heard in that quiet meadow. Both men poured with sweat. Into the dark eyes of St.

Cheviot there had crept a new look — an expression of failing confidence in himself. *And the first fear he had ever known*.

"This for the black brat your fine daughter spawned," he snarled as he attempted to gain mastery. But they were the last words Denzil St. Cheviot was ever to utter. For with a fearful cry, Harry Roddney lunged and with all his strength drove forward; the point of the sword passing straight through the Baron's heart. And Harry cried out those words that he had uttered in the Taylors' house last night: "*Die, dog, die!*"

Without a cry, with only a pink froth bubbling from his lips, Denzil St. Cheviot dropped his sword and sank on to the grass. The red blood slowly dyed his fine shirt. The melting snow on the grass turned a deep crimson.

Dr. Barnstaple rushed forward and knelt beside the Baron. He examined the fallen man for a brief instant then looked up at the others, his face scared.

"His lordship is dead," he said in a sepulchral tone.

"*Deo gratias*," said Harry Roddney,

and wiped his bloodied sword on a handkerchief, and the sweat from his brow.

Ivor turned and slunk through the archway. He began to run towards the house.

Fleur and Peveril came forward. The girl disengaged herself from her lover's embrace and ran to her father. He folded her to his heart.

"God has been merciful. I have avenged you and the dear mother who bore you," he whispered.

There was a brief silence while Harry dressed himself and Dr. Barnstaple covered the dead Baron with his cloak.

A while later, one of the gentlemen who had been witnesses, after staring in silence at St. Cheviot's corpse, looked up towards the house.

"Great God — there is a fire — *look*!" he cried.

All eyes turned to Cadlington House. Sure enough, a flame like an orange tongue flicked up into the morning sky, followed by a billow of black smoke. Peveril exclaimed:

"*It is the tower*. The tower is ablaze!"

Fleur, very pale and avoiding the sight of that body that lay so still on the grass, trembled from head to foot.

"Something must have happened there, we ought to go back and see," she said.

Dr. Barnstaple said:

"I will give orders for his lordship's servants to carry his body to my house. Let us all go to the House, for every hand will be needed."

What accident had occurred remained a mystery to them. The Welshman was at this very moment running like a rat down Cadlington hill seeking to escape from the vengeance which he knew would fall upon him.

As soon as he had realized that all was over and that he could no longer hide behind St. Cheviot for protection, he had hurried to tell Mrs. Dinglefoot what had happened.

Hearing of her master's death, that terrible woman had uttered a cry of grief. She and she alone had truly loved the vicious young nobleman upon whom she had waited on since his infancy. But sorrow speedily gave place to a desire for self-preservation. She, too, was

514

horrified and startled to hear that Sir Harry — father of the one-time Lady St. Cheviot — was alive — and here. She had just been regaling herself with a tankard of stout during her breakfast, brooding upon the thought of young Peveril Marsh's impending death which would afford her great satisfaction. Ivor's news came as a horrid surprise. St. Cheviot *dead*. Peveril alive. And with a rich and powerful man like Harry Roddney behind him! What a calamity!

"Say nothing to the rest of the servants, but let us two get away," she said to Ivor. The very moles on her face quivered; her small eyes almost disappeared in the wobbling fat of her cheeks.

"Such is my intention," Ivor replied grimly.

But although Ivor made his escape, Martha Dinglefoot was not so lucky. Out of her own avarice and greed, she managed to destroy herself.

For many years, Mrs. D. had been stealing in a quiet and unobtrusive fashion from the hand that fed her. She had always controlled the domestic purse-strings for Lord St. Cheviot's household, and she had managed to fill a deed box with gold. She did not keep the box in her own room. She did not trust the servant girls who cleaned or entered the apartment in her absence. So she had conceived what she thought to be the brilliant idea of hiding the money in the one place where it was least likely to be found; the studio in the haunted tower. For none of the staff dare venture there except when Peveril was in residence.

Up there, under one of the loose boards, was a hole in which she had placed her box which every week grew heavier with the golden guineas she pilfered.

Now that she knew St. Cheviot was dead and that she, herself, might be called to account by Sir Harry Roddney for her cruelty to her young mistress, she made haste to find her savings. She must escape.

She took with her a small oil lamp, for there was little light in the long neglected passage which ran between the main portion of the house and the tower.

Panting and puffing, Mrs. D. climbed

the circular staircase, reached the studio and went down on hands and knees. She found the loose board and drew out her treasure. Her eyes glittered with triumph. All was well. She could live comfortably on the money she had so carefully put away. She might, she thought, even have time to pocket one or two of the jewels which St. Cheviot, in his careless fashion, used to toss into a drawer. Jewels he had intended to give to his second bride. But the foolish giggling Georgina would never now become Lady St. Cheviot. The Master of Cadlington lay dead and there was no heir. It was the end, thought Mrs. D. and managed to squeeze a tear, blinking her sandy lashes as she hurried downstairs again.

Holding the lighted lamp in one hand and the heavy box in the other, she could not cling to the banisters for support. In her haste, she caught the heel of her boot in a hole that the rats had bored. That for Mrs. Dinglefoot was dire calamity. She stumbled, clutched at air, and pitched down the stairs, uttering a fearful cry. The box clattered before her. The lamp broke, the oil spilled and caught alight.

In a moment, the dry rotting wood of the narrow banisters ignited.

When Mrs. Dinglefoot recovered consciousness a few minutes later it was to a satanic world of hot darkness, of black suffocating smoke; and with the crackle of burning timber in her ears.

A wail of despair was drawn from her throat, ending in a gurgling moan. *The tower was on fire.* She was pinned here with her legs broken under her. She could not move. Soon she would not be able to breathe. Her voice was inaudible above the terrible sound of that ever-increasing furnace. Her cries could not be heard. As the flames drew nearer to lick at her face and singe her hair, the housekeeper uttered a last frightful cry. It seemed that every crime and abomination of cruelty that she had practised, rose to confront her now. It seemed, too, that she caught a glimpse of a young pale face with violet eyes full of pain and grief. It was as though Fleur St. Cheviot, the young bride, who had been brought to Cadlington three years ago, stood beside her now with clasped hands, watching; crying aloud for vengeance.

"Mercy . . . *mercy!*" yelled Mrs. Dinglefoot, writhing in her torment and feeling that hell, itself, was already her portion. Then a piece of timber from the ceiling fell from a great height and crushed her skull. She knew no more. The purifying flames melted her fat and frightful body.

Later, when the tower had burnt itself out and scavengers came, they found the twisted box of gold; but of the woman who had hoarded it, and who had caused so much suffering to others, nothing remained save a few charred bones.

The rest of the servants escaped from the big house with ease. One or two attempted to show loyalty to a dead master by throwing a few treasures out on to the lawn. Gardeners and farm hands attempted to pour water on the flames that advanced all too rapidly from the direction of the blazing tower. But it was futile. A brisk wind this cold February morning fanned those flames into a merry conflagration.

The heat from some buildings nearby which had also caught fire shattered the panes of glass in the famous orchid houses. The lovely poisonous blooms writhed and danced in the hot blast like horrid marionettes jerking to their death. They shrivelled and blackened until nothing was left.

As the smoke belched into the heavens and the fire rose higher, licking greedily through the dry old wood of the great hall, hundreds of people in the valley saw it and watched in awe and horror. It was an epic fire; that great fire of Cadlington which burned and smouldered late into the night. It was to be chronicled in history and remembered by old and young in the district as long as they lived.

Little remained of the famous mansion in which generations of St. Cheviots had been born and had died; it became a charred ruin with yawning apertures for windows. One by one the painted smirking faces of the barons and their ladies that had hung in the galleries, had melted, crumpled and become thin black fragments to be tossed by the mischievous wind into complete disintegration.

6

IN the humble parlour of the small house in Monks Risborough occupied by Dr. Barnstaple, the dead Baron of Cadlington lay on a bier like a figure of wax, his nose already thinning with the sharpness of death. And even in death, the expression on that face remained arrogant and brutal. The upper lip was drawn slightly back from the teeth in a sneering smile.

Candles burned at the Baron's head and feet. White linen covered his body — drawn up to his chin. But those on his estate who came to pay their respect to Denzil St. Cheviot did not find him a pleasant corpse. Few truly mourned him save one creature, and that, a dog.

Alpha the wolfhound had escaped from the burning mansion and nosed her way to the doctor's house. She laid herself down beside the bier of her master and refused to leave it, showing her fangs, until at length one of the men on the estate, in obedience to the doctor's orders, put a bullet through her head.

Meanwhile, Harry Roddney and his daughter, with the young man who was her chosen love, and Luke Taylor, travelled in their coach back to London.

Harry, despite his age and the exhaustion that had followed his fight with St. Cheviot, was in good spirits. Peveril bandaged and pale from loss of blood, was also capable of smiling, for his fingers were locked in Fleur's, and her warm sweet presence remained close to him while they rolled through the deserted countryside.

None spoke of St. Cheviot. Death had wiped him out. In Harry Roddney's mind there remained only two more things to be done — to settle an account first with Caleb Nonseale, then with Cousin Dolly, Lady Sidpath. Neither should go free, he decided. For they were the two who were most culpable. Had they not sold Fleur into the hands of the monster Baron?

Pillars, The Little Bastille, all his and Hélène's possessions, would in due course be restored to Harry. Once again he could live in comfort and elegance as a gentleman of means. And already Fleur had expressed the hope and wish that she and her young husband might share the beauty of her old home with him, the father, to whom she owed everything.

This new day for Fleur had dawned like a miracle of joy and renewed hope. Nature itself was rejoicing. The snows were melting. All the way through Buckinghamshire and into London, pale sunlight persisted, and with it the golden promise of the approaching spring.

Behind them they had left Cadlington in ashes. Her dear Peveril had been spared to her. She felt that her cup of good fortune was overflowing, and that the doom had been lifted at last from her head.

It was afternoon when they entered the busy city and drew near to St. Martin's le Grand. They saw the final touches being put to the array of flags, banners and bunting. A spirit of excitement rippled through the entire populace this afternoon. Then the little party in the coach turned to each other, remembering the circumstances and the date.

The marriage of the Queen! This was her wedding eve.

Tomorrow, the young Victoria would stand beside Prince Albert. The young sovereign would have a Consort to cherish and support her in the tremendous duties that lay ahead of so great a queen.

Fleur's heart beat quickly. Her shining eyes turned to Peveril.

"Let us pretend that the bells are ringing for us, too, my dear love," she whispered.

"It is no pretence. They shall also ring for us very soon now, my love," he said.

"Oh, Peveril," she said, "what happiness to know that I have a father to turn to before I take you for my husband. For now I need not walk alone to the altar. *He* will walk with me."

"If his lordship is willing," put in Luke, "we will now proceed direct to my house where Alice will give us refreshment."

"I shall be happy to receive it, my boy," said Harry kindly, "and afterwards to rest awhile before I call upon Mr. Nonseale."

Fleur shivered.

"I always hated that man."

"I owe you an apology, my darling," said Harry ruefully. "Your dear mother abhorred him, too. It seems that my judgment (and my uncle's) were at fault."

Peveril had felt the tremor that went through the slim form at his side. He pressed Fleur's arm close to him.

"Turn your thoughts from all things sad and let us remember our love and contemplate our future together," he said.

She lifted his bandaged hand and put her lips to it.

"Alas that your wonderful fingers were mutilated for my sake," she said, "I cannot get over *that*."

"But, my dearest, Dr. Barnstaple said that in a few weeks both shoulder and hand will be healed and I shall soon be able to paint again," he comforted her.

Harry Roddney opened sleepy blue eyes and smiled at the young man who was to become his son-in-law. The more he saw of Peveril Marsh, the more he liked him. There was nothing dashing or spectacular about Peveril. But the lad was charming and an idealist. He adored Fleur. He had helped her to escape from what might have been a terrible martyrdom at Cadlington. Added to which, Harry had been moved, as only a much stronger man could be, by the thought that the young artist had embarked upon that fearful duel with St. Cheviot, knowing that he had not the slightest hope of winning it.

"You shall paint me when your hand is recovered, Peveril," he said with the old gay smile that used to enchant Hélène. "Scars and all, eh?"

"Scars can be truly honourable, sir," said Peveril.

"Quite so," said Fleur softly and once more raised her lover's bandaged hand to her lips.

As the little party stepped down from the coach a merry fellow, arm linked with that of another, passed by them. One well in drink paused and clapped Peveril on the back.

"Long live the Queen and her Consort!" he ejaculated.

Peveril winced a little from the pain of his wound, but smiled and echoed the good-natured young gentleman's words:

"Long live the Queen and her Consort."

And then it seemed that all the church bells in London were ringing. Fleur linked hands with her father and her lover. She thought of the young Victoria in her Palace preparing for tomorrow's great event.

"Oh, my dear young Majesty," she whispered the words to herself. "God bless you and may your happiness be as great as mine!"

And she could no longer see the faces of the two whom she loved so dearly; for at long last Fleur wept, not for sorrow, but for the joy of being alive.

THE END

THE WILDERNESS WALK
Sheila Bishop

Stifling unpleasant memories of a misbegotten romance in Cleave with Lord Francis Aubrey, Lavinia goes on holiday there with her sister. The two women are thrust into a romantic intrigue involving none other than Lord Francis.

THE RELUCTANT GUEST
Rosalind Brett

Ann Calvert went to spend a month on a South African farm with Theo Borland and his sister. They both proved to be different from her first idea of them, and there was Storr Peterson — the most disturbing man she had ever met.

ONE ENCHANTED SUMMER
Anne Tedlock Brooks

A tale of mystery and romance and a girl who found both during one enchanted summer.

CLOUD OVER MALVERTON
Nancy Buckingham

Dulcie soon realises that something is seriously wrong at Malverton, and when violence strikes she is horrified to find herself under suspicion of murder.

AFTER THOUGHTS
Max Bygraves

The Cockney entertainer tells stories of his East End childhood, of his RAF days, and his post-war showbusiness successes and friendships with fellow comedians.

MOONLIGHT
AND MARCH ROSES
D. Y. Cameron

Lynn's search to trace a missing girl takes her to Spain, where she meets Clive Hendon. While untangling the situation, she untangles her emotions and decides on her own future.

NURSE ALICE IN LOVE
Theresa Charles

Accepting the post of nurse to little Fernie Sherrod, Alice Everton could not guess at the romance, suspense and danger which lay ahead at the Sherrod's isolated estate.

POIROT INVESTIGATES
Agatha Christie

Two things bind these eleven stories together — the brilliance and uncanny skill of the diminutive Belgian detective, and the stupidity of his Watson-like partner, Captain Hastings.

LET LOOSE THE TIGERS
Josephine Cox

Queenie promised to find the long-lost son of the frail, elderly murderess, Hannah Jason. But her enquiries threatened to unlock the cage where crucial secrets had long been held captive.

THE TWILIGHT MAN
Frank Gruber

Jim Rand lives alone in the California desert awaiting death. Into his hermit existence comes a teenage girl who blows both his past and his brief future wide open.

DOG IN THE DARK
Gerald Hammond

Jim Cunningham breeds and trains gun dogs, and his antagonism towards the devotees of show spaniels earns him many enemies. So when one of them is found murdered, the police are on his doorstep within hours.

THE RED KNIGHT
Geoffrey Moxon

When he finds himself a pawn on the chessboard of international espionage with his family in constant danger, Guy Trent becomes embroiled in moves and countermoves which may mean life or death for Western scientists.

TIGER TIGER
Frank Ryan

A young man involved in drugs is found murdered. This is the first event which will draw Detective Inspector Sandy Woodings into a whirlpool of murder and deceit.

CAROLINE MINUSCULE
Andrew Taylor

Caroline Minuscule, a medieval script, is the first clue to the whereabouts of a cache of diamonds. The search becomes a deadly kind of fairy story in which several murders have an other-worldly quality.

LONG CHAIN OF DEATH
Sarah Wolf

During the Second World War four American teenagers from the same town join the Army together. Forty-two years later, the son of one of the soldiers realises that someone is systematically wiping out the families of the four men.

THE LISTERDALE MYSTERY
Agatha Christie

Twelve short stories ranging from the light-hearted to the macabre, diverse mysteries ingeniously and plausibly contrived and convincingly unravelled.

TO BE LOVED
Lynne Collins

Andrew married the woman he had always loved despite the knowledge that Sarah married him for reasons of her own. So much heartache could have been avoided if only he had known how vital it was to be loved.

ACCUSED NURSE
Jane Converse

Paula found herself accused of a crime which could cost her her job, her nurse's reputation, and even the man she loved, unless the truth came to light.

CHATEAU OF FLOWERS
Margaret Rome

Alain, Comte de Treville needed a wife to look after him, and Fleur went into marriage on a business basis only, hoping that eventually he would come to trust and care for her.

CRISS-CROSS
Alan Scholefield

As her ex-husband had succeeded in kidnapping their young daughter once, Jane was determined to take her safely back to England. But all too soon Jane is caught up in a new web of intrigue.

DEAD BY MORNING
Dorothy Simpson

Leo Martindale's body was discovered outside the gates of his ancestral home. Is it, as Inspector Thanet begins to suspect, murder?

A GREAT DELIVERANCE
Elizabeth George

Into the web of old houses and secrets of Keldale Valley comes Scotland Yard Inspector Thomas Lynley and his assistant to solve a particularly savage murder.

'E' IS FOR EVIDENCE
Sue Grafton

Kinsey Millhone was bogged down on a warehouse fire claim. It came as something of a shock when she was accused of being on the take. She'd been set up. Now she had a new client — herself.

A FAMILY OUTING IN AFRICA
Charles Hampton and Janie Hampton

A tale of a young family's journey through Central Africa by bus, train, river boat, lorry, wooden bicycle and foot.

THE PLEASURES OF AGE
Robert Morley

The author, British stage and screen star, now eighty, is enjoying the pleasures of age. He has drawn on his experiences to write this witty, entertaining and informative book.

THE VINEGAR SEED
Maureen Peters

The first book in a trilogy which follows the exploits of two sisters who leave Ireland in 1861 to seek their fortune in England.

A VERY PAROCHIAL MURDER
John Wainwright

A mugging in the genteel seaside town turned to murder when the victim died. Then the body of a young tearaway is washed ashore and Detective Inspector Lyle is determined that a second killing will not go unpunished.

DEATH ON A
HOT SUMMER NIGHT
Anne Infante

Micky Douglas is either accident-prone or someone is trying to kill him. He finds himself caught in a desperate race to save his ex-wife and others from a ruthless gang.

HOLD DOWN A SHADOW
Geoffrey Jenkins

Maluti Rider, with the help of four of the world's most wanted men, is determined to destroy the Katse Dam and release a killer flood.

THAT NICE MISS SMITH
Nigel Morland

A reconstruction and reassessment of the trial in 1857 of Madeleine Smith, who was acquitted by a verdict of Not Proven of poisoning her lover, Emile L'Angelier.